CASTAWAYS

"Relentlessly frightening and viscerally brutal, *Castaways* combines nonstop action with an old school horror abandon that gives readers scarce time to come up for air."

—Dark Scribe Magazine

"You've got all the things here a horror fan craves: the violence, the mayhem, and the blood and guts. Much like Laymon, Keene provides all kinds of thrills here....But Keene has his own voice, too, one just as good as the late great master, Richard Laymon."

—SFRevu

"Bloody, vile, violent and nasty *Castaways* is a can't put down page turner....There is no one writing any better horror right now than Brian Keene."

—House of Horrors

GHOST WALK

"Keene returns to creepy LeHorn's Hollow with enthusiasm and with a formidable chunk of evil in Nodens...Keene demonstrates an authoritative grasp on primal fears and on a rural America cut off from the mainstream."

—Publishers Weekly

"Keene has easily grown to be my favorite writer, and until he proves that he can no longer write anything good anymore, he most likely will hold that title for a long time. *Ghost Walk* is another one...to add to the pile of greatness."

—The Horror Review

DARK HOLLOW

"Keene keeps getting better and better. Given how damn good he was to start with...soon, he will become a juggernaut."

—The Horror Fiction Review

"*Dark Hollow* is a powerful novel—it is Brian Keene presenting his 'A' game....Brian Keene is a unique voice and talent...."

—Fear Zone

DEAD SEA

"Delivering enough shudders and gore to satisfy any fan of the genre, Keene proves he's still a lead player in the zombie horror cavalcade."　　　　　　　　　—*Publishers Weekly*

GHOUL

"Bursting on the scene with an originality and flair, it seemed that Keene was responsible for breathing new life into the zombie story for a vast number of hungry readers in the horror genre. With the publication of his newest novel, *Ghoul*, Brian Keene has finally cemented himself in as a leader of . . . the horror genre. . . . "　　　—*Horror World*

"If Brian Keene's books were music, they would occupy a working class, hard-earned space between Bruce Springsteen, Eminem, and Johnny Cash."

—John Skipp, *New York Times*
bestselling author of *Jake's Wake*

THE CONQUEROR WORMS

"Keene delivers [a] wild, gruesome page-turner...the enormity of Keene's pulp horror imagination, and his success in bringing the reader over the top with him, is both rare and wonderful."　　　　　　　　　—*Publishers Weekly*

CITY OF THE DEAD

"Brian Keene's name should be up there with King, Koontz and Barker. He's without a doubt one of the best horror writers ever."　　　　　　　　　—The Horror Review

THE RISING

"[Brian Keene's] first novel, *The Rising*, is a postapocalyptic narrative that revels in its blunt and visceral descriptions of the undead."　　　　　—*The New York Times Book Review*

"Hoping for a good night's sleep? Stay away from *The Rising*. It'll keep you awake, then fill your dreams with lurching, hungry corpses wanting to eat you."

—Richard Laymon, author of *Dark Mountain*

"Here kitty, kitty, kitty ... "

The voice didn't belong to Javier. Indeed, it barely sounded like it belonged to anything human. It was harsh and ragged, the words slurred, and there was an unmistakable hint of maniacal glee in the tones. Heather covered her mouth with her hands and tried not to make any noise. Despite her best efforts, a pitiful whine slipped past her lips and fingers.

"It's okay, kitty," the thing in the dark responded. "Come on, now. If you come out now, I'll twist off your head and make it real quick, so you don't feel it when we eat you."

The voice sounded like it was all around her. Heather crouched low to the floor, ignoring the pain in her hands, and concentrated on taking slow, deep breaths and remaining motionless. She inhaled, exhaled, and forced herself to calm down. A few more breaths and she was clear-headed again—still terrified, but not paralyzed by fear.

She heard shuffling footsteps, as if the hunter was dragging one foot. It was coming from her left. Then she heard the belt crack. It sounded very loud in the darkness. Her spirits soared. It was Javier. She knew he wouldn't abandon her.

"Javier?" Her cry echoed in the chamber.

"No. I'm Scug. Was Javier the guy with the belt? Cause it's mine now. And you are, too."

Other *Leisure* books by Brian Keene:

CASTAWAYS
GHOST WALK
DARK HOLLOW
DEAD SEA
GHOUL
THE CONQUEROR WORMS
CITY OF THE DEAD
THE RISING

ACKNOWLEDGMENTS

Thanks to my family; Don D'Auria and everyone else at Leisure Books; Larry Roberts; my assistants—Big Joe Maynard, Joe Branson, and Dave Thomas; my pre-readers—Tod Clark, Kelli Dunlap, and Mark Sylva. Thanks also (for various reasons) to James A. Moore, Bryan Smith, Tom Piccirilli, J. F. Gonzalez, Nate Southard, Tim Lebbon, Christopher Golden, John Urbancik, Geoff Cooper, Mikey Huyck, Mike Oliveri, Paul Synuria, the Drunken Tentacles, and Mike Lombardo (for the Phillipsport shirt). Finally, as always, a very special thanks to the message board regulars at Brian Keene.com and the loyal members of the F.U.K.U.

ACKNOWLEDGMENTS

Author's Note

Although this novel takes place in Philadelphia, I have taken certain geographical liberties with the city. If you live there, don't look for your street corner or block. You won't like what's lurking beneath the sidewalks.

URBAN GOTHIC

CHAPTER ONE

"Shit happens," Javier grumbled from the backseat.

A car rolled slowly past, its underside so low to the ground that it almost scraped against the road. The windows were tinted, and they couldn't see the driver, but the vehicle's stereo was turned up loud enough to rattle their teeth.

Brett sighed in frustration. "Now's not the time, Javier."

But he's right, Kerri thought, gazing out of the passenger window. *Javier is right. There's no rhyme or reason to it. Sometimes, events just spin out beyond our control. Sometimes, no matter how careful we are, no matter how much we try sticking to the script or routine, our day gets off track, and nothing we say or do will fix it before night comes around. Shit happens. And when it does, things get fucked up.*

Like now.

However, while the situation they were in now was indeed fucked up, it wasn't just a simple case of "shit happens"—at least, not entirely. Perhaps some of it could be blamed on fate, but the rest of it was purely Tyler's fault.

Kerri wondered how it was possible to simultaneously love and hate her boyfriend—because that was how she felt.

They'd driven in from the suburbs of East Petersburg to attend the Monsters of Hip Hop show at the sprawling Electric Factory club in downtown Philadelphia. While the venue wasn't in the best part of the city, the show had definitely been worth it. Headliner Prosper Johnson and the Gangsta Disciples had gathered together some of the biggest names in hard-core, gritty hip-hop for a nation-wide benefit tour—Lil Wyte, Frayser Boy, T-Pain, Lil Wayne, Tech N9ne, The Roots, Mr. Hyde, Project: Deadman, Bizarre, Dilated Peoples, and Philadelphia's own Jedi Mind Tricks. The girls preferred hip-*pop*, rather than hip-hop, but they tagged along anyway because it was an excuse for all of them to hang out together and get out of East Petersburg for a night. They were in Philadelphia, after all. It sure beat the hell out of hanging around Gargano's Pizzeria for another evening.

Kerri and Tyler.

Stephanie and Brett.

Javier and Heather.

They'd been friends since elementary school—long before they'd actually started dating and paired off into couples. Now things were changing. Graduation was over. College loomed. Adulthood. The real world. Although none of them verbalized it, they all knew that this could very well be the last time they'd all be together like this. Most of them were going their own way in a few months, so they were determined to live it up. One last great time before life intruded.

When the concert was over, all six of them had shuffled out to the parking lot with the rest of the crowd. They piled into the old station wagon Tyler had inherited from his brother Dustin, after Dustin went off to Afghanistan. Dustin had always kept the car running like it was fresh off the factory floor. The engine had been tuned to purr when it idled and to roar when Dustin stomped the accelerator. When he'd first gotten the car, Tyler had made an effort to keep it in perfect shape. But eventually, he ran it ragged, just like everything else in his life. When Kerri asked him about it, Tyler's excuse was that he wasn't as good with his hands as his brother had been. He'd never been mechanically inclined. Tyler's talents lay elsewhere—scoring a bag of weed or six third-row tickets for this concert. He liked to call these things "acquisitions." He was the closest thing to street smart they had in East Petersburg, and he knew it, too.

Half-deaf from the concert, and adrenalized by the late hour, they'd driven out of the parking lot with the windows down, laughing and shouting at one another. It was summer and they were young. Happy. Immortal. And all the bad things out there in the world?

Those bad things were supposed to happen to someone else.

Until they'd happened to them.

It started when, five minutes after pulling out of the lot, Tyler decided to visit a friend of his on the other side of the river, in Camden. No one in their right mind went into Camden, New Jersey, after dark, but Tyler swore that he knew what he was doing. He'd promised them this friend had great weed.

Tyler navigated the station wagon through a bewildering maze of city streets, insisting that he knew where he was going. They drove past block upon block of row homes, seeing only the occasional business—a mattress store, a Laundromat, a pizza shop and a bail bondsman. A group of men were hanging out on the stoop of one of the row homes, watching as they drove by. Their intense stares made Kerri nervous.

Despite his insistence that he knew where he was going,

Tyler got flustered when the road he needed was under construction and closed. Orange-and-white oil drums topped with flashing yellow lights barred their passage.

"What the fuck is this all about?" Frowning, Tyler pointed at the large, dented ROAD CLOSED sign.

"It's blocked off," Brett told him.

"I know it's blocked off, shithead. Thanks for your help."

"You need a GPS," Stephanie said. "My parents bought me one for my birthday last year. I *never* get lost."

Tyler's frown deepened. "Your parents buy you everything, princess."

Stephanie shrugged. "Well, if you had a GPS, we wouldn't be sitting here now, would we?"

"I'm surprised you know how to program the fucking thing."

"Hey." Brett spoke up, trying to defend his girlfriend. His tone was nervous. "Chill out, Tyler."

"Shut the fuck up, Brett."

"There's no need for that. Knock it off or I'll . . ." Brett's voice trailed off. He squirmed uncomfortably.

"You'll what?" Tyler teased. "Beat me at chess? Sit back and shut the fuck up, pussy."

Sensing his growing agitation, Kerri tried to calm her boyfriend. "Tyler, why don't we just turn around and go home. We don't need weed that bad."

Tyler's handsome features pinched together for a second, and she saw him trying to control his temper. In private, when it was just the two of them, Tyler could be really sweet, but he also had anger issues. When his temper got the better of him, things usually ended badly. He'd never hit her or anything like that. But he said things—words more hurtful than any blow.

He shook his head. "It's all good. I can get around this. I just have to go down one block and then back-track."

Ultimately, the detour took them in the opposite direction of the Ben Franklin Bridge. Tyler's calm demeanor cracked when they found themselves driving on a meandering stretch of the Lower Carlysle Thruway, winding through some of the worst parts of Philadelphia. Hookers roamed the streets, looking hollow and emaciated. A woman with haunted eyes and fire-engine red hair gave them the finger as they drove by. A huge herpes sore dotted one corner of her mouth. Brett waved at her. Steph nudged him in the ribs with her elbow.

The road was rutted and cracked. The car bounced over a gaping pothole, thumping and rattling in ways that would have surely sent Dustin after his little brother with an assault rifle. Something scraped along the underside of the vehicle. Brett gasped from the backseat, and the others cringed at the sound as the car continued to scrape along.

"Fuck me," Tyler whispered under his breath.

"You wish," Kerri replied.

He smiled, but there was no humor in the expression.

They'd continued down the street, slowing to a crawl. The landscape grew steadily bleaker. They drove past a cluster of seedy-looking bars, patrons lounging outside, bathed in garish neon. Then the bars gave way to pawn shops and liquor stores and rundown, shoebox housing.

"Jesus," Brett gasped. "Look at these houses. How can anybody live like this?"

They'd stopped at a red light. Thumping bass from the car next to them rattled their windows. A large group of black youths stood on the street corner, peering in at

them. When one of the teens sidled up to the station
wagon and gestured, Tyler gunned it, racing through the
light. A car horn blared behind them.

"Lock the doors," Heather urged, staring wide-eyed.

Tyler ignored her request, but everyone else rolled
their windows up. After a moment, he begrudgingly did
the same.

"Where the fuck is the turn?"

From the back of the station wagon, Javier said, "Dude,
there's a sign for Route 30. Doesn't that take us back to
Lititz?"

"I don't want to go back to Lititz. I want to go to
Camden."

"Fuck Camden," Javier shouted. "Have you looked
outside? You're gonna get us carjacked!"

Tyler stared straight ahead. "You guys worry too much.
For fuck's sake, we just came from a rap concert. Now
y'all are worried about driving through the city? Bunch
of white-bread motherfuckers."

"In case you haven't noticed," Brett said, "you're white
too, Tyler."

"I'm not white. I'm Italian."

Javier sighed.

"Everybody just calm the fuck down," Tyler continued. "We'll be fine. Long as you don't fuck with anybody, they won't fuck with you."

He'd kept his voice calm, but his teeth were clenched.
Kerri knew from experience that his anger was building
inside again.

The last of his facade shattered when the engine light
came on and steam began billowing out from under the
hood, blanketing the windshield.

"Shit!"

The engine sputtered, then died. The radio and headlights died with it. Their speed decreased from forty miles an hour to five. They'd rolled a few more yards and then came to a halt. Another car horn blared behind them, the driver impatient. Tyler tried turning on the emergency blinkers, but they didn't work.

"Motherfucker." He opened the door, got out, and waved the other car around them. Then he ducked back into the station wagon and pulled the hood latch.

"Stay in here," he said, then stomped off to the front of the car.

And now here they were—broken down in the middle of the hood.

Tyler's fault.

Kerri shook her head and sighed.

"Shit happens," Javier grumbled again.

Heather nodded in agreement. "He just *had* to go to Camden tonight. If he'd listened to us, we'd be on the turnpike by now."

"Maybe we should go out and help him," Brett suggested. "I mean, Tyler doesn't know shit about cars. Dustin was always the motor head. What's he gonna do out there?"

Kerri frowned. "Tyler said to stay in the car."

"Screw that," Brett said. "It's hot in here, and there's no way I'm rolling the windows down."

"You're afraid to roll the windows down," Heather said, "but you'd rather stand outside with Tyler?"

"Yeah," Javier said. "What's that about, bro?"

Smirking, Heather adopted a baby-talk tone. "He knows Tyler will beat up the big bad gangbangers if they mess with us. He's afraid."

Brett's ears turned red. Instead of responding, he opened the door and got out.

"You know," Stephanie said, turning to Heather. "That was a real bitch move."

Heather's smile died. "I was just kidding."

"Well, Brett's sensitive. You know that."

Sighing, Javier and Heather got out of the car to apologize to Brett. Stephanie remained seated, rummaging through her purse. She pulled out a pink cell phone and flipped it open. The display glowed in the darkness.

"Who are you calling?" Kerri asked.

"My parents. They've got Triple A. They can send a tow truck for us."

"Hold off on that. Let's just wait a minute and see what's wrong with the car first."

"Screw that," Stephanie said. "I'm not sitting around here waiting to get mugged. Have you taken a look outside? It's like Baghdad out there."

Kerri rubbed her temples. A headache was forming behind her eyes.

"Please, Steph? Let's just wait a few minutes. If you call them now, you're just going to piss Tyler off even more."

"I don't care."

"I know you don't, but you're not the one who has to deal with him when he's angry. Please? Do it for me?"

Stephanie shook her head. "I don't know why you put up with that shit. If Brett treated me that way, I'd have dumped him a long time ago."

"Brett lets you walk all over him. He's done that since middle school. He's a pushover."

"Maybe. But he's sweet, and he treats me the way I deserve to be treated. He respects me. Like I said, I don't know why you put up with Tyler. He doesn't respect anyone or anything. Not even himself. "

"I won't have to put up with it for much longer. Once I'm at Rutgers, things will be different. We'll drift apart."

"Why not just break up with him now?"

Kerri paused before answering. "Because I care about

him, and I don't want to hurt him. I'm afraid of what he might do if I did."

"To you?"

"No. Not to me. To himself."

Stephanie didn't respond. She quietly closed her cell phone and stuffed it back into her purse.

Kerri murmured, "I don't think Tyler likes himself very much."

"You think?" Stephanie's tone was sarcastic. "What was your first clue?"

"It's so easy for you, isn't it? Pretty little Stephanie, who gets everything she wants. Some of us don't have it that easy, Steph. You're supposed to be my best friend. I don't need that shit from you. You gave Heather shit for picking on Brett, but then you're going to turn around and do it to me?"

Scowling, Kerri opened the passenger door and stepped out into the street. Stephanie quickly followed her, offering apologies. They joined the others huddled around the open hood. The guys were peering down at the engine intently. Steam rose from the radiator. The motor smelled of oil and antifreeze. Heather was smoking a cigarette. Kerri bummed one from her. Stephanie made a disgusted sound when she lit up.

Tyler raised his head and looked at them. "I thought I told you guys to stay in the car. Doesn't anyone ever listen to me?"

"It's hot in there." Stephanie tossed her head. "Want me to call my parents? They've got Triple A."

"No." Tyler returned his attention to the engine. "We can figure this out."

"You're doing a great job so far."

Tyler's knuckles curled around the car's front grille, clenching tightly. Kerri and Brett both motioned at

Stephanie to be quiet. Another cloud of steam drifted up from the engine.

Even though the sun had gone down, it was still excruciatingly hot outside. The heat seemed to radiate off the sidewalks and the pitted blacktop in waves. The air was a sticky, damp miasma. Kerri tugged at her blouse. Between all the sweating she'd done at the concert and the temperature here on the street, the sheer fabric stuck to her skin. She took another drag off the cigarette, but with the extreme humidity, it was like inhaling soup. She smelled food cooking. Gasoline. Piss. Booze. Burned rubber. Hot asphalt. Stephanie's perfume. The mix was nauseating.

Coughing, Kerri breathed through her mouth and looked around, nervously studying their surroundings. She'd heard the term urban blight before, but had never really understood it until now. Most of the streetlights weren't working, and the few that were operational cast a sickly yellow pall across the neighborhood. Combined with the moonlight, it made for an eerie scene.

They were surrounded by decrepit row homes, none of which looked hospitable. In the gloom, the squat houses seemed like monoliths, endless black walls with deteriorating features. Dim lights burned behind dirty curtains or through broken windows—some of which were covered with clear plastic or stuffed with soiled rags. Many of the buildings were missing roof tiles, and the outside walls had gaps where bricks or boards had crumbled away. Some were covered with graffiti—gang tags and names she didn't understand. None of the homes had yards, unless you counted the broken sidewalks, split by the roots of long-dead trees and cracked by blistering summers and frigid winters. Cockroaches and ants scuttled on the sunken concrete amidst crack vials, cigarette butts and glittering shards of broken glass. Ruptured garbage bags sat on the curbs, spewing their rotten contents into the street.

The sidewalks and stoops were deserted, except for a surly-looking gang of youths lurking on the street corner about a block away. Kerri's gaze lingered on them for a moment, before moving on. The only businesses on the street were a pawn shop, a liquor store, and a newsstand. All three were closed for the night, shuttered with heavy steel security gates. Many of the businesses also had graffiti painted on them. So did some of the junk cars sitting along the curb. A few of the vehicles looked abandoned—shattered windshields, missing tires replaced with cement blocks, bodies rusted out and dented, bumpers hanging off or bashed in.

She turned in the opposite direction and looked farther down the street. It seemed to terminate in a dead end. Beyond the row homes was a large swath of debris-covered pavement, as if all the buildings in that section had been knocked down. The moonlight was stronger there, and the headlights of passing cars illuminated the scene. Chunks of concrete and twisted metal girders jutted from the devastation. Beyond that was a single house, much larger than the rest of the row homes. Kerri thought it must be at least a hundred years old, judging by the architecture. Maybe one of the original buildings in this neighborhood, standing there long before the slums had been erected. She supposed at one time it had been very pretty. Now it was a desolate ruin—in even worse condition than the other row homes. It seemed to squat at the end of the street, looming over the block. Beyond it was a vacant lot, overgrown with weeds and brambles. Behind that was a tall, rusted chain-link fence.

Kerri stared at the house. She shivered despite the

heat. She had the uncanny impression that the abandoned building was somehow *watching* them.

Tyler cursed, rapping his knuckles against the car, and Kerri's attention returned to her friends. As she did, she noticed that the street had emptied of traffic. They were suddenly all alone.

"Maybe we should call Steph's parents," Brett suggested. "It's pretty late, and we're in a bad neighborhood."

Tyler glanced up at him, opened his mouth to respond, and then stared over Brett's shoulder. Kerri saw his face twitch. Then she and the others turned around to see what had attracted his attention.

The group of black men she'd noticed a moment before was slowly approaching. The boys appeared to be about the same age as they were. Most of the youths were dressed in either athletic jerseys or white tank tops. Their pants, held up only by tightly cinched belts and the tongues of their high-topped sneakers, sagged almost to their kneecaps, exposing their boxer shorts. Gold rings and necklaces completed the ensemble. A few of them wore backwards ball caps on their heads. The one in the lead wore a black do-rag on his head. Gold hoops glittered from each of his ears. He reminded Kerri of a pirate.

"Oh shit," Brett whispered. "What the hell do they want?"

Stephanie whimpered. "We're going to get mugged."

Brett nodded. "This is bad. This is really fucking bad."

"Calm the hell down," Javier said. "You guys automatically assume that just because they're black, they're gonna mug us?"

"Look at them," Brett insisted. "They sure as hell don't look like they're here to sell us Girl Scout cookies."

Javier glared at him, speechless.

The group shuffled closer. All of them walked with a sort of lazy, loping gait. Kerri's nervousness increased. She wanted to agree with Javier, but then she considered their situation and their surroundings. Panic overwhelmed her. She reached for Tyler's hand, but he was stiff as stone.

"Shit," Brett moaned. "Fucking do something, you guys!"

Javier shoved him. "Dude, chill out. You're acting like an asshole."

When the group was about ten feet away, they stopped. The leader stepped forward and glared at them suspiciously. Slowly, his friends stepped alongside him.

"The fuck y'all doing around here? You lost?"

His voice was deep and surly. He stood tensed, as if ready to spring at them.

Stephanie and Heather clasped hands and took a simultaneous step backward. Brett slipped in behind them. Javier stepped out from behind the car and faced the group. Tyler slowly slammed the hood, then joined him. Kerri stayed where she was. Her feet felt rooted to the spot. Her heart pounded beneath her breast.

Another of the black youths spoke up. "Man asked you a question."

"We don't want any trouble," Tyler said.

Kerri cringed at the plaintive, pleading tone in his voice.

"Well, if you don't want no trouble," the leader said, grinning, "then you're in the wrong place."

His friends chuckled among themselves in response. He held up a hand and they immediately fell silent.

"Come into this neighborhood after dark," he continued, "then you *must* be looking for trouble. Or dope. Or be lost. So which one is it?"

"Neither," Javier challenged. "We had a little car trouble. That's all. Just called for a tow truck and they're on the way." He paused. "Should be here any minute now."

The leader elbowed the gangly kid next to him. "You hear that shit, Markus? He said a tow truck is on the way."

Markus smiled and nodded. "I heard that, Leo. What you think?"

The leader—Leo—stared at Javier as he responded. "I think this esse be bullshitting us, y'all. Ain't no tow trucks come down here after dark. Not to this street."

Javier and Tyler glanced at each other. Kerri saw Tyler's Adam's apple bobbing up and down in his throat. She turned to Stephanie, who was slowly pulling her cell phone out of her purse.

"Now for real," Leo said. "What y'all doing down here? You looking to score?"

"M-maybe," Tyler said. "What you got?"

Leo stepped closer. "The question is, what you got? How much money you carrying?"

Oh shit, Kerri thought. *Here it comes. Next, they'll pull out a knife or a gun.*

"W-we came from the M-monsters of H-hip Hop," Brett stammered, hidden behind the girls. "We're j-just trying to g-get home."

The group broke into raucous laughter. Kerri couldn't tell if it was over the all-too-apparent fear in Brett's voice, or the fact that a bunch of white, obviously suburbanite kids had been at a hard-core rap concert.

Leo glanced at the car, then at each of them. Kerri felt his eyes lingering on her. She shuddered. Then his gaze flicked back to the car again.

"Alright," he said, "let's handle this shit nice and easy. Tell you what we'll do. Y'all give us—"

"Fuck you, nigger!"

Kerri was just as surprised as Leo and his cronies. She heard feet pounding on the pavement, and turned to see Brett running away, racing toward the large abandoned house at the end of the block. A second later, Stephanie and Heather dashed off after him. Stephanie's cell phone slipped from her grasp and clattered onto the pavement as she fled. She didn't stop to retrieve it. Tyler chased after them, shouting. Javier and Kerri stared at each other for the beat of one heart, and then he grabbed her arm and pulled her along.

"Come on!"

"Hey," Leo shouted. "The fuck did you just call me?"

"Oh Jesus," Kerri gasped. "Oh my God . . ."

"What the hell is wrong with you guys?" Javier called after their fleeing friends. "You assholes are gonna get us killed."

"Shut the fuck up and run," Tyler answered, not bothering to look over his shoulder and see if Kerri was okay.

"Yo," Leo yelled, "get back here. Hey, motherfuckers. I'm talking to you!"

Kerri screamed as she heard them give chase. Leo had stopped shouting. Their pursuers moved in silence, save for grunts, gasps, and the sound of their feet slapping the sidewalk.

"Go," Javier said, shoving her forward. He kept up the pace behind her, putting himself between Kerri and their pursuers. He paused only to duck down and retrieve Stephanie's cell phone.

The chase continued down the street—Brett in the lead, followed by Stephanie and Heather, then Tyler, with Kerri and Javier bringing up the rear. The strap on one of Heather's sandals broke, and the shoe flew off her foot. She slowed for a second, and Tyler shot past her, not stopping. Crying, Heather kicked off her other shoe and sped up again, running barefoot. Kerri noticed in horror that her friend was leaving bloody footprints. Heather must have cut her foot on some of the broken glass littering the sidewalk. Kerri wondered if Heather even realized it, or if adrenaline and instinct had overridden the pain.

They fled past the row homes and entered the wasteland of jumbled debris. The streetlights in this section weren't functioning, and the shadows deepened around them. Kerri heard something scurrying behind a pile of crumbled masonry and nearly shrieked. Behind them, the sound of pursuit halted.

"Yo," Leo bellowed. "Get the fuck back here. You all are asking for trouble you keep going."

Ignoring him, they made a beeline for the abandoned house. It loomed before them in the darkness. Heather stumbled and fell behind, but Kerri and Javier helped her. Even though the pursuit had stopped, they didn't slow. Kerri's breathing became jagged, more frantic. She tried to calm herself by looking at her friends. Stephanie was mouthing the Lord's Prayer. Brett's face was set in a worried scowl, his steps drunken and dazed. Tyler's eyes were wide and panicked, and beads of sweat dotted his forehead.

Kerri glanced back and saw Leo and the rest of his gang lurking at the edge of the wasteland, slowly milling back and forth. He shouted something, but they were too far away to hear him. Probably another threat. Kerri wondered why they'd given up chasing them so easily. Maybe they were content to busy themselves with Tyler's car. She felt a pang of sorrow. Poor Tyler—Dustin would be livid when he found out.

Javier urged them on faster, careful to step over the worst holes, guiding them around piles of debris. Brett mumbled something, his voice low and on the edge of hysteria.

"Shut the fuck up," Javier told him. "It's your stupid ass that got us into this mess. What the hell were you thinking, you dumb motherfucker?"

Instead of responding, Brett quietly sobbed.

Javier handed Stephanie her cell phone.

"Thanks," she mumbled.

"What now?" Tyler asked, conceding to Javier.

"In there." He nodded at the abandoned home. "We hole up inside and call the cops."

"But they'll see us go in," Heather whispered.

"I don't think so," Javier said. "We can see them back there because of the streetlights. But here it's dark. I noticed as we were running up—you can't see shit from back there. Just shadows. Long as we're quick and quiet, we should be okay."

Stephanie eyed the house warily. "What if somebody lives there?"

"Look at it," Javier said. "Who's gonna live inside a shithole like this?"

"Crackheads," Kerri answered. "Homeless people. Rats."

Instead of replying, Javier pushed past them, plodding up the sagging porch steps. They groaned under his weight, but held. The handrail wobbled when he grasped it for support, and small flakes of rust and paint rained down onto the pavement. The others followed. Kerri studied the rough brick and mortar of the exterior wall. It was covered with sickly, whitish green moss. The windows were all boarded over with moisture-stained plywood sheets. Curiously, unlike the occupied row homes, this abandoned house was free of graffiti.

When they were all on the porch, Javier explored the

pitted wooden door. It was misshapen and water-warped, and several coats of paint peeled off it, revealing a variety of sickly colors. He found the doorknob, an old cut-crystal affair, and turned it. The door opened with a grating squeal. Dirt and paint flecks fell onto his forearm and dusted his hair. Standing back, Javier brushed the debris away.

"Hello?" Brett's voice was a hoarse whisper. "Anybody home?"

There was no answer.

They peered inside, but the interior was hidden within a deep, oppressive darkness. Kerri had the impression that if she reached her hand out, the darkness would be a tangible thing, capable of sticking to her fingers like tar.

Javier shoved forward, stepping into the gloom. Kerri followed him. Stephanie and Heather hesitated for a moment before proceeding. Heather limped, still leaving bloody footprints in her wake. Brett trailed along behind them, followed by Tyler, who slammed the door shut once he'd stepped through it. The sound echoed throughout the structure. The others glared at him in annoyance. Tyler shrugged defiantly.

"We need some light," Kerri whispered.

She pulled out her cigarette lighter and flicked it. The shadows seemed to converge around the flame. Tyler opened his lighter and did the same. Heather, Javier, and Stephanie flipped open their cell phones, adding the weak, green illumination from the display screens.

Kerri turned in a circle, sweeping the lighter around. A cobweb brushed against her cheek. She shuddered, brushing it away. They were standing in a dank, mildewed foyer. A hallway stretched into the darkness. Several closed doors led off from it into other parts of the house. Yellow wallpaper peeled away from the dingy walls in large sheets, revealing cracked bare plaster splattered with black splotches of mildew. There were holes in the baseboards where rats and insects had chewed their way through.

Something scurried in the shadows—a dry, rustling sound. Heather stifled a shriek.

"Hear anything?" Javier asked Tyler, nodding toward the door.

Tyler leaned close and listened. Then he shook his head and shrugged. "Nothing. This lighter is burning the shit out of my fingers, though."

He released the button and the flame disappeared. Somehow, even with the other lighter and the cell phones still glowing, it suddenly seemed darker.

"Maybe they're gone," Brett suggested. "Maybe they gave up."

"And maybe," Tyler said, "they're fucking up Dustin's car while we're standing here. Fuck this shit."

He reached for the doorknob.

"What are you doing?" Kerri whispered.

"Taking a peek outside. I'm just gonna open it a crack."

His hand turned. The knob didn't move. He jiggled it, but it remained motionless. Frozen.

Stephanie squeezed closer to Brett and peered over his shoulder, watching Tyler. "What's wrong?"

"It's stuck or something. Fucking thing won't open."

Javier groaned. "Did it lock behind you?"

"How the hell should I know?"

"Chill, bro. Keep your voice down. We don't want them to hear us."

"Fuck that. I ain't staying in this shithole all night. My fucking brother's car is out there."

"You should have thought of that before."

Tyler wheeled around, facing him. He jabbed a finger into Javier's chest.

"This shit isn't my fault. Brett's the one who called them niggers."

Javier stiffened. His jaw clenched. For a moment, Kerri thought he was going to punch Tyler, but then he relaxed. He held his hands up in surrender.

"Okay," he whispered. "Okay. Relax. But we can't go breaking that door down, man. If they're still out there, they'll hear us. Our best bet is to go into one of these rooms, find some windows, and see if we can peer through the cracks in the boards. Maybe we can figure out where they are."

Tyler nodded, slumping his shoulders.

"You're right."

He strode forward and opened the first door on his left. The rusty hinges creaked as the door swung slowly, revealing more darkness. Kerri stepped up behind him, holding her lighter over his head to illuminate the room beyond.

"Hurry up," she whispered. "My lighter's getting hot."

Tyler hesitated.

And in his hesitation, everything changed.

Shit happened.

Kerri saw the looming, shadowy figure standing on the other side of the doorway. She knew that Tyler saw it, too, because his entire body stiffened. He made no sound. Kerri tried to speak, tried to warn the others, but her mouth suddenly went dry, and her tongue felt like sandpaper. Her breath hitched in her chest.

The person inside the room was impossibly large. She couldn't make out any features, but its head must have nearly been touching the ceiling. The figure's shoulders were broad, and its torso was thick as an oil drum. There was something in the figure's hand. It looked like a giant hammer.

Tyler moaned.

There was a flash of movement.

When she was twelve years old, Kerri's older brother had managed to get some M-80 firecrackers. They were as big as the palm of her hand and made her nervous when she held them. Her brother and his college buddies had shoved the explosive deep inside a watermelon just to see what would happen. When they lit the fuse, there was a titanic clap of thunder followed by a massive spray of seeds and pink pulp and rind.

That was what happened to Tyler's head. Only it wasn't seeds and rind, it was bone and hair and brains. Warm wetness splashed across Kerri's face and soaked through her shirt and bra. She tasted it in the back of her throat. Felt it running down her head and inside her ears. Something hot and vile and *solid* trickled over her lips. She gagged and dropped her lighter.

Tyler stood there for a moment, jittering. Then he toppled over with a thud.

Kerri opened her mouth to scream, but Brett beat her to it.

The giant figure lunged toward them.

CHAPTER TWO

"Fuck this shit," Leo muttered. "I ain't going any further."

Markus and the others gaped at him. They'd halted at the edge of the streetlights, about fifty yards from the abandoned house at the end of the block. A group of clouds had passed over the moon, and the area was now pitch-black.

"You just gonna let them get away with that?" Jamal asked. "You hear what they said?"

Leo nodded. "I heard. But look at the facts, Jamal. Six white kids. Judging by their clothes and shit, I'd say they were from the suburbs. Come into the city, got lost, broke down in the hood—and then *we* come walking up. Probably scared the piss out of them."

"True that," Markus said. "They probably thought we were slinging crack or something. Probably sit at home, watching *The Wire* and shit, and thinking everyone in the hood is a drug dealer."

"That's fucked up," Chris replied. He was the youngest of the group and looked up to them all. Leo and Markus, especially. Wanting their approval, he always went along with whatever they decided. "So what are we gonna do?"

Leo paused, considering their options. He stared at the

house and the darkness surrounding it. It had been a good evening. They'd gone to a party, met some girls, had a fun time. All was right with the world. They'd been walking home, bullshitting with one another and laughing, when they'd come across the broken-down station wagon. They knew right away that the teenagers inside needed help. They didn't belong here. They were outsiders. Easy prey. This was a bad neighborhood during daylight, but at night—at night, it really was a jungle. At night, there were monsters on the streets.

And even worse things in the shadows.

Crack, heroin, and meth whores roamed up and down the street, opening their diseased mouths and other orifices for ten or twenty bucks—enough to get the next fix. Drug dealers controlled everything—the street corners, the houses, the apartment buildings, and all that lay between them. The homes had rats, mold, mildew, roaches, and all sorts of other health hazards. A broken sewer pipe spilled shit and piss into the street, yet the public works department did nothing about it. The cops didn't come down here unless they were passing through on their way to another call. Neither did the ambulances or firemen. To serve and protect didn't mean much in this part of the city.

Two years ago, an obese woman who was too fat to get out of her house, had suffered a heart attack in front of the television while watching Judge Judy. Her family had called 911. Twice. And then the next day. And the day after that. A week passed before paramedics arrived. By then, the dead woman had begun to lose weight.

Just another day in paradise.

A year ago, a twelve-year-old girl with cerebral palsy had died just a few doors down from where they were now standing. She'd lain for days on top of a feces-and-urine-covered bare mattress in a fetid, sweltering room, begging for water. Her family ignored her cries. Malnourished and dehydrated, she was covered with maggot-infested bedsores and her muscles had begun to atrophy. When she was finally discovered, the little girl weighed less than forty pounds. The outline of her body was imprinted on the mattress. The Department of Human Services could have helped her—but the social workers never came to this section of the city.

No one did.

And the shunned house at the end of the street was very hungry.

Leo's gaze was drawn back to it again. He didn't want to look at the structure, but its terrible allure was magnetic. He *had* to look. He shivered and hoped the others didn't notice. He didn't want them to know he was scared—even though he knew damn well that they were, too.

Everyone was scared of the house at the end of the block. Better to let your kids play in the middle of the Interstate than to play down there.

People who went inside that house were never seen again.

They were heard sometimes—faint, muffled screams that ended abruptly.

But they were never seen.

Every neighborhood—even theirs—had a haunted house.

Leo shook his head. Why did those white kids have to react like that? He and the guys were just having a little bit of fun. He was about to say, "Alright, let's handle this shit nice and easy. Y'all give us twenty bucks and we'll fix the car for you." And they could have, too. Angel Montoya ran a chop shop two blocks down, and Angel liked Leo and his crew. He let them hang out at the garage sometimes and gave them free sodas from the dusty machine out back. He'd have fixed the car if they'd asked him to. But before Leo could finish the sentence, the kid with the glasses had shouted "Fuck you, nigger" and then they'd fled. Leo had been momentarily stunned by the reaction. It wasn't the first time a white person had called him that, but he hadn't been expecting it tonight—not under these circumstances. He'd felt angered and hurt, and it took him a moment to recover from his shock. Then he'd shouted after them, trying to warn them not to go any farther, not to run into the darkness at the end of the street, not to venture near the house. He didn't know if they'd heard him or not. They kept running. Hell, the one girl had dropped her cell phone and left it there. Another dude had picked it up, but obviously, she wasn't too worried about it. None of them had even glanced back. In hindsight, looking at it from their eyes, he couldn't blame them if they had heard his shouts and just ignored him.

He probably shouldn't have called them motherfuckers. Not the best way to win friends and influence people, in hindsight.

The distant sound of gunshots rang out from several blocks away. Neither Leo or the others even bothered to duck. They were used to it. The noise was as common as traffic or sirens or pigeons or any other city sound. Leo's older brother used to say that the sound of gunshots helped him sleep at night.

Now his brother was upstate at Cresson, serving twenty years to life on some bullshit charges. Leo wondered what sounds lulled him to sleep at night in prison.

"What are we gonna do?" Chris asked again. "We just

gonna walk away and pretend we didn't know they were here?"

"I like the sound of that," Jamal said. "Better if we mind our own business. Safer that way. Know what I'm saying?"

Leo glanced at his friends, studying their faces. Then he turned his attention back to the house.

"I'll tell you what we're going to do. We're gonna call the po-po."

Markus laughed. "Five-oh ain't gonna do shit. Might as well call in the National Guard."

"You're probably right," Leo agreed. "But it ain't right, letting them go in there. You all know the stories about that place. Any of you feel like going in to rescue them?"

Markus stared at the ground. Jamal and Chris glanced at each other. The others looked away.

"None of you want to play hero?" Leo teased. "None of you want to rush in with guns blazing?"

None of them responded.

More gunshots rang out, then faded. A sleepy, laconic-sounding police siren started up from far away.

"Well," Leo said, after a pause. "That's okay. Because I don't want to, either. Not in that place."

He turned around and stared at the house again.

"Not in there."

CHAPTER THREE

As the looming figure lunged into the foyer, Kerri and Javier backed away, nearly knocking over Stephanie, Brett, and Heather. Bits of Tyler's hair, scalp, and blood dripped from the weapon the killer clutched in its gnarled hands—a rough-hewn chunk of granite the size of a watermelon. The boulder was affixed to a length of iron pipe. Together, they formed a crude but effective war hammer. Stunned, Kerri wondered how it was possible to lift such a thing, let alone swing it. Then her gaze turned to their attacker, and she wondered no more.

He drew himself up to his full height, raised the hammer, thrusting it before him, and bellowed—whether from rage or laughter, Kerri couldn't tell. Perhaps both. He stood well over seven feet tall. His chest, arms, and legs were corded with thick slabs of muscle. His skin was the color of provolone cheese and covered with large brown moles and festering sores. Bloody saliva dripped from his open mouth, leaking around gums that had receded from his black, broken teeth. His breathing was harsh and ragged. His head was bald and misshapen. He glared at them with eyes that were almost perfectly round, rather than oval-shaped. His pupils were black. He was nearly nude, clad only in black garbage bags held together with frayed duct tape. They rustled as he moved.

His penis—as big as the rest of him—bobbed and swayed, jutting from between the plastic bags. Kerri gagged at the sight. He was uncircumcised, and the foreskin looked infected. Pus dripped from the putrid member, splattering onto the floor. Worst of all was the attacker's stench. It was revolting—sour milk mixed with feces and sweat. Kerri's nose burned.

She noticed all of this in a matter of seconds, but it was the longest moment of Kerri's life. Time seemed to pause.

Then it came rushing back with a wallop.

The hulk backhanded her, knocking Kerri off her feet. She slammed into the opposite wall and slumped to the floor. Spitting blood, Kerri spotted her cigarette lighter. Without thinking about it, she reached out and snatched it. The madman laughed. Kerri scrambled to get to her feet, but she slipped in a spreading pool of Tyler's blood.

Their attacker laughed again. With his other hand, he swung the mallet. Kerri watched, cringing as Javier dodged the blow, narrowly avoiding having his chest crushed.

The five teens scattered. Shrieking, Heather ran to the end of the hall and flung open one of the doors, disappearing through it. The only signs of her passage were the bloody footprints she left in her wake. Javier shouted after Heather, but if she heard him, she showed no sign. While the figure menaced Brett and Stephanie, Javier kneeled over Kerri and thrust out his hand. She grasped it, and he pulled her to her feet. They ran down the hallway in blind panic, forgetting about Stephanie and Brett. Forgetting about Tyler. Even forgetting about each other. The only thing their minds comprehended was survival.

They followed Heather's crimson trail through the

open doorway. Kerri glanced back once and saw what was happening to Stephanie, but her feet kept moving.

Their friends' screams faded behind them.

"Open, you fucker!"

Sobbing, Stephanie clawed at the entrance, trying to get back outside. She beat at the locked door with her fists. Tears coursed down her mascara-stained cheeks. She babbled a string of nonsense—jumbled prayers and pleas for her parents to come and get her.

Brett tugged at her arm. "Steph, come on!"

She shoved him away.

A massive shadow fell over them both, and the hammer whistled through the air. It slammed into Stephanie's curled fist with a sickening crunch. Blood and pulp squirted out from beneath the stone. Stephanie wailed, gaping at the pulverized flap of meat where her hand had been. The attacker pulled the hammer back for another swing, and Stephanie flailed helplessly. Blood jetted from her crushed appendage. Brett moved to help her, but before he could, the man swung the hammer again. This time, the blow crushed Stephanie's head.

Brett froze, helpless, feet rooted to the floor. All flight instinct had left him. He stared at Stephanie's body, trying to understand what he was seeing. Put him behind a chessboard and everything was crystal clear. Give him a trigonometry problem and he'd solve it. Those things made sense to him. They had logic and order. Rules.

There was no logic here. No order. There were no rules that he could see and understand. Instead, there was some kind of monster (because it couldn't be a man—no, his mind wouldn't accept that this *thing* was human). It had killed Tyler. And now it . . .

Brett screamed.

Something was wrong with Stephanie's face. He saw it as she slid down to the floor. Her features were mashed together. Her eyes and nose and mouth—they were too close. Her lips—lips he'd kissed just an hour ago—were smashed almost beyond the point of recognition. Her head wasn't round anymore. Instead, it looked like a deflated basketball. The top of it was split open, and inside that red chasm was something that looked like curds of jellied lasagna.

Her brains, Brett thought. *Oh, Jesus, that's her brains.*

Brett winced as the bile rose in the back of his throat. It burned. He glanced up at the killer.

The killer laughed a third time—hoarse and booming.

In that instant, Brett fell back on what he knew best— logic. This was nothing more than a puzzle. A real-life video game. All he had to do to survive was figure it out. As their attacker raised his bloody weapon, Brett ran through the possibilities. Then he did the last thing he hoped the monstrosity would expect—he raced right past it and flung himself into the room from which it had emerged. The man-thing roared, clearly enraged.

Even as he wept, Brett couldn't help smiling.

Weren't ready for that, were you, fucker?

He ran, charging across the room. Ahead of him was another door. It led deeper into the house. Brett dashed through it without hesitation, plunging into the darkness, heedless of where it might lead.

His pursuer's feet plodded along behind him, shaking the wooden floor.

Somewhere beyond the walls, perhaps in another room, Kerri started screaming, her voice broken and shrill.

Brett knew just exactly how she felt.

CHAPTER FOUR

Kerri's world had shattered before her eyes. Tyler was dead. Stephanie was dead.

Shit happens . . .

Stephanie had been her best friend since kindergarten. They'd gone to the same classes at St. Mary's Catholic School from first grade through seventh, at which point they'd both switched to public school. They'd studied together. Grown up together.

Kerri's breath caught in her throat as Javier urged her along through the darkness. Although their vision had adjusted, their only source of light was Javier's cell phone, which he held open. Her hands were shaking too much to hold her cigarette lighter. Kerri heard Javier's nose whistling as he breathed. She tried to speak, tried to tell him to slow down, to ask him if he'd called 911, but she couldn't find her voice. Kerri shuffled forward a few more steps and stopped. She felt dizzy all of the sudden. There was pressure building behind her eyes.

She closed them, hoping the pain would go away.

Maybe Steph wasn't dead. Maybe she was still alive back there. After all, she and Javier had been fleeing. Maybe what she thought she saw happen hadn't actually occurred.

Kerri heard the sound again. That awful noise the hammer had made when it . . .

Tyler . . .

Tyler and Steph . . . Steph and Tyler . . .

They were definitely both dead. And she'd done nothing to help them. Instead, she'd run away. How was that possible?

Tyler had taken Kerri's virginity. Steph was the one who listened to all the details afterward, just like she had when Steph lost her virginity under less pleasant circumstances a few years earlier. Steph was her sister in every way that mattered and now she was dead.

Tyler wasn't just her boyfriend. He'd been her world. Yes, things had been difficult lately. They'd been fighting a lot. Fed up with his immaturity, she'd been thinking about leaving him. But all the arguments and annoyance— those things just proved how much they'd really loved each other. You didn't fight with somebody if you didn't care about them. And now he was gone. Dead. Lying on the floor at the front of the house, cooling and coalescing, his blood mingling with Steph's.

The pressure in her head boiled over. Kerri opened her eyes and screamed. It was a deep, raw, throat-stripping shriek that seemed to go on forever—

—until Javier clamped his hand over her mouth and pressed tight.

"Stop it," he whispered. "Just stop."

She struggled against him, and his grip tightened. Kerri felt her snot running between his fingers. She tried to talk, tried to tell him that they had to go back for Tyler and Steph, but he stared into her eyes, unblinking, and shook his head.

"I know. I know. I'm feeling it, too. But we've got to keep going. Got to find Heather and the others, and then get out of here. You keep screaming and that fucking *thing* will find us first. Now, stop it. Okay?"

His long-fingered, almost feminine hand remained on her mouth, but the pressure decreased. His eyes glittered in the open cell phone's dim light.

Kerri blinked.

Javier removed his hand and she sobbed. He pressed a finger to her lips, silencing her again.

"No. Not here. Not anymore. We have to leave here."

After a moment, Kerri nodded. Javier removed his finger. She regretted it almost immediately. His touch— that tiny bit of human contact—had been reassuring. Now panic and grief threatened to overwhelm her once more. When she spoke, her voice was barely a whisper. "Did you call someone?"

"I can't get any bars in here. Old place like this? Probably asbestos in the walls or some shit."

Kerri frowned. Could asbestos block cell phone coverage? She didn't know.

"What now?" she asked.

"We sit a minute and listen. I think it went after Brett and Stephanie."

"Steph's . . . it got her."

"How do you know?"

"I saw it as we were running away. It . . . that thing smashed her head with the hammer."

"What about Brett?"

"I don't know."

"Shit." Javier took a deep breath and paused. "We need to find Heather. Then we find a way out."

"What about Brett? And we can't just leave Tyler's and Stephanie's bodies behind."

"We're not going to do them much good if we're dead."

He beckoned her to follow him, and crawled behind an old couch that had been covered with a filthy, moldy tarp. Kerri crawled along behind him. They sat there, huddled together in the darkness, and waited. They heard no sound, save their own breathing. Kerri glanced around the room, trying to discern their surroundings. She couldn't see much. The shadows were too thick. Maybe it had been a living room at one time, but now it was a junk heap. The very atmosphere seemed full of the same despair she felt inside. Garbage lay strewn across the dirty wooden floor—empty cans, broken bottles, shattered drug vials, a shriveled condom. She wondered what had happened to the people who'd left the trash there. Had they been slaughtered, just like Tyler and Steph? In addition to the sofa they were hiding behind, there were a few other pieces of broken furniture in the room. She could make out their shapes, sitting beneath tarps in the gloom. Above her, a cracked, smudged mirror hung askew. The nail it was hanging from was slowly working its way out of the plaster. Kerri considered that they were lucky their passage through the room hadn't caused it to crash to the floor, alerting their pursuer to their location.

She pulled out her lighter and flicked it. The small flame did little to dispel the gloom, but it made her feel better.

They spotted a few bloody footprints on the floor, but there were less of them now. Kerri assumed that Heather's wound had started to clot.

Javier held the phone up to his face and squinted at the display. Kerri stared at him, hoping to see a positive expression. Instead, he merely frowned and shook his head.

She looked up again and caught her reflection in the cracked mirror. Her blue eyes were nearly perfectly round and the freckles on her face stood out in the faint cell phone glow and lighter flame like black spatters of paint. There were dark circles under her eyes that hadn't been there an hour before.

Javier lowered the phone again. Then he grabbed Kerri by her elbow and forced her to move, directing them to another door on the far side of the room. She put her lighter back in her pocket. They crawled on their hands and knees, and Kerri winced as a long splinter of wood pricked her palm. She pulled it out with her teeth and spat it aside. A thin bead of blood welled out of the cut. She glanced back down at the floor and saw another drop of her blood there. As she watched, it disappeared, almost as if the floorboards were drinking it up.

Maybe that's why we're not seeing as many of Heather's footprints, she thought. *The house is gobbling them all up.*

They reached the open door and Javier leaned forward and peeked around the corner. Then he nodded at her, indicating that the coast was clear. They crawled through the doorway into another hallway. Above them, an ornate lamp hung from the ceiling, draped with spiderwebs. The floor was covered with worn, stained carpet the color of lima beans. Several closed doors lined the narrow hall. Kerri shook her head, trying to get a sense of the house's layout.

Javier must have been as puzzled as she was. He said, "Place is like a goddamned maze. I can't figure it out."

"Well, we know what's back that way." Kerri pointed.

"Yeah, but we don't know what's ahead. Or where Heather is."

"She'll be okay. We'll find her."

"I hope so," Javier said. "I don't know what . . ."

His voice trailed off, choked with emotion. Kerri felt him trembling beside her. She touched his shoulder.

"It'll be okay," she whispered.

He glanced up at the ceiling and frowned. Kerri followed his gaze. A crude string of electrical cords and bare lightbulbs dangled from the ceiling. They didn't look like part of the house. To Kerri, it appeared as if they'd been added as an afterthought.

"Weird," Javier muttered.

She nodded.

Javier stood and helped Kerri to her feet. Moving cautiously, they tried the first door. It opened easily, revealing a brick wall.

Javier grunted. "What the hell is this shit?"

Kerri tapped him on the shoulder. "Do you think Heather came through here?"

"Through the wall?"

"No! Through this hallway."

Javier shrugged. "She must have. I don't see any more footprints, though."

"Maybe her foot stopped bleeding."

He turned back to the bricks and placed his palm against them. Kerri studied them, too. The mortar was cracked and covered with moss and mold, but the wall still stood firm.

"We can't just stand here," she said. "That thing could come back at any minute."

Nodding in agreement, Javier started forward. The floorboards creaked slightly as they walked. They froze, waiting to see if the sound had attracted attention. The house remained quiet. Kerri pulled her lighter out and flicked it on again. Dust swirled around the flame. Moving on, they stopped at the next door, on the opposite side of the hall, and listened. Hearing no sound from inside, they opened it.

Kerri slapped her hand over her mouth and bit down, trying not to scream.

Beyond the door was a small room devoid of furnishings save for an old, rusty heater sitting against one wall—

—and the scattering of bones that littered the floor.

There was no question that they were human remains. The two and a half human skulls were a dead giveaway. The other bones were too big to belong to an animal—at least, any kind of animal that would be found in a Philadelphia ghetto. One of the hands still had a wedding ring on its finger. The flame from her lighter glinted off of it.

"Jesus." Javier turned to her. His eyes were wide and wet. "Jesus Christ, Kerri. What the fuck have we stumbled into here? What is this?"

The scream she'd been suppressing turned into a giggle. The sound alarmed her, but she couldn't help it.

"It's like you said, Javier. Shit happens."

Then the laughter bubbled over. Javier hissed at her to shut up. Kerri could tell by his expression that she was freaking him out. Hell, she was freaking herself out. But the laughter came anyway, and echoed off the walls.

It didn't stop until another door on the other side of the hallway crashed open and a figure jumped out at them.

CHAPTER FIVE

Perry Watkins peered out his smudged window and shook his head. Behind him, his wife, Lawanda, made a clicking noise with her tongue and mirrored the motion with her own head.

"What the hell was that all about?" Lawanda's tone was shaken. "I heard shouting. Those slingers fighting for the corner again?"

Perry shook his head harder, picked up an empty beer can, and spat a wad of phlegm into it. His heart was beating fast, and his knees felt weak and rubbery. The house at the end of the block had always had that effect on him. Had since he was just a little boy. Still did. Especially when someone went inside.

"Damn fools. That's what it's about. Goddamned fools."

"Who?"

"Bunch of white kids. Looks like their car broke down or something. Leo and that group of kids he hangs out with tried to help them, but the white kids run off."

Lawanda paused. "Which way did they run?"

Perry lowered his voice. "Guess."

"Oh Lord." Lawanda's eyes grew wide. "No one goes near that building. Not if they want to live. Everyone round here knows that place is haunted."

"Everyone around *here*," Perry stressed. "But I'll be damned if them kids were from around here."

"Come on, baby." Lawanda pulled nervously at his shirt. "Get away from the window. Somebody might see you."

Perry resisted the urge to pull away. "Who's gonna see me? The ghosts in the house? They're busy right now. They've got . . . company."

"You know what happens when folks don't mind their own business with that place."

"What? You think they care about an old man looking out the window? They gonna come up through our basement? Get me while I'm sitting on the toilet? Bullshit, Lawanda. There ain't nothing supernatural in that house. It's just crazy, inbred crackheads."

"Since when did you stop believing the stories about that place? After all the folks that have gone missing?"

"I ain't saying I don't believe. Sure, the place is dangerous. Spooky. But it ain't monsters. Whatever it is that lives inside there, they don't bother anyone unless folks go sticking their noses inside. It's just like everything else in this neighborhood—the best way to stay out of trouble is to not get involved. Long as we stay out of it and don't go bothering them, we'll be alright. You know how it is around here. You've got to watch your back and take care of your own shit. If you don't, sooner or later the street will get you."

He pulled back the shade and peered outside again. He noticed that several of his neighbors were looking through their windows, as well—just as worried, just as perplexed.

Just as guilty of inaction as he was.

But what were they supposed to do? Storm in there with torches and pitchforks? It had been tried, and the neighborhood had paid the price in blood. Call the police or the fire department? That had been tried before as well, with even worse results. Picket city hall and demand action? Hell, city hall was part of the problem. They knew all about the house. They just didn't care. Wouldn't do to have something like that show up in the press. Not with its history—not with the string of murders and disappearances. No, city hall was content to sweep it under the rug, just like they did with all the other problems down here.

"Now if it was happening in the suburbs," Perry muttered under his breath, "you know damn well they'd do something about it."

"What are you mumbling about?"

"Nothing. Leo and them boys are coming back this way. They probably gonna steal the car."

"You always think the worst of people."

"Maybe I do, but can you blame me? Leo used to be a good kid, but he don't come around no more. He's probably into drugs. You know how all these kids down here turn out eventually. Rotten. Or dead. It's like this place poisons them."

"Not always," she said, even as she nodded in reluctant agreement. "What are they doing now?"

"It looks like they're . . . oh, hell no. They're coming up on our porch. What the hell do they want? I ain't getting involved in this shit."

As if on cue, there was the sound of footsteps plodding up their porch stairs, followed by somebody beating on their door. It sounded like the knocker was using their fist. The door rattled in its frame, and the chain lock at the top jingled.

Still muttering, Perry rose from his seat. Lawanda grabbed his arm.

"Don't answer it, Perry."

He pulled his arm free. "If I don't, they gonna knock the damn door down. Now stay here."

The pounding increased—thunderous blows that seemed to shake the entire house.

"Hold your horses, goddamn it! I'm coming."

In the corner, next to the door, were a coatrack and a small rolltop desk. Perry opened the desk drawer and withdrew a revolver nearly as old as he was. He didn't have to check to make sure that it was loaded. He never took the bullets out of the weapon. Stuffing it in his waistband, he moved toward the door. The pistol felt snug against the small of his back.

He opened the door and saw Leo with his fist raised, ready to knock again. Behind him stood Jamal, Chris, Markus, some kid they called Dookie (Perry didn't know his real name) and some other youths Perry didn't recognize.

"Mr. Watkins," Leo said. "You sleeping?"

"Does it look like I was sleeping, boy? Why you beating on my door this time a night?" His eyes narrowed suspiciously. "You on drugs?"

"No, we ain't on no fucking drugs! You know me better than that, Mr. Watkins."

"Maybe," Perry admitted. "Can't be too sure these days, though. I thought maybe y'all was coming in here to rob me or something."

Leo looked genuinely offended. "Now why would you go thinking something like that?"

"What happened with them white kids? Y'all spook them?"

"We didn't do shit," Jamal exclaimed, but fell silent again when Leo glared at him.

"Maybe a little bit," Leo admitted, turning back to Perry. "But we didn't mean nothing by it. We were just goofing around and shit. We were gonna help them with their car."

Perry scowled. "Help them? You ain't no mechanic."

"No, I ain't. But Angel is. We were thinking—"

"The fella who runs the chop shop?"

"Yeah. We figured those kids had money, right? I mean, they were wearing nice clothes and it was pretty obvious that they ain't from around here. We'd hook them up with Angel, get him to fix the car, and then we'd get a payment—you know, like a finder's fee and shit."

Perry threw his head back and laughed. "A finder's fee? Boy, you ain't Triple fucking A."

Leo ignored the taunt. "Can we use your phone, Mr. Watkins?"

"For what?"

"To call the police. Tell 'em about those kids."

"Ain't y'all got cell phones?"

The youths shrugged and shook their heads.

"No," Chris said. "We can't afford them."

"Well, I ain't got no phone either," Perry lied. "The damn phone company shut it off two weeks ago. Said I—"

He fell silent as Lawanda crept up behind him and gently pulled him away from the door.

"You boys come on inside. But mind your shoes. Take them off at the door. I don't want you tracking dirt up in here. I just cleaned this morning."

Smiling, Leo stepped into the house and did as he was told. The big toe on his left foot stuck out of a hole in his sock. One by one, the other kids followed him inside and removed their shoes.

Perry groaned. "Oh, for God's sake, Lawanda . . ."

She shushed him with a stern look. "Leo and his friends want to get involved and do the right thing. That's a sure sight more than anyone else wants to do around here these days. If they want to use our phone, then you darn well better let them. A fine example you're setting, Perry Watkins."

Leo beamed. "Thank you, Mrs. Watkins."

"Never you mind, Leo," she scolded, turning her attention to him. "Not that I think that calling the police will do a lick of good, but I ain't about to stop you from doing the right thing. But none of y'all should be out this late. You know what these streets are like after dark. The phone's in the kitchen. Leo, you go make your call. The rest of you sit down. I'll fix you something to eat."

While they got settled, Perry shuffled toward the refrigerator and pulled out a can of beer. Before popping the top, he pressed the cool can against his forehead and sighed. It was going to be a long night. There was nothing Lawanda liked more than playing den mother to a bunch of teenagers. They'd never been able to have kids of their own, and she absolutely doted on all the kids who lived on the block. Every week when they went to church, Lawanda asked God to watch out for them all.

Perry shook his head again and wondered if God was watching out for the kids who'd run into the house at the end of the street.

He hoped so.

But he had doubts. Serious doubts. He'd lied to Lawanda before. He believed everything that was said about the abandoned house.

Like most other people, God didn't have any business inside of that place.

But if you listened to all the neighborhood rumors about the place, the devil sure did.

CHAPTER SIX

Heather felt like her heart was going to explode. She sat in absolute darkness, unable to think or move—barely able to breathe. She shivered—partly from shock and partly from the cold wetness soaking her underwear and jeans. She'd peed herself at some point, and hadn't even realized it until now. Her foot still hurt, but at least it had stopped bleeding. She'd been afraid to look at the wound, but she had to. It wasn't deep, but it was long and filled with dirt and debris. She knew she'd have to clean it soon or risk infection.

Heather shook her head, exasperated with herself. Infection was the least of her worries right now.

She listened intently, expecting to hear the heavy, plodding footsteps of their pursuer, but the bizarre house was quiet. Somehow the stillness was more disconcerting than if she'd heard screaming. When she was younger, Heather used to play hide and seek with her two older brothers. She'd find a good hiding spot—the shrubs in front of the house, the toolshed down by the garden, the basement—and hunker down, but then her brothers would stop hunting for her and go play video games instead. It used to frustrate her, and she'd end up shouting, trying to lure them to her hiding place. For a brief moment, Heather considered yelling now—just standing up and hollering, *You're getting colder!* like a game of hot and cold.

But the only thing growing cold was Tyler's corpse.

Heather bit the inside of her lower lip to stop from braying nervous laughter. Why was this happening? She felt a sudden surge of anger for Tyler. Dead or not, this was his fault. He had to come out and get his fucking drugs. He couldn't wait for another time. No, he had to screw everything up again because he was an asshole. What had Kerri ever seen in him?

She pulled her knees up to her chest and hugged them, shivering. She felt a twinge of guilt over that thought. Tyler was dead, after all, and no one was supposed to talk ill of the dead, at least not according to her mother.

She considered pulling out her cell phone and calling for help, or at least using the display pad's light for illumination, but she was worried that if she did, the killer might hear the tones as she dialed or see the light from under the door.

Her thoughts turned to Javier. She hoped he was okay. Instead of following her, he'd stayed behind to help Kerri. Despite her fears, Heather felt pangs of jealousy. Why would he do that? Javier was her boyfriend, not Kerri's. Kerri's boyfriend was dead. She didn't need to get Heather's boyfriend killed as well.

Heather rocked backward and something soft brushed against her head. Stifling a scream, she batted at it. Her hand came away sticky. A spiderweb.

She wondered what else was in here with her in the darkness.

Out in the hallway, she heard a floorboard creak. Heather froze, holding her breath.

The sound was not repeated.

Heather's fingernails dug into her palms, drawing

blood. She barely felt it. She imagined the killer waiting outside the door, standing in the hallway, foot poised over the creaky floorboard, waiting for her to come out. She waited, expecting at any moment to hear his terrible cry, or for the big hammer to smash down the door.

Instead, she heard somebody start laughing—a high-pitched, frantic sound, almost veering into crying.

Kerri?

It sure sounded like her.

The laughter came again, followed by a harsh, male voice that, despite the whispered tones, was familiar.

Kerri and Javier! It had to be. Heather was sure of it.

She jumped to her feet and stumbled toward the door, flinging it open. Even though the hallway was dark, it was still lighter than the room she'd been hiding in, and at first, Heather couldn't see anything. Before her eyes could adjust, she was greeted by screams.

Brett held his breath and crept across the old sagging floorboards, trying to tread as lightly as possible. He'd lost count of the number of rooms he'd fled through, running headlong, not stopping to examine his surroundings, just trying to lose his pursuer. He was left with the vague impression that the derelict house wasn't laid out like a normal dwelling. There were too many doors—some of them leading to nowhere, as he'd soon learned, much to his chagrin. There were hallways that seemed to double back and rooms that served no logical purpose. A bathroom with a loveseat propped against one deteriorating wall. A bedroom with shattered porcelain shards from a toilet strewn across the floor. Perhaps most bizarre was the absence of windows. From the outside of the house, he'd noticed many boarded-over windows on both the first and second floors. But here, inside the abandoned dwelling, all of those windows were missing. Someone had constructed walls over the panes. He'd also noticed that some of the rooms and hallways had makeshift lighting installed—a rough series of lightbulbs connected by a frayed power cord. So far, he'd found no way of turning them on.

As baffling as the layout was, he hoped his pell-mell dash through the labyrinthine construct would confuse the killer as well.

He peeked his head through the open door in front of him and found a kitchen. Quickly verifying that the room was clear, Brett ducked inside the kitchen and shut the door behind him. The hinges groaned, and flecks of rust fell onto his hand. The door had no lock, and the doorknob itself jiggled in his hand. Brett felt for the light switch. It was sticky. He pulled his fingers away in disgust, reprimanding himself for forgetting that there was no power in the house anyway. He'd tried the light switches in the other rooms and none had worked. He fumbled for his cell phone, flipped it open, and used the meager light of the display screen. At least it was good for illumination; he'd had no signal since entering the house.

He scanned the shadowy corners, looking for something to blockade the door with. He spotted two other doors. One looked like it led into a pantry. He assumed that the other door led out of the kitchen, unless it was another false door, opening up into a brick wall. The kitchen counters were cracked and warped, and covered with inch-thick layers of dust and grime. Cobwebs hung from the ceiling like party streamers, and the corners and sink were full of rat droppings and dead flies. The air was thick with the smell of mildew. Brett stepped closer to the sink. The stainless-steel basin was encrusted with brownish red stains and there was some sort of shriveled organic matter in the strainer over the drain. Wrinkling his nose, Brett turned his attention to the oven. The door had a brown handprint on it. Brett assumed it was blood, but long since dried. His eyes settled on an old, dented refrigerator. If he could move it over to the door without making much noise, it would serve as a decent blockade.

The memory of Steph's head suddenly appeared in his mind. Moaning softly, Brett gritted his teeth and forced the image away.

Flipping his cell phone shut, Brett tiptoed across the kitchen and pushed on one side of the refrigerator. It scuffed along the floor with a loud groan, moving only a fraction of an inch. Something rolled around inside of the appliance, jostled by the sudden movement. Brett opened the door and peered inside. With the darkness and his state of shock, he didn't comprehend what he was seeing at first. A jumble of whitish yellow forms filled the refrigerator's shelves. Slowly, he reached out and touched one. It was dry and textured, and felt fragile. He picked it up and pulled it out for a closer look.

It was a rat. The refrigerator was full of rat skeletons.

Gasping in disgust, Brett flung the bones to the floor and wiped his hands on his cargo pants. As he closed the refrigerator door, he heard footsteps approaching. Rather than the powerful, plodding steps of the guy who had been chasing him, these were lighter. More hurried.

Brett scampered across the kitchen and hid inside the pantry. He'd barely closed the door behind him when the other door on the far side of the kitchen opened and another figure entered the room.

Another one? Brett's fear grew strong again, threatening to overwhelm him. *How many of these freaks are in here?*

The new arrival was carrying a lantern, and its soft

glow filled the room. Brett peered through the slatted cracks in the pantry door, watching. This one was female. She was shorter than Tyler and Stephanie's killer, and more misshapen. She was naked and hairless. Both her head and her vagina were shaved. Her breasts hung low and flat, stretching almost to her belly, and barely moved as she walked. Something was wrong with her skin. It seemed too smooth, too shiny. And there were strange black lines crisscrossing her flesh—around her waist, up each leg, down her abdomen and encircling her neck. He stared harder, realizing what they were. Stitches.

The woman's skin wasn't her own. She was wearing someone else's.

Jesus, he thought. *Is she even a woman?*

As if sensing his presence, the freak turned toward the pantry, giving him a full frontal view. The tip of a pale, flaccid penis dangled from between the tanned, dead vagina.

Well, that answers that *question . . .*

The new arrival wasn't a hermaphrodite. It was a man wearing a dead woman's skin.

Maybe.

It was too dark for Brett to be sure.

Brett gaped, trying to keep as still as possible. The pantry was musty, and dust filled the air, getting into his nose and throat. His shoe brushed against something soft. He looked down and saw that it was a dead mouse—the carcass alive with wriggling, bulbous gray-white maggots.

The intruder shuffled closer. She/he raised its nose and sniffed the air. Then it was suddenly seized by a violent bout of harsh, ragged coughing. The figure doubled over, hacked up a wad of phlegm, and spat the fluid into its hand. It rolled the pinkish mucus between its finger-tips and then wiped it on its human vest. Then it raised its fingers to its nose and inhaled.

Grunting, it stepped toward the pantry door. It was close enough now for Brett to smell it. The stench was cloying—an overpowering mix of sweat, feces, urine, and blood. It reached for the door and Brett tensed, ready to leap out and clobber it as soon as the door was opened. His only advantage was the element of surprise.

Before the creature could open the door, however, it was distracted by the sound of approaching footsteps. Brett recognized them immediately. They were the same footsteps that had been chasing him through the house.

The kitchen door opened and the hulk that had killed Tyler and Stephanie appeared. He walked backward, dragging their corpses into the kitchen. Each of his hands clutched one of their legs. Its hammer was slung over its misshapen back and tied with a length of frayed exten-sion cord.

The other creature giggled.

"What you got there, Noigel?" Its voice sounded like someone gargling with broken glass. The tone answered for certain the question of its gender. Brett was pretty sure that no woman could ever sound like that. Besides, its shoulders were too broad to be a female's. It coughed again, and hocked up another wad of phlegm.

The big one—Noigel—grunted in response. Then it let go of Stephanie's leg. Brett winced as her foot thudded on the floorboards. He wanted to scream. Wanted to charge out of the pantry and kill the fucker who'd done this to her. Instead, he stood there, quaking. His terror filled him with shame and guilt. Javier would have fought back. He wouldn't have let Heather be murdered like that. Tyler would have kept it from happening to Kerri.

Brett felt snot and tears running down his face. What had he done to save Steph? Nothing. He'd been too scared.

He'd run away.

Enraged—at both himself and the killers—Brett looked through the slats again.

Noigel held up four fingers.

"Four more?"

Noigel nodded, then whined. Brett was reminded of a dog, begging for a treat.

"No," the other one said. "You get those two down below. Let the others have some fun. Been too long since we had company. We let the little ones up to play. They haven't had a chance to hunt in a while."

Little ones, Brett thought. *Children?*

Noigel's malformed lips stuck out in a pout. The smaller one crossed the kitchen and smacked him in the chest.

"Do what I said." The smaller one bent over and examined the corpses. "Look at this, Noigel! You smashed their heads. That's the best part. Why you wanna do that for?"

Noigel groaned apologetically.

"It's okay, you big baby. Long as I get one of their hearts, that's okay. Or this one's dick. I could go for a good man-chew. Better than beef jerky! Come on, I'll give you a hand."

The man in the woman suit leaned over and grabbed Stephanie's leg. Noigel whistled.

"I wish you'd learn to talk. What's wrong now?"

Noigel held up four fingers again.

"It doesn't matter. Not like they're gonna escape. Only way out is down below, and they'll never make it past the rest. Besides, the little ones will find them long before then. They out searching the house right now."

The thing called Noigel grunted. His friend cackled with laughter, which in turn gave way to another bout of coughing.

They dragged the bodies out of the room. Brett caught a glimpse of Stephanie's corpse, and hot tears streamed down his cheeks. The two cannibals left the room, disappearing through the second door that he'd noticed when he first entered the kitchen. The door slammed shut behind them. Brett could still hear the guy wearing the woman's skin talking, but now it sounded like they were beneath him. Brett assumed the door must lead down to a basement level. Brett listened to their footsteps fade, but when the silence returned, he stayed inside the pantry, too afraid to move. Noigel's friend had mentioned that there were more of them inside the house and "down below." Brett assumed that meant in the basement. How many, and more importantly, where were they right now? The man wearing a woman's body had said they were searching the house. Were they on this level, hiding in the shadows, waiting for him to pass by? Hunting his friends?

He had to find Javier, Heather, and Kerri. Had to warn them. Had to escape. But when he willed his feet to move, they rebelled. His knees trembled. His balls tightened and shrank. He glanced back down at the dead mouse and wondered how long it would be before the maggots started working on Tyler and Steph.

Then he imagined them going to work on himself.

Damn it. I can do this. I can't just hang out here in the closet and wait for them to come back.

Brett reached out with one shaking hand and pushed the pantry door open. Then he hurried across the kitchen, heading back in the direction he'd come. He reasoned that if there were other hunters on this floor of the house, they were probably in other areas and rooms. Otherwise, he'd have seen them during his escape from the foyer to here.

He took a deep breath, exited the kitchen, and tried to remember which direction he should go. He felt like crying.

CHAPTER SEVEN

Leo leaned forward in the chair and peeked through the curtains.

"How many times you gonna stare out that damn window?" Perry asked Leo. "You think the police will show up any quicker if you keep looking?"

Shrugging, Leo let the curtain fall back into place and slumped down in the chair.

"Gawking out that window," Perry continued, "ain't gonna do nothing but attract unwanted attention."

"Leave that boy alone," Lawanda scolded her husband. "You were doing the same thing just a little while ago."

Chris, Dookie, Markus and Jamal chuckled in the corner.

Perry took another swig of beer and shot his wife a dirty look over the rim of the can. It had been fifteen minutes since they'd called 911, and so far no one had responded to the call. Perry had suggested the boys wait outside for the cops to show, but Lawanda had shut that idea down in a hurry, inviting them to wait in the living room. Now he was stuck entertaining them when he should be getting ready for bed. On the television, a studio audience laughed as Tyler Perry ran around in drag. Perry groaned, wondering why the man had to dress like a fat woman in all his shows and movies. He hated Tyler Perry's sitcoms, but he watched them because Lawanda usually controlled the remote. Every evening, he resigned himself to episodes of *Dancing with the Stars* and bullshit sitcoms.

"The cops ain't gonna show," Markus said. "We're wasting time, yo."

"Maybe," Leo agreed. "Maybe not. But at least we did *something*."

"That's a good outlook," Lawanda praised, offering them a plate of cookies. "You'll go far in life if you keep it."

Leo smiled, but Perry could tell that the youth was merely humoring Lawanda.

"Go where?" Jamal asked. "The next block? Shit, Mrs. Watkins. There ain't no escape from this place unless you can rap or play basketball. Or want to sell drugs."

"You got that shit right," Dookie said.

"I'd appreciate it if you boys wouldn't curse in my house." Lawanda set the cookies down. "Mr. Watkins does it, but that's because he's old and set in his ways."

"Sorry." Dookie slumped down.

"That's okay. And listen to me. Don't be saying that there's no way out of this neighborhood. Don't think that way. There are always opportunities. There are always doors. You just have to wait for the right door to open. Y'all can be anything you want to be. People said there would never be a black president, and they were wrong, weren't they?"

"He ain't black," Jamal said. "His momma was white."

Lawanda frowned. "Show some respect. The man is your president. Do you know how hard he had to struggle to get to where he is today? You should look up to him, instead of these rappers."

"Maybe," Jamal agreed, "but that don't change the fact that his momma was white."

"So what if she was?" Lawanda said. "It doesn't matter. He's as black as you or me."

"He's damn sure blacker than Chris," Markus teased. "Ain't nobody more yellow on this street than Chris."

"Fuck you, motherfucker," Chris said, raising his voice. "Knock it off. I told you before about that shit."

"Yo," Leo shouted. "She asked us to watch our language, you dumb shits. Now quit swearing!"

Perry took a deep swig of beer and silently cursed his wife's sense of charity and community responsibility. He glanced at the television again, then added her choice of quality entertainment programming to his list of things to curse.

Headlights flashed across the wall, bleeding through the curtains, tracing across framed photographs and the clock that Perry and Lawanda had received as a wedding present. Leo pulled the curtains back and glanced outside again.

"Is that the po-po?" Markus asked. "They finally show up?"

"No," Leo said, staring more intently. "It's an old van. Cruising by real slow, like they're looking for something or somebody."

"SWAT," Perry suggested. "Or maybe some undercover boys."

"I don't think so." Leo shook his head. "It looks pretty beat up. White dude driving it, though. Can't see him real well, so I can't be sure, but I don't think I ever saw him around here before. The van either."

"Where's he going?" Perry asked.

"Oh, shit . . ." Leo turned around and stared at the group. His eyes were wide. "Toward the house."

Perry sat his beer down. "Well, then it's *got* to be the cops."

"Let's go outside and watch," Jamal suggested. "Might see some shit go down."

The boys stood, but Lawanda raised her hand, motioning at them to sit back down again.

"Just hold up," she said. "We don't know what's gonna happen. If there's shooting or something, then y'all are safer in here."

Perry jumped to his feet. "Oh, let them go look. Ain't no harm gonna come to them, long as they don't go down there."

And besides, he thought. *It will get them out of our house that much sooner.*

Lawanda scowled at him. Perry scowled back. They stared at each other for a moment, and then Perry's will broke. He turned away with a sigh.

"Come on, y'all," Leo said, moving to the door. "We took up too much of your time already, Mrs. Watkins. We should get going. Thanks for letting us use your phone."

"Boys!" Lawanda leaped up from her chair, flustered. "I really wish you'd stay inside."

Leo glanced from Perry to his friends to Lawanda, and then shook his head.

"That's okay. We'll be alright. Like Mr. Watkins said, ain't nothing gonna happen as long as we stay up here."

"Shit," Markus muttered. "On this block, something can happen no matter where we stand. Motherfuckers be tripping twenty-four seven."

Lawanda put her hands on her hips, pressed her lips together tightly and nodded at Perry.

"You go out there and wait with them."

Perry opened his mouth to protest, then thought better of it. He'd seen the expression on his wife's face before. If he defied her, he'd be sleeping on the couch again. He hated the couch. It fucked with his hip and his arthritis. He was defeated and he knew it. Worse, so did Lawanda. Shoulders slumping, he walked toward the door and followed the teens out onto the stoop. The strange van was just passing by the house at the end of the block. They watched the brake lights flash as it slowed. Then the driver shut off the headlights. A moment later, the vehicle disappeared into the shadows. There were clouds covering the moon, and that end of the street was shrouded in gloom.

"That's weird," Leo mumbled. "What the hell's he doing?"

The street was silent. It made Perry uncomfortable. The street was *never* quiet. He glanced at Leo and his friends and noticed from their stance that the stillness was making them nervous, too.

Then gunshots rang out from a few blocks away, and they all relaxed.

"Think he's driving around?" Markus asked. "Scoping shit out before he goes up to the door?"

Perry shrugged. The van was still out of sight.

"Whatever he's doing," Leo muttered, "he'd better hurry his ass up. They been inside there a long time now."

The other boys murmured their agreement. Perry nodded, but didn't respond. Personally, he figured it was already too late for the kids inside the house.

With one hand on the steering wheel, Paul Synuria eased the van toward the curb. His other hand clutched a Styrofoam cup of lukewarm coffee that he'd bought at a rest stop along the Pennsylvania Turnpike. He'd spiked it with a splash of Johnnie Walker Black Label whiskey, the half-empty bottle of which was wedged under his seat. With the headlights off, he couldn't see very well; there were no working streetlights or other homes near this abandoned house, and a bank of thick, slow-moving clouds covered the almost-full moon. His front driver's side tire bumped up over the curb. The van shook and vibrated, and then slammed back down to the road again, jostling him. Coffee spilled all over his crotch. Cursing, Paul put the van in park. Then he set the coffee in the cup holder and rummaged around until he found a fast-food bag with a napkin inside. He wiped and blotted his pants. It looked like he'd pissed himself. At least the coffee hadn't been hot.

On the van's stereo, Slipknot's "New Abortion" gave way to Jimmy Buffet. Paul liked to tell people that his eclectic musical tastes reflected that he was a man of contradictions. He'd say that he was the only Maggoty Parrothead around. But the truth was that he'd never heard Slipknot until a few months ago, when he found a carrying case full of compact discs at a construction site he'd been sneaking around. All the CDs were heavy metal— or what passed for heavy metal these days. No big hair. Just vocals that sounded as if Cookie Monster were fronting a band. He'd sold the stash at a pawn shop, but had held on to the Slipknot discs. He liked their melodies, and their shtick reminded him of KISS, from back in the day. Their music pumped him up before he scavenged a site.

Like now.

Paul turned off the engine so that the idling motor wouldn't attract any unwanted attention. Then he blotted at the coffee again and shook his head, wondering, not for the first time, how he'd come to this. He'd once been the site coordinator for a group home that served people who had mental illnesses. He'd loved the job.

Sure, it was stressful sometimes, but that tension had evaporated each day when he came home to his family— his wife, Lisa, and their two kids, Evette and Sabastian. But then the group home had been bought out by a bigger corporation, and they brought in their own people to fill many of the positions. After fourteen and a half years, Paul found himself out of work.

When his unemployment ran out, Paul still hadn't found a job. There were no other group homes in his area, and when he searched beyond his region, he found that many of those facilities were also downsizing. Desperate, he'd taken a job at a metal scrap yard.

And that had led to this.

At first, Paul had been amazed. He'd had no idea that scrap metal recycling was such a big business. It was a booming, sixty-five-billion-dollar industry, thanks to an increasing global economy and the current social movement toward environmental awareness. Scrap metal was America's largest import to China, after electronic components. Before getting the job at the scrap yard, Paul had always envisioned recycling centers as something out of *Sanford and Son* reruns. The truth was something different. There was money to be made in junk.

Especially on the black market.

He'd started simply enough. Legally, too. He'd been at the yard for a week. On his first day off, Paul explored his basement and the corners of his garage and toolshed. The assorted, castaway debris of their lives had been tossed into cardboard boxes, plastic milk crates, garbage bags, and footlockers and left forgotten in these places. Paul was pleasantly surprised by the amount of recyclable material he discovered—aluminum soda can tabs (saved for some long-forgotten charity but never turned in), brass fittings from an old cutting torch he no longer owned, bits of copper wire that he'd saved from various home wiring jobs, copper and brass pipe fittings, and other assorted junk. He'd hauled it all to the scrap yard the following Monday and made enough cash to cover one of his and Lisa's payments on their auto loan.

So Paul went looking for more. Before this, he'd never broken the law. Sure, he had a few unpaid parking tickets, and there was a citation for public drunkenness when he'd been in college, but that was all. He took to black-market metal thievery like it had been what he was meant to do all along. Looking back on it, maybe he'd been bitter about how things had turned out—giving most of his adult life to a company only to be tossed aside like so much garbage. He told himself he was doing it for Lisa and the kids—the money he brought in was more than he'd ever made in his life, and although they didn't know how he was earning it, they were happy with the results. But the truth was, he enjoyed it. After a life behind a desk, a life of board meetings and memos and stress, being a metal thief was exciting. Liberating.

He broke into construction sites, new homes that were not yet occupied, storage areas, foundries, warehouses, abandoned buildings, and even other recycling facilities. He scavenged electrical cables, aluminum siding and gutters, pipes, manhole covers, railway spikes and plates, electrical transformers, bolts and screws—anything he could resell. He even managed to score one hundred and twenty feet of steel and copper from an old abandoned radio tower in a remote section of Adams County.

Paul was smart about it. He didn't steal near their home, preferring instead to scavenge throughout the rest of the state, and even into Ohio and West Virginia. He used the van, which wasn't registered to him, and changed the tags each time he made a run. He drove the speed limit and obeyed all the traffic laws so he wouldn't get pulled over. Since most scrap processors required a driver's license for each transaction, Paul had obtained two phony licenses. When he sold scrap, he did it under the aliases of Mike Heimbuch or Jeff Lombardo. He'd practiced signing their names on sheets of paper until both signatures looked different from each other—and nothing like his real signature.

Since the economy's downturn, he'd had to scavenge more metal than ever. Prices for copper, lead, and zinc had plummeted to levels lower than those during the Great Depression. Paul had come to Philadelphia because he'd heard that the pickings were good, and he hoped he could make up for the lower prices with a higher take. He'd never been to the city before, so he'd just driven aimlessly until he found a location that looked promising. The deeper into the city he went, the worse the neighborhoods became. Paul locked the doors and stared straight ahead, not wanting to attract attention.

Now, as he gazed out at the decrepit old Victorian home across from him, he wondered if he should scout around for another location. Surely this place had been picked clean already. It looked positively ancient—older and bigger than any of the row homes located farther up the block. He studied it for a moment longer and decided that he should at least take a closer look.

Paul got out of the van and quietly closed the door behind him. He glanced up and down the street, making sure nobody was watching him. Farther up the block, he saw a group of people gathered on a porch step, but he couldn't tell if they were looking in his direction or not. Near them, on the other side of the street, a lone hooker leaned against a brick wall, adjusting her skirt. Otherwise, the street was deserted. No cars or pedestrians. Paul turned his gaze skyward. The clouds were still covering the moon. He was pretty sure that even if the group on the porch steps was looking his way, they wouldn't be able to see him. It was dark.

He made his way to the rear of the van, opened the door, and pulled a large toolbox toward himself. Inside were various items that he used from time to time: flashlights, wire cutters, metal shearers, bolt cutters, crowbars, a tool belt, screwdrivers, wrenches, hammers, chisels, leather gloves, and a small, handheld acetylene torch. He slipped on the gloves and flexed his hands. Then he grabbed a flashlight and a flathead screwdriver. His intention was to quickly check the house. If it looked promising, he'd return to the van and retrieve the tools for the job.

Paul approached the house cautiously, alert for any sign that squatters or other undesirables inhabited it. The structure was silent. He tiptoed up the sagging porch. The boards groaned beneath his feet. He reached out and tried the door. It was locked. He rattled the brass knob, surprised at its resilience, and made a note to pry it off later. While not as in demand as copper, brass still fetched a good market price.

Paul moved around to the side of the house, glancing over his shoulder to make sure the coast was still clear. When he got out of sight of the street, he approached one of the first-floor windows and peered inside. It was pitch black. He turned on the flashlight and shined it into the window. The light reflected back to him. It took Paul a moment to realize that the glass had been painted black. A quick check verified that the rest of the windows on this side of the house had also been painted over. Shaking his head, he listened one more time. The house was still quiet. Paul pulled out the screwdriver and rapped the corner of one pane. The glass cracked, but did not shatter—exactly what he'd hoped would happen. Using the screwdriver, he pried the triangular wedge of glass loose from the window, then shined his light inside, peering into the hole.

He saw nothing but brick.

Somebody bricked over the window?

Now he was intrigued. If someone had taken the trouble to prevent entry in that manner, then there was a possibility that the building had remained free of squatters or looters. There was no telling what he might find inside.

He moved on to a second window and repeated the process. Behind it, he found another brick wall, but the masonry was a different color and texture. Paul assumed that it had been built at a different time than the previous wall.

No way I'm getting in here.

He walked around the house and found a back door. It, too, was locked and just as sturdy as the other. Paul had no doubt that he could break either door down, but doing so would make a lot of noise and might attract unwanted attention. Instead, he decided to see if the place had a basement, and if so, if there was outside access—storm doors or even just a set of stairs. He searched for several minutes, and while he determined that the building did indeed have a basement, there was no access from out here. There was, however, a nearby manhole cover. Paul wondered if the tunnel led into the cellar somehow. That happened sometimes in these old houses.

He returned to the van and fetched a thin but strong cable. Then he went back to the manhole cover. He threaded the cable through the lid, braced himself, then lifted the cover, grunting with exertion. Pain coursed through his lower back, and the tendons stood out on his neck, but the manhole cover moved. An inch. Then two.

Finally, he moved it out of the way, revealing the hole. He let the cover drop on the ground with a muffled clang.

Sweat dribbled down his forehead. He wiped it with the back of his hand. Manhole covers were always a bitch—but they were also worth good money. He'd have to load this one into the van before he was done.

Paul picked up his flashlight and shined the beam down into the shaft. A rusty iron ladder had been built into the side. It was dark at the bottom. He heard the sound of trickling water. A noxious stench wafted up from the tunnel. Paul winced, turning his head aside. He smelled sewage, obviously, but there was something else, as well. Something he couldn't identify.

"Fuck it," he muttered. "I came this far. Might as well check it out."

He returned to the van and put on the tool belt, adjusting it to fit around his prodigious belly. He equipped himself with a variety of tools—the portable acetylene torch, bolt cutters, crowbar, screwdrivers, and other items. There was no telling what he might need once he got inside, and he didn't feel like running back and forth to the van. Satisfied, he returned to the hole. Then, tucking the flashlight under his arm, Paul started down the ladder and disappeared from sight.

CHAPTER EIGHT

Javier clamped his hand over Kerri's mouth before she could scream again. She squirmed against him, her mouth hot on his palm, and let loose with a string of muffled squeals. Javier squeezed her tighter, and Kerri's hands flailed, slapping at him. He barely noticed. Instead, he stared wide-eyed at Heather, who had just emerged from a room to their right. Her expression of astonishment matched his own.

"Javier?"

"Heather! Holy shit, where have you been? Are you okay?"

Kerri went slack. Javier released her and embraced Heather, hugging his girlfriend tight.

"Are you okay?" he repeated. "When you took off like that . . ."

"I'm fine . . . now." Sighing, Heather slumped against him. "Feel like I'm going to throw up. That's probably the adrenaline."

He stroked her hair. "Are you sure? You cut your foot."

"It stopped bleeding, but it still hurts. I lost my shoes. I'm a little banged up, but nothing serious. I was so worried that you guys were . . . that he'd gotten you."

Javier squeezed her tighter. "We got away. So did Brett."

"Where is he?" Heather glanced around, looking for him.

"We don't know. Kerri saw him take off in the other direction. We're guessing that thing went after him."

"Oh my God. I hope he's okay. And Steph, too."

Neither Javier or Kerri responded.

Heather's eyes grew wide. "Steph's okay, right? She got away, too?"

"She's dead," Javier said. "That . . . big guy got her."

"Steph . . ."

Something scratched behind the walls—light, feathery scuffling noises. Heather and Kerri both jumped, startled by the sound.

"Just a rat," Javier whispered. "Ignore it."

Heather wiped her nose with the back of her hand, then brushed tears from her eyes. Javier watched her, cracking a slow smile.

"What's so funny?" she asked. "How can you be smiling, with everything that's happened?"

"Your mascara," he explained. "It's running. You look like a raccoon."

She pushed away from him. "Asshole."

"Hey, come on. I was just kidding."

Heather gave Kerri a quick hug.

"Are you okay?" she asked.

Kerri shrugged.

"I'm sorry about Tyler," Heather said. "I know you guys were having trouble lately, but still . . ."

Before Kerri could respond, Javier interrupted.

"We need to—"

A door slammed. All three jumped at the noise. Footsteps shuffled toward them, but they sounded weird—as if the person was hopping on one foot and dragging something along behind them. They heard a faint electric hum from somewhere in the house. The string of lightbulbs hanging from the ceiling flickered to life. After growing accustomed to the darkness, the sudden brilliance blinded them for a second. They squinted, shielding their eyes from the glare.

"What do we do?" Kerri's voice trembled.

Javier motioned toward the room Heather had just emerged from. When the girls didn't move, he shoved them forward.

"Hide."

They ducked into the room, and Javier shut the door behind him, quickly but as quietly as possible. He held his breath, hoping the hinges wouldn't squeak. They didn't. His cell phone was their only source of light. Heather's and Kerri's faces seemed almost ghoulish in the illumination. It didn't help that his night vision was all screwed up now, thanks to the hallway lights. He glanced around the room, only able to see a few feet in any direction. The room was sparse, but he found a piece of termite-eaten wood about the length of a baseball bat. A long, rusty nail jutted from one end. He picked it up and tested its weight. It wasn't much, but it made him feel better. More confident.

In the hall, the strange footsteps grew louder, accompanied by wet, raspy breathing and a slightly sour stench. It didn't sound like a human being's breathing. Instead, it sounded like an animal.

"What if it's Brett?" Heather whispered.

"Shhhh," Javier hissed, motioning at them to go to the back of the room. He stuffed his cell phone back in his pocket as the girls retreated. They vanished from sight almost immediately, swallowed by the shadows, and Javier reluctantly wished that he'd told them to stick by his side instead. The room seemed more sinister without their presence, and even though he knew they were still close by, their absence seemed greater. He couldn't believe how dark it was inside the room. Hefting the piece of wood, he flattened himself against the wall next to the door and waited. His heart beat faster. A strand of cobweb brushed against his face, sticking to his hair and skin.

Something pawed at the doorknob. Javier tensed. The door slowly swung open. The light in the hallway seemed like a mini sun. The sour stench became over-whelming. A shadowy form stepped into the room. Its asthmatic wheezing seemed to fill the space. With a cry, Javier whirled, swinging his makeshift club at the space where the intruder's face should be. The length of wood whistled through the air and smacked against the door-frame. The shock vibrated through Javier's arms. Dust and plaster from the ceiling rained down on his head.

I fucking missed?

Javier's eyes adjusted to the light. He glanced down at the figure and saw why he'd missed. The intruder was a midget.

With a very large knife clutched in one gnarled fist.

"Gotcha," it wheezed, and then slashed at his crotch with the blade.

Heather and Kerri screamed.

Javier leaped backward, narrowly avoiding the attack. He winced as the tip of the blade brushed against the fabric of his jeans. Luckily, it went no farther. Javier swung the club again, this time in a downward arc. The midget shrieked as the nail tore a ragged gash in his lumpy fore-head. Blood ran into his eyes. He stumbled around, squeal-ing with rage. Not pausing, Javier swung a third time. The nail caught the dwarf just beneath the chin. His jaws slammed shut as the nail sank deep into the flesh.

With a cry, Javier jerked the nail out. Part of the

midget's jaw and throat came with it. The skin stretched, and beneath it, muscle and gristle ripped and snapped. Blood gushed from the gaping wound. The intruder's eyes opened wide with shock. Dropping the knife, he brought his hands to his ruined throat. Blood jetted out across his fists and ran down his stubby forearms. He squawked, then toppled backward. Emitting choking noises, the midget jittered and shook on the floor. Blood continued to pump from the wound.

Heather and Kerri continued to scream.

Javier let the club drop to the floor. He wiped the sweat from his brow with the back of his hand and turned to the girls.

"Shut up!"

Grimacing, he bent over and grabbed the midget's feet. The dead man wore no shoes. The bottom of one grimy foot was covered with thick yellow calluses. The other foot was terribly malformed—more of a withered stump than an appendage. His skin felt rough and flaky. His ankles were covered with scabs and insect bites. His legs twitched in Javier's grip. The midget uttered one last warbling cough, and then he was still. The stench roiling off his unwashed body was revolting. Turning away, Javier dragged the corpse into the room. He let the legs flop to the floor, then shut the door again—leaving it slightly cracked so that a thin sliver of light crept into the room.

"It's okay," he whispered to the girls. "He's dead."

There was a rustling in the shadows as Heather and Kerri crawled forward. Javier pulled out his cell phone again and opened it. He aimed it at the midget and took a picture. All three of them blinked at the flash.

"What are you doing?" Heather asked.

Javier shrugged. "Evidence. I'm documenting every-thing."

"Why?"

"So that when we get out of here, I can show the police."

Kerri stared down at the corpse. "You killed him."

"Yeah," Javier said. "I did. And please don't give me any shit about it right now. You guys saw it. He tried to cut my fucking dick off. Not to mention that—"

"No," Kerri broke in. "That's not what I was going to say. I'm not arguing with you. But this isn't the guy who killed Tyler and Steph. This is someone different. That means there's more than one."

The three teens stared at each other.

"H-how many?" Heather thrust an index finger into her mouth and began gnawing on the nail.

As if in answer, another set of footsteps shuffled down the hall. The approaching gait was much stealthier than the midget's had been.

And much faster.

Javier scooped up the knife and ducked behind the door. Kerri grabbed the club and flattened herself against the wall where Javier had previously been positioned. Heather melted back into the shadows.

Outside in the hall, the footsteps paused, then continued. Javier pressed his ear to the wall, listening. They paused again.

Somebody's checking the doors, Javier thought. His muscles tensed. His palms grew damp with sweat. He tightened his grip on the knife handle and tried to remain still.

The footsteps continued down the hall, louder now. Then they paused again. The light shining into the room from underneath the door flickered. Then the door opened. An inch. Then two. Javier heard heavy, panicked breathing. The door opened a few more inches, and Javier flattened himself against the wall, holding his breath and sucking his stomach in so the door wouldn't hit him. He had the sudden urge to piss. Javier gritted his teeth and tried to ignore it. He contemplated slamming the door shut on the intruder, but that would just leave them trapped inside. Better to let the lurker enter the room completely, and then creep up behind them and slit his throat. Javier could see it all in his head. The brutality didn't shock him. Although he was scared, he had no qualms about the killings. This was survival. It was no different than a video game, except that now, if he died, he died for real.

With the door open, light flowed into the room, stretching across the floor. As the door swung wider, the light reached farther. Alarmed, Javier realized that he could see both Heather and the dead midget's feet.

So could the figure in the doorway, because the heavy breathing turned into a gasp.

The intruder said, "Heather?"

Before Javier could register that the intruder knew Heather's name, he lunged forward, slamming the door into his opponent. He pushed with all his weight, knocking the figure to the floor. The intruder grunted. Kerri charged out of the shadows, the club held over her head. Before she could swing it, Heather shouted, "No!"

"Jesus Christ, you guys," the figure on the floor moaned. "What the fuck is wrong with you?"

Gaping, Javier and Kerri stared down at Brett.

"Holy shit," Javier said. "You okay?"

Heather crawled out of the shadows, and Kerri lowered her weapon while Javier stuck out his hand and helped Brett to his feet.

"You okay?" he asked again.

Brett nodded. "I will be. Knocked the wind out of me."

"Sorry about that. We thought you were one of them."

Brett's eyes widened in surprise. "You guys have seen them, too? The guy wearing a woman's skin?"

"We killed one." Javier pointed. "Some kind of deformed dwarf."

Brett walked over to the corpse, stared down at it, and shivered.

"No," he said. "This isn't one of the ones I saw."

While he told them about Noigel and the other killer who'd been wearing a suit made out of a dead woman's skin, Kerri shut the door again. They huddled closer together in the darkness, whispering to one another.

"So you heard him say they're hunting us?" Javier asked.

Nodding, Brett removed his glasses and wiped the lenses on his shirt. Then he put them back on and pushed them up with his index finger.

"How many?"

"I don't know," Brett said. "He mentioned something about more of them being down below, too."

"A basement?"

Brett shrugged. "I guess. He mentioned that it was the only way out. We were in such a hurry when we broke in here, and it was dark out there. I didn't notice if this place had any basement windows or not. Did any of you guys?"

Kerri and Heather shook their heads. Javier cleared his throat and then checked his cell phone again, hoping for a signal. There was still nothing. He cursed softly in Spanish.

"Do you still have your phone?" he asked Brett.

"Yeah, but there's no service in this place. It's like they're blocking it or something."

"So what do we do now?" Kerri asked.

Javier realized that they were all staring at him. Somehow he'd become the leader. He reached out, pulled

Heather toward him, and held her close. He kissed her forehead.

"How's your foot? Can you walk?"

"Yeah, it's better."

"Hang on a second," he told the group, and then walked over to the corner. Shivering, Javier pulled down his zipper, freed his penis, and aimed for the wall. The others couldn't see him in the darkness, but he knew they could hear him, because he heard Kerri make a disgusted sound a second later. Javier shook himself, zipped up, and returned to the group.

"Did you really have to do that here?" Brett asked.

"Yeah, I did. And while I did, I was thinking. We can't go out the way we came in. Obviously, we need to find another way out of here. I don't know about heading down into the basement, though. They get us down there and we might be cornered. Maybe we should look for a back door or an upstairs window."

"The upstairs windows are probably blocked off, too," Brett said.

"Maybe," Javier agreed. "But we don't know for sure. Fact is, we don't know shit, and we're gonna continue to not know shit until we leave this room and find out for ourselves."

"You don't have to be a dick about it."

"Yeah, Brett, actually, I do. Because it's your fucking fault we're in here in the first place."

"Dude, maybe it hasn't occurred to you, but I just saw my girlfriend's brains get bashed out all over the fucking place!"

Javier edged closer to him. "Which wouldn't have happened if—"

Heather patted Javier's shoulder. "That's not helping."

"We could just stay in here," Kerri suggested. "Hide.

It's dark in here. Those lights out in the hall don't penetrate that far into the room. We could stay against the back wall and hide until someone rescues us."

Javier paused before replying, choosing his words carefully. "Listen. We're on our own here. Nobody knows where we are. Our folks are all sleeping. Chances are they won't even notice that we're missing until tomorrow morning. We might not have that long. We can't rely on anyone else. We have to rely on ourselves."

"But the gangbangers," Kerri protested. "Somebody must have called the cops when they chased us. Somebody will notice Tyler's car."

"I doubt it. The car is probably stripped by now. And I don't think this is the sort of neighborhood where people call the cops right away. We've wasted enough time. While we stand here arguing, they could be coming down the hall. Everybody find a weapon—anything at all—and then let's get the hell out of here."

They quickly searched the room. In addition to Javier's knife and Kerri's makeshift club, Brett found a long, jagged shard of broken glass. He tore off a small strip of his shirt and wrapped it around the shard to avoid cutting his fingers. Then he clutched it like a dagger. Heather found a brick. She carried it daintily, as if unsure what to do with it.

"If they attack us," Javier told her, smiling, "sneak up behind the motherfuckers and bash them on the head."

Nodding, she returned his smile. Her expression quickly faltered.

"Come here." He pulled her close again and kissed her forehead. "Listen. It's gonna be okay. I'll get us out of here."

"I know. I believe you."

"Your foot gonna be okay to walk?"

"I think so."

"Then let's go."

He listened at the door. Determining that the hallway was deserted, Javier opened the door and, after one glance back at the dead midget, he led them out into the light.

Heather squeezed her boyfriend's hand as they crept down the hall, deeper into the house. Despite everything that had happened, she felt amazingly calm now. Having Javier beside her was the reason. His presence was soothing. In truth, she'd been surprised at the change that had seemed to overcome him in the last hour. Although decisive, Javier was usually the quietest member of their group and rarely made the decisions. He'd always just gone along with whatever everyone else decided— usually Tyler. He'd been the same way in his relationship with her. He usually deferred to whatever she wanted.

But now . . . Heather wondered if she was finally seeing the real Javier. Confident. In control.

She thought about the way he'd killed the dwarf. He'd seemed emotionless, like a man taking out the trash or performing some other menial, everyday task. Some of that could probably be chalked up to shock, but still—it was a little disconcerting. While it was true that the little man would have probably killed them, Javier's actions had seemed so sudden. Perfunctory. It was a little scary. And yet his presence here was soothing at the same time. She knew that the conflicting emotions made no sense, but she couldn't help it.

What was even scarier was that it had turned her on.

Not that she'd ever admit it to her friends. Not even to Javier. What would they think of her? Heather wasn't even sure what to think of herself. Steph and Tyler had been dead less than an hour, and here she was, on the run from the killers inside an abandoned house—and horny.

Javier released Heather's hand and slipped away, tiptoeing down the hall and motioning at the three of them to stay where they were. Heather chewed her bottom lip and watched him go. She felt bad. While not fighting (it was impossible to really fight with Javier because he always let her have her way), she'd been giving him the silent treatment off and on for the last few days, even when they were hanging together and with the gang. Recently, he'd been bringing up the future, asking her what it held for them—indeed, wondering if there would even *be* a "them." She wanted different things than he did, and no matter how many times she told him that, Javier didn't seem to understand. Was it right? No. Was she probably being a bitch? Yes. Did it matter? No. What was the point if she couldn't be with a person who wanted the same things?

None of which meant a damned thing now. Not in this place.

Jesus, Heather thought. *I'm a fucking mess. I'm scared. I'm soothed. I'm horny. I don't know what the hell I am.*

Heather heard Kerri sniffle. She turned and saw her friend wiping her eyes with her sleeve. Brett stared down the hallway in the direction they'd come from—keeping watch or trying to give Kerri her privacy. Or maybe both. Heather wasn't sure. She put her arms around the other girl. It was all that she could think of to do. Kerri let out a snuffling, stifled moan and hugged her tightly. Kerri's hot breaths blew against Heather's neck.

"Shhhh. It'll be okay. Javier will get us out of here. We just have to be brave, alright?"

Nodding, Kerri sniffed again. Heather rocked back and forth slowly, and made placating noises until Kerri pulled away from her and straightened up again.

"Sorry," Kerri said, wiping her nose. "Just . . . seeing you and Javier together . . . it made me think about Tyler . . ."

Heather wasn't sure what to say, so she didn't respond.

Javier motioned at them to come ahead. They crept through an open door and into another hallway. This one ran in the opposite direction of the previous passageway. Like the other, it was illuminated with a string of bare lightbulbs hanging from the ceiling.

Heather glanced in each direction and whispered, "Which way?"

Shrugging, Javier pointed with the knife to the right. They started in that direction. Javier went first, followed by Heather, then Kerri. Brett brought up the rear. Javier held the knife out in front of him. The lights glinted off the blade. Heather shifted the brick from one hand to the other. It was heavy, and her arms were beginning to ache. Plus, the hard, rough surface was giving her blisters. Heather noticed that Kerri allowed the club to dangle at her side, as if she'd forgotten she was carrying it.

"Um, guys?"

Brett's voice trembled. They turned and noticed that he'd stopped a few feet behind them.

"Where did we come in?"

"Out front?" Kerri sounded confused.

"No," Brett said. "I mean this hallway. Where's the door we just came through?"

"Right behind you . . ." Javier's voice trailed off as he gaped. Heather was about to tell him that he needed to quit blaming Brett for their predicament and quit being so short with him—but instead, her attention was drawn to the spot where they'd come in.

"See?" Brett pointed. Instead of an open doorway leading out into the previous corridor, there was now a wall. "The door's gone."

"What the fuck?" Javier whispered.

Heather heard real fear in his voice this time, and for a second, she thought it might be Javier's turn to start crying. Instead, he strode toward the new wall.

"Doors don't just get up and walk away." Javier knocked the wall with the hilt of his knife. He grunted. The others gathered around him in confusion.

"Watch our backs," Javier told Kerri. Then he turned his attention back to the wall. He handed Heather his knife and placed both hands on the paneling. He shoved and pushed in different directions, but the slab didn't move. Brett moved to help him, but Javier waved him away.

"It ain't budging," he whispered. "It's a trapdoor of some kind."

"But why would they only seal off this end?" Brett asked.

"To keep us heading forward, maybe? An ambush?"

Heather pushed past both of them and ran her hand over the wall. It wasn't plaster or paint or even wallpaper. It was solid wood—smooth, like a tabletop.

Or a coffin lid, she thought.

Heather squatted and let her hands run along the surface until she found the floor. She felt the edge of the wooden surface there. The wall had slid in front of the door—quietly enough that none of them had heard it.

She stood back up again. Brett and Javier were still discussing the blockade. Heather was about to suggest that instead of standing around talking about it, maybe it would be more prudent for them to hide again, but she never got the chance. As if in response to Javier's words, the lights blinked out. Darkness engulfed them once more.

Strange, cruel laughter boomed down the hall.

Heather, Javier, Kerri, and Brett screamed in unison.

The laughter grew louder, almost drowning out their cries.

CHAPTER NINE

As their screams echoed off the walls, the sinister laughter brayed out a third time. Then, as suddenly as it had started, the noise ceased. The sudden darkness seemed to amplify the stillness. The silence terrified Kerri even more than the laughter had.

She scuttled back down the hall, groping with one outstretched hand, and nearly tripped over Heather. Both girls squealed in fright.

"Quiet," Javier whispered. "Listen."

Kerri had to hand it to him. Just moments ago, when the door had disappeared, Javier had sounded as scared as the rest of them. But now, with danger once more imminent, his cool, no-nonsense demeanor had returned. He kept his voice calm. Almost detached.

"Where are they?" Brett moaned. "I don't—"

"Everybody hold hands," Javier interrupted. "Heather, give me the knife back, but be careful not to stick me with it."

They fumbled around in the darkness, seeking one another. Someone's hand encircled Kerri's. The palm was sweaty, and thick calluses rubbed against her skin. She squeezed tightly, seeking comfort, and the hand squeezed back. Long, pointed nails grazed her wrist. Kerri froze. Her stomach lurched and her muscles tensed. Brett and

Javier had short fingernails. So did Heather. She complained about it anytime that she, Kerri, and Steph got together for a day trip to the spa. Every time she tried to grow them out, they got brittle.

The hand squeezed harder.

Kerri shrieked. She tried to pull her hand away, but the stranger's grip tightened. The nails dug into her skin. In the darkness, she heard Javier, Brett, and Heather crying out in confusion, but she was too panicked to warn them. The club slipped from her other hand and clattered onto the floor. The attacker jerked her forward, and Kerri nearly fell. She felt hot, rancid breath on her face, as something warm and wet slithered across her cheek. She realized it was a tongue. Shuddering in revulsion, Kerri opened her mouth to scream again. The slick appendage slipped between her lips. Half in shock, Kerri chomped down.

Now it was her attacker's turn to scream. It did so in short, muffled bursts because its tongue was firmly clenched between Kerri's teeth. Blood filled her mouth. Nauseated, Kerri released the tongue and stumbled backward. Something groaned in pain. Seconds later, footsteps pounded down the hallway as the wounded attacker fled.

"Kerri?" It was Javier. "What's wrong?"

She tried to answer, but all she could do was wail. She fumbled in her pocket with one trembling hand, pulled out the cigarette lighter, and flicked it on. The flame jittered. Brett, Heather, and Javier stared at her in concern.

"What's wrong?" Javier repeated. "What the hell happened?"

"There . . . there was something in here . . . with us. It grabbed me. At first I thought it was one of you, but . . ."

She couldn't finish. Stomach roiling, Kerri sank to her knees, released the lighter wheel, leaned forward, and vomited. She heard small sounds of shock and dismay from her friends, but when she tried to answer them, her stomach heaved again. The stench rising from her own puke made her throw up a third time. Javier, Brett, and Heather pulled out their cell phones and used the display screens to give her light. Heather stood over her, holding Kerri's hair back. She rubbed her friend's back and whispered soothing words. Kerri stayed there for a few moments more, retching. Finally she tottered to her feet and wiped her mouth.

"Are you hurt?" Brett asked.

"No, I—" She turned away and vomited again.

"Sorry," she said when she was finished. "I'm not hurt, but I definitely hurt it—whatever it was. I think I might have bitten its tongue off."

They shined their lights toward the floor and found dime-size splotches of blood.

"I'll say you did," Heather agreed.

Kerri spat, trying to rid her mouth of the horrible taste. Her teeth, tongue, and the insides of her cheeks felt like they were covered with slime.

"Can you bleed to death from your tongue?" Brett asked, eyeing the scarlet droplets. "I wonder how badly it's injured."

"Let's not stick around to find out," Javier said. "Come on."

Using his cell phone, he snapped a quick picture of the hallway. Then he crept down the passage. Kerri picked up her club, and she and Heather followed. Brett balked.

"Hold up."

"What now?" Javier asked, annoyance creeping into his voice.

Brett pushed his glasses back up onto his nose. "We're not going that way?"

"There's no other way to go."

"Yeah, but whatever it was that attacked Kerri—it went that way, too."

"Good," Javier replied. "If it ain't dead yet, then we'll finish the job if we run across it."

He started forward. The girls followed. Sighing, Brett trailed along behind them.

When the lighter grew hot again, Kerri put it back in her pocket. With the flame gone, the darkness seemed denser. The cell phones did little to lessen the gloom. As far as she could tell, there were no rooms along this corridor. The walls were featureless.

Javier halted, staring ahead into the darkness. The others followed his lead.

"This doesn't feel right," he muttered. "There's no doors leading off. No rooms. It just keeps going. If Kerri's attacker came this way, I don't know where he went."

"I told you," Brett said. "We ought to go back."

"We can't go back," Kerri reminded him. "Remember? The hall is blocked."

Brett didn't respond. Heather rolled her eyes.

Javier cursed in Spanish again. "I don't know what to do, guys. I guess we just keep moving forward. See where it goes."

Without another word, he started down the hall again. After a moment, the others followed. Kerri slid her hand into her pocket, but her lighter was still too hot to flick. The floor changed under their feet, becoming uneven. The floorboards began to squeak and groan with each footstep. They slowed their pace, almost tiptoeing.

The dark hallway ended in three doorways—one directly ahead of them, and one on each side. All three doors were wide open. Each doorway opened into more windowless rooms full of junk and debris. Kerri moved up to the front of the group and stood alongside Javier. Their arms touched, and she felt a momentary flush of warmth. The sensation comforted her. She glanced at him, but Javier seemed oblivious. He stared at all three exits, his eyes flicking from one to the next as if waiting for something to jump out at him. When nothing happened, he held his cell phone aloft like a torch and stepped into the room directly ahead of them. Then he stopped and turned.

"Let me see your lighter?"

Nodding, Kerri handed it to him. Javier winced as his fingers came in contact with the hot metal.

"Sorry," she apologized. "It hasn't cooled down yet."

Javier pocketed his cell phone and held the lighter high over his head. Then he checked the room thoroughly. He stepped around a rusted bunk-bed frame and thrust the flame into the corners. Then he returned to the hall.

"It's empty," he whispered, "but it's a dead end. No way out."

His voice sounded resigned, as if he hadn't expected anything less.

"What about the other two?" Brett asked.

Scowling, Javier entered the room on the right. A few moments later, he emerged from the room and reported the same. He handed Kerri her lighter and then sucked his thumb and index finger.

"Burned the shit out of me."

"Sorry," she said again, and returned the lighter to her pocket.

Kerri watched as Javier stepped into the third room. He pulled out his cell phone and fumbled with it as he walked. He'd only gone a few feet into the darkness when the floor disappeared beneath his feet. One moment he was there, glancing around the room and opening the cell phone. The next instant, he plummeted from sight, as if the house had opened up and swallowed him. He didn't even have time to scream. The only sound was a crash. To Kerri, it sounded like a million glass windows breaking.

One heartbeat. Two.

And then Javier began shrieking.

Gasping, Heather pushed past Kerri and dashed through the door. At the same time, Brett made a noise behind them, and there was a loud thud. Kerri leaped forward, grabbed Heather, and looped an arm around her waist, pulling her back. Heather struggled, shouting for Javier.

"Stop it," Kerri warned. "Don't run in there."

"Get off me," Heather yelled. "Let me go! He's hurt."

Kerri tightened her grip. "It's a trap! I think there's something wrong with the floor. We have to go slow."

As suddenly as they'd begun, Javier's screams stopped. He didn't cry out. Didn't plead for help.

Kerri thought that the abrupt silence was even more terrifying.

Heather pushed away from her, but Kerri grabbed her shirttail and tugged.

"Listen to me," she urged. "Watch your step."

And then Brett began shouting, his voice rising in pitch.

"Get it off me . . . Oh Jesus, get it the fuck off me!"

Kerri whirled around, distracted by his frantic cries. Heather broke loose from her grip and ran to help Javier. Kerri barely noticed. Javier and Heather were no longer her primary focus. She gaped, horribly transfixed by what she was seeing, needing time for her brain to process it. She almost wished that her eyes hadn't adjusted to the darkness, that instead, she was groping blindly, because then she wouldn't have to watch. Brett was on all fours in the middle of the hall. His lips peeled back in a sneer of pain. A shape clung to his back, trying to crush him to the floor. Kerri squinted, trying to see whatever was behind him more clearly. The figure's arms and legs looked out of proportion to its body. Brett slapped at it repeatedly, but each time he did, the figure smashed him to the floor again. His glasses, cell phone, and the shard of glass he'd been carrying all lay nearby, but out of reach. Blood streamed from his nose. His eyes locked with hers.

"Kerri . . ."

Before he could finish, the figure clutched a fistful of Brett's hair and rammed his face down. Brett's cries became muffled. The thing on his back chattered insanely, babbling nonsense words and noises.

Kerri raised the club and tried to appear menacing.

"Hey," she shouted.

The thing still clung to Brett's back, but it ceased pummeling Brett and glanced up at her. White teeth flashed in the darkness.

"Let him go," Kerri warned, trying to keep her voice from shaking.

The attacker spat at her. Something warm and wet and sticky splattered against her cheek and clung there. It slowly rolled down the side of her face, leaving a sluglike trail. Disgusted, Kerri wiped at it with her fingertips. The stench was revolting.

Brett took advantage of his attacker's momentary distraction and pushed himself upright. Still kneeling, he reached behind him and punched the thing in the head. It must have hurt, because then Brett jerked his hand away and shook his fingers as if they'd gone numb. The thing tumbled off his back and staggered. Then, squealing in what sounded like frustration, it waddled forward again. Its movements were jittery. Spasmodic. But it was incredibly fast. Shouting, Kerri dashed toward Brett, as well, praying that she reached him first.

Brett screamed.

As she closed the distance, Kerri finally got a good look at their foe in the light of Brett's cell phone. Like the previous attacker, this one was a dwarf, but it was even more repulsive than the last one had been. It was naked, except for a swath of dirty cloth sticking out of its vagina. The cloth was soaked with fresh blood. Kerri realized with horror that the cloth served as some type of tampon. The woman's body was lean but heavily muscled, and her face, even obscured by the darkness, was clearly malformed. Her forehead bulged, and her mouth seemed to curve around her face. What hair she had was long and stringy and matted with filth. Her eyes were too large for her face, and the pupils seemed to almost completely fill in the irises. The thing's arms were longer than its body and rippled with bulging muscles. By contrast, her legs were mere nubs—withered and useless. Despite this, the freak moved quickly. It waddled toward Brett, running on its arms, and reached him before Kerri. Brett tried to roll out of the way, but the female dwarf stood on one hand and slapped him in the head with the other. Brett collapsed to the floor, stunned.

"Get away from him, bitch."

The female laughed at Kerri—a high-pitched keening that drowned out Heather's shouts from the dark room.

Kerri felt a sudden but slight draft of air on her face. She glanced upward. Directly above Brett, there was a hole in the ceiling—a dark spot, blacker than the rest of the hallway. An open trapdoor dangled there. Kerri grunted in fearful awe as it dawned on her what had happened. Their captors had sealed off the hallway, turned off the lights, and then waited for them to pass beneath the trapdoor. The dwarf had dropped out of the ceiling, directly onto Brett.

The dwarf growled, eyeing Kerri's weapon.

"Get away from him," she repeated.

Before Kerri could strike, Brett regained his senses and lashed out at his attacker with his right hand. His movements were sluggish. He cried out, and Kerri noticed that his voice was slurred. His fingers scraped across the dwarf's shoulder. The woman lunged forward. Her wide open mouth clamped down on Brett's fingers.

Brett tried to pull his fingers back and moaned in disgust. Kerri gasped. She knew what was about to happen as surely as if she were watching footage that had already been filmed—and even as she raised the club, she knew she'd never be able to stop it in time.

The woman bit down. Blood flowed from around her lips and streaked down Brett's forearm. Brett shrieked. His eyes opened wide. The thick lips on the dwarf's face quivered. Then the woman reared back, shaking her head savagely. Kerri heard the crunch of Brett's fingers breaking, even over her own screams.

Brett wailed. His voice rose in octaves and echoed off the empty walls and ceiling as the dwarf wrenched her head back and forth, ripping at the prizes caught in her jaws until they finally peeled away from Brett's hand.

The dwarf growled again. Kerri edged closer and caught a good look at the shadowed, malformed face. It seemed garish in the cell phone's light. The creature glared at her as it chewed. It sighed, clearly relishing the meal. A black froth of spittle dripped from the open maw. The woman's teeth ground meat and gristle and bone into paste. Her throat bulged as she swallowed.

Brett thrashed on the floor, eyes rolling and teeth clenched. His remaining fingers clawed at the wood. Blood jetted from his stumps, running down his hand and forearm as he kicked and jittered. He wasn't screaming, but Kerri could tell he was trying to. His neck muscles were corded, and his mouth hung open, but the only sound he made was a low, pitiful whine.

The dwarf hunkered down and grunted, almost barking as it charged toward Brett again, propelling itself forward on its elongated arms. Brett tried to defend himself with his good hand, but he wasn't fast enough. The creature rushed to his side. Her head darted forward, slavering mouth open wide, aiming for his nose.

And then Kerri swung the club in a wide arc and buried the nail in the dwarf's eye.

It shrieked, a rough, gurgling noise, and spun around so quickly that the weapon was wrenched from Kerri's hands. The dwarf scuttled backward. The length of wood dangled from its face; the tip dragged across the floor. The thing tottered back and forth, swaying, then lurched forward, glaring at Kerri with its remaining eye. It tripped over Brett's outstretched feet and fell face-first onto the floor. It lay there, jerking spasmodically. Its bowels and bladder erupted, spraying the floor and Brett with foul, yellow feces the consistency of vegetable soup.

Kerri reached down, grabbed a fistful of the dwarf's greasy hair, and jerked its head up. Then she wrenched the club free. The pulped eyeball came with it, dangling on the edge of the nail like a squashed, oversized grape. A strand of tissue stretched like taffy from the empty eye socket. Kerri twisted the weapon in her hands and the ropy gristle snapped. Cringing, Kerri shook the club until the eyeball fell off. It landed in a puddle of feces and blood.

Kerri watched, forgetting about Javier or Heather or even Brett. She stood there trembling, absolutely transfixed as the dwarf's motions slowed. Amazingly, it was still alive, despite the massive amount of damage it had endured. The thing rolled over and tried to crawl, failing miserably in all efforts to rise even to its knees. Kerri stared, horrified. It looked toward her, one eye rolling wildly while dark fluid gushed from the red, raw, empty socket. Then it breathed out one long, shuddering sigh and lay still. A strange expression of calm seemed to come over its misshapen face.

Despite everything the freak had done, Kerri felt a sickened sense of pity for it.

She moved past the corpse and crouched next to Brett. Without a word, she pulled at his belt until it came loose from his jeans and slipped it over his wrist. Two hard yanks and the leather strap was tight, pinching the flesh until the skin beneath was bone white. Brett let out a yelp but didn't struggle.

"Lie still," Kerri soothed. "I've got to stop the bleeding. And then I've got to help Javier and Heather."

"W-wh-where . . ."

"Don't talk. Just lie still."

Kerri retrieved Brett's cell phone and eyeglasses. She glanced around for his makeshift glass knife, but it had shattered at some point during the struggle. All that was left were tiny slivers. She put the glasses on his face. The frames had been bent during the attack, and they hung crooked—one side higher than the other. Using the sharp, white light from the phone, she examined Brett's injuries. The three center fingers of his right hand were gone. Raw meat and jagged bone showed clearly past the remaining shreds of flesh. The remaining digits were already bruised and swollen. His nose had stopped bleeding and didn't appear broken. Kerri doubted that would comfort him, though.

Brett coughed and then moaned. Frothy spittle dripped from the corner of his mouth. He tried to speak again, but she put a finger to his lips. Then she handed him his cell phone, hoping that the light might give him some comfort.

"Stay here. I'll be right back. You need to stay awake, okay? Can you do that? You need to holler if you hear any more of them coming."

Brett whimpered, but nodded in understanding. He clutched the open cell phone to his chest with his good hand. Kerri felt like crying as she left him lying there.

She made her way to the end of the hall and peered into the darkened room. Heather was kneeling on the floor, sobbing. Dark streaks of mascara ran down her cheeks. Kerri moved up beside her, and Heather jerked in surprise.

"It's okay," Kerri said. "It's just me."

They were at the edge of a deep pit. From somewhere far below, they heard Javier groan. He sounded weak and afraid.

Kerri leaned forward and examined the floorboards. They'd been sawed off about five feet into the room. The trap ran the entire length, from wall to wall. Heather held her cell phone over the pit, and Kerri peered down into the hole, but all she could see was more darkness.

"Is he alright?" Kerri asked. "Has he said anything?"

Heather shook her head. "Not yet. I think he might have passed out or something. All he does is groan."

Kerri leaned farther over the pit and called out for Javier. She kept her voice low—if there were any more creatures in here with them, she didn't want to give their location away. When Javier didn't answer, she glanced up at the ceiling, wondering if it concealed a trapdoor as well, like the one in the hallway. If so, she didn't see it. The plaster was water stained and cracked, but there were no seams indicating a hidden door or compartment.

"Javier," she tried again, "are you okay?"

He groaned louder, and then coughed. He stirred in the darkness, and once again, Kerri heard the distinct sound of clinking glass.

"If you can't talk, just cough again. Okay? Let us know you can hear us, at least. Can you do that?"

"I can hear you." His voice was stronger now, but tinged with pain. "Shit . . ."

"Are you hurt?"

"Yeah." He paused. More glass tinkled. "But I'll live. I think. Nothing's broken, at least."

"How far down are you?"

"I don't know. It all happened so fast. Fuck me running. I can just barely see you guys. I dropped your lighter and my cell phone. Lost my knife, too. They're down here somewhere, but I can't find them."

"Can't you feel around?" Heather asked.

"No."

"Why not?"

"There's broken glass all over the floor. I'm sitting in it right now. The less I move around, the better."

"Jesus . . ." Heather gasped.

Kerri frowned, trying to figure out how to free him.

"Everyone else okay?" Javier asked.

"Brett's hurt really bad," Kerri said.

"What happened?" Heather glanced over her shoulder and out into the hallway.

"Another of those dwarf things popped out of the ceiling and attacked him. He's been bit. He lost three fingers."

"Oh shit!"

"Yeah. I stopped the bleeding, temporarily at least, but it doesn't look good."

Javier let out a choked, muffled yell.

"Babe?" Heather leaned out over the edge of the hole. "What's wrong?"

"I think a fucking rat just crawled over my leg. Get me the hell out of here, okay?"

"Okay," Kerri promised. "Just hang on."

"We don't have any rope," Heather said. "What are we going to do?"

Kerri stood up. "Take your clothes off."

"Wh-what?"

"You heard me. Take your clothes off. You said it yourself, Heather. We don't have any rope. We need to get him out of there before more of these . . . whatever they are, come for us. And Brett needs a hospital."

Without another word, Kerri began peeling off her dirty, sweaty, blood-soaked clothes. They were stiff and sticky, and in a way, it felt good to be free of them. Heather watched her for a moment, and then emptied her pockets and did the same. They piled their keys and other belongings on the floor. Both girls shivered, and goose pimples prickled across their flesh. Despite the stifling lack of airflow in the barricaded house, it was chilly. When they were down to their bras and underwear, Kerri gathered the discarded clothes and began tying them together.

"You guys still there?" Javier sounded worried.

"Yeah," Heather told him. "We're here. Kerri's making a rope. We'll have you out of there soon. Just hang on."

Kerri tugged on the makeshift rope. Satisfied that the knots were tight, she lay down on the filthy floor and inched herself out over the pit. Then she lowered the rope into the hole.

"Grab my legs," she told Heather. "Don't let me fall, okay?"

"I won't. Just hurry."

Out in the hallway, Brett moaned.

"Javier," Kerri called. "I'm sending a rope down. Can you see it?"

"No . . . wait! Yeah, I see it. Just barely."

"Can you reach it?"

"Hang on." He grunted. Then there was the sound of glass crunching again. Javier cursed loudly. "I can't do it. Too much glass on the floor. I can't see shit."

Kerri glanced back over her shoulder. "Heather, give me your cell phone."

Heather fished it out of the pile of belongings on the floor and handed it to Kerri. She flipped it open and held the open display screen out over the pit. Her other hand gripped the rope. At first, she couldn't see anything. She lowered the phone farther, and waited for her eyes to adjust. Kerri gasped. The cell phone's light glittered off the bottom of the hole. The pit was covered with broken glass—bottles, lightbulbs, windowpanes—sharp, glittering shards at least a foot deep. The glass around Javier was bloody. She saw cuts shining on his forearms and face.

"Holy shit . . ."

"What is it?" Heather asked, edging closer.

"He wasn't kidding about the broken glass."

"Yeah," Javier said, glancing around his prison. "Gotta admit, it's even worse than I thought it was."

"How badly are you cut?" Kerri asked.

"I'm okay," he insisted. "None of it pierced my shoes or anything. If you keep the light there, I think I can make it over to the rope."

Brett's moans drifted to them.

"Okay," Kerri said. "But please, try to hurry. Brett's in pretty bad shape."

Groaning, Javier stood slowly. Shards of broken glass fell from his body. Kerri noticed a few small fragments jutting from his arms, and winced as Javier plucked them out and cast them aside. He carefully plodded forward and grabbed the line. Kerri sat Heather's cell phone aside and braced herself, gripping the rope with both hands while Heather grabbed on to her legs again.

"Okay," Kerri grunted. "Let's go."

"Don't let him fall," Heather pleaded.

Kerri locked her arms and clenched her jaw. Javier's weight nearly pulled her down into the pit with him, but she managed to hold on until he'd reached the top. He clambered out of the hole and collapsed next to them, breathing hard. While he examined his cuts, the girls untied the rope and got dressed again. Kerri noticed that even under duress, Javier copped a glance at both her and Heather in the nude.

"Thanks," Javier said when he'd recovered.

"How bad is it?" Heather asked, brushing tiny pieces of glass from his hair.

"Nothing too deep. Just scratches mostly. Could have been a lot worse."

"Let's see to Brett," Kerri said.

They hurried out into the hallway and knelt next to their friend. Brett was conscious, but obviously in pain and going into shock. His teeth chattered uncontrollably, and his face was pale. Despite this, he smiled when he saw them.

"You look like shit," Brett told Javier.

"So do you. I hope you got the number of the truck that hit you."

Kerri heard the tension in Javier's voice, even though

he tried to joke with Brett. His eyes were focused at the three bloody stumps on Brett's hand.

Brett nodded toward the mutant's corpse. "See for yourself. Kerri fucked it up good."

Javier stood and stared at the dead thing. He prodded it with his toe.

"Heather, get a picture of this. My cell is down there in the pit."

Without a word, Heather touched a button on her phone and aimed the screen toward the dwarf. Kerri held Brett's good hand and watched. Up close and illuminated, the thing looked worse than it had in the darkness. The skin was pasty and pale, blotched with red areas that appeared to be advanced patches of eczema. The remaining eye was not merely large, it was malformed, with an oblong, hazel iris and uneven pupil. In the stark light, the whites of its eye appeared slightly yellowed. The nose on the woman was wide and flat, the skin on each side pulled back to accommodate a wide slash of a mouth and the thick teeth inside. The jaw was broad and angular. Kerri understood now how it had chewed through Brett's finger bones so easily. Kerri's attack had ruined any possible symmetry in the thing's face, but staring at it now, she was sure that no part of it had ever truly been balanced. The thin hair running along the dead woman's scalp sporadically painted the jaw line. It was hard to judge how old the mutant might have been.

Then Kerri noticed something else. Earlier, when she'd been attacked in the dark, she'd bitten down on what could have only been her attacker's tongue. The tongue of the woman on the floor was uninjured, and while the hand that had clutched Kerri's hand was equipped with long, talonlike fingernails, the corpse's nails were blunt and cracked.

Javier shook his head. "Midgets. Giants. What's next?"

"Let's not stick around to find out," Kerri said. "This isn't the one that attacked me earlier. That makes at least five of them, counting the two we've killed, and the two Brett saw earlier."

"Brett," Javier whispered, "can you walk?"

Licking his lips, he nodded.

"Where's your cell phone?" Kerri asked him.

"I put it in my pocket," Brett explained. "I didn't want the battery to get low. We might need it later."

"So you sat here in the dark?"

"Y-yeah."

"You dork." She patted his hand.

"We can't go back the way we came," Javier said, his Spanish accent growing more noticeable for a moment. "And we can't go forward any farther, unless we want to swim in broken glass."

"And all the other doors and windows are bricked up," Heather said. "So how do we get out of this shithole?"

Kerri cringed. Heather's voice was shrill and stressed.

Brett moaned again. "Seriously. I need bandages, or a real tourniquet."

"I'm going to need your belt, anyway," Javier told him.

"What? Why?" Kerri frowned.

"Because I lost my knife, and I need a weapon, and you're in no shape to fight if we get attacked again."

Brett chuckled and winced. "Yeah, well, I think I need it more than you right now, dude."

"You can use my club," Kerri said.

Javier smiled. "No, you're keeping that. By the looks of this thing, you're pretty good with it."

Heather sighed impatiently. "Well, if the doors and windows are all blocked, why don't we try hammering our way out? I've still got my brick."

Brett answered before anyone else could. "There's no way we're getting past that barricade. Not without a sledgehammer or something."

Javier looked down at his hands for a moment and then back at each of his friends. "So we find a different way out of here. And I know how."

"What do you have in mind?" Kerri's voice was low and soft, but every word was clipped. She'd noticed that Brett's breathing was growing erratic.

Javier looked up at the trapdoor in the ceiling. "We have one doorway that isn't blocked."

Heather shook her head. "No fucking way."

"How are we going to get Brett up there?" Kerri asked. "Look at his hand. He can't go crawling around on it."

"He has to. Either that, or we hide him here and go for help."

"I'll go along," Brett whispered. "I can do it."

"We follow it to wherever it lets out," Javier said. "Then we look for this basement that Brett told us about. It's the only choice we have left. Either we find a way out, or we find something to help us get past the barricades."

"Maybe if we all tried to move them together?" Kerri suggested.

"No," Javier's voice was low and firm. "I tried moving the barrier, too. I think something is locking it in place."

Coughing, Brett sat up and started taking off his bloody T-shirt. "Somebody want to help me here?"

"What are you doing?" Kerri tried forcing him to sit back against the wall.

"I need to use my shirt as a tourniquet. Javier needs my belt."

Kerri slipped her hands under her shirt, and unhooked her bra. Then she slipped it out of her sleeve.

"Try this. It should do the job a little better."

Brett grinned. "Impressive."

"Yeah. Tyler used to . . ."

She trailed off, unable to complete the sentence. Kerri was surprised. With everything that had happened, she'd forgotten about Tyler while they were trapped in this hallway. She guessed that she'd pretty much gone insane after Tyler died—freaking out and everything. But here in the corridor, she'd pushed past all that. She'd killed the mutant, made a tourniquet and a rope, rescued Javier, and then made another tourniquet with her bra like she was MacGyver with breasts. Now her take-charge attitude evaporated as it all came rushing back to her.

"That's perfect." Javier took the bra from her and knelt next to Brett. His hands moved quickly and deftly, wrapping the still warm undergarment around Brett's wrist and pulling it tight. A moment later he pulled the belt away and examined Brett's fingers.

"Heather, can you light his hand?"

Heather shined the screen over Brett's hand, and they all leaned closer. His remaining fingers were swelling. Kerri winced as she looked at the damage. She didn't know how Javier could study the wounds with such clinical detachment.

"Good," Javier said. "The blood flow has stopped. Cutting off the circulation was a quick fix, but if we don't get you to a doctor soon, you'll have bigger worries than a few fingers. You need blood in your hand or you'll wind up losing it. So it's good that the flow has ceased."

Brett cleared his throat and moved his hand out of the light. "So, let's get going. Fuck this sitting around shit."

His tone was lighthearted, but Kerri could hear the fear in his voice. She knew how he felt. Brett had always been one to make jokes or talk tough when he was nervous or insecure or scared. This time was no exception, but he couldn't mask the terror. It was there in his voice, no matter how hard he tried to hide it.

It mirrored her own.

CHAPTER TEN

"Still no po-po," Leo sighed. "This shit is fucked up."

Their other friends had wandered off down the street, bored with waiting around and looking for some other form of entertainment. He, Markus, Jamal, Chris, and Dookie were still standing on the corner, watching the house at the end of the block. The derelict building seemed to loom larger as the night grew darker. Mr. Watkins stayed outside with them as well, not saying much. Just listening. Privately, Leo wondered if Mr. Watkins suspected they were going to fuck with the white kids' car and was hanging around to make sure they didn't.

"Yo," Chris said. "Y'all remember when them NSB boys were outrunning the cops, and they holed up inside the Mütter Museum and took hostages and shit?"

The others nodded.

"Yeah," Leo replied. "So what?"

"I watched that shit on television. This shorty I knew from back in the day was banging a dude from NSB's crew."

"Only shorty you know," Markus teased, "is the one that gave you the drips."

"Shut the fuck up." Chris frowned. "Anyway, there were cops all deep around that museum, in like, five minutes and shit. Now why do they show up for that, but not for this?"

"Because," Leo told him, "there ain't no tourists flocking to see our neighborhood like they do for the Mütter Museum."

The boys chuckled. Leo glanced at Mr. Watkins. The older man's eyes seemed to sparkle, and there was a slight grin on his face.

"Mr. Watkins," Leo said, "you know you don't have to hang out here with us, right? I mean, if you gotta go to work tomorrow, then you probably want to go to bed. It doesn't look like the police are gonna show, anyway."

Shrugging, Perry took a drag off his cigarette and exhaled smoke into the night air. "That's okay. Lawanda don't like me smoking in the house, so you boys are doing me a favor. The longer you hang out, the more nicotine I get in my system." He lowered his voice and leaned forward conspiratorially. "And believe me, living with her, I need all the nicotine I can get."

Their chuckles turned to laughter, and Perry's grin transformed into a broad, beaming smile.

"And I'll tell you boys why the police haven't shown up yet." He sat down on the top step of his porch. Leo and the others took seats around him or leaned against the railing. Leo thought that Mr. Watkins seemed surprised—and maybe a little pleased—by their undivided attention.

"Now, it's true," he continued, "that the cops are slow to respond down here. Sometimes it takes hours. About ten years ago, I saw a young man get gunned down right over there." He pointed. "Took the police three hours to respond, while he lay there and bled to death. It ain't no thing for them to be late. Most nights, it pisses me off, but sometimes I can't really say that I blame them. With the economy the way it is, they're even worse about showing up. Ain't just the big corporations going broke. It's the governments, too. All levels. Municipal, city, state—even the Feds. It doesn't matter who's in charge. Hell, California almost filed for bankruptcy last year. California—an entire goddamned state!"

"What's that got to do with us?" Jamal asked.

Perry took another drag off his cigarette. "I'll tell you what it's got to do with you. People ain't got no money, so they don't pay their taxes or other bills. Then the city goes broke. Starts looking for ways to cope with the budget crisis. Ways to save money. First they go after all the programs they don't think are necessary—the programs that a lot of folks down here count on to survive. But then they're still coming up short of cash at the end of the month, so they start laying people off. Parking meter attendants, garbage men, maintenance workers— and cops. Always the cops. In the end, the city ends up with fewer cops, but just as much crime. Hell, more crime even. The worse the economy gets, the higher crime rises. But now there aren't as many cops to deal with it, and the ones who are left—they've got priorities. And our neighborhood ain't very high on that list."

The boys were silent, pondering his words, weighing them. Finally, Leo spoke up. "It shouldn't be that way."

"No," Perry agreed. "It shouldn't. It definitely shouldn't. But it is. Been that way long as I can remember, and I've lived here a long time. On television, the president talks about change, and I'd like to believe that he means it, but down here, ain't a damn thing changed."

One by one, their gazes were drawn back to the house at the end of the street. Perry's cigarette tip glowed orange in the darkness.

Leo frowned. "What is it with that place, Mr. Watkins? I mean, I know not to go in there. Ever since we were little, we've been told it was haunted. Hell, it *looks* haunted. Nobody goes inside. Everybody knows that the people who go inside don't come out again."

"True that," Jamal said. "Not even the crackheads or meth skanks go near there anymore."

"But why?" Leo insisted. "What's it all about? What happens to the folks who vanish? There's got to be a story behind it all."

"You asking me for the history of that place?" Perry watched them nod, then sighed. "No one knows, boys. No one knows. At least, not anymore. Maybe folks did at one time, but if so, then those folks are dead by now, or old and senile. This neighborhood ain't got no sense of history. Not like the rest of the city. You think about that for a moment. There's over a million people living in Philly proper—almost six-million if we count the whole metropolitan area. We're the fourth largest city in the country. With that many people, you'd think *somebody* would know the story behind that house over there, but they don't. They can tell you all about the Liberty Bell and Ben Franklin and the Underground Railroad and the influenza outbreak. They can even tell you about when the police declared war on MOVE and firebombed their house back in the eighties. But none of that happened on our street or on our block, so we don't matter. We don't even rate a footnote. Only thing that happens here is black folks killing other black folks, and that don't make the news unless it's a bumper between sports and weather."

He made a broad, sweeping gesture with his hand and continued. "Look around you. You kids see anything to be proud of? You see anything here worth noting or remembering? Of course you don't. We've got no pride because there's nothing here to be proud of. There's nothing here that we want to remember. And when that happens—when the folks in a neighborhood lose their pride in where they live, then their history—and the history of that neighborhood—gets lost, too. If you took a drive out there to the suburbs, you know what you'd find?"

The boys shrugged and shook their heads. Dookie admitted that he'd never been outside of their neighborhood.

"Well, if you boys took a drive out there, you'd learn that folks in the suburbs don't know each other. They go to work. They come home. They go inside with their families. Maybe they know their next-door neighbor, enough to nod at him and shit, maybe exchange some pleasantries—but for the most part, they can't tell you who lives down the street, or the name of the family three houses down from them. All they know about each other is what their neighbors are driving and which political sign they had in their yard during the election. That's all. Down here, we know each other. Hell, most of the block is all up in each other's business. We know when somebody is sick, when they've been fighting, when they've broken up, when they get arrested, or when they lose their job. We can't help knowing our neighbors because they're stuck here with us. But they don't know each other out there in the 'burbs, and I'll tell you something else they don't know—their history."

"So they're just like us," Chris murmured. "That's what you're saying?"

"No," Perry said. "They ain't just like us. People around here don't know our neighborhood's history because they don't give a fuck about it. Out in the suburbs, they don't know their neighborhood's history because in most cases, there's no history there *to* know. Most of those suburban neighborhoods didn't exist until twenty years ago. It's all new housing and new developments, and all that was there before were cornfields and forests. If there was history there, they'd be all over it—erecting commemorative signs and shit. But they can't because there's nothing there *to* remember. That's an advantage we have here. Our neighborhood is old. We have history. All we have to do is embrace it. Learn it. But we don't. And in the end, we're no better than them. So, maybe I'm wrong. Maybe you're right, Chris. Now that I'm sitting here thinking about it."

"What do you mean?" Markus asked.

"The fact is, boys, people don't give a shit, no matter where they live. They've got too many other things to worry about. Down here, we worry about drugs, paying the rent, keeping our children out of jail, all these crazy sons of bitches shooting up street corners and playgrounds. The boogeyman living in the haunted house at the end of the block just doesn't rate when compared to all of those other things. Especially when the only time something happens is when somebody is stupid enough to go inside. It ain't like most of us can afford to move away from it. So you learn to live with it. Ignore it. Maybe even accept it. As long as it ain't them or their loved ones going inside that house, people could care less. And if the people down here could care less, then why should the cops and the politicians give a fuck?"

He paused, flicked his cigarette butt out into the street, and then continued. "Shit. This used to be a nice neighborhood. Folks used to hang around together outside, like we're doing now. Used to have big block parties and work on people's cars and carry groceries for one another. Now it's just dark, all the time, even in the daylight—just like that place down there. But you know what? Even when this block was a nice place to live, we still had that fucking house looming over us. We didn't talk about it, but we knew it was there, just the same. It's kind of hard to miss. We used to whisper about it then, the way people do now. But that was all we did—whisper. Who knows what goes on in there? Your guess is as good as mine. Some folks figure it's drug dealers. Personally, I call bullshit on that. Can't be drug dealers, because this shit's been happening long before drugs were ever a problem here."

"Then what do you think it is?" Leo asked. "What's happened to all them people over the years?"

Perry shrugged. "I don't know, and I don't *want* to know. I mind my own business. I expect the house to do the same. Maybe someday the authorities will take an interest or people will give a shit again. I keep hearing about all sorts of people wanting to buy up all the sub-prime real estate in Philly so they can get into their urban renewal programs, but so far no one has come knocking at my door or offered me a shitload of money. Maybe they will one of these days. Maybe they'll buy us all out. Relocate us somewhere nice. The idiots in New Jersey are already fixing up Camden—which is like trying to beautify a two-dollar whore—but sooner or later those same idiots will want to do the same here. Then they can deal with that house. Let them."

Frowning, Leo grew quiet. His expression was one of deep thought. Perry was about to ask him what was the matter, when Jamal interrupted. "Damn, Mr. Watkins."

"What?"

"I ain't never heard you talk so much," Jamal said. "I thought you were always grumpy and shit."

Smiling, Perry lowered his voice. "I don't talk much

because Mrs. Watkins doesn't give me a chance to. Every time I open my mouth to speak, she interrupts me."

They all laughed, but the sound seemed strange to Perry, as if the concrete and darkness were unused to it. Soon enough, the laughter died. They fell silent after that. Perry lit another cigarette. The wind was picking up, and he had to cup his hand over the flame to light it. The brown leaves of a stunted, dead tree jutting up from the split concrete sidewalk rustled in the breeze. It sounded like a death rattle.

They watched the house and waited.

Perry was no longer sure what they were waiting for.

Paul's nose wrinkled in disgust as he reached the bottom of the shaft. The air smelled like rotten eggs. A thin stream of foul water trickled along the tunnel floor, disappearing into the darkness. The tunnel itself was actually a large sewer pipe, big enough to allow for the flow of residential and industrial waste water and sewage, as well as runoff from the city's storm drains. He was actually surprised that there was so little water flowing through the pipe. Given the number of houses in this part of the city, there should have been more.

He shined the flashlight around, surveying his surroundings. The tunnel was big enough for him to stand upright. The top of his head brushed against the ceiling, and flecks of rust and sticky strands of spiderwebs fell into his hair. He wondered idly if there was a way to rip these sewer pipes up from under the pavement. They'd be worth a gold mine in scrap metal.

Once he got his bearings and his vision had adjusted, Paul slogged off in the direction of the house. He walked bowlegged, his feet planted on the sides of the pipe rather than the floor, so that he wouldn't have to wade through the water. The flashlight beam showed old high-water marks on the walls. Apparently the stream had been much higher and more forceful at some point. Now the sides of the pipe were covered with garbage. His feet shuffled through leaves, wrinkled condoms, cigarette butts, plastic bags, crumpled food wrappers, empty bottles, clumps of toilet paper, tampons, crushed beer cans, and other trash that had been washed down from the streets or flushed from one of the dwellings above. He considered fishing the aluminum cans out of the debris, but then decided they wouldn't be worth the effort. Chances were good that he'd find much more valuable scrap inside the abandoned house.

The stench grew thicker as he proceeded down the tunnel, and Paul concentrated on breathing through his mouth. The air was humid but cold. Occasionally a fresh breeze caressed his face. Paul wondered where it was coming from. He wondered, too, about the potential for disease. Although he'd salvaged scrap from a variety of locations, this was his first time wading through a sewer. He hadn't seen any turds floating by yet, and the water wasn't yellow, but that didn't mean the place was sanitary. What if there were bacteria on the walls or floating in the air? Were bacteria airborne? He didn't know and found himself wishing that he did. There was no telling what kind of infections he could pick up down here. But he plodded dutifully on, determined to gain access to the house now that he'd come this far. Cockroaches skittered around him, running up the curved walls. The sewer was quiet, and the darkness seemed oppressive. Paul clutched his flashlight tightly, thankful that he'd brought it along. He couldn't imagine being stuck down here without some sort of light.

Paul estimated that he'd gone about twenty yards in a

straight, horizontal line, when he suddenly emerged into a crossroads of sorts. Ahead of him, the tunnel split into three pipes, each one of equal size. He shined the flashlight around, weighing his options. One pipe veered sharply to the right. Another curved slightly to the left. The one in the middle continued on straight ahead. The left and right pipes had water trickling out of them, but the middle pipe was bone-dry, save for a tiny pool of stagnant, scummy water at its opening. Tiny insects squirmed in the pool. He assumed the middle pipe was his best chance of getting under the house. The lack of water flowing from it suggested that the pipe was unused. If it was connected to the abandoned home, then that made sense. He decided to try it and forged ahead.

Immediately the air grew fouler. There was the ammoniacal tang of urine and the sharper reek of feces, but there was something else, as well. Something he couldn't identify. It reminded him of the meat department at the grocery store, but he wasn't sure why. Paul cringed at the stench. His eyes watered. Instead of watching his step, he shined the light ahead, trying to find the stench's source. His attention remained focused on the walls. He'd only gone a few more feet when the floor suddenly disappeared beneath him.

With a startled cry, Paul plummeted downward. He managed to hang on to his flashlight, even as he splashed into a pool of cold, greasy liquid. The stench grew overwhelming. Sputtering, Paul kicked his feet, trying desperately to find a bottom. Instead, his feet found empty space. He dog-paddled and glanced around, terrified. He realized that the revolting liquid—whatever it might be—was more like paste than water, as if it was semicongealed. There was solid matter floating in it, but he couldn't tell what it was. The space was pitch-black, save for his flashlight beam, which was pointed above. He readjusted it and shined the light around.

Paul shrieked.

He was swimming in a toxic, brown and gray and black stew of human waste and toilet paper and . . . something else. It stunned him when he realized what the other matter was. Human bones—skulls, femurs, mandibles with teeth still attached, clavicle, ribs, and shattered, unidentifiable fragments—all coated with the viscous, stinking liquid. A quick glance confirmed that there were enough human bones in the pool to assemble dozens, if not hundreds, of skeletons. There were animal bones, as well—rats, birds, and other city creatures; he even spotted a few dog and cat skulls. He recognized what they belonged to from several family trips to various natural history museums. The stench rising from the pool filled his nose, threatening to overwhelm him. He flailed, reaching up with his arms. Gray and brown sludge dripped down them, splattering his face. The foul liquid had the consistency of syrup.

Despite his terror and overwhelming disgust, Paul remembered a newspaper article he'd read several years ago, about a government agent—ATF or FBI, he couldn't remember which. The man had been staking out a group of domestic terrorists in the backwoods of West Virginia. His cover got blown. When they caught him, the group killed the agent by drowning him in an outhouse. Paul couldn't think of a worse way to die than drowning in shit.

"Help," he screamed. "Somebody help me!"

His voice echoed back to him from somewhere to his left. Paul shined the light in that direction and gasped. There was a stone ledge rising several feet above the pool. Beyond it was a vast chamber that seemed to be a natural cavern. Limestone glinted in the flashlight beam. Gagging, Paul swam for the ledge. His fingers slipped on the stone as he tried to pull himself up. Inch by inch, he worked his way free, making squelching noises as the slime sucked at his shoulders, waist, and legs. When he'd finally freed himself, Paul collapsed on the ledge, sobbing. The stone felt cool against his face. He squeezed his eyes shut. Filth bubbled out of his nose and ran out of the corners of his mouth. He retched, but was unable to vomit. He desperately wanted to, if only to clear his system of the foulness he'd ingested. Paul opened his eyes again and groaned. The cave seemed to be spinning. Paul thought that he might pass out.

Then something grabbed him, and he did pass out, but not before he got a glimpse of it.

He was still screaming when his consciousness faded.

CHAPTER ELEVEN

Kerri, Heather, Javier, and Brett crawled through the stifling horizontal shaft. Javier was in the lead. He had Brett's belt coiled around his clenched fist and kept the buckle beneath his fingers so it wouldn't jingle. Javier was followed closely by Heather. Kerri squirmed along behind her. Brett brought up the rear, struggling to keep up with them. They kept stopping so he could catch up, but then he'd quietly urge them to keep going. Kerri supposed that Brett knew just how serious his situation was. He was trying to sound brave, but the fear in his voice was still there. He left a bloody trail in his wake.

The crawlspace tunnel was snug, and the walls brushed against their shoulders and hips as they crawled forward. The air smelled stale and there was a thick smell of feces. Not the nasty odor of rat droppings—that was bad enough, but this was far worse. It was a cloying, nauseating stench. Kerri tried to figure out what the crawlspace had been used for, but she couldn't come up with any rational explanation. It was made of wood rather than metal, so it couldn't be ductwork for heating or air-conditioning. The shaft appeared newer than the surrounding building materials. She wondered if it had been constructed more recently than the house, and if so, by whom. And again, for what? Had the midgets built it, just to drop down on unsuspecting victims after they'd trapped them in the hallway below? Kerri shivered. If so, how many other people had been in this situation? How many people had died in this place?

She lost track of how far they crawled. At one point, she caught a faint hint of vomit in the air and assumed they must be over the spot where she'd thrown up. They moved slowly and in silence, speaking only when they stopped for Brett, and then, communicating in hushed, short whispers and frantic hand signals.

When a door slammed below them, Kerri nearly shrieked. All four of them froze. They kept their cell phones open, so that they could see and had adjusted the backlight options so that they wouldn't turn off suddenly. Without that meager illumination, the tunnel would have been completely dark. Kerri wondered, however, if they should close the phones. What if the light shined down through the ceiling, or what if one of them suddenly got a signal and it rang while they were hiding? Then those thoughts vanished, replaced with more immediate fears. She heard the sounds of heavy, thudding footsteps coming from below. Kerri held her breath, afraid that if she didn't, she'd cry out. The fine hairs on her arms and the back of her neck rose up as she contemplated what might be making the noises. She had a pretty good idea. The footsteps sounded just like those of the man—thing— who had killed Tyler and Stephanie. Brett had told them its name was Noigel. She didn't know what kind of a name that was, but she was certain it was him down there. And when Heather turned around and glanced at her, wide-eyed and trembling in the cell phone's garish glow, Kerri knew that her friend suspected it, as well. Kerri shuddered, remembering his garbage-bag clothing and that swollen, infected penis that had dripped pus all over the place.

The footsteps stopped almost directly beneath them. Then Noigel, if indeed it was him, moaned, deep and mournful. He sounded sad. The moan rose in pitch and volume, turning into an anguished cry. The crawlspace thrummed as Noigel voiced his rage. Brett reached out and squeezed Kerri's ankle with his good hand. Heather squeezed her eyes shut and chewed on her hair. Javier remained motionless. Kerri caught a whiff of something— that same sour milk mixed with feces and sweat stench that she'd smelled when Noigel attacked them in the foyer. That left no doubt in her mind that Tyler's killer was directly beneath them, pissed off and intent upon finishing the job. That meant they hadn't gone very far at all.

Time seemed to halt. The sorrowful, enraged cries continued. Something slammed into the wall, hard. Then it struck the wall again. Kerri realized that Noigel was lashing out. By the sound, he was punching holes through the walls. She heard crumbling plaster and falling dirt and debris. Then the thing below them paused and fell silent. Kerri crossed her fingers, willing him to go away. Instead, Noigel sneezed three times—great, wet explosions that sounded like rifle shots. It followed this with a series of guttural snorts. Then the footsteps began to plod away, while the creature softly cooed to itself. The revolting stench dissipated.

It found the corpse, Kerri thought. *Noigel found the midget's corpse and he's upset. Not that he wasn't unreasonable to begin with, but now we're doubly fucked. I killed his friend.*

Brett slowly let go of Kerri's ankles as the thunderous footsteps faded. She turned around and gave him a reassuring smile. He returned the gesture, but his expression was weak and his face had grown paler. Kerri turned back to the others in time to see Heather tap Javier on the foot. He held up his hand, palm outward, indicating for them to stay still and silent.

The waiting was worse than Kerri would have thought possible. Even with Heather, Brett, and Javier right there with her for moral support, all she could do while they crouched in the darkness and waited, was listen to the sounds of the house settling around them. She jumped at every creak and groan, no matter how slight, convinced that each sound was a sign of the killer returning. She knew it hadn't been long, but it seemed like hours. Her mind swam, overwhelmed with disjointed thoughts and conflicting emotions. She was scared. Angry. Worried about Brett. Distraught over Tyler and Steph. She wanted to scream aloud until the killer found them, if only so he would put her out of her misery. She wanted to run, pushing past her friends, abandoning them if she had to, all in a desperate ploy to live. She wanted to hide—to find a dark nook somewhere in this house of horrors and just stay there until help arrived. Most of all, Kerri wanted to cry.

So she did.

Hot tears rolled down her face and dripped from her chin onto the crawlspace floor. Her shoulders and head shook, but she made no noise, weeping in terrified silence. Brett squeezed her ankle again. Eventually, the tears ceased. Kerri took a deep breath and let her body sag. Her eyes burned from the crying jag, and her face felt hot and tight. Somewhere in the back of her mind, the sight of Tyler dying reared up again. She pushed it away once more, afraid that if she began weeping again, she'd be unable to keep silent. But the image was still there, like an endless echo of things best forgotten.

They waited a few minutes longer. Finally, Brett spoke. "What now?" he whispered.

Without a word, Javier motioned them forward. They crawled even slower than before, moving cautiously, afraid to make even the slightest sound. The area below them remained quiet. No footsteps or garbled cries or slamming doors. Rats scratched and scampered deep inside the walls, and at one point, Kerri's palm came down in a pile of tiny, hard mouse droppings. She warned Brett so that he wouldn't get them in his wounds. There was no telling how many diseases the feces was crawling with.

Eventually, Javier stopped and the others halted behind him. They listened, but the house remained still.

"Dead end ahead," Javier whispered. "There's another trapdoor here. I'm gonna open it."

Kerri heard the creaking of hinges. Then, the shaft was suddenly filled with light. She flinched, shielding her eyes with one hand. Spots danced in her vision.

"We're on the other side of the barrier," Javier reported. "They've got the hallway lights turned back on. You guys stay here. I'm going to check it out."

Squinting against the light, Heather grabbed his ankle. "Don't."

"I have to, Heather. If there's anyone down there, maybe I can get them before they know we made it out of the trap. Or maybe I can lead them away from the rest of you."

"That's crazy."

"No, crazy is a rundown Victorian-style home in the middle of the hood with a bunch of sick fucks inside trapping and killing innocent people. Now stay here and be quiet."

The light in the crawlspace dimmed again as Javier squeezed through the trapdoor. After he'd dropped down to the floor, it got even brighter in the cramped space. The dazzling brilliance gave Kerri a headache.

"Javier," Heather whispered. "Do you see anything?"

His response was an angry hiss. Heather fell silent. Kerri listened to Javier creep down the hall. She could tell by his tread that he was trying to be stealthy, but she could still hear him. She wondered if anything else could, as well. Eventually, they heard his footsteps returning.

"I think the coast is clear," he called in hushed tones. "No sign of Noigel or anyone else. We're in a different part of the house, but near where we went into the last hallway. Come on down, but keep quiet."

Heather went first, followed by Kerri. Javier helped both of them out of the crawlspace. Then the three of them aided Brett's descent. Kerri was taken aback by his appearance. Under the fluorescent lights, he seemed more dead than alive. He swayed on his feet, smiling slightly. Then Kerri realized that it wasn't a smile, but a grimace. His complexion was pale, and there were dark circles under his eyes. His ruined hand was swollen and bruised, and his entire arm was soaked with blood, except where the sweat had washed it away. Despite their crawl through the shaft overhead, he was the only one sweating. Kerri wondered if that was a symptom of shock, and if so, what they could do about it, other than getting him some medical attention soon. She had applied the tourniquet competently enough, especially under pressure, but most of her medical knowledge came from watching *House*.

She realized that she wasn't the only one staring at Brett with concern. They all were. Brett must have noticed, too, because he shook his head ruefully.

"Jesus, guys," he murmured. "I'm not dead yet. Don't look at me like that."

Javier placed a hand on Brett's shoulder and squeezed. "Don't worry, dude. We're gonna get you out of here."

"I know you will."

"Listen," Javier continued, "what I said earlier about this being your fault and everything—I'm sorry about that. I didn't mean it. You're smart. Always looking at things logically. I'm glad you're with us right now, because we might need that brain of yours to get out of this place. So again, I'm sorry."

Brett winced in pain. "It's okay, man. Seriously. You were scared and upset. We all are. I know you didn't mean it."

"So we're all right?"

"Everything is copacetic."

Nodding, Javier turned to the girls. "Let's go, before Noigel or his friends come back. Kerri, you bring up the rear. Watch behind us. Keep an ear out in case they try to sneak up behind us. Brett, you stay between us, okay?"

Kerri took a deep breath and gripped her club tighter. The dwarf's congealing blood glinted on the nail sticking out of the wood. She glanced around the room. Like the others, it was devoid of furnishings. There was a single door, splattered with what looked like old blood and rat holes in the walls and baseboards. Black mold climbed the corners, spreading from the floor to the ceiling in grotesque spiral patterns. Dead flies and rat feces carpeted the bare floor. She'd had hopes that there might be a chair or even a table lying around, something they could have used for another weapon, something better than the belt, but there was nothing. She supposed that it was possible they could peel some wainscoting from the gouged, water-stained walls, but even that wouldn't make much of a weapon.

Javier opened a door with his left hand. The hinges squealed in protest, and he frowned at the noise. His right hand was drawn back, the belt wrapped into his fingers and the buckle dangling down like a short bullwhip.

They hurried down the hallway, moving as quickly but quietly as possible, retracing their steps through the house. As they passed the room where Javier had killed the first midget, he ducked inside. When he emerged again, his expression was troubled.

"What's wrong?" Heather asked.

"The body is missing."

"What body?"

"The midget. The one we killed before Brett found us. I hid it in there, back in the shadows, and now it's gone."

"Maybe it was still alive," Brett suggested.

Javier shook his head. "No. No way. I made sure it was dead. Noigel or one of the others must have found it."

"Maybe that's a good thing," Kerri said.

"How the hell can it be a good thing?"

Kerri's voice grew excited. "Noigel knows we've killed at least two of his friends. Maybe he'll decide that makes us even. Maybe he'll decide we're more danger-ous than their average prey, and he'll let us go."

Javier stared at her, unblinking.

"Do you really believe that, Kerri?"

Her expression crumpled. "No."

"I don't think Noigel is smart enough to think that way," Brett said. "From what I saw, he might be men-tally retarded."

"You think so?" Heather's tone was sarcastic. "I'd say he's more than retarded. I'd say that he's batshit fucking crazy. Retarded people don't go around bashing people's heads in."

Kerri choked back a sob as images of Tyler's death flashed through her mind again.

"Shut up, Heather," Brett whispered. "That's not help-ing."

"I agree," Javier said. "Now, come on."

Without another word, he led them forward again. Heather reached for his hand, but he brushed her away. Pouting, she followed. Brett shuffled along behind them with his head drooping low. Occasionally, he veered off course and bumped into the walls. After a few times of this, Kerri walked beside him, and let Brett lean on her. They crept back through the maze of hallways and rooms, finally emerging into the foyer again. The space was now lit by a single dirty bulb hanging from the ceiling. Kerri tried to remember if the lightbulb had been there when they came in. She didn't recall. Everything had happened so quickly.

She watched as Javier tried opening the front door, but it still refused to budge. Grunting, he tried harder, exerting himself hard enough that his muscles and sinew hardened like granite, and his veins stood out as if they were about to burst from his flesh. Kerri moved to help him, but before she could, Javier went slack again. Back to the door, he slid down into a crouch, panting for breath.

"It's no use," he mumbled. "I can't get it open. I could kick the fucking thing down, maybe, but not without them hearing us."

"Maybe there's somebody on the other side," Heather said. "Maybe somebody out there will hear us and go for help."

"Who?" Javier lifted his shirttail and used it to wipe beads of sweat from his forehead. "The guys who chased us in here? A fat lot of good that will do us."

"Better them than the freaks in here." Heather's voice got louder. "At least the guys outside weren't killing us!"

Javier stood up suddenly and clamped a hand over her mouth.

"Quiet," he warned. "What the hell is wrong with

you? Get your shit together, babe. Do you want them to find us?"

Heather's eyes were wide. She blinked twice. Javier released her and removed his hand from her mouth. They all stood quietly for a moment, listening for sounds of pursuit or discovery, but the house was silent as a graveyard.

"I'm sorry," Heather apologized.

"It's okay," Javier said. "We're all on edge. But we need to focus. We need to stop wasting time."

"Well," Kerri said, "let's go then."

"Hang on," Javier said. "First, I want everyone to check their phones. We're closer to the outside now. I'm wondering if we might be able to get a signal."

They checked their remaining cell phones, but none of them had service.

"Shit. I'd love to know how they're blocking it." Javier turned to Brett. "You think you remember how to get back to this kitchen you were in?"

Brett nodded, licking his lips. Kerri noticed that even his tongue had turned paler.

"I can find it," he muttered. "Are we really going down into the basement, though?"

"Yeah," Javier confirmed. "We are. I don't like it any more than the rest of you. But unless we find another way out of here, I don't see that we have much choice."

Brett slumped his good arm over Javier's shoulder and leaned on him for support. Then he took the lead, guiding them through an increasingly bewildering labyrinth of twisting passageways and doors. Kerri and Heather walked behind the boys. Kerri kept glancing over her shoulder, making sure that they weren't being followed. She also tried to keep track of each turn they made, but the task was impossible. All of the rooms looked the same—empty and desolate. There were doors that led into other hallways, doors that led into more barren rooms, and doors that led into nothing but brick walls. She noticed that there wasn't a single window anywhere in the building. The lights hummed overhead. The sound was simultaneously comforting and disturbing.

"You sure you know where you're going?" Javier asked Brett.

Brett nodded, unable to speak. He appeared even more exhausted than before. He led them through a few more rooms and passages, and then through a door that opened into the kitchen. The makeshift lights glowed overhead.

"I need to rest for a minute," Brett said. "There's no lock on the door, so one of us should stand guard."

Javier leaned Brett against the wall and eased him down to the floor in a kneeling position. Then he began looking around. "Let's find something to prop against the door. Slow them down if they try to get in."

"Forget it," Brett gasped, tottering back and forth on his knees. "I looked already, when I was here before. There's nothing."

Kerri glanced down at the floor and realized that she was standing in a large swath of fresh blood. The stains led to a closed door at the rear of the room. It looked like somebody had dipped a mop in a bucket of blood and dragged it across the floorboards. Alarmed, she choked in disgust and stepped aside. Her shoes left red footprints.

"That's . . ." Brett's throat worked soundlessly. "They brought Steph and Tyler through here. Noigel and the other one."

Kerri's hand fluttered to her mouth. She closed her eyes and tried to remain strong.

"The other one," Javier said. "You said he was wearing a woman's skin over his body?"

"Yeah. I get sick just thinking about it."

"Did you get his name?"

"No. Although Batshit-Crazy Man would suit him well."

Javier picked up a chunk of white plaster and drew a small line on his forearm. Then he drew another one beside it. He followed this with a shorter line.

Heather leaned closer to him. "What are you doing?"

"You never saw *Die Hard*?"

"No."

"I'm keeping track of how many are left—that we know of. This mark is for Noigel. This mark is for his cross-dressing friend."

"What's the half mark for?"

"The one that got its tongue bitten by Kerri. We don't know if it's alive or dead."

Brett sagged onto his rump and looked up at the lights. "I wish I knew how they were turning those on and off. I tried the light switches before, but none of them worked. They must be using a central breaker or something."

Kerri spotted the refrigerator and walked toward it. She breathed through her mouth. The air reeked of mildew and filth. Dust floated in the beams of light, swirling like tiny snowflakes. More of the sickly black mold sprawled across the walls. There was a bloody handprint on the appliance's door. It appeared old—the blood was more like dirt than liquid. She glanced behind the unit and saw that the electrical cord had been cut off at some point. The frayed wires dangled like veins from a severed human limb.

"Somebody help me out here," she said. "We'll slide this fridge in front of the door."

"Forget it," Brett replied. "I tried doing that before.

It's heavy as hell and it makes too much noise. And besides, you shouldn't disturb a burial ground."

"A what?"

"A burial ground," he repeated. "The fridge is full of rat bones."

Kerri scampered backward, sputtering in disgust. "Jesus Christ . . ."

Brett, Heather, and Javier laughed softly. After a moment, she joined them. It felt like a release. All the negative emotions drained out of her.

"Come on," Javier said, helping Brett to his feet again. "Let's check out the basement and find the exit."

Javier led them to the cellar door as if approaching a hornet's nest. The floorboards creaked. When he opened the door, they all felt a faint breeze on their faces. The odor was terrible and indefinable, but the breeze felt luxurious. Kerri didn't know if it was that or their earlier bout of laughter or just the new surge of adrenaline coursing through her body, but she suddenly felt more positive—upbeat. For the first time since they'd entered the home, she dared to hope. She held on to that emotion, drawing strength from it as they stood at the top of the basement stairs and prepared to descend.

Javier stared down into the darkness for a moment. With the kitchen lights behind him, his night vision was messed up. The basement wasn't just dark, like the rest of the house. It was pitch-black. He doubted that even their cell phones would pierce the darkness. He sniffed the air, trying to identify the repulsive stench wafting up on the slight breeze. It wasn't rot or putrefaction or sewage, but it was similar. Maybe a combination of all three? Finally, he gestured with his left hand and started down the stairs, urging silence with a backward glance.

As if in mockery of him, they heard distant, thudding footsteps—Noigel's unmistakable tread. At first, Javier thought the giant must be below them, climbing up the stairs toward them, but then he realized that the footfalls were actually coming from the corridor on the other side of the kitchen door.

"Hurry," he whispered, taking the stairs faster.

He heard Kerri shut the door behind them, and the stairwell turned even blacker. Brett or Heather—he couldn't tell which—stumbled behind him. Javier listened, his head cocked slightly to the side. He didn't hear the footsteps anymore, but wasn't sure if that was because the door was shut or because Noigel had stopped. Gripping the belt with one hand and trailing his other hand along the wall, Javier continued down the darkened staircase, moving as carefully as possible without sacrificing his speed. The others stumbled along behind him. He held his breath, certain that Noigel would hear them and come charging along in pursuit. The stairs were old and narrow and half of them sagged under his footsteps as if they were ready to collapse. Still, he continued without hesitation. It was only when they'd finished their descent that Javier allowed himself to breathe.

"Everybody huddle together," he whispered, so low that he was unsure whether they'd heard him until he felt their hands reaching out to brush against him.

"Are we all here?" Kerri asked.

"I am," Heather said. "Brett?"

"Yeah, I'm here."

Javier frowned. There was something in Brett's voice—pain, certainly, but something else beneath it. "You holding up okay?"

"No," Brett sighed. "My hand is starting to hurt like a bitch. I mean, worse than it was—and that's a lot."

"Just hang in there a little bit longer."

"I don't hear him up there," Kerri said. "Do you guys think he stopped?"

"Maybe," Javier admitted. "Who knows what the fuck the crazy bastard is doing? Maybe he's searching somewhere other than the kitchen. Let's put some distance between us and him, before he comes back."

Javier reached into his pocket for his cell phone and then remembered that he'd lost it in the pit. He asked Brett for his instead. Brett passed it up the line, groping in the darkness. Javier flipped it open and used the weak light to look around. His spirits soared when he spotted a dusty, cobweb-covered, antique oil lamp hanging from a rusty nail in one of the cellar's wooden support beams. His enthusiasm quickly dissipated when he realized there was neither a wick nor oil to be found anywhere in the basement. Indeed, the sublevel was as empty as the rooms above, save for a pile of rotting burlap sacks, a heap of broken masonry, a few glass bottles, and some moldering cardboard boxes. The cell phone's light did little to penetrate the shadowed corners, but he was certain they'd be empty, as well. He wondered how the spiders and other insects lived in such a desolate place. It was just proof that life could exist anywhere, even in a location as dismal as this.

"How the hell are we supposed to find our way around down here?" Heather's voice had an edge of despair. "I can't see shit. It's worse than upstairs."

Javier shrugged, knowing full well that she couldn't see the gesture. "Let's just find a way out, okay? Before anything else can happen."

Kerri made an agreeable grunt and Brett stayed quiet.

"I know it's dark, but maybe we'd better use one

phone. That way we can save the batteries in the others, just in case."

They murmured their displeasure, but did as he said.

Javier took Heather's hand and settled it on the back of his jeans. "Hold on to me. Don't let go for any reason. We don't want to get separated down here."

She hooked one finger through a belt loop, and then, while Javier held up the light to guide them, Heather found Kerri's hand and placed it on her pants. Then Kerri did the same with Brett. His wounded hand hung limp by his side. A moment later they were moving again. Javier led them through the darkness, taking small, measured steps with only the cell phone's dim glow to guide him. Brett's belt dangled from his hand, the buckle smacking silently against his leg with each step. He felt Heather tug at his pants as they walked slowly forward, and it brought to mind another time she'd done that. A year before, the six of them had driven out to York County for a night so that they could attend a Halloween haunted attraction in LeHorn's Hollow. Everyone at school had been talking about it since the ghost walk had first been announced, and they'd arrived with eager anticipation. They'd been standing in line waiting to buy tickets and Heather had hooked her index finger through his belt loop and pulled him to her suddenly, kissing him deep and earnestly. The suddenness had surprised and excited him. Sadly, their evening had been cut short when some kind of riot ensued inside the ghost walk. A bunch of people died. The police and the firemen arrived, and it was shut down. They'd driven back to East Petersburg, frustrated and bored. But not Javier. On the way home, he'd sat in the backseat of Tyler's brother's car, smiling, one arm around Heather, pulling her close, the kiss still lingering like an echo in his mind. It was a memory that Javier returned to often—and fondly. He held on to it now, as well, and it was enough to keep him going. As they crept forward, she came close enough a few times that he felt her breath on the back of his neck. It was warm in contrast to the unseen breeze that blew through the dark space. Javier just wished he could find the source of that breeze, because he was willing to bet he'd also find their escape route.

Still listening intently for any indication that Noigel was on their trail, he held the phone higher, trying to see. The darkness wasn't complete, but it was close enough. Javier kept his eyes wide and his attention focused ahead of him and used his right hand to feel along the cold, damp basement wall. His fingers trailed over cracks and crevices and tore through cobwebs. He ran into a corner and felt along it for a moment before deciding to go to the left. It made sense, as he was fairly certain the street was in that direction. Hopefully, so was the exterior wall of the house and maybe a set of storm doors or even a sewer entrance. It occurred to him that an old place like this might even have a coal bin or root cellar attached to the basement, points of access that had been necessary in the past. He just hoped that the freaks who lived here hadn't blocked them up. There *had* to be another way out down here. Brett had overheard them say it, and it made sense. The things living here couldn't very well stroll out the front door—not without everyone seeing them. There had to be a hidden exit.

But he wasn't having much luck finding it.

"Shit happens," he murmured, reciting his mantra but not thinking the others could hear him.

"Yes," Kerri responded. "It does. And tonight, it's happened to us."

Javier was about to reply when the wall opened up

unexpectedly. He stopped. The slight breeze grew stronger as it flowed from the opening. It held a musky scent, age and mildew and something else that he couldn't easily identify. He felt along the edge of the opening and realized that he might have found exactly what he was looking for. Holding the cell phone high, Javier stepped forward and felt for the wall ahead of him. The wooden boards disappeared, replaced with a hard, packed clay surface.

"What the hell?" he spoke softly, but his voice carried more than he'd expected. Chastising himself for doing exactly what he'd gotten on Heather about, he reached out and touched the spot, seeking any indication that the change might indicate a broken section of wall or an exit. The breeze gusted against his face. Heather pushed closer to him. Her breasts slipped along his back and her hands moved up to touch his shoulders. Had he been facing her, they'd have been close enough to kiss.

"Sorry." Heather's voice was a sighed whisper. Her body turned sharply and her voice grew a note sharper. "Watch it!"

Kerri's voice was louder, even sharper. "I can't. Brett's wobbling back here. You okay?"

"Sorry," Brett apologized. His voice was slurred. He sounded tired. "Lost my balance."

Javier shook his head, pressing his lips together in irritation. He was about to remind them to whisper when a new noise came from somewhere far ahead of them, deep in the darkness—a long, warbling howl, a sound that made as much sense in the basement of a crumbling, inner-city Victorian home as cannon fire in a confessional. The howl didn't sound like a wolf, but more like a human throat doing a poor imitation.

Javier froze, his heart pounding in his chest. He felt

Heather jerk upright behind him, clinging tighter to his shoulders. Shrugging her off as gently but firmly as possible, he listened intently, trying to guess at the distance or even a general location of the cries. At a guess, the howls came from at least a hundred feet away and directly ahead of them.

"What the hell was that?" Brett's slurred voice was terrified. The echoes rang through the basement.

Javier flinched again.

"Everyone shut up."

He listened to the still-reverberating echoes. They told him more than the howl had. There was some kind of tunnel directly ahead of them—a long tunnel, judging by the sound. Javier frowned, wondering why such a thing would be in a basement. Before he could tell the others his suspicion, another wail pierced the darkness, twice as loud as before.

And closer. Much closer.

It was followed by another cry. This one had a different pitch and inflection.

And then another sounded out.

And another.

There were at least five different voices in the darkness. Javier closed his eyes. His skin prickled. The air blowing out of the wall turned foul.

Behind them, they heard the basement door open. The darkness lessened, cut into by the kitchen lights from above. Then the all-too-familiar heavy footsteps thundered down the stairs. Noigel voiced his garbled cry, joining the others.

"Oh shit," Heather moaned. "We are so fucked."

Brett had allowed himself to be distracted by the feel of Kerri in front of him. Yes, it was wrong. He knew that.

Especially when his girlfriend and her boyfriend were dead, murdered, their corpses lost somewhere inside this hellhole. But thinking about her body, feeling the way her hips swayed against his hand with every step was taking his mind away from the throbbing pain shooting up his arm and throughout his body. He'd just bumped against her ass—and it had been an accident, but a nice one—and was apologizing when the first howl erupted from the darkness.

Suddenly he needed to pee very badly. The pressure in his bladder almost overrode the pain surging from the stumps of his severed fingers.

Although he hadn't told the others, Brett was having trouble with his vision. He could see, but everything was a faded monochrome, a dusky black and white that leeched away all details and colors. Part of it was his injuries, he knew, as well as the deep sensation of lethargy and exhaustion that had overcome him since escaping the hallway. The almost complete darkness in the basement was another contributing factor. He didn't like Javier's idea about using only one cell phone, but he silently went along with it just like the girls, because Javier had obviously taken charge. Brett didn't care. Let him. Logic was helpful on a chessboard, but in this house, it was a wasted effort. Nothing about this place was logical.

His eyes had finally adjusted as much as they were likely to, when the door crashed open behind them and the kitchen lights shined down the stairs. Standing at the rear of the group and closest to the stairs, Brett was momentarily blinded as his eyes struggled to cope with the sudden change. He listened to the footsteps and to the strange and terrible howls coming from both in front of and behind them, and did his best not to scream.

"What do we do?" Heather yelled, her voice frantic. "Javier?"

If he heard her, he gave no indication. Javier was silent, seemingly paralyzed by fear and indecision.

Our fearless leader is out to lunch, Brett thought. *And Heather's right. We are so fucked.*

Logic dictated that they run, but where? Even as the howls drew closer, the footsteps behind them increased in speed. The staircase sounded like it was shaking. Kerri said something, but Brett couldn't hear her over the intensifying cacophony. She turned around and faced him, her eyes nothing more than two wide smudges in her shadowy face. Her hand settled on his chest for a moment. She clutched a fistful of his shirt and sobbed. Brett nodded his head, realizing what had to be done. His fear evaporated as he embraced the inevitable. This was no more difficult than solving a trigonometry problem.

Kerri didn't deserve to be here. She was already suffering enough. He could see it in her, how ruined she was by Tyler's death and Stephanie's, too. His face flushed red with anger. Kerri was a wonderful, sweet girl, and he didn't want to see her hurt any more. She was a little bitty thing, and until today, he'd have thought her too small to defend herself. She'd proven that wrong, of course, going up against the thing that had bitten off his fingers. During that struggle, Brett had caught a glimpse of the strength inside Kerri, roiling beneath the surface. Such strength deserved to live on. She had too much yet to offer the world. She couldn't die in this shit pile. Therefore, someone needed to give her—and the others—a chance to escape. That someone was him. It was logical, after all. He was severely wounded, in shock, and had lost a lot of blood. There was no telling how many different infections he'd picked up already, and the chances of reaching a hospital were getting slimmer with each passing second.

It had to be him.

Check and checkmate.

All of this went through his mind in seconds. Brett didn't say it aloud, of course. Kerri, Javier, and Heather wouldn't have been able to hear him even if he had told them. The strange sense of calm deepened as he prepared himself. The pain racking his body went away, turning into nothing more than a distant hum, like the drone of a gnat hovering around his face, too small to bother with, more of an annoyance than anything else.

Noigel's footsteps plodded across the basement floor, each one reverberating like a shotgun blast. Brett turned to face him and immediately wished he hadn't. For one split second, his resolve almost shattered. Noigel was a massive shadow amidst the darkness. He seemed to glide toward them. Brett could make out the huge hammer clutched in one hand. Other than his footsteps, the giant moved silently. He made no more cries or howls. Brett couldn't even hear his breathing. Steeling himself, Brett stood his ground and risked a glance behind them. Several humanoid shapes emerged from the darkness. Unlike Noigel, they weren't silent. If anything, their frenzied howls increased as they drew closer. In the dim light of Javier's cell phone, Brett couldn't make out much about them, except that they varied in size and shape. Some were of normal height and weight. Others were diminutive in stature, like the thing that had attacked him. A few were tall like Noigel, but thin and scraggly rather than possessing his girth. One seemed obscenely obese, lumbering forward in a see-saw–type motion. All of them shared one common characteristic—even in the darkness, they were brutal looking, predatory rejects that moved in slowly and carefully and with an almost palpable self-assuredness, taking their time and jockeying among one another for position.

Perhaps it was their appearance that snapped Javier out of his trance, or maybe it was Kerri and Heather's frantic, pleading screams. Whatever the cause, Brett saw the steely determination return to his expression. Javier snapped the cell phone shut and stuffed it in his pocket. For a second, Brett didn't understand why, but then Javier explained.

"We're gonna run straight past them," he said. "There's a tunnel up ahead. That's got to be the way out."

"Are you fucking crazy?" Heather shrieked.

"It's the only way. We'll run in the dark. They can't see us if we don't have a light."

Brett shoved Kerri forward with his good hand. "Move! Get away! Get the fuck out of here. I'll distract them. Run!"

Kerri jerked with each word as if he'd slapped her. She stared past him, watching Noigel's approach in the glare from the kitchen lights, her eyes wild and terrified, her lips peeled back in a feral grimace that looked too much like the freaks menacing them.

Then Noigel laughed. The sound was deep and guttural, and boomed across the basement like artillery blasts.

Brett's resolve shattered. Thoughts of logic and sacrifice and heroism fled as he shoved her forward again. He forgot all about Kerri's hidden and remarkable reserves of bravery and strength. Forgot all about his sympathy for her. He was not a hero. He had never been the sort to consider others before himself. It wasn't in his nature. He wasn't truly thinking of Kerri or any of the others as he pushed her forward a third time. He was just trying to get them all moving, because instinct told him to flee, and there was no way he could get through them without falling on his ass. Unable to hold it anymore, his bladder let go, and the front of his pants grew warm and wet.

Brett was aware of Noigel as the hulk loomed behind him and came to a halt. The madman's massive form blocked the remaining light. The loathsome stench roiling off him was overpowering, cloying around Brett like a smoke. Brett didn't turn around. He couldn't. His feet felt like they were stuck in concrete. He stared straight ahead, watching Kerri's expression as she looked up and over his shoulder, her eyes impossibly wide, her mouth open to scream but no sound coming out. He watched as the rest of the freaks fell silent, then charged, moving low to the ground and loping toward them en masse. Brett blinked as one of the creatures did the impossible and leapfrogged over the others, diving through the air, narrowly missing the ceiling as it jumped. He sighed as Javier charged forward to meet the attacker, shouting challenges in Spanish. Brett smiled slightly as Heather and Kerri ran.

Then a massive hand grabbed his hair and jerked him backward, and all Brett saw was the ceiling. He tried to scream, but only managed a gobbling choke as Noigel jerked his head back even farther. Brett felt like he was being bent over backward. Then he got a good look at the giant's face. The hulk's mouth was open, smiling, and bloody saliva dripped onto Brett's face and ran into his eyes. Noigel's breath was like an open sewer. His bald, misshapen head seemed to be surrounded by a halo of kitchen light, and his round, black eyes glittered with malicious glee. It leaned closer, drooling more foul saliva into Brett's gaping mouth. Instinct took over and Brett's hand came up in a fast arc to block the flow. He realized as it rose just how foolish he had been, but it was too late to stop the reflective action. Brett's wounded, bloodied hand slammed into Noigel's face, leaving trails of crimson on the waxy, pocked flesh. He felt his stumps bend backward. Pain jolted through him, electrifying his raw nerve endings. Grunting, Noigel jerked him off his feet with one hand and swung him through the air by his hair, turning round and round like a top.

Then the creature let go, and Brett felt himself sailing through the darkness.

Mercifully, his vision—already weak from the surrounding darkness—completely failed before he slammed into the basement wall, and although he felt his bones snap and heard his skull crack apart, he did not see the red explosion his impact made or hear the wet sounds of his brains splattering across the stone blocks.

CHAPTER TWELVE

Leo stood suddenly, hitched up his sagging pants, and addressed the others.

"Fuck this shit. I'm tired of just waiting around for something to happen. I'm going in there."

His friends gaped at him. Mr. Watkins seemed bemused. He exhaled smoke and stared at Leo, as if unconvinced of his sincerity and waiting to see what Leo would do next.

"For real," Leo said. "I ain't playing. This is bullshit. What Mr. Watkins was saying? That shit is true. People down here don't give a fuck anymore, and that's a big part of the problem. And the cops don't give a shit either. It's our neighborhood. We need to deal with it. If not us, then who?"

"Go ahead," Markus said. "My ass is staying right here and waiting for five-oh."

Leo shook his head, disgusted. "Let me ask you something. How would you feel if it was us in there? How about if we took a drive out to Amish Country or some shit, and our car broke down, and we were trapped inside some old barn? Wouldn't you want someone to help us?"

"Yeah," Jamal said, "but they called us niggers, yo. I say the hell with them. They can rot, for all I care. You know what I'm saying?"

"True that," Chris agreed. "All we were trying to do was help them."

Dookie and Markus nodded.

Leo impatiently waved them off. "Man, they were scared. And it was only the one guy who called us that— the Poindexter-looking motherfucker. The others just ran away. In hindsight, I can't say as I blame them. We were pretty pissed off after he called us that."

"So why you want to help them?" Dookie asked.

"Because it's the right thing to do. Don't you get tired of people assuming we must be drug dealers, just because of where we live or how we look or dress? Don't you get tired of not doing anything to change our situation? This is a chance to make a change—real change, not that bullshit the politicians go on and on about."

Dookie and the others seemed to mull over Leo's sentiments, but Markus was adamant. "I ain't going inside no haunted house," he said. "No way. Fuck that noise."

"How do you know it's haunted?" Leo challenged him. "You ever see a ghost peeking out the window at you? Ever hear chains rattling around and shit? No? Neither have I. And neither has anyone else that we know of. It's like Mr. Watkins said—nobody really *knows* what happens in there. All we know is that we're told to stay away from it because people who go inside don't come back out. And usually it's the crackheads or dope slingers or homeless people, and who gives a fuck if they disappear, right? Except that this time, it ain't them. It's somebody who will be missed. At the very least, when word gets out that those white kids went missing and the last folks they encountered was us, what do you think is going to happen? We're going to be the number-one suspects."

Markus stared at the cracked pavement, frowning with

concentration. Leo could tell that his friend was thinking it over.

"Maybe you're right," Chris admitted, "but that don't change the fact that we still don't know what's in there. Sure, maybe it ain't ghosts, but what if it's some serial killer motherfucker, like that crazy dude killing people on Interstate 83? You see him on the news?"

"Can't be him," Jamal said. "Interstate 83 is a long way away. Down near Maryland and shit."

Markus glanced up and appeared confused. "I thought 83 was the one that runs up through State College?"

"No," Jamal corrected, "that's 81. Interstate 83 runs from Baltimore up to Harrisburg."

"Would y'all shut up?" Leo glared at them. "We're getting sidetracked here. The point is, you're right, Chris. We don't know what's in there. And we should. This is where we live. It's our responsibility to find out. Who knows? Maybe it's something as simple as a rotten floor, and folks have been falling through over the years. Or maybe it *is* a serial killer. Fact is, we won't ever know unless we go look. But first we need guns."

Mr. Watkins's eyes grew wide. His mouth fell open and his cigarette tumbled to the ground.

"Guns," he sputtered. "What the hell do you need guns for?"

"If I'm going in there," Leo said, his tone the same as he used when talking to his little brother, "then I'm going in strapped. I'm not stupid. If the cops ever bother to show up, you think they're going to walk inside that house without their guns?"

Sighing, Mr. Watkins pulled out his crumpled pack of cigarettes, shook another one out, stuck it in his mouth, and then flicked his lighter. A moment later, he spat it out.

"Goddamn it, I lit the filter. Look what you made me do, talking all this nonsense about guns."

Leo and the others said nothing. They simply watched him, waiting.

Mr. Watkins shook his head. "Listen. Let me call 911 one more time first. This time, I'll report it as a fire. That should get them down here quicker."

Leo eyed him doubtfully. Now that he'd decided on a course of action, he was eager to proceed. "How long's that gonna take?"

Before Mr. Watkins could answer, Dookie interrupted. "Yo, I got it! Check this shit out. I know how to get them down here. We set the fucking house on fire. They'll come in a hurry if we do that."

Leo, Chris, Jamal, and Mr. Watkins stared at him without speaking. Markus reached out and slapped him hard on the back of his head.

"Owwww . . ." Pouting, Dookie rubbed his head and glared at his friend. "What the hell did you do that for?"

Markus slapped him again, softer this time. "We can't set the house on fire, you stupid motherfucker. There's people trapped inside of it. How we supposed to save them if the fucking thing is burning down?"

"Oh, yeah. Guess I didn't think of that."

"No shit."

"You boys just wait here a minute." Groaning, Mr. Watkins stood up and brushed off his pants.

He went inside his house, and they waited. Leo heard him talking with Mrs. Watkins, but he couldn't make out what they were saying. Judging by their tones, they were arguing about something. Then it grew quiet. A black Nissan with tinted windows and purple running lights rolled slowly past. The subwoofer in the car's trunk rattled the windows of the nearby homes. It made a slow turn at the corner. The boys watched it fade from sight.

"You know what?" Dookie's voice was low and thoughtful, and he looked up at the sky as he spoke. "I don't want to die here."

"We ain't gonna die in there," Jamal said. "We're just gonna look around. Help those white kids out."

"No, I don't mean in there. I mean *here*, on this block. I don't want to get all old and shit and never have gone farther than North Philly. Mr. Watkins was talking about the suburbs and stuff. I want to see it. Maybe it ain't no different than here, but I want to find out for myself."

None of the boys responded. Secretly, Leo harbored the same desires. He was positive that the rest of his friends did, as well. The farthest from home he'd ever been was six years ago, when he was ten. His mother had signed him and his brother up for a summer program, where inner-city kids went to live with a family out in the country for two weeks. Their adopted family, the Gracos, had been all right. Mr. Graco wrote comic books for a living, and his wife, Mara, was an insurance agent. They had two kids—Dane, who was Leo's age, and Doug, who was about the age of Leo's little brother. The Gracos lived in a big farmhouse with an even bigger yard, and lots of woods and fields around. It had scared Leo at first. He'd felt uncomfortable there, and although he had a good time that summer, he'd been grateful to return home. But sometimes, late at night, Leo would lie in bed and listen to the sounds of the city and think about that place so far out in the country and how quiet it had been. He wondered what it would be like to live there all the time, to not go through life scared, to not have to be constantly aware of his surroundings or worried about his loved ones. Of course, even people like the Graco family probably had things they were scared of. There were monsters everywhere. All you had to do was turn over their rocks, and you'd find them, hiding in the dark.

A few minutes later, Mr. Watkins emerged from his house. He had a plastic bag in one hand.

"Well?" Leo asked. "Did you call them again?"

He nodded. "Yeah, I called them alright."

"What did they say?"

"They didn't say anything. I couldn't get through. All I got was a goddamned message telling me that all circuits were busy and I should try my call again later."

"That's fucked up," Jamal said.

"Yes," Mr. Watkins agreed, "it is."

Leo turned away from them and faced the house at the end of the block. "Well, you all can do whatever you want. I'm going in."

"We got to get some guns first," Chris reminded him. "Want to try Cheeto or Tawan? They can probably hook us up. Or maybe Terrell?"

"We'll go see Terrell," Leo said.

"You boys ain't doing any such thing," Mr. Watkins stepped down onto the sidewalk. The plastic bag rustled as he reached inside of it. Grinning, he pulled out his pistol. Then he handed the bag to Leo, who glanced inside and saw several flashlights.

"I'm going in there with you," Mr. Watkins said, "and I'll go first, because I've got the gun. The rest of you can carry the flashlights."

"Well, shit," Leo said, grinning, "why didn't you say so?"

CHAPTER THIRTEEN

"Go," Javier shouted. "Fucking run!"

Heather's breath caught in her throat as Javier punched the nearest attacker in the jaw. He shook his hand, wincing in pain, as the creature crumpled to the floor. Javier leaped over the writhing beast and yelled, urging the girls to follow him. He lashed at another creature with the belt, trying to clear a path, and then dashed into the darkness. Heather ran, desperate to keep up with him. Javier seemed to have snapped. That cool self-assuredness that he'd displayed so far was gone. His actions now were frantic. Manic. He shouted again, this time in Spanish.

He's afraid, she thought. *But that doesn't mean he's going to abandon us down here. He wouldn't dare. He loves me. He wouldn't leave me behind. He wouldn't leave Kerri, either.*

Heather bit her lip. Despite the immediate danger looming on all sides, she couldn't help wondering whether Javier had feelings for Kerri. They'd spent time alone together in the aftermath of Tyler and Stephanie's death, while Heather was hiding. And when they'd all found each other again, Kerri and Javier seemed closer somehow. Was it her imagination, or had something happened?

Javier shouted a third time, but Heather couldn't understand what he said. She couldn't even tell whether it was English or Spanish. She could barely hear him over the enraged and excited chatter of their foes. The bizarre howls had been replaced with guttural growls and grunts. Most surprisingly, a few of them spoke. The things they said were somehow more terrifying than their appearance. They promised the teens a multitude of mutilation and torture and deviancy once they'd caught them.

Heather had no intention of letting that happen. She ran, not glancing over her shoulder to see if Kerri and Brett were following. It sounded like there was a struggle taking place behind her. She heard Brett screaming. Then his cries turned to one long, extended wail that was suddenly cut short. Heather plunged ahead, narrowly avoiding the grasping hands of one of the freaks. Long, ragged nails scratched at her skin, slicing into her shoulder. She shrugged them away and kept running.

"Get them," one of the cellar's inhabitants screeched. "Don't let them get away."

"They're fast," another called. "My legs aren't as long as theirs."

"You won't have any fucking legs if you let them get away, 'cause we'll eat those instead."

An impossibly obese hulk loomed over her, wheezing with exertion. Heather dodged it easily, but not before glimpsing two pale, ponderous breasts swaying amidst mounds of sweaty, jiggling flesh. It was female—and naked. The woman reached for her with cold, clammy hands. Her skin had the consistency of wax. Heather shuddered in revulsion.

"Javier? Where are you?"

In response, something tittered in the darkness.

"Here," he called, his voice distant. "Heather?"

Another mutant lunged for her as she followed Javier's voice, realizing too late that she was fleeing right into the midst of their attackers. Heather was out of range of the kitchen lights now, but the thing was close enough that she could make out some of its features, even in the darkness. It had a face and snout like a baboon, and its short, squat body was mostly hairless. Its eyes were definitely human, and they smoldered with rage. She darted to the left, out of reach of her pursuer, and then dodged to the right again. Her heart pounded in her chest. She breathed through her mouth to avoid the stench roiling off the creatures.

She thought she heard the belt crack up ahead, followed by a cry of pain. Heather ran in that direction, determined not to get separated from Javier. The ground was uneven and sloped downward. Even in the darkness, she could feel the descent increasing drastically. She winced as what felt like sharp, jagged stones poked her bare feet, but she shoved past the pain, not daring to slow down.

The sounds slowly dimmed, then ceased, but she kept running. She had no way of knowing whether she was still being chased. This part of the basement—if she was even still in the basement—was pitch-black, and she didn't want to risk stopping to pull out her cell phone. She heard no footsteps behind her, but that didn't mean that they weren't still there, lurking, waiting to attack. Without stopping, Heather instinctively glanced over her shoulder, forgetting that she probably wouldn't be able to see anything anyway. As she did, her foot came down in something wet, and she slipped, bouncing off a wall. Her hands shot out to break her fall, and sharp rocks sliced into her palms. Sitting up, Heather gasped, but managed not to scream. She crouched there, cradling her hands in her lap. She could feel her blood trickling down her palms but couldn't tell how bad the cuts were. She wondered if her feet were lacerated as well. They hurt, but she didn't know whether that was from the earlier wounds or brand-new ones. She didn't know how badly she was injured. She didn't know where her boyfriend or her friends were. She didn't know where her pursuers were. All Heather knew was that she was suddenly alone in the darkness.

"Javier?" she whispered, her voice quavering. "Kerri?"

There was no answer from either. Heather stood and listened, but the only sound she heard was her own harsh breathing. If Javier or Kerri were still nearby, then they were unwilling—or unable—to respond. She glanced around in the darkness, no longer sure of where she was or which direction she'd come from. She'd lost her bearings during her tumble. Far off in the distance, she spotted a tiny dot of illumination, and after a moment, she determined that it was the kitchen lights shining down into the basement. But it was so far away—as if the cellar were larger than the house above it. Maybe it was. Or maybe she'd run into a cave attached to the basement or something. She couldn't tell. Her hands began to burn. Deciding to risk it, Heather fumbled for her cell phone, intent on at least examining her wounds. She patted her pockets, felt the reassuring bulge of the tiny cell phone, but then decided against using it, after all. What if one of the killers heard it or saw it? Darkness and silence were preferable to that.

"Kerri?"

Nothing.

Pouting, Heather tried to figure out what to do next. She couldn't stay where she was, no matter how strong her urge was to curl up into a ball and just hide herself away. In the darkness, she had nothing but her hands and her sense of hearing to guide her. Both seemed useless right now. She couldn't risk using the phone, so what did that leave her with? She patted the floor, wincing in pain as her cuts brushed against the rough surface. Eventually she located the wall and pressed herself against it. The cold, clammy surface felt good against her skin. She rested there, catching her breath and weighing her options again. Javier and Kerri had to be somewhere up ahead. They *had* to be, because the alternative was far too terrifying to consider. What if Javier had left her here? What if Kerri had wound up with Brett when whatever had happened to him back there in the darkness—something dreadful, by the sound of it—occurred?

What the hell would she do if everyone else was dead?

Somewhere off to her right, she heard a slight scuffling noise.

"Javier," she tried again. "Is that you?"

This time she got a response.

"Here kitty, kitty, kitty . . ."

The voice didn't belong to Javier. Indeed, it barely sounded like it belonged to anything human. It was harsh and ragged, the words slurred, and there was an unmistakable hint of maniacal glee in the tones. Heather covered her mouth with her hands and tried not to make any noise. Despite her best efforts, a pitiful whine slipped past her lips and fingers.

"It's okay, kitty," the thing in the dark responded. "Come on, now. If you come out now, I'll twist off your head and make it real quick, so you don't feel it when we eat you."

The voice sounded like it was all around her. Heather crouched low to the floor, ignoring the pain in her hands, and concentrated on taking slow, deep breaths and remaining motionless. She inhaled, exhaled, and forced herself to calm down. A few more breaths and she was clearheaded again—still terrified, but not paralyzed by fear.

She heard shuffling footsteps, as if the hunter was dragging one foot. It was coming from her left. Then she heard the belt crack. It sounded very loud in the darkness. Her spirits soared. It was Javier. She knew he wouldn't abandon her.

"Javier?" Her cry echoed in the chamber.

"No. I'm Scug. Was Javier the guy with the belt? 'Cause it's mine now. And you are, too. You're going to be my new suit of clothes."

Screaming, Heather sprang to her feet and fled. Laughter bubbled up behind her, nipping at her heels. The belt whistled through the air again, striking the wall. Flinching, Heather kept running. In the darkness, she never noticed when the tunnel forked, veering off in several different directions.

Kerri fled, plunging headlong into the blackness, heedless of the misshapen forms grasping at her from all sides. Heather vanished in front of her, swallowed up by the shadows. Brett screamed behind her, but when she turned to see what was happening, a tall, lanky form loped toward her, swaying from side to side. It wasn't Noigel—this attacker was too skinny to be the murderous giant. As it drew closer, she noticed a rusty hacksaw in its hand. Kerri turned and ran, forgetting all about Brett. She pushed past two figures and ran straight into a third. Both Kerri and the creature tumbled to the floor. She sprang up again, kicked the fallen mutant in what she assumed was its face, and continued on. She'd managed to hold on to her club all this time, but had forgotten about it. She swung it as another shadowy figure lunged at her. The club vibrated with the impact and the nail at the end of it drove deep into the creature's brain. When Kerri tried to tug the weapon free, it remained stuck in the corpse's head. She let go of it and ran.

Something squeaked to her left, and tiny, childlike fingers clawed at her thigh, trying to grasp her jeans. She lashed out with her hand, struck flesh, and heard the thing grunt. The fingers slipped away and she ran again. She darted to the right, then the left, dashing aimlessly through the wide-open space, seeking only to avoid being caught. A multitude of footsteps pounded along behind her, accompanied by a chorus of grunts, gasps, howls, and laughter. Something whistled through the air and struck her back hard. Kerri cried out, but didn't slow down. She heard the object—a rock, perhaps—clatter to the floor. Two more whizzed by in the darkness, close enough that she could feel the air shift at their passing.

Kerri swerved again, changing direction. She stumbled around and gasped, her hands touching nothing, no one, her security lost in the darkness. She heard a cry of pain, but couldn't tell which direction it had come from or who had made it. Brett? Heather? Javier? One of the things? She ran on, her hands held out in front of her, deflecting the walls as she drifted too far to the right and then too far in the other direction, overcompensating. Her foot came down in a pool of something cold and wet. She heard a splash, and then her sneaker was soaked. Her socks squelched around her toes with each step she took.

Her breaths hitched in her throat and chest and Kerri felt the tears start. Not that they mattered in the black pit where she was running blind. It was too much. All of it. How had the evening gone so horribly wrong? How had all this happened? This morning, she'd been thinking about college and her relationship with Tyler. Now Tyler was dead and college . . .

. . . college was probably something she'd never live to experience.

Breathless, she slowed her pace but did not stop. Images of Tyler and Steph came to her again, unbidden. She could hide from her pursuers in the darkness, but when it came to her own memories, there was nowhere to go, no way to hide. She pushed thoughts of Tyler and Stephanie away, thinking instead of her family. She was four years old, and her father's face wavered, reminding her that there was never a right time to be stupid as he picked up the shattered remnants of the glass she'd dropped. He'd swatted her hand briefly, but that was nothing in comparison to the look of disapproval on his face. He was a wonderful man, gentle and warm and loving but never one to forgive stupidity or ignorance. She wondered how he'd react to the situation she was in now. Would he tell her that it was her own fault—that she should have listened to him when he'd said time and time again that Tyler was no good and that he'd only lead to trouble? Of course, Daddy had probably been thinking about her ending up pregnant or in a car crash, or maybe even in jail. She was pretty sure that even her practical, nononsense father couldn't have imagined that her relationship with East Petersburg's bad boy would lead to his daughter being trapped in an inner-city slaughterhouse and hunted like a rabbit by a bunch of mutated freaks.

Kerri was startled from her ruminations as her fingertips brushed against a wall. She stopped running and listened for sounds of pursuit, but the chamber was now eerily quiet. Could their attackers still be out there, hiding in the darkness, lying in wait? Were the bastards just toying with them? Making them think they had a chance at escape before finally jumping out and killing them the way they had Tyler and Steph? Kerri wiped her tears away

and squeezed her eyes shut. Her legs ached and her lungs
burned. She was exhausted, both physically and emotion-
ally. She suddenly didn't care whether they found her.
She needed to rest.

She leaned against the wall. Slick, wet clay soaked
through her dirty jeans. Despite the danger of her situation, Kerri was intrigued. She explored the wall with her
hands, running them along it. She'd been expecting
stone blocks. That's what the cellar walls had been constructed of. She'd noticed them when they first entered.
Instead, rough, wooden planks formed the wall in this
section of the underground warren. Wide gaps between
the boards let the wet dirt spill out in a thick sludge. This
close to the wall, the air was thick with a deep scent of
stagnation. It aggravated her throat. She tried to stifle her
coughs, not wanting to give away her location, and
moved a little to the right. Both of her feet came down
in another puddle. This one was wider and deeper than
the last, and she clasped her arms around her shoulders
and shivered as cold water soaked through both shoes.
The sensation just made everything worse.

"Shit."

Her voice was very small, barely even audible to her
own ears, but something else heard it. One of their pursuers howled from nearby. She heard it sniffing like a
dog. Kerri dropped to her knees and started crawling
through the wet clay. It squirted between her fingers as
she slunk away. Gone was the basement floor. This
was—somewhere else. She didn't know where. A cave,
perhaps. The water was everywhere, and her hands became slicked with mud.

She felt the ground begin to slope under her, slightly
at first, then suddenly steeper, and she had to struggle to
keep from sliding downward headfirst. Then the ground

changed, and she did indeed begin to slide. The soft, slick mud was still there, but her palms didn't sink in as much as they had before, and she felt the texture of wood under her hands again. Kerri stopped her forward slide and felt along the wood. If it was hard enough, she might be able to use it as a club if she could pry some loose. That would at least make up for the one she had lost earlier. Her hands shook from nervous exhaustion and adrenaline alike as she felt the edges of the plank and tried to yank it loose. A quick exploration revealed that it wasn't a single board, but several lengths nailed together. She kept digging, her fingers pulling the mud away from around the wood, searching desperately for something that she could use to defend herself—anything was better than nothing.

She paused, tilting her head and listening. The snuffling thing was gone—or at least silent again. Kerri tried to do the same, working as quietly as possible. With little to go by but her sense of touch, she eventually uncovered the wood's dimensions. It was bigger than she'd imagined. She pulled along the first edge and got nothing for her efforts. The second edge had a bit of yield, and the third edge lifted awkwardly a few inches, slowly and with a wet sucking sound.

It's a door, she realized. *But to where? A sub-basement? Who puts a door in the floor of a cave?*

The air billowing up from below smelled different. Not fresher, but less vile. It was a welcome change. Taking a deep breath, Kerri slid her arm into the black space and felt the coolness beneath. Her fingers failed to touch anything but open air. Whatever might be hidden below was too far down for her to reach it. She stretched farther, trying to feel for some stairs or a ladder, when behind her, there came another noise. It sounded like something metal being scraped across stone. Several guttural voices echoed from either side of her. As she listened, they turned to whispers.

Cautious but quick, Kerri slipped her body lower. The wooden slab dropped as she did, scraping along her shoulder blades and then her back. It was heavy enough to pin her in place. She struggled with it, still trying to stay quiet, and pushed the door up long enough to slide the rest of her body beneath it. Her feet touched something solid. Standing on it, she ducked her head and lowered the door back into place. Then she explored this new area. Her left hand scraped along what felt like a stone wall. It was dry and cool. She raised one foot and thrust it out into the darkness. Kerri sighed with relief when she found another stair. She slowly started down it, wondering what was at the bottom.

Javier had lost his belt. He remembered that much upon regaining consciousness. He fumbled around in the darkness, searching for the makeshift weapon, and then it all came rushing back to him. The belt had been ripped from his hands by a shadowed opponent during his escape. But then what? He lay on the ground, defenseless and aching, trying to remember what else had happened. His face hurt, and a nauseating mix of blood and mud blocked one of his nostrils and filled his mouth. Coughing, Javier pushed himself up into a sitting position and shook the muck from his face and hair.

What the hell had happened?

He remembered running. Shouting at the others to follow him, trying to clear a path for them by taking the creatures on himself. And he had. He'd cut through the motherfuckers like a buzz saw, relishing each of their grunts or cries of surprise and pain. Whoever these people were (because despite their deformities, Noigel and his friends were clearly human), they obviously weren't used to having their prey fight back. He'd been doing fine until he lost the belt. Then they'd closed in on him, and his fear had overtaken his bravado, and Javier had fled.

Javier couldn't remember anything past that, no matter how hard he tried, so he decided to take a different tack. He gingerly felt his body, wincing as his fingers found dozens of shallow cuts and bruises. He didn't think he was injured too badly, however. He listened, hoping to hear Heather or Kerri or Brett, but the darkness was silent. It seemed to press against him, as if trying to climb inside his body. Javier mentally pushed back. Satisfied that he'd live, at least for the moment, he felt around him, patting the ground. Then he reached out into the black void. His fingers came in contact with a stone wall.

Then he remembered. The wall. He'd run into it in the dark. He hadn't known what it was—he hadn't been conscious long enough to wonder. All he'd known was that he'd run headlong into something hard. Then he'd woken up again. He now assumed that he'd hit the wall with enough force to knock himself stupid.

His luck had held twice tonight—first with the glass pit and now with this . . . whatever *this* was. He assumed caverns of some kind. Natural or man-made. Or maybe both.

He slid over to the wall and rested his back against it. The silence deepened. There was no sign of his girlfriend or his friends. No sign of their pursuers, either. He was on his own down here. The realization filled him with shame and worry. He felt responsible for all of them. No, it wasn't his fault that they were in this mess, but as far as he was concerned, they were under his protection. And they wouldn't have entered the house in the first place if he hadn't been the one to suggest it after Brett's stupid outburst.

"What the hell was I thinking?" He muttered the words to himself and spit a trail of saliva and mud away from his lips. "Should have confronted those guys and just apologized for my idiot friend. Or called the police right there."

He fumbled for Brett's cell phone. He'd still had it in his hands when they were attacked, but now it was gone. He tried to remember whether he'd stuck it in his pocket as he ran. He wasn't sure. If he had, his pocket was empty now. Javier's heart sank. It must have fallen out of his grip during his dash through the cellar or when he crashed into the wall. He patted the ground, searching for it, but his efforts were futile. His hands came up empty. Javier was overcome by a wave of confusion, fear, and despair. Heather, Brett, and Kerri might be dead and he was lost underground, in total darkness, with no weapons to defend himself.

"Well, fuck that noise."

Javier listened to his words echo. Wherever he was, it sounded like a wide-open space. Grinding his teeth, he slowly got to his feet, taking his time and trying to keep his balance. His legs felt a little wobbly and his head light, but he had neither the time nor the inclination to allow that. Javier had been in bad situations before—situations nobody knew about. Not even Heather. They'd happened when he was younger, before his family had moved to East Petersburg. Ancient history. He'd lived through them, and he intended to live through this one, as well. He forced himself to move forward, trailing his hand along the wall so that he had a frame of reference in the darkness. Javier told himself that he didn't need the cell phone anyway. Using it to light his way at this juncture would have been foolish. The last thing he needed to do was advertise his position to the cannibalistic freaks.

He made a silent vow to buy Brett a new phone as soon as they got out of here, and then wondered if he'd ever see his friend again long enough to keep that promise.

Water dripped down on his head. Javier glanced upward and then felt foolish. He couldn't see anything. He made his way through the subterranean chamber, determined to find the girls and Brett if he could, but to also find a way to escape. It had to be down here somewhere. Brett had overheard the killers say so. Javier stopped in his tracks, chilled by a sudden terrifying thought. What if Noigel and the guy wearing a woman's skin had just been fucking with Brett? What if they'd known he was hiding in the kitchen and rather than killing him right then and there, they'd toyed with him instead, leading him to believe that the basement was the only way out of the house?

If so, there was nothing he could do about it now. Javier seriously doubted that he'd be able to find his way back to the basement stairs, even if he did find Heather and the others. He started walking again. His back felt tight and his neck was stiff with tension. He ignored the aches and pains, doing his best to listen for any possible sound, but other than the occasional drip of water, the area remained deathly still.

Paul woke up in transit and captive. He'd been trussed upside down on a long, metal pole. Steel, judging by its texture and weight. It would have probably fetched him a nice price at a scrap yard. Rough cords cut into his wrists and ankles, chafing his skin. He bobbed and swayed as his captors carried him along, trekking through some sort of underground tunnel. Paul was staring at the ground, so he raised his head a little and glanced at the walls. They seemed natural, rather than man-made. A cave, maybe? He'd never heard of caverns beneath Philadelphia, but the idea wasn't so surprising. Pennsylvania was riddled with limestone caverns and shafts, as well as abandoned iron ore and coal mines.

As his full senses returned, he wondered how he was able to see if he was indeed in an underground cavern. Then he felt a slight breeze on the back of his neck. Despite his terror and confusion, the sudden gust of air momentarily soothed him. When Paul opened his eyes again, his wits had returned. For a second, he wished that they hadn't, because with his wits came memories of what had transpired—his trip into the sewers, falling through the hole, landing in that foul pool of liquefied bodies and sewer water, and finally—the things that had been waiting for him there in the darkness. Paul raised his head and stared at his captors. His mouth went dry. He drew in breath to scream, but before he could, a particularly hard jostling knocked the air from his lungs again.

They were all around him. He counted at least eight—two on each end of the pole he was dangling from (he saw now that it was some sort of sewer pipe and iron rather than steel), their muscles bulging, grunting with effort as they carried him along. In addition to the pole bearers, there were several more beings scampering along ahead of them, as well as at the rear of the procession. He tried to figure out what they were. Humanoid, certainly, but Paul wasn't positive that they were actually human. They varied in size and shape, and each was cursed with unique birth defects. Some of the mutations were almost mundane, while others were utterly horrifying. One of his captors was bare chested and covered by a thick mat of curly black hair, out of which peeked four dime-sized nipples. Another seemed to have double the amount of joints in his legs, arms, and fingers. Paul stared at a mis-shapen lump of flesh jutting from the thing's left shoulder, and then realized that the lump of flesh was staring back at him with one small, watery eyeball—a second head, a Siamese twin, not fully developed. What looked like a ragged pink scar was really a tiny mouth. A third crea-ture, a female, appeared relatively normal, but she was obviously pregnant with either quintuplets or a giant lone fetus. Her distended belly stuck out before her, glis-tening, the bare flesh a sickly, swollen kaleidoscope of purple and black hues. Her massive breasts slapped her ribs as she walked. Clear fluid dripped from her mauled nipples. He wondered if she'd given birth before, and if so, whether it was her offspring that had chewed her nipples like that. Her wild thatch of pubic hair was filthy and matted. She gibbered as she loped along, a thin line of drool running from her mouth and dangling to a spot directly in the middle of her obscene cleavage. Her facial features were similar to that of someone with Down's syndrome, but her expression was cruel and savage.

Despite the variations in height, weight, and physical characteristics, they all shared a few similar traits. Their skin pigmentation was a mix of gray and alabaster. They weren't Caucasian or African-American or any other race he could think of. Nor did they appear to be of mixed racial heritage. These beings were something else, but he didn't know what.

"H-hey," he stuttered, working up enough saliva to speak. "W-what is this?"

An albino dwarf with pink, rheumy eyes and six fin-gers on each webbed hand darted forth and hissed at him. Its breath smelled worse than the sewer had. Its teeth were black and broken. Paul screamed, and the thing slapped him in the face. His jaw stung, and he bit the inside of his cheek. Paul's fear gave way to sudden anger and humiliation.

"Hey, you little shit! What do you think you're—"

Growling, it slapped him again. Then it grabbed a fistful of his hair and yanked hard. Paul screeched as his hair came out by the roots. The dwarf scampered away, clutching its prize. The procession never slowed.

Paul began to sob. He was embarrassed by the reaction, but he couldn't stop himself. Snot bubbled out of his nose and curdled on his lip.

"Let me go," he pleaded, hoping they understood him. "Listen, I've got a wife and kids. Please let me go. Please? What is this? Tell me!"

"This is where we live," the thing with two heads answered. Its voice was deep and somber.

For a moment, Paul was too stunned to reply. "W-what?"

"This is where we live. All of us."

"I d-didn't know. I'm sorry. I didn't know I was trespassing. I thought the house was deserted, you know?" Paul heard the plaintive, whiny tone in his voice, but he didn't care. "I was lost. Just looking for directions. I didn't know that . . . p-people lived here."

They walked on in silence, not answering him; not even bothering to look at him. Paul heard distant howls from somewhere up ahead. They sounded inhuman.

"I didn't know," he tried again. "I'm really sorry. If you'll just let me go, I can—"

"You brought tools," Two-Head said, matter-of-factly.

"What?" Paul frowned, unsure if he'd heard the freak correctly. He had no idea what it was talking about.

"Tools."

The creature took one hand off the pole and snapped

its fingers. Another mutant ran forward. This one had a long, withered, tentacle-like appendage where its left arm should have been. The right arm was normal, and in that hand it clutched Paul's tool belt.

"You lie." Two-Head sighed. "You say you are lost, but you came with tools. You came to fix the sewer pipes."

"No," Paul protested. "I don't work for the city. I'm from Uniontown, for Christ's sake! I'm just here be-cause—"

"It doesn't matter. Either way, we still have to kill you."

The statement brought a fresh round of pleas and cries from Paul, but his captors refused to respond. They marched along, almost methodically. Some of them carried crude lanterns. A few had flashlights. Most of them were naked or covered with some type of dried red clay. A few wore tattered, dirty scraps of clothing. One—a child or another dwarf, he couldn't tell which—looked especially bizarre. It was naked from the waist down, clad only in a once-white T-shirt that said, I GOT CRABS IN PHILLIPSPORT, MAINE. Another was nude, but wore a backward ball cap with a logo for Globe Package Service. Paul wondered if the odd scraps of clothing had belonged to other victims, and if so, what their previous owners' fates had been.

His thoughts turned to Lisa, Evette, and Sabastian. He quietly wept, wondering if he'd ever see them again, wondering if they'd miss him, if they'd ever find out what had happened to him, if they'd go on with their lives without him. He wasn't resigned to his fate—not quite yet—but things weren't looking good. The cords binding his ankles and wrists were strong and tight. No way he could snap them. And some of his captors were physically impressive. Maybe he could have kicked their asses twenty years ago, but middle age had softened him. He swore to a God he wasn't even sure he believed in that if he got away from here, he'd go straight. He'd get a real job again, something legal, and do right by his family. Sure, he'd justified stealing scrap metal as a means of supporting his loved ones, but look what it had led to?

Paul sobbed. His broad chest hitched with each shuddering, labored breath. The temperature in the tunnel grew slightly warmer. The breeze remained steady. The stench of his captors was foul, but there were other smells in the air. Mildew. An earthy odor—maybe clay or dirt or minerals of some kind? And something else, something that smelled like animal fat cooking in a frying pan. It wasn't until one of the lanterns sputtered and hissed that he realized what the smell was. They were using fat as fuel. Paul had a sinking feeling that he knew what kind of animal the organic matter had come from. Bile burned his already raw throat. He opened his mouth to scream again, but paused as they came to a sudden stop.

They had emerged in a vast underground chamber—a true limestone cavern, just like the ones he'd taken the kids to a few times. It was brightly lit. Fires flickered in an assortment of rusted fifty-five-gallon drums scattered throughout the space. Stalactites and stalagmites dotted the rocky landscape. Paul found himself trying to remember which one was which, and then uttered a crazy laugh. What the hell did it matter? Geology wasn't his main concern right now. Regardless, thoughts of high school fluttered through his head. Back then, he remembered the difference by calling stalactites "stalac-titties," because tits hung. Hence, stalactites hung from the ceiling.

His laughter turned into a choked sob.

There were more creatures in the cave. Some of them were sprawled out on boulders, relaxing, staring at him with intense interest and amusement. Others were engaged in various tasks. Two-Head and the rest of his captors carried him to the center of the great chamber. Paul noticed a series of steel barrels had been set up here. There was some sort of makeshift rack above them, manufactured from angle iron, wooden beams, and pipes. Something dangled over two of the drums—something raw and red and glistening. It took him a moment to realize what he was looking at. Corpses. Two butchered human corpses. Each one had been strung upside down over one of the barrels, then skinned and gutted. Paul was reminded of the deer processing center during hunting season. The bodies were headless, and he couldn't tell what sex they had been. They'd been slashed open from neck to groin and spread wide, emptied of their internal organs. These had been people once. Now they were just hollowed out carcasses.

"Oh God. Oh my God . . ."

They hoisted Paul higher into the air and sat the pole into the rack. He dangled over an empty drum, the top of his head just inches from the rim.

"Hey," he yelled. "Don't do this! Please don't do this. We can talk about it, right? You don't need me. You've got two already. I can pay you. I can give you anything you fucking want, okay? Just please don't do this!"

His pleas turned into nonsensical babble as Two-Head and the others calmly strolled away. Another mutant approached. Paul blinked, staring at the creature from his upside-down vantage point. It stared back at him, blinking with its one, lone eye, which was affixed in the center of its face, giving it the appearance of a mythological Cyclops. Its head was smooth and hairless, and its ears stuck out at odd angles from the side of its head. They reminded Paul of cauliflower. It smiled at him with a broad gash of a mouth, revealing sharp but rotten teeth. In its hand was a long, broad carving knife. The silver blade glittered in the firelight.

"Let me go. Hey, listen to me, man. Do you understand me?"

The Cyclops nodded slowly, still grinning. "I understand you. Some of the younger ones don't. They never learned the above speech. But us older ones still know it. A few of us can even read."

"What . . . what are you?"

"I'm Curd."

"I-is t-that your n-name, or your r-race, or what?"

The Cyclops tilted its head and frowned, staring at him with deep concentration, as if trying to determine Paul's meaning.

"My name is Curd."

"Okay. Now we're getting somewhere. My name is Paul. Paul Synuria."

"I don't care."

Paul licked his lips. "I know, and that's okay. But listen . . . Curd. Listen. You don't have to do . . . whatever it is you want to do. I can make it worth your while to let me go. What do you need?"

"For you to be quiet."

"Okay. I can do that. But before I do, tell me what you *really* need? I'll get it for you, no matter what it is."

"You have everything we need right here. Your brains and heart and kidneys and lots and lots of meat. We'll even use your bones."

"No . . . listen . . . oh God . . ."

"If you were a woman, Scug would want your skin, but he's busy with them other women right now, so we'll use it for something else."

Paul sputtered in confusion.

"You're not the only one here tonight," Curd continued, slapping one of the bloody corpses with his free hand. "Noigel killed these two. Smashed their heads up, so we couldn't use the brains, but that's okay, because there are plenty more of you left. Scug and the others are hunting them right now. We'll be busy tonight."

He raised the knife and stepped forward, seizing Paul's hair in his fist and entwining his fingers through it.

"No," Paul screamed. "No, goddamn it! Didn't you hear me? I can give you whatever you want."

"You didn't hear me. I already said, you've got everything we want right here with you. We'll use all of you, after I've bled you out. That's how we were taught, and that's how we teach the little ones. Every single scrap of you will be put to use."

Paul's eyes widened. Laughter bubbled out of him again, and this time, he couldn't control it. It echoed across the cavern.

"Scraps," he wailed. "Oh, it all comes down to scrap! Scrap . . . scrap . . . scrap . . ."

"It's time for you to be quiet now."

Curd yanked hard on Paul's hair, exposing his throat. Then he brought the knife up and made a slashing motion. Paul shut his eyes, anticipating a flash of pain, but there was none. His neck felt a little hot, but it was warm inside the cave. He heard water running and tried to turn his head to see where the sound was coming from, but Curd held him firmly in place. Paul noticed that Curd had blood on him. Fresh blood, splattered across his ugly, misshapen Cyclops face, and all over his arm. Paul tried to ask him where the blood had come from. Tried to beg him one more time, to tell him why the scrap comment had been so funny, tell him about Lisa and the kids. But when Paul tried to speak, he found that he couldn't. He heard a faint wheezing sound and wondered where it was coming from. The running water grew louder, and the heat on his neck faded. He shivered, suddenly growing cold and sleepy and nauseated. Curd's grip on him slackened, and Paul's gaze drifted downward into the barrel that he was suspended over. He blinked. The barrel was filling with . . .

. . . blood?

Whose blood? Where was it coming from?

And why was it so cold in here all of the sudden?

Then Curd raised the knife again, grabbed a fistful of his hair and began sawing his head off with savage, sweeping thrusts of the knife. He whistled while he worked. Realizing what was happening, Paul willed himself to pass out, but he was dead before he could. The last thing his eyes registered was his own decapitated body, when Curd lifted his head up to show it to him. Blood pumped from his neck like water from a garden hose.

If Paul had been able to, he would have screamed.

CHAPTER FOURTEEN

"So what's the plan?"

Leo stopped in his tracks, and the rest of his friends did the same. Chris, Jamal, Markus, and Dookie had accompanied them. Some of their other friends who had wandered away earlier had returned, and Perry had told them to stay behind to direct the police on the off chance that they actually responded to the 911 call.

"What?"

"What's the plan?" Perry asked again. "You were the one who was all fired up to do this. So, what's your plan once we get inside there?"

"I don't know." Shrugging, Leo frowned. His expression was doubtful. "I guess I figured we'd just go in there all hardcore and shit, and find those kids. Fuck up whoever was holding them captive—if there *is* someone else."

Perry shook his head. "You boys have watched too many movies. This ain't *Black Caesar*."

They all stared at him, and he could tell by their expressions that they were clueless about his reference.

"You mean you kids have never watched *Black Caesar*? *Hell up in Harlem*? *Superfly*?"

"Hell, no," Markus replied. "I don't watch TV."

"Your daddies didn't watch them with you when you were little?"

"I ain't got no dad," Leo said. "Never knew him."

Chris nodded. "My old man's doing twenty up in Cresson."

"Only thing my dad ever watches," Jamal said, "is wrestling."

"I watch anime," Dookie told Perry. "You ever watch that, Mr. Watkins?"

"No," Perry admitted. "I don't even know who she is."

"Who?"

"This Anna May woman that you just said you watch."

Now it was Dookie who was confused. "What?"

"Never mind." Perry sighed and caught Leo's eye, making sure he had the young man's attention. "Look, just forget about the movies. My point is, we can't just go barging in there. We don't know what's going on inside. If there really is someone in there up to no good, then we could get those kids killed if we rush in. Hell, we could get *ourselves* killed. We've got to be smart about this. Careful."

"Okay," Leo said, "so what do *you* think we should do?"

Perry paused, cupped one hand over his cigarette, and lit it. Then he stuffed the lighter back in his pocket and grinned.

"I don't know yet. That's why I wondered if you had a plan. Let's just check it out first. No sense worrying about things until we know what we're actually up against."

They reached the end of the block and crossed over into the debris-covered wastelands that separated the old house from the other homes on the street. Perry and Leo walked side by side, taking the lead. The others slunk along behind them, casting nervous glances in every direction. Each chunk of concrete or twisted girder took

on sinister forms in the dark, transforming into lurking
dangers, waiting to jump out at them, gun or knife in
hand. The overgrown weeds in the vacant lot became a
prime hiding place, and they approached with trepida-
tion. The tall, rusted chain-link fence jingled and swayed
in the wind, sounding like the rattling chains of a ghost.
The house groaned, as if disturbed by their arrival. Or
perhaps anticipating it.

They paused at the bottom of the porch steps. Perry
took a deep drag on his cigarette. The tip glowed orange, providing their only source of illumination. Shivering, he turned to Leo and told him to turn on one of
the flashlights. The young man did as he was told, but
Perry noticed that his hands were trembling. He was
scared. Perry scanned the other boys' faces. They were *all*
scared.

Well, he thought, *at least I'm not the only one.*

"Keep that pointed at the ground," he whispered to
Leo. "If there are bad people inside, we don't want them
seeing the flashlight through the windows."

Leo nodded, but didn't reply.

Swallowing hard, Perry dropped his cigarette butt to
the ground and stepped on it, grinding it into the dirt
with his heel. Then he walked up the porch steps and
approached the front door. The old boards creaked and
popped, bending under his weight. He stopped a few
paces from the door and turned around. The boys remained where they were, watching him.

"Ain't y'all coming?"

"You go ahead," Jamal whispered. "We got your
back."

"From down there?"

They shuffled their feet and stared at the ground, except Leo, who took one faltering step. He perched on the

bottom stair, hitching his pants up with one hand and leaning against the railing, which wobbled at his touch.

Shaking his head, Perry turned around and tiptoed the rest of the way across the porch, cringing each time a board creaked. He stopped in front of the door and took a deep breath. There was an empty hole on the right where a doorbell had once been and worn, faded screw holes indicating that there had been a knocker on the door at one time—probably stolen. There was a tiny peephole in the center of the door, but when he leaned forward and tried to get a glimpse through it, all he saw was darkness. Perry was suddenly overcome with the uncanny impression that there was someone on the other side of the door, staring back at him. His arms prickled with gooseflesh, and the hair on the back of his neck stood up.

"Well," Dookie whispered, "what you waiting for, Mr. Watkins?"

Gritting his teeth, Perry raised one fist and knocked on the door. The wood thrummed beneath his knuckles, but nothing happened. The door remained closed, and there was no noise from inside. Perry knocked again, louder this time, but got the same result. He rapped a third time, more insistent, then stepped back and waited. After a moment, he glanced back over his shoulder.

"You boys run around the sides and check the windows. Don't let anybody see you. But peek inside and see if there are any lights on or anything."

They hesitated, obviously afraid to split up. They looked at one another and then up at him, their expressions unsure.

"Go on," he urged.

"You heard the man," Leo said. "Do it."

Jamal and Chris went to the right of the house, while Markus and Dookie took the left. Perry and Leo watched them disappear around the sides. To their eyes, it looked as though the shadows simply swallowed the four boys whole. Perry still couldn't shake the feeling that they were being watched. He decided not to mention it to Leo. The teens were already spooked. There was no sense in making them any more uneasy.

"What do you think we'll find in there, Mr. Watkins?"

Perry studied Leo for a moment before responding. A bright, inquisitive intelligence burned in the boy's eyes. Perry had never noticed it until now. He suddenly felt guilty. His ears burned with shame. Many times over the years, he'd thought the worst of Leo and his friends, and why? Sure, they got up to no good once in a while, but what boy didn't at some point in his life? No, the truth, Perry realized, was that he'd had no good reason to be suspicious and derisive of the kids all these years. They meant well, Leo especially. They were the future, and maybe the future wasn't as bleak as Perry had always assumed it would be. Maybe they'd make a difference in the world—provided they made it out of this neighborhood alive.

"I don't know, Leo. I don't know what we'll find in there. But I want you to promise me something."

"What's that?"

"I want you to promise me that you'll stay behind me, and that if something happens, you'll run, and let me handle it."

"Shit. I ain't no punk. I can take care of myself, Mr. Watkins."

"I know you can. And that's why it's important to me that you do as I say. So promise me, okay?"

Leo shrugged. "Sure, whatever."

Perry smiled, looking at the teen with a sudden, immense swell of admiration. The sensation of being watched had passed. Leo shifted his feet, clearly uncomfortable with the scrutiny.

"Um, no offense, Mr. Watkins? But I think I liked it better when you were grumpy and shit. I ain't much for this touchy-feely Oprah shit, you know?"

Perry snorted, trying to stifle his laughter. Leo chuckled along with him. They were still smiling when Chris, Jamal, Markus, and Dookie returned. All four were solemn.

"What'd y'all see?" Leo asked.

"Nothing," Chris said. "The whole damn place is locked down tight. The windows are boarded over or bricked up. No back door, at least, not that we saw. Whoever is in there, they don't want folks getting in."

"But people *do* get inside," Perry reminded them. "If people couldn't get inside, we wouldn't be here right now. So, why would someone secure the whole house but not board over the front door, too?"

"Dealers," Markus said. "It's gotta be. And we're standing on the porch of their whole operation. We should jet before somebody sees us."

"It can't be dealers," Perry replied. "Normally, I'd agree with you. Ain't no shortage of crack houses and meth labs in this city. But if this was a regular operation, we'd see people coming and going all the time. Fact is, we don't. Usually this place is quiet. Even when somebody goes missing, there's no disturbance or anything. No gunshots or screams."

He turned back to the door, studying it carefully. Then he motioned at the boys to follow him. They stepped back up onto the porch.

"Stay behind me," Perry told them. "I mean it. I don't want any of you playing badass when we go in there."

The boys nodded in silence.

Perry reached out and grasped the doorknob. It was cold and damp against his palm, despite the dry air. He turned it.

"Shit."

"What's wrong?" Dookie whispered.

"The goddamned thing is locked."

Leo sighed. "So what do we do now?"

Scowling, Perry shook another cigarette out of his pack.

"Mr. Watkins? What do we do now?"

"Hold up," Perry said, fumbling for his lighter. "I'm thinking."

"You'd best think faster."

CHAPTER FIFTEEN

Heather had almost resigned herself to never seeing light again when she noticed a glow in the distance. At first, she thought that her eyes were playing tricks on her, but the glow remained in place, slowly getting bigger as she walked toward it. She gasped, then coughed. The air still reeked of mud and filth, and each time she breathed through her nose, she felt like vomiting, so she tried to breathe through her mouth as much as possible. Her bare feet were numb beyond the point of pain. She was cold and wet and dirty and miserable, bleeding from dozens of shallow cuts and scratches, half out of her mind with fear, but all of that seemed to fade as the glow grew brighter. When she realized that she was actually able to see her surroundings now, albeit in shadow, Heather almost cried, overwhelmed with a conflicting mixture of relief and dread.

The details of the walls around her were not overly encouraging. As she continued on and her eyes adjusted even more to the light, she noticed the rough wooden planks and half-rotten plywood sheets that had been used to shore up the sides of the sloping passageway. Black and red-tinted seepage trickled through the gaps between the boards like perspiration. The clay behind the wood was deep red, but she also noticed limestone peeking out between it. She recognized it from the semester they'd studied geology. Apparently this point of the tunnel joined up with a natural limestone cavern.

She wondered whether Javier, Kerri, or Brett were still alive. If so, she hadn't heard them since getting lost. She hadn't heard her pursuers, either. The silence was oppressive and added to her misery. Heather focused on the light ahead. It was definitely getting brighter. She knew it for certain when she looked at her hands and saw the light pink color of her nail polish where before there had only been a vague gray hint of fingernails.

The passageway began a sudden downward descent. She had no choice but to follow it. The makeshift walls vanished, replaced by natural stone. The air quality changed. Gone was the damp, bitter smell of mold and mud. As she continued forward, the air became acrid, drier than she would have expected. There were other new scents, as well. She smelled salt, of all things, and something that reminded her of mothballs.

The ceiling grew progressively lower, and Heather was forced to crouch as she walked. Within another twenty feet, she had no choice but to drop to her hands and knees and crawl. Sharp rocks jabbed at her knees and palms, and water dripped from crevices in the stone ceiling above her, splattering onto her head and back. Then the ground leveled out again, and the tunnel rose slightly. The light grew bright enough to make her squint, and finally, Heather saw something other than more tunnel ahead of her.

She crawled forward into a chamber that had been cleared out and shored up with thick columns of wood and metal pipes old and new. A few stalactites hung from the ceiling and stalagmites jutted from the floor, but most of the space was wide open. Heather had never been great at figuring distances, but she guessed the cave was about fifteen feet long and three times as wide as the tunnel had been. There were no other entrances or exits, save a small, irregular hole in the back wall. The crevice looked barely wide enough for a dog, let alone a human being. Satisfied that no one was hiding in the room, Heather clambered to her bare feet, flexing her joints and staring around in disbelief.

There was furniture down here. All of it was old and in a sad state of repair. Four metal cots ran along one wall, end to end, each of them with a scattering of moldering blankets, mildewed clothing, and scraps of newspaper covering them like nests. The fabrics appeared as old as the furniture, and most were nothing more than shreds. A card table sat crookedly against the opposite wall. The table was covered with yellowed papers and a few pieces of lumpy, misshapen pottery that looked crafted by a grade-school student.

Heather moved into the chamber, squinting against the glare, and saw that the light came from an old kerosene lantern hung above the table. The flame was banked low, but even so, thick, oily smoke billowed from it. That explained the smell of salt and odd chemicals she'd noticed before.

Most of the papers on the table were held down by whatever had enough weight to keep them still. Though there was little by way of a breeze, the smoke trail drifted toward the far wall, where it was swallowed up by the crevice.

She didn't know how long the room would remain deserted or if her pursuers were still on her trail. Heather scanned the papers quickly, just to see if she could find any information that might help her situation. They crinkled when she touched them. Heather frowned. The papers made no sense. Rather than ink, they looked like they'd been written using mud—or blood. The penmanship was crude, illegible. She pushed them out of the way, looking for anything that could be used as a weapon. A scattering of old photographs fell to the ground. She bent over and studied them. They were wrinkled and faded, but she could make out the faces well enough and the houses in the background. Judging by the clothing the people in the photographs were wearing, she guessed they dated back to the thirties. All of the homes looked like the one topside, except that they were new. Indeed, a few of the pictures seemed to feature this very same house.

Heather placed the photographs back on the table. Then she shook her head and pinched her eyes shut for a moment. None of it made any sense. The photographs. The room. The booby-trapped dwelling. The caves. The killers. In the movies, there was always an explanation eventually, but this was real life, and so far, no answers were forthcoming. She'd watched her friends get butchered, and she still didn't know why—or by whom.

It occurred to Heather that since she was in a cave, maybe she was no longer beneath the house. She didn't know how far underground she was, but maybe there was a slim chance she could get a cell phone signal. Deciding that it was safe enough to risk the light from her phone again, she pulled it from her jeans and slid it open. The cell phone showed no signal. She tried to dial 911 anyway. The phone beeped once, and the words CALL FAILED scrolled across the screen. Sighing, Heather took pictures of the paperwork, photos and the chamber, remembering that Javier had suggested they document as much as they could so that they could show it to the authorities once they escaped. He'd be proud that she'd remembered, if and when they were reunited. Biting her lip, she finished capturing the images and then put the phone away again. There was no sense in running the battery down while she still had another source of light.

She shuffled some more of the papers around and found a tarnished butter knife that had been sharpened to a point. It wasn't much, but it was enough to make her feel a little better. Next to the knife were some odd drawings—stick-figure diagrams of human anatomy and scenes of torture and mutilation. All had the same crude traits as the other papers. They seemed like the work of an evil, demented child.

Before she could consider them further, something coughed in the distance, the sound echoing through the tunnel that she'd already left behind. Moving quickly, she snatched up the butter knife and carefully lifted the kerosene lantern from the hook on the wall. A small knob on the base of the lamp kept the flame low. She turned it to the right, and the knob moved with a grating squeak. As she twisted, the wick rose higher and caught fire, brightening the flame inside the lantern. Thick, black smoke guttered into the lamp's chimney.

Satisfied, Heather hurried over to the crevice at the rear of the cave. It would be a tight fit, but she had no choice. Kneeling, she crawled into the cramped space and crept forward. She found herself in another tunnel. The lantern hissed and spit as it was repeatedly jostled. The walls seemed to press in on her, and in a few places, she had to squeeze around rocks to make it through. Despite the tight quarters, she felt more at ease this time, due to the lantern and the knife. The tunnel rose steadily, and she followed it, hoping it led all the way to the surface. She thought about the neighborhood above, and how frightening and otherworldly it had seemed as they drove through it. Now she couldn't wait to see it again.

As far as Heather was concerned, compared to her current surrounding, the ghetto was heaven.

She prayed as she continued her desperate ascent.

Exhausted, Kerri lay still for a long while with her eyes closed. She had no idea how long she lay there. When she snapped out of it, her head and muscles ached, and her jaw was sore from gritting her teeth. She turned over slowly and licked her lips, tasting mud. She idly wondered what she looked like right now, after wallowing in filth and blood the entire night. What would Tyler think if . . .

"Tyler . . ." Her voice cracked.

No. She didn't have time for that. It seemed all she'd done since his death was to bounce from one emotional extreme to the other. She'd been a wreck, then a female Rambo, and then a wreck again. She wanted to sleep. Just lay there in the mud and drift away.

For a few minutes, she'd been having the most wonderful daydream—half memory and half flight of fancy. Toward the end of the last summer, she and Tyler and the gang had driven into New Jersey and made their way to Cape May one morning. The houses there were all beautiful and brightly painted, and there was a lighthouse where they all went to the top of and took pictures. Later, when that got boring, they'd strolled along the boardwalk in Wildwood, riding the roller coasters and feeding french fries and funnel cakes to the seagulls. It had been a great day. Tyler had been in a great mood. In the arcade, he'd won her an atrociously pink stuffed gorilla with false eyelashes. She'd made him carry the oversized thing around for the next couple of hours. Somewhere at home was a picture of her, the ape, and Tyler all sitting together on the Ferris wheel, grinning like crazy, both of them sunburned to a darker red than the stuffed animal. That part of the daydream was all accurate memory.

The fantasy involved all six of them going to Wildwood again. Tyler was right there with her, holding her hand and smiling as she talked with the others about how they were going to get out of the crazy house and the tunnels underneath it. He kept smiling, and so did all of the others. They behaved like there was nothing wrong, even when the dark shapes strode out of the ocean and stalked toward them down the boardwalk, stinking of mud and blood. Noigel was in the lead, and his hammer dripped blood.

That was what had woken Kerri from her stupor.

She spat, trying to clear the mud from her mouth. Then she sat up and groaned as her stiff muscles protested. There was a strange odor in the air, dry and autumnal. It wafted down from somewhere ahead of her. The darkness was impenetrable—a solid curtain of black. She wiggled her fingers in front of her face, but couldn't see them. That was okay as far as Kerri was concerned. As much as she feared the dark, she feared being killed by Noigel and his fucked-up friends even more. If she couldn't see anything, then maybe nothing could see her, either.

Kerri crawled. The surface beneath her was stone, not mud, and while it was cold and felt as damp as the level above her had, there was no actual moisture beneath her hands. It was hard to tell which direction she was going in the dark, but she had a sensation of veering slowly to the right, farther and farther away from the trapdoor. She tested the floor and the walls and finally the ceiling, and discovered that the area was large enough for her to stand up. A moment later she did just that. It felt good to be walking again, even if she couldn't see where she was going. She held her arms out in front of her, fingers stretched as far as they would go, feeling her way.

She'd gone a few more steps when something snagged her hair and pulled. Kerri screamed. Her hands fluttered to her head, slapping and clawing at the attacker. A second shriek died in her throat as she touched the impediment. She'd been expecting a hand, but what her fingers came in contact with instead was long and thin and made of wood. It didn't fight back when she grasped it. Didn't move at all. At first, she couldn't figure out what it might be. A wooden tentacle? Some new booby trap? Then she realized what was tugging her hair. It was the bottom end of a tree root. She calmed down as she removed it from her hair. Kerri couldn't remember seeing any trees in the area when they'd fled from the street gang. True, they'd had more immediate concerns and she hadn't really been paying attention at the time, but she thought she'd remember if there had been trees. Here was a root, dangling down from unseen heights. She lifted her arms over her head and waved them around. Her fingertips brushed against more roots. There were definitely trees overhead. That meant either she was farther away from the house than she'd originally thought, or the trees were all dead and gone and their underground root systems were all that remained—nothing more than ghostly fingers, pulling her hair in an effort to remind humans that they'd once existed before the pavement and houses and concrete. She shivered at the thought. Kerri wondered whether the network of roots was keeping the ceiling from collapsing on her. If so, that was a good thing.

The trapdoor that had led into this subterranean chamber was somewhere behind her, but she wasn't sure of its exact location anymore. She assumed that since she was close enough to the surface to discover tree roots, the ground beneath her feet would begin to climb higher, but it was hard to tell in the dark.

She kept moving. The air was still, without even the hint of a breeze.

Which was why she stopped in her tracks when a puff of rancid hot air suddenly blew across her face. Startled, Kerri lurched forward. Her arms bumped into something in front of her—something soft and slick and yielding. Flesh. Two powerful, hairy hands grabbed her wrists and yanked her forward. She stumbled as another blast of the creature's breath assailed her senses. It stank like rotten eggs and feces.

Kerri screamed, and the thing in the darkness laughed. Then its arms snaked around her body and squeezed.

Just when he was beginning to think that he wouldn't be able to take the silence for a second longer, Javier stopped and listened. There was someone up ahead of him. No, not just someone. There were at least two. Maybe more. His spirits rose for a second in the hopes that it might be the girls or Brett. But then his hopes were dashed. What followed was a bewildering series of noises—snatches of what sounded like conversation, but like no language he'd ever heard. It sounded like gibberish, constructed to almost make words. He couldn't tell how far away they were. The voices weren't alarmed, so he was pretty certain that they weren't aware of his presence.

His bladder ached. He needed to piss, but Javier was afraid that if he did, the sound or smell would give his location away.

The sound of shuffling footsteps caused him to hunker down. They were coming from a different direction than the hushed voices. A moment later, a third speaker joined the fray, but unlike the others, this new addition was understandable—if barely. His voice sounded like he had a throat full of barbed wire.

"What are you two doing? I thought I told you to hunt! Bad enough we lost them all earlier, in all the confusion. The longer they're down here running loose, the worse it will be."

This elicited a garbled, excited response. Then the new arrival spoke again.

"See, this is why you should have stayed put and helped make man-pudding or tended to the fires. I knew you two weren't old enough to hunt yet. Get on back. Noigel and the others will handle this."

More chatter. This time, they sounded dejected.

"I don't care. You can't hunt if you're standing around playing with each other's peckers and making the milk come out. Now go on. Tell Curd I sent you back to help him. He's got one hung up now, freshly cleaned and skinned. I want you to take all the bones and smash them open and pull out the stuff inside. The eyeballs, too, and his poop tubes. We'll make a good pudding with it all."

Another unintelligible response.

"Don't be stupid. You can't milk a man once he's dead. Now get going."

Javier heard them scurrying away. A moment later, the third set of footsteps faded, as well. He waited another ten minutes, until he was absolutely certain that he was alone again. Then, unable to hold it anymore, he pulled down his zipper and pissed. He wanted to groan with relief, but he held his breath instead. Javier shuddered at the sensation. The stream was hot and heavy and splashed back against his legs. He forced himself not to gag as the piss wet his shoes and cuffs. Then his fear evaporated and the anger came back, a deep and abiding rage that nestled in the back of his skull and pulsated with a life all its own.

Although he couldn't be sure, it sounded from the conversation he'd just eavesdropped on that one of his friends had been caught and killed. He wondered who it was. Then it occurred to him that maybe the speaker had been referring to Tyler or Stephanie—or maybe somebody they didn't even know. Somebody from the neighborhood, perhaps? Some drug addict or homeless person.

Who it was didn't really matter. He intended to kill every single one of these fucking things he came across just the same. No more hiding. No more pissing on himself. No more being a victim. Javier shook his feet one at a time, grimacing at the feel of his wet socks rubbing against his soles. Then he moved forward again, walking carefully and doing his best to be completely silent.

He wasn't sure how far he'd gone or how many minutes had passed before he heard the voices again. They were muffled and distant. He slowed his pace and crept forward, summoning all the stealth he could manage. His hands trembled and his teeth chattered from the adrenaline and anger coursing through his body. Javier resisted the urge to charge blindly forward, shouting with rage and lashing out in the darkness.

As he progressed, he noticed a spark of light ahead, coming from the same direction as the voices. When he got nearer, he saw that it was a flashlight beam—weak, but still effective in this near total darkness. He paused, waiting for his eyes to adjust and then moved forward again. The conversations continued, the speakers oblivious to his presence. He tiptoed closer, until he could see their silhouettes. Then Javier paused, waiting for his eyes to adjust to the sudden light. He took slow, shallow breaths and tried to remain completely still.

There were three of them. He couldn't see them clearly. They were too close together, but he could make out

enough to disgust him. The only similarities he could see
in them was their utter *wrongness*. Two were malformed.
Their skin was slicked with greasy perspiration, and their
brittle, matted hair was thin and long, as if it had never
been cut. They wore no clothing, but they'd painted
themselves with mud and wiped it away in strategic places
to act as distinct markings. Both were decidedly female.

The third figure was a man. At first, Javier mistook
him for a female, but when he looked closer, he saw that
it was really a man wearing a woman's tanned and pre-
served skin. He wondered if this was the same maniac
Brett had encountered, or a different one with a similar
fetish. The man seemed older than the females. He was
taller and equipped with broad shoulders that bulged
through his suit of skin with each small move he made.
Horrified, Javier wondered how he'd fashioned the
gruesome outfit to cling so tightly to his body. *Skin
tight*, he thought, and had to bite his lip to keep from
screaming.

He studied the man more intently. As far as Javier
could see, there was no fat on his body. The woman-skin
suit didn't bulge from a potbelly or prodigious abdomen.
Javier had little doubt that the thick fingers on the man's
hands could gouge through the hard-packed dirt around
him with ease, and the length of his fingernails suggested
that digging like a mole wouldn't be anything new for
him. Most surprisingly, Brett's belt dangled from the man's
clenched fist. This was the same attacker that had ripped
it from Javier's grasp during the initial fight!

Javier turned his attention back to the women. The
one holding the flashlight had hard muscles along her
bare back. Her fingers, however, had fused together with
thick knots of gray flesh that made her look as if she were
wearing baseball gloves on each hand. The same excess

skin covered the rest of her body, beneath the mud, from her face to her legs, like obscenely swollen scar tissue.

The other female looked very young, maybe a pre-teen, and while the hair on her body was fairly thin and plastered down with mud, it covered her entire frame. Her eyes seemed too large for her head, in much the same way as the Japanese cartoons seemed malformed, but without the same symmetry. One eye was oval shaped but oversized. The other was almost perfectly round and seemed to bulge from the socket.

"We haven't seen anything, Scug," the woman with the flashlight was saying to the man. Javier had to strain to understand her. The woman's voice was slurred and slow, as if she were speaking with a wad of cotton balls inside her mouth. The man, Scug, leaned forward, also listening to her intently. Javier wondered if the scar tissue on her body was also present on her tongue or the roof of her mouth.

"I didn't ask if you'd seen anything," Scug said, and Javier recognized his voice as the one he'd heard earlier, chastising the other freaks. "I asked where you've been."

She pointed around with the flashlight, and Javier ducked to avoid being seen as the beam swept overhead.

"All over down here. They couldn't have come through here. Maybe Noigel got them all."

Scug sighed. He sounded exasperated. He grabbed the belt with both hands and cracked it. The women jumped.

"Noigel couldn't have killed them all," he said. "Because when I left Noigel, he was still playing with the one he'd killed."

The females giggled.

"Was he doing that thing with his pecker?" Scar-Face asked.

Scug nodded. "Yeah. He split the guy's head open on

the wall and then fucked the crack. Don't know how he keeps from cutting himself on the skull fragments. Them things can be sharp. But he loves it. Maybe he'll let you lick the brain juice off his pecker later on."

"Un-uh," Scar-Face protested, her eyes wide. "He's too big for my mouth, and last time, there were fleas biting my face. He's got a nest of them down there."

"That's protein. You should just pick them off and eat them. Might be all you get anyway. Worthless as you are, it ain't like you've done anything to earn tonight's feast. And we ain't had a bounty like this in a long time."

Scar-Face pouted. "Be nice to us, Scug. I've been teaching the young ones how to talk."

"Well, it ain't working. Now let's get back to it. One of the females gave me the slip earlier. Need to catch back up with her again. The rest of them, too."

The hairy, silent female suddenly whipped her head in Javier's direction and sniffed the air. Her lips quivered, and her eyes seemed to grow even wider. A thin line of drool dripped from her open lips.

"What's wrong with her?" Scug asked. "Shine that light-tube over that way."

Before he could move, Javier found himself pinpointed in the flashlight beam. All three freaks cried out in surprise and alarm. Javier knew exactly how they felt. Before he could even breathe, the hairy girl was in motion. She ducked low and charged him, her fingers spread like talons.

Javier tried to block the attack by throwing up an arm, but he'd been motionless too long, and his legs were wobbly. Instead of countering her charge, he stumbled off balance and slammed against the wall. He had enough presence of mind to turn his hip and protect his privates, but he was too late to stop the assault. The girl hit him hard and fast, her ragged fingernails ripping into his sleeve and into the flesh of his arm. Screaming in pain, Javier tumbled backward. The girl held on to his arm and fell over with him, landing astride his chest. She snarled, sounding more feral than human, and drove a fist into his abdomen. The air whooshed out of Javier's lungs. She followed up the punch with a second to his balls.

Javier fought back about as effectively as a toddler. He tried to sit up and push her off him, but the girl swiped out with one arm, backhanding him. The force of the blow slammed his head against the packed earth beneath him. Stars danced across his vision. Her nails tore into his arm again. Javier felt a burning sensation, and then warmth trickled down his wrist and forearm. The pain was intense, and his stomach roiled.

The girl's face moved in as fast as a striking cobra, and Javier snapped his head to the side just in time to avoid having her teeth peel part of his cheek away.

"Jesus Christ! Get off me, bitch."

"Let's give her a hand with this one," he heard Scug say. The freak's harsh, phlegmatic voice was tinged with amusement.

The girl uttered a grunt and tried to hit Javier again, even as she used her legs to pin him in place. Her head darted forward, teeth snapping. Behind her, Scug and the other woman came closer, their expressions wild and ravenous. The flashlight in the woman's hand was metal rather than plastic, and Javier knew that if she managed to hit him with it, the tool could do some damage to his head.

"This one's still got some fight left in him," Scug said. "We'll have to bleed him out a little before we take him back. Make him weaker. Not enough to kill him, though. I hate dragging their bodies back. It's much better if they can walk on their own. Curd says so, too. He says the fresher the kill, the fresher they taste."

Javier tried again to force the girl from him and sit up, but before he could, the others fell upon him, pinning his arms and head in place. They stretched his arms out, pressed their talonlike fingernails against the soft flesh of his wrists, and slashed across, drawing blood. Javier squirmed and bucked, but their combined strength was too much for him. All he could do was scream.

"That's enough," Scug advised the women, licking his lips as he watched the blood flow. "Don't go any deeper or he'll bleed out too quick. We just want him weakened. Not dead. Not yet, at least."

"You motherfuckers," Javier gasped. "You filthy goddamned—"

Scug struck the side of Javier's head with his knuckles. Javier tried to bite the freak's hand, but Scug jerked it out of the way before he could. His teeth snapped down on nothing but air. He felt warm wetness streaming down his hands and dripping from his fingertips.

Scug dangled the belt, swinging it back and forth in front of Javier's face. "You been looking for this? Your girlfriend recognized it earlier."

Javier felt veins throbbing in his forehead and neck. "What did you do to her, you fucking freak?"

"Don't worry," Scug taunted. "She got away, but she won't be free long."

"This one's dangerous," Scar-Face observed. "We'll have to take his teeth out. Want to do it now or wait till we get home?"

Horribly, Javier was reminded of an old Bugs Bunny cartoon he'd watched as a child. Elmer Fudd was hunting Bugs, but the wascally wabbit had convinced the hapless hunter to shoot at Daffy Duck instead. What followed was a routine in which Bugs had asked, "Would you like to shoot him now or wait till you get home?" Despite his terror, despite his pain, even despite the feel of his own warm blood trickling down his wrists like syrup, Javier grinned at the absurd memory.

"We'll wait," Scug said. He climbed off Javier and motioned for the females to do the same. Freed of the weight, Javier drew a deep breath. His chest hitched.

Scug slapped Javier again. "On your feet now. Don't make me ask twice. If you do, I'll cut off your pecker and stick it in your mouth to wipe that stupid grin off your face—bleeding out or no. Bet it would be the first man-chew you've ever had, huh?"

Something in the man's tone told Javier that Scug wasn't exaggerating. He would do that very thing. Javier didn't know what the bizarre term "man-chew" meant, but the rest of the lunatic's intent was crystal clear. Groaning, Javier slowly got to his feet. Each of the women seized one of his arms, and with Scug leading the way, they marched him into the darkness.

CHAPTER SIXTEEN

Leo and Dookie both leaned against the door, their ears pressed to the rough wooden surface, listening intently.

"Still don't hear anything," Dookie said. "It's all quiet and shit. If they're in there, then they ain't talking."

Mr. Watkins nodded. "I just wish we knew for sure before we go kicking that door down. I didn't tell you boys before, but earlier, while you were checking the windows, I could have sworn that somebody was watching us through the peephole."

"Did you see them?" Leo asked.

"No, I didn't see anything. It was more of an impression. I *felt* them standing there, you know?"

Chuckling, Markus elbowed Chris in the ribs and whispered, "Mr. Watkins is all psychic and shit. He's like the ghetto version of the motherfucking Ghost Whisperer, yo."

"Shut the fuck up. Show the man some respect." Leo glared at them both. Then he turned his attention back to the older man. "So who do you think it was?"

"I don't know," Mr. Watkins said. "I've been wondering about that myself. If it was those kids you spooked earlier, then I would think that they'd have called out for help when they saw us. Unless they're more scared of you guys than they are of whatever is inside that house."

"If there's even anything inside that house," Markus muttered.

Mr. Watkins made a sweeping gesture with his arm. "Well, step on up and be my guest, sunshine. You can be the first one through that door."

"Can't," Markus said.

"Why not?"

"'Cause you ain't got the door open yet."

"I told you, I'm thinking."

Markus grinned. "Sounds more to me like you're talking, rather than thinking. Maybe you don't want to go inside. Maybe all this talk about doing the right thing and helping out our neighborhood and change is just bullshit."

Leo stepped toward his friend, fists curled. Anger coursed through him. He couldn't believe that Markus was being so disrespectful. Sure, Markus always had an attitude. He'd walked through life with a chip on his shoulder for as long as Leo had known him. And yeah, until tonight, Mr. Watkins had been a grumpy old fart. But regardless of any of that, Mr. Watkins didn't deserve this shit. He was just trying to help. After all, they had knocked on his door. If it hadn't been for them, he'd probably be asleep by now.

"Yo, I told you to show him some respect. The hell is wrong with you?"

"Screw you both."

"Come on," Jamal pleaded with Leo and Markus. "Both of you just need to chill out."

Markus refused to back down. "The fuck you gonna do, Leo? You want some of this?"

"You want to fight? Well, come on."

Dookie, Jamal, and Chris backed away.

"Come on," Leo challenged again.

"Don't think I won't. I've had it with your bullshit."

"The fuck are you talking about, Markus?"

"You ain't the boss of me. You ain't our leader. You ain't shit. Talking about change and doing the right thing and helping people out—when has anybody ever helped *us* out? Nothing ever changes for us. All you're doing is dreaming, Leo. You're a damn fool."

Leo was momentarily stunned by Markus's invective. He struggled not to show it. He couldn't display any weakness or doubts right now, or the others would begin to have misgivings, too.

"If you don't like it, Markus, then get the fuck out of here. We don't need your sorry ass."

"I ain't going nowhere. You damn sure don't run this street. I'll stay if I want."

Leo's fists clenched and unclenched. "Suit yourself. But if you're staying, then you'll damn sure quit talking shit and apologize to Mr. Watkins."

"Fuck that. What's this old man ever done for me, except look at me funny when I'm out too late? You remember a couple of years ago on Halloween, when somebody broke all the car windows on the block and egged the houses? Remember how he looked at us after that?"

Mr. Watkins stirred. Before he could speak, Leo interrupted.

"Did he accuse you, Markus? Huh? Did he accuse any of us?"

Markus smirked. "He didn't have to. You could see it in his eyes."

"You know what? Just get the fuck out of here. Go on home."

"You can't make me do shit, Leo. And you keep stepping to me like this, I'm gonna knock you the fuck down."

"I hear you talking, but I don't see you moving."

"Fuck you, motherfucker."

"No," Leo said, poking his friend in the chest with his index finger. "Fuck you. That's your ass, Markus."

"Enough!" Mr. Watkins stuffed the pistol in his waistband, stepped between the teens, and placed a hand on each of their chests. "That's enough. Knock this bullshit off. What the hell is wrong with you both? Do you think this is helping somehow?"

Leo tensed. "He started it. I was just sticking up for you."

"I don't need you to watch my back out here," Mr. Watkins said, nodding at the house. "I need you to watch in there. We need to watch out for each other." He paused, then turned to Markus. His hand was still on the young man's chest. "I know why you're doing this."

"Oh yeah? Why's that?"

"Because you're scared."

"Fuck you, old man. I ain't scared of shit."

"Yes, you are," Mr. Watkins said, ignoring Markus's curled fists. "You're terrified."

Leo had to give him credit. Mr. Watkins had balls. He could tell by Jamal, Chris, and Dookie's expressions that they were impressed as well. Markus's eyes flashed to the handgun in Mr. Watkins's waistband. Leo held his breath, ready to spring if Markus went for the weapon.

"Don't even think about it," Mr. Watkins warned. Then his voice became soothing again. "I know you're scared because I'm scared, too. We all are. Hell, we'd have to be some crazy motherfuckers not to be scared, walking into this place. But this? This ain't helping. Okay?"

Markus paused, glancing at each of his friends. Then he looked down at his feet.

"Yeah," he muttered. "You're right."

"Apologize to the man," Leo said.

"He doesn't need to," Mr. Watkins said. "There's no reason to apologize for feeling the same thing that the rest of us are feeling. But I'll tell you what you *can* do, Markus."

"What's that?"

"Run on back up the street to my house. Tell Lawanda to go down in the basement and get my crowbar and my sledgehammer. Then bring them back here."

"You're gonna smash the door down?" Chris asked. "Won't they hear us?"

Mr. Watkins shrugged. "If there is anybody else inside that house other than them kids, then you can bet your ass that they already know we're here. Especially with all the hollering and carrying on. We've lost the element of surprise. Now we're just going to bum rush them."

As Markus trotted up the street, Mr. Watkins pulled out his pistol and faced the front door.

Grinning, Leo playfully punched the older man in the shoulder.

"Damn, Mr. Watkins. I had no idea you were so hardcore. Original fucking gangsta!"

Mr. Watkins didn't smile. He paused, lighting another cigarette. When he spoke again, his voice was quiet and seemed sad.

"I'm no gangster, Leo. What I am is a pissed-off, middle-aged black man whose gut sticks out over his pecker now and who can't get any from his wife except on holidays and gets hollered at for smoking in the house and hates his shitty job and is tired of watching this neighborhood turn to shit, because this neighborhood is all he has left in this world. And there ain't nothing on Earth more hard-core than that."

They waited, and when Markus returned, they moved

with grim purpose. Without a word, Mr. Watkins handed the gun to Leo and the crowbar to Chris. Grunting, he wielded the sledgehammer. It's bright yellow, fiberglass handle seemed to glow in the darkness.

Mr. Watkins tossed his cigarette butt out into the street and stepped forward.

"Okay, boys. Let's go knock on the door again."

They clomped up the porch, no longer bothering to conceal their presence. Then Mr. Watkins raised the sledgehammer and swung, putting all his weight into it. The door shuddered in its frame. Wood splintered with a loud crack.

"Listen," Dookie gasped.

From inside the house, they all heard the sound of fleeing footsteps.

"You think it's those white kids?" Leo asked, nervously fumbling with the gun.

"Only one way to find out," Mr. Watkins said, and swung the sledgehammer again.

CHAPTER SEVENTEEN

Heather clutched the sharpened butter knife in one hand and the sputtering lamp in the other. Both items jittered from her uncontrollable trembling. Although she'd willed herself to stop, the shaking continued. Worse, even though she could see her breath in front of her, appearing as white puffs of cloud each time she exhaled, Heather was bathed in sweat. Neither condition was conducive to escaping. She didn't know if it was shock or fear or the temperature or a combination of all three, but it was maddening and aggravating. It was hard enough listening for sounds of pursuit behind her without having to do it over the chattering of her own teeth. The only part of her not shaking was her feet. They were completely numb. She'd tried pinching the soles, but she felt nothing other than a vague twinge. She could still walk, but she had no sensation in them.

Since leaving the strange grotto behind, the ground beneath Heather had been rising steadily as she progressed through the small tunnel. She'd lost track of time and had no way of knowing how long she'd been crawling. The darkness and her own fatigue weighed heavily on her, and it was getting harder to concentrate. Her mind kept returning to the bizarre collection of photographs and drawings, trying to mine some meaning from them—some explanation for the evening's horrifying events. She grew increasingly frustrated trying to figure it out. Nothing about this situation made sense. It all just seemed so random. So unexplainable. How could such a race of beings exist undetected beneath a city the size of Philadelphia for so long? And what were they? Mutants, obviously, but from where? And from whom? They didn't seem to have any single racial characteristic or genetic background. How long had they been here? How many people had they killed?

She had no way of knowing. In fact, all that Heather knew for sure was that her legs hurt, her back hurt, and her eyes felt gritty from sweat and dirt. There were blisters on her palms and knees, and the cut on her foot was bleeding again. Lantern smoke drifted lazily into her face, obscuring her vision and making her choke. Each time a new round of shaking overtook her, Heather's teeth clamped together. She'd bitten her tongue and the insides of her cheeks several times. The slow, steady taste of blood made her stomach roil.

Heather wondered how much farther she'd have to climb before she could escape this nightmare. By all rights, she should have been above ground by now. And yet here she was, still stuck in a damned tunnel with the weight of the entire city over her head. She wished it would all just come crashing down, squashing everything flat. Even that would be preferable to this miserable, torturous scurrying around in the dark. Heather stifled a laugh. Her brother would have loved this shit. He was always playing his dungeon crawl games online. He'd have been right at home here.

A deep, thunderous rumble echoed from somewhere behind her, reminding Heather of her immediate danger. She forced away the self-pity and crawled on, clinging to the hope that she'd get somewhere if she just kept going the same direction she was headed. Then again, it wasn't like she had much choice. There were no branching tunnels. Her options were moving forward up the slope or retreating back the way she'd come—and she knew what awaited her there. All roads have to lead somewhere. That was what her dad always said, at least. She wondered if her parents were worried about her yet. Would Kerri's or Steph's parents be looking for them? Would they have called the police by now? Or Javier's mother, maybe? No, she worked nights, and Javier hadn't seen his father since he was three years old.

The air changed up ahead. She felt it shift, running across her face like the touch of light fingers. The sensation was amazing after what seemed like forever in the stifling dampness of the caves. The lantern flickered and hissed, and the flame danced around as if also enjoying the breeze. She had no idea what was up ahead of her, but if there was fresh air, then surely that meant there was a way out.

Heather's spirits soared. She forgot all about her family, about Javier and Kerri and Brett, and focused solely on survival and escape. She crawled faster. Then the air shifted again, bringing a new stench—a thick, pungent odor of rot and filth, stronger than any she'd smelled so far tonight. Despite her best efforts to ignore the scent, Heather gagged, choking. Ropes of spittle hung from her open mouth. Her stomach heaved. If she'd had anything inside it, she would have vomited. Instead, the muscles in her abdomen cramped, expanding and contracting painfully. Heather wiped her lips with the back of her hand and gasped, trying not to gag again. The flickering lamplight glinted off the sharpened butter knife. She focused on it. When she'd calmed down again, she proceeded onward, breathing through her mouth as she crawled. That didn't help much; she could *taste* the repugnant aroma on her tongue. Soon, whatever was ahead of her became too much. Her eyes watered, blurring her vision, and her gag reflex refused to stop. She closed her eyes and fought the urge to puke.

At least her uncontrollable trembling had ceased.

She turned around, raised the lamp, and looked back down the tunnel and into the darkness. If her pursuers were still back there, they were being quiet. She was so close to the surface. She *had* to be! But she didn't think she could make it any farther, struggling against that reeking miasma. She debated turning around and returning to the small room.

Heather was still considering her options when she heard chattering laughter behind her, coming from the same direction as the stench. The sound was high pitched and excited. She spun around again, holding the lantern high and thrusting the butter knife out in front of her. Shadows scurried toward her, growing larger with each passing second. Then the creatures skittered into view. Heather shrieked, and something tore in the back of her throat. The things that came for her were obscenities, barely even capable of being called humanoid. These weren't mere mutations, like the others she'd seen. These organisms were utter blasphemies.

The one at the very front of the horde was horrific enough to leave her staggered, even in the dim light of the lantern. The monstrosity had no body that she could see—at least, not in the traditional sense. Instead, it consisted of a giant head, three times the size of a normal human's, with a thick, tubular mass of pink and gray flesh beneath it. Something that might have been large fingers or tiny legs or maybe tentacles flailed and bumped. The creature slithered closer. Heather saw its sides expand and contract as the muscles within hunched and strained. Despite its odd extremities, the thing was fast. The appendages beneath its tumorlike body helped propel it forward, clinging to the tunnel floor and pulling with frightening efficiency. Heather gaped, unable to move. The beast was almost mesmerizing in its atrociousness. It stared back at her with wide, wet eyes the size of tea saucers. Its gibbering, drooling mouth was pulled back in a sneer. Gobs of green-yellow snot dripped from its bulbous, misshapen nose.

She barely had time to absorb the shock of the first beast before the second came into view. It had nothing in common with the first. Her mind flashed back to her junior year, and Mrs. Atkins's biology class. One day, while discussing birth defects, Mrs. Atkins had shown slides of several different fetuses that had failed to mature. The second creature to scramble down the tunnel toward her looked like one of those fetuses brought to life. The eyes in its head were enormous. Its eyelids were so thin that she could see the eyeballs moving clearly beneath them. The mutant's nose and lips were translucent, and like its eyes, they seemed much too large for its hideous face. The head itself was bloated and misshapen, more of a lopsided oval than anything resembling round. The beast crawled forward on small warped legs and arms. Heather cried out in disgust and horror. Clearly, it should have died in the womb, but it hadn't. Here it was, an affront to nature and evolution, hurrying along behind its friend and baring blunt, stumpy teeth that filled its mouth. They flashed in the lantern light as it licked its thin lips and squeaked.

A third creature had a harelip that split its upper mouth all the way to its flared nostrils. It had no nose—just two gaping holes where its nose should have been. Uneven teeth and gums were visible through the harelip. Its body was stunted and wrinkled.

There were worse things behind the first three. She heard them gasping and wheezing, squealing with high-pitched voices. Their labored breaths echoed off the tunnel walls. Their fingernails scratched against stone. They poured toward her, a mutant tide of crawling, hopping and in some cases, slithering monstrosities, mewling like hungry babies—which was, in effect, exactly what they were.

The combined stench of the horde grew overwhelming as they bore down on her. It snapped Heather out of her stunned paralysis. She flung the lantern at them and pivoted around on her knees, facing the opposite direction. She heard glass breaking and metal clanging as the lantern caromed off the rocks behind her. There was a brief but bright flare, and the creatures screamed. Heather screamed, too. She bounced off the tunnel wall with bruising force and started crawling back the way she'd come. She hurried, heedless of the damage her mad scramble across the stone floor was doing to her palms and knees. The light dimmed and then fizzled. Darkness enveloped the tunnel once again. Heather didn't care. She knew the way back to the room. There were no branching passageways for her to get lost in. Most importantly, in the darkness, she couldn't see the pursuing horrors.

She could hear them, though. With the fire extinguished, their cries grew frenzied. They chased after her again, and while their malformations and handicaps slowed them down, they sounded tenacious and enraged. Heather crawled faster, her teeth bared and her eyes wide, trying desperately to see. Her heart thundered in her chest, and her lungs worked like a bellows. Her gasps seemed to echo back to her. She ignored the pain each time a rock sliced through her palms or scraped her arms. Spurred on by adrenaline and fear, and unable to navigate except by touch and sound, Heather struck her head on a low-hanging outcrop. The force of the blow knocked her flat on her belly. She cried out, and the creatures cheered. Warm blood flowed into her left eye. Her fingertips explored her forehead. There was a cut above her left eyebrow. She winced as she touched it. Heather wiped the blood away and tried to sit up.

Thick, clammy fingers clutched at her ankle. Screaming, Heather kicked, and the fingers slipped away. They returned a second later, gripping more forcefully this time. Other appendages joined in the effort—tendrils, fingers, teeth, and things she was too afraid to identify. Heather spun around and swung wildly with her knife. Several of the creatures howled and spat. Her foot scraped along something that felt like a rib cage. She stabbed the knife downward, slashing at a small hand squeezing her thigh. The tunnel filled with shrieks—hers and theirs. Something warm and wet—blood or spittle—splashed across her cheek. Heather lunged backward, kicking and slashing, and the creatures fell back. She started to scuttle away, but something leaped onto her chest and slapped her face. Despite the mutant's diminutive size, it was a powerful blow. Her cheek stung and her ears rang. More blood flowed into her eye from the cut above her brow.

Another monster gnawed at her arm. Judging by the feel, it was toothless. Heather lashed out at it and felt scaly skin. She swung her arm, knocking the beast on her chest backward, and slashed at the scaly one with her sharpened butter knife. Both fell away. Heather flipped over and scurried forward again. The knife slipped from her grasp.

"No. No nonononono . . ."

Sobbing, Heather pawed at the ground. Her hand closed on the cool, metallic handle and she seized it. Then she froze, muscles stiffening, her mouth open in a silent scream. She tried to cry out, but all that came from her lips was a fluttering sigh.

Heather was no stranger to pain. When she was seven years old, Heather had fallen from a tree and dislocated her shoulder. The pain had made her nauseous. A few years later, when she'd impaled her calf on a stick while playing tag with her brother and some neighbor kids, the pain had been intolerable. She'd had a few bad weeks where she was almost certain she would never be able to walk without discomfort again. Neither of those experiences came close to what she was feeling now. Dozens of sharp teeth sank into the back of her calf, just two inches below her knee. The pain bloomed like a flower, slowly spreading into something bright and vivid.

Talons slashed at her ankle and the teeth sank deeper into her calf. A hot, sandpapery tongue lapped at the blood welling from the wound. Heather lashed out with her free leg, ramming her heel into the face of the creature behind her. It jerked backward, but not before taking a few pieces of meat with it. Heather spun around and slashed blindly in the dark with the knife. Something hot splashed across her arm and hand. Her attacker emitted a horrid, bubbling squeal and snatched the knife from Heather's grip. She heard it thrashing and howling instead of trying to attack her again. Above its cries, she heard the rest of the horde closing in.

Hoping that the body of their wounded comrade would slow the rest of the creatures, Heather turned around and limped toward the tunnel's exit again. When she reached the grotto, she felt her way out of the crevice. Unlike before, the strange room was pitch-black.

Some of the fallen papers rustled beneath her feet as she plunged forward.

Behind her, the sounds of pursuit continued.

Javier tried to swallow, but his mouth was dry. His head drooped as they forced him onward. His eyelids fluttered. Fatigue had settled over him like a coarse, heavy blanket. Each shuffling step seemed to take an enormous amount of physical effort, and when he slowed, Scar-Face and the hairy girl shoved him forward. What he wanted more than anything at that moment, even more than escaping, was to lie down and take a nap. He fought against the desire, still retaining enough alertness to know that if he did that now, he would surely die.

The truth was he was probably going to die anyway, unless he figured out something soon. His captors were ruthless and showed no remorse. They'd cut his wrists with the same practical efficiency and disregard that someone making a salad might show toward a stick of celery. He wasn't sure how long he'd bled, but when they deemed him sufficiently weakened, Scug had called a halt, and they'd tied his wounds with scraps of damp, mildew-covered cloth. Then they'd applied pressure before marching him forward again. His wrists still hurt, but the bleeding had stopped. He was sure that it would start again—and from more places than just his wrists—when they arrived at their final destination.

"Where are you taking me?" he asked, his voice slurred.

His captors didn't answer.

"Hey," Javier tried again. "Where are you—"

Scug backhanded him, splitting Javier's lip open. Wincing, Javier spat blood before he could swallow it.

"No more talking," Scug warned, cracking the belt

again. "Do it again and I'll gut you right here. Let your insides slip out and show you what they look like, all wet and shiny. Ever strangled a man with his own intestines? I have. Plenty of times. It's always a funny sight, watching them flap around and choke, eyes bugging out of their heads, faces turning as purple as the guts wrapped around their throats. I'll do it to you, too, if you don't keep walking."

Deciding to take a gamble, Javier just shrugged his shoulders and did his best to smile. It hurt his mouth, but got the man's attention. Blood welled out of his split lip.

"What are you grinning about?" Scug asked. "You smile too much."

"I'm just thinking that it doesn't matter anyway. Do what you want. The police will be here soon. We called them before we came inside."

"No, they won't. The police never come. And even if they did, do you think we care? This is our home. Our place. They can't hurt us here. No man can hurt us here."

"How long have you lived here?"

"We have always been here. Our people were here before the city, before the buildings and the cars and everything else, and we'll be here after it's all gone. Us and the cockroaches and the rats."

"Your people? What are you, exactly?"

Scug didn't answer. Javier repeated the question, and again his captor refused to answer, so Javier decided to ask something different.

"Why do you wear women's skin over your own?"

Scug's lips pulled back in a sneer. Spittle foamed at the corners of his mouth. He rushed forward, fist raised over his head, ready to strike Javier again.

"This is *my* skin! My fucking skin. Got it? Now, no more talking. Move!"

Scar-Face and the hairy girl forced him to pick up the pace, and Javier struggled to keep up with them. He tried to keep track of each twisting passageway and of each turn that they made, but he was soon hopelessly disoriented. The weak flashlight beam did little to dispel his confusion. The only thing he was sure of was that the ground seemed to be staying relatively flat, rather than sloping upward or deeper into the earth. His mind began to wander again, and the pain in his wrists and lip dulled. His feet moved automatically, in time with those of his captors. He didn't come to his senses again until the dwarf popped out of the wall.

One minute, it had just been the four of them in the tunnel. The next, there was a dwarf standing by Scug's side, chattering excitedly in a guttural, ugly language Javier couldn't understand. Some of the words were rudimentary English. Others seemed nothing more than a collection of snarls, grunts and homeless syllables. Javier raised his head and noticed a small passageway to their right. He assumed that the new arrival must have come from there. The dwarf was completely hairless, and its naked body was covered with thick black scabs. He listened to its conversation with Scug, and tried to figure out what they were talking about.

"Anyone catch her yet?"

The dwarf shook its head.

"Well, I'll look into it myself. It's my fault for letting her give me the slip earlier. Can't have her hurting the babies."

The dwarf spoke again. It seemed agitated.

"When it rains, it pours." Scug shook his head. "How many are there?"

The dwarf held up six crooked fingers.

"I'll check the nursery," Scug told it. "Take care of the

bitch once and for all. You go find Noigel. He's probably still fucking that kid's brains out back near the basement steps. Tell him we have more visitors up top."

The dwarf squealed a reply.

"You do as I say and interrupt him," Scug replied. "He won't hurt you if you tell him I sent you. Can't be many brains left in that kid's head by now anyway. He can worry about spraying his ball juice later. We need him on the hunt."

The dwarf made an almost comical salute with one hand, then turned and dashed back up the side tunnel.

"And tell him not to fuck these six in the head after he's killed them," Scug called after the fleeing form. Then he turned to the women and pointed at Javier. "One of this one's friends—I'm guessing the girl I was chasing earlier—is near the nursery. The babies are worked up. I'm going to go tend to that because none of the rest of you seems to be able to fucking handle it. You get him situated. Tell Curd that there are more on the way. A bunch of new arrivals just showed up. They're at the door now. Tell Curd that Noigel will be bringing them down. Give him a hand butchering if he needs it."

They nodded their assent and Scug skulked away, disappearing into the darkness, heading back down the passageway. Javier tried to make sense of what he'd just heard. New arrivals? Who could it be? The police? The gangbangers who had chased them in here in the first place? Maybe their parents, come to look for them after discovering the car? And who was at the nursery—whatever that was? Scug had indicated that it was one of Javier's friends and that it was a female. That meant it had to be Heather or Kerri. He felt like calling out, regardless of whether they could actually hear him, and telling them to hide because Scug was on the way, but such an effort would only waste energy. He'd be more help to them if he was free. Then another thought occurred to him. Scug had twice mentioned Noigel and something about him skull-fucking somebody. The first time, Javier hadn't paid attention, but this second time, Scug had indicated that the assault was taking place near the basement steps. Could the victim be one of his friends? Could it be Heather?

Javier's heart pounded. A sense of urgency swept over him. He needed to get free and he needed to do it now—both for his friends and for himself. With Scug's departure, the odds were a little more even. He sensed that this might be his last opportunity to escape. He concentrated on his breathing as they marched him forward again, trying to simultaneously calm himself and wake himself up. He allowed the females to lead him onward until he was certain that they were out of Scug's earshot. Then he took a deep breath and made his play.

Javier lurched forward, shifting his weight. At the same time, he squirmed, trying desperately to free his arms from their grip. His ploy worked, but not without consequences. The woman's flashlight clattered to the floor. His right arm slipped easily enough from Scar-Face's grip, but the hairy girl squeezed harder on his left arm. Her nails sank into his wound, and blood flowed again. Screaming, Javier wrenched his arm free and stumbled forward, slamming into the tunnel wall.

He shook his head, trying to regain both his senses and his footing. The women lunged for him. Javier turned to face them. The hairy girl grabbed his left hand and jerked him toward her. She twisted his arm at the same time, so that his wounded wrist and his palm were face up and his fingers were folded back. Her head darted forward. Her eyes and teeth glinted in the darkness. As her mouth came down on his hand, Javier grasped her upper lip with his fingers and pulled. The girl uttered a muffled shriek and let go of his hand. He pulled harder, savagely yanking the lip toward him. It stretched like warm bubblegum that had been left on the sidewalk on a summer day. Javier felt the skin start to tear. Then Scar-Face broke his grip with a blow to his forearm. Both Javier and the hairy girl stumbled backward.

He landed on his rump and his teeth clacked together painfully. Javier tried to get up, but before he could, Scar-Face leaped on him, slamming him back to the floor. Behind her, the hairy girl was moaning and crying, patting at her mouth with the back of her hand. Her lips were bleeding, and Javier felt a surge of savage joy. It vanished a second later when Scar-Face's fingernails opened four ragged, bloody furrows on his cheek. Her mouth opened and her teeth tried for his injured wrist even as he pulled back to strike at her again.

Javier rolled sideways and did his best to dislodge her, but the woman held on to his legs with her *feet*. Too late, he realized why. Her double-jointed toes clutched at him like hands. They felt like what he imagined a monkey's feet would feel like, capable of clutching not only the fabric of his jeans but the skin beneath them, as well. She held on and rolled with him. Her teeth snapped as she tried to find a way past his defenses. He blocked her again and struggled to get free. Behind them, the hairy girl continued to whine.

"Get the hell off me, bitch!"

Scar-Face snarled, well past the point of any coherent speech. Her teeth flashed. Her fingers wrapped around his wrist and pulled on the ragged edges of the wound. Javier wailed. Her nails opened new gashes beneath the first cut. Fresh blood flowed. Hissing, Javier twisted his arm, breaking her grip enough that he could push his fingers and palm up against her chin. She couldn't bite if she couldn't open her jaw. Scar-Face turned her head and tried to get away, but he wouldn't let her. He didn't dare. Sharp as her fingernails might be, her teeth were much more dangerous. Javier thought of the attack on Brett earlier in the evening. He couldn't risk losing a finger. A muffled cry of frustration slipped past her closed lips and Javier grinned in response.

"That's right. What you gonna do now, you crazy fuck?"

Scar-Face continued to struggle. Over her shoulder, Javier noticed that her companion was shaking off her fugue and preparing to rejoin the battle. He had to finish this quick. He reached out with his other hand and grabbed her ear, clenching it in his fingers. He noticed that fresh blood was running down the inside of his forearm, but it was only trickling, rather than gushing. He squeezed her ear, pulling and twisting as hard as he could. Javier both heard and felt the cartilage snap. She shrieked in agony and he yanked a second time, trying his best to pull her ear off completely. She was too preoccupied with her pain to attack him, and the hairy girl cowered against the tunnel wall, suddenly afraid. Javier pulled a third time. The woman thrashed on top of him as he twisted. He screamed right along with her, no longer caring if any of the other creatures heard him. He was focused only on tearing her ear from her skull. They rolled out of the range of the flashlight beams, and Javier heard something rip. A moment later, he was free—her severed ear still clutched between his fingers.

Scar-Face howled in the darkness. Javier clambered to his feet, tossed the ear at her and then kicked her in the face. Her nose exploded beneath the sole of his shoe. He kicked again, catching her in the ribs. His third kick slammed her in the temple. The hapless woman went limp. Javier didn't care. He was aiming a fourth kick when Scar-Face's companion leapt onto his back. Her bloodied, swollen lips pressed against the back of his neck, but he felt no teeth. Javier realized that she was either too panicked to bite him or he'd damaged her mouth even more than he had first thought. One of her arms wrapped around his throat. The other clawed at his face. Her fingers sought his eyeballs. Moving fast, Javier stumbled backward, slamming her into the rock wall. Then he lurched forward and did it again. After several collisions, the hairy girl slipped from his back, unconscious.

Panting for breath, he studied them both. Their chests rose and fell slightly, but their eyes were closed. He didn't think they were faking, but there was only one way to be certain. He cocked his head, listening. The tunnels were quiet. If the sounds of their battle had been noticed, then whoever was lurking in the darkness was remaining silent. Javier didn't think that was a possibility, though. He was positive that they were alone—for now.

Kneeling, he leaned over the hairy girl, wrapped his bloody fingers around her warm neck, and squeezed. Her eyes shot open, bulging in their sockets.

"Auullkgh!"

The sound was not a word, though perhaps it was meant to be one. Javier did not know and didn't care. His fingers pressed in on her carotid artery, and on the thick vein that mirrored it on the other side of her delicate, grimy neck. Both veins throbbed beneath his fingertips. He could almost feel the blood surging through them.

She tried one last time to get away and her fingers sank into his thighs as he squeezed harder still. He ignored the pain, and watched her, relishing the expression on her face when she realized that she could not breathe. Her swollen lips parted, and Javier increased the pressure. Every muscle in his arms and legs stood out. He shivered with strain. His sweat and blood from his wounds dripped onto her face and chest. Javier was dimly aware that he was panting.

The strong pulse under his fingertips slowed and stuttered and then stopped. Still, she tried to breathe. Still, he kept his grip firm. Her legs thrashed, kicking and flailing. She slapped and clawed at the floor. Javier maintained his vise grip and squeezed as hard as he could. His grin grew wider.

A moment later, she stopped struggling.

Javier held her a moment longer than that, then finally released his hold. The hairy girl didn't move. Not satisfied, he seized her head in both hands and turned it to the side until her neck snapped. It was one of the most satisfying sounds he had ever heard.

He rested a moment with her corpse in his lap and caught his breath. He examined the cuts on his wrists. Both were bleeding, but not badly enough that he'd die or lose consciousness. Although the fight had reopened them, both wounds were clotting satisfactorily. They'd need to be cleaned and stitched later, but he couldn't worry about that right now. His main concern was fatigue. He'd need to rest soon, if only for a few minutes. He listened again, but the tunnel remained quiet. The only sound was the unconscious Scar-Face's low, shallow breathing. Javier shoved the hairy girl from his lap. Her corpse sprawled across the tunnel floor. He stared down at her and spat in her face.

Then he turned his attention to the other one.

He kicked and stomped on Scar-Face, turning her to jelly. He relished every breaking bone, every shattered rib, and every ruptured organ. He laughed when one eyeball spurted from its socket and when shards of broken bones tore through her flesh. Then, still not satisfied, he leaped into the air and jumped up and down on her corpse. Flesh and blood and hair matted between the treads of his shoes. Then he dipped his index finger in her remains, and used her blood to add two more slash marks to the scorecard on his arm.

When he was finished, Javier picked up the flashlight. His body trembled and ached. His teeth were chattering.

He'd never felt more alive than he did at that moment.

"Ready or not," he called, "here I come!"

He ran back the way they'd come, calling out for Scug to come and play.

Kerri grabbed the arms that had encircled her in the darkness and tried to dislodge them, but it was like trying to push stone. Although her assailant's flesh was soft and slippery with sweat, solid, massive muscles bulged beneath the skin. They rippled as the creature squeezed harder. Kerri tried to scream but could barely even breathe as the air was forced from her lungs.

The thing laughed again. Its grip slackened just enough that Kerri had time to draw a breath. She inhaled the foul air it had just exhaled, and then the creature squeezed again, mashing her breasts and abdomen against its body. Her arms were now pinned to her sides. Her hands flailed helplessly.

"Hugs," the monster rasped in an oddly childish voice. "I give you hugs."

"*Get . . . off . . . ME!*" Her demand was half scream, half gasp, and it only seemed to amuse the creature even more. Its laughter echoed through the darkness, seeming to come from every direction at once. There was no hint of menace in its laugh. It sounded more like glee and wonder.

"Nice. Pretty."

Kerri thrashed in the mutant's viselike grip, shaking her head furiously back and forth, but nothing broke its hold.

"Kisses," it said. "I give you kisses."

"Oh, God . . ."

Something long and wet and smelling of sulfur and rotten meat touched her face, licking her eyes and then her nose and then slipping between her lips. She thought of earlier in the night, when she'd bitten a previous attacker's tongue off, and steeled herself to do the same again, when the proboscis was suddenly pulled away. Stinking, hot saliva dripped from Kerri's face.

"Stick you," it panted. "I stick you now. I stick you in the wet place."

Kerri closed her eyes, anticipating the thrust of a blade or other weapon into her body at any moment. Instead, she felt something warm and hard pressing against the fabric of her groin. Shuddering, she realized what it was.

"No!"

"I stick you now," the creature repeated. "I stick you in the wet place."

Its breathing grew harsher and more rapid. The length of flesh pressing against her crotch stiffened even more, seeming to pulsate in the darkness.

"Let me go," she wailed. "Goddamn you, let me go. Don't do this! Stop it!"

The creature froze, muscles locking up. It groaned softly, and then Kerri's jeans grew wet. At first, she wasn't sure what had happened but then she caught a whiff of something ammonia-like. Fishy. It reminded her of how sidewalks smelled after a rainstorm. She knew what it was. Under normal circumstances the smell might have brought back fond memories of all the times she and Tyler had made love. Instead, it simply repulsed her.

"Uhhhh," her captor groaned. "When you wiggle, I go boom."

At least it can't rape me now, she thought. It's *already shot its wad.*

But then the penis pressed against her again, seeking a way inside her jeans, and Kerri realized that if anything, the creature's erection had grown bigger.

"I stick you now," it promised. "You not wiggle so much this time. You be good. I don't want to go boom too early like before. Okay?"

Its tone was gentle. Almost loving. With a cry, Kerri ripped one of her arms free and slapped at the darkness, connecting with her would-be rapist's face. Surprised, it released her. Kerri fell to the ground and backpedaled as quickly as she could. She was nowhere near fast enough. A massive hand seized her ankle and dragged her back across the floor. A moment later, she was being lifted into the air again. The fingers that caught her face were rough and callused, and stretched her lips almost to the point of rupturing them as they muffled her next scream.

"I tell you to stop wiggling. You'll make me go boom again. Not time yet. No fun for you. Want you to have fun. Want you to like me. Then you stay and we not eat you."

Kerri tried to pull away, but she was no match for the beast's impressive strength. It carried her to the hard stone floor, and she felt its body pressing against her. It kissed her again, slobbering all over her face. Its tongue flickered across her cheeks and neck, as if the creature were slowly savoring the taste of her. Kerri moaned in revulsion. The thing misinterpreted the sounds as ones of anticipation. Sighing, it pawed at her jeans. Kerri tensed as the fingers trailed across her zipper. Then she reached out with one hand and grabbed its erect penis. At the same time, her head darted forward and her teeth snapped shut on what she could only assume was the creature's nose.

The thing's penis was wet and sticky and her hand slipped free of it when she tried to pull. Her other attack was more successful. She clamped her jaws shut and ground her teeth together, biting hard. She felt its nose burst inside her mouth like a chocolate-covered cherry. She bit harder, shaking her head back and forth. Screaming, her attacker tried to pull away. It sat up, but Kerri hung on, squeezing her jaws with all of her remaining strength, determined not to let go. More blood ran down her throat. Her attacker leapt to his feet. Suddenly, Kerri's teeth came together, severing its nose completely.

She stumbled upright and spat the knobby piece of flesh onto the ground. The monster wailed, totally ignoring her now.

"Dy dose," it shrieked. "Do dit dy dose off!"

She stumbled to the side and pressed her back against the wall. Then she crouched, waiting, trying to block out the terrible screams. The thing cried and howled for what seemed like an eternity. Kerri slowly crept away, keeping her back to the wall. There was silence for a moment. Then it screamed again from a different point in the distance.

"Der dar do, ditch? Der dar do?"

It's going in the opposite direction, she thought. *Just keep quiet and let it go.*

It screamed again from even farther away.

She waited until it was gone. There was silence again after that, except for the sound of her breathing. Kerri huddled in the darkness and felt the tears again, but not from panic this time. Not really. These tears were caused by loss. She was horrified by what she'd just done—by everything that she'd done so far to stay alive. She felt like she'd lost a part of herself in the transition, an important part that she'd never be able to regain. Every tragedy she'd endured in the past eighteen years felt insignificant in comparison to the horrors of this evening.

She shivered, feeling the slick of her attacker's vile seed drying on her jeans. His stench was on her body. Earlier she had smelled of lavender perfume and the Axe body spray Tyler favored. Now she smelled like a dead animal. Even though he hadn't succeeded in raping her, she felt as if her attacker had still violated her. She needed to get out of this dark crevice, no matter what the cost. Even if it led her directly into the hands of more of these freaks, she needed to get away from this subterranean chamber. She doubted anything else would ever matter as much again as that simple, desperate need. Her hands shook with controlled fury. Every part of her hurt, shook, and shivered as if electrified. Her mouth tasted sour and she spit again and again, hoping to get rid of his taste.

Kerri sat there in the darkness for a long time, mourning not only her boyfriend and her friends, but also herself.

CHAPTER EIGHTEEN

Perry swung the sledgehammer again, smashing its broad head into the door. There was a loud crack and more wood splintered as the hammer broke through the barrier. Behind him, several of the boys cheered. Wood-boring insects squirmed around the edges of the hole. Sweat ran into his eyes, stinging them. Blinking, Perry swung again. This time, he aimed for the ornate brass doorknob. He connected hard. The vibration ran up through the hammer handle and into his arms, numbing his hands. He set the sledgehammer down, leaning it against the porch railing. Then he turned around and held his hand out to Chris.

"Let me see that crowbar."

Chris handed it to him, and Perry went to work on the doorknob. It gave way easily enough, tumbling to the porch and rolling across it before landing on the sidewalk. Dookie started to run after it, but Perry stopped him.

"Leave it."

"But that's brass," Dookie protested. "You know how much that shit is worth down at the scrap yard?"

"Leave it alone," Perry repeated, turning back to the door. "We've got more important shit to worry about right now."

His knees popped as he stood, and his hands ached

from the exertion. Perry knew that he'd regret it tomorrow when his arthritis was flaring, but right now, he didn't care. He pushed on the door, leaning his weight into it. Still, the heavy barricade refused to move.

"What the hell?" he muttered. "I think there's something on the other side of this thing."

Leo rushed to the door, bent over, and peered through the jagged hole made by the sledgehammer. His eyes widened. Then he glanced up at Perry.

"It looks like a big piece of metal or something."

"Shit." Sighing, Perry wiped his forehead with the back of his hand. "Okay, you boys help me get this door out of the way. Then we can see what we're dealing with."

"Well," Jamal said, "now we know, right?"

Perry pried at the door's hinges with the crowbar. "Now we know what?"

"That whoever is inside there must be holding them white kids hostage. Why else would there be metal blocking the doorway."

"The kids could have put it there themselves," Markus pointed out. "Try to keep us out and shit."

"They didn't know we were coming," Leo said.

"Maybe not. But they damn sure heard us trying to break through this door."

"Yeah, but then we would have heard them dragging the metal in place."

Perry snapped the hinges free, set the crowbar down, and grabbed the door. The boys ran to his aid. Together, they hefted the wooden slab out of the doorframe and carried it down the porch steps and into the yard. Then they inspected the second obstruction. It was indeed metal—steel, in fact. It completely blocked the opening. Perry could see no rivets or welding marks. It was one solid piece, as best he could tell. He rapped on it with his knuckles and then struck it with the crowbar, but it had no effect—not even a dent.

"Shit."

"Can you smash it down with the sledgehammer?" Chris asked.

"I can try," Perry said. "But I don't think that's gonna get us anywhere. That son of a bitch sounds pretty damned thick."

Leo cocked his head, studying the steel blockade. "There's a hole in it."

Perry frowned. "Where?"

"Up near the top." Leo pointed. "See? It's small, but it's there."

They all glanced at where he was pointing. Perry squinted, and then saw it. The hole was about five inches from the top of the barrier and very tiny, no bigger than the tip of his pinky.

"It looks like a peephole," Chris said.

"I think that's exactly what it is," Perry replied.

"Can you hammer it there?" Dookie asked. "Maybe it's weaker around that spot."

Perry shook his head. "No. That steel is still pretty thick. I don't think hitting it there will do any good."

Leo took the crowbar from Perry's hand and reared back, clutching it in both hands. Then he shoved forward, slamming it into the bottom of the door, right into the part where the metal met the floor. Dookie shone the flashlight on the doorway. Leo looked up at Perry.

"Hit it."

"That's not going to—"

"Go on," Leo insisted. "If we can get the crowbar wedged in under the metal—even a little bit—maybe we can raise it up or move it out of the way."

"Yeah," Perry agreed slowly. "Maybe so. But that

means you're going to have to hold the crowbar in place, and if I miss when I'm swinging, I could break your hand or worse."

Leo grinned. "Then don't miss, Mr. Watkins."

"Nobody likes a smartass, boy," Perry said, returning his grin. Then he glanced at Dookie. "Keep that flashlight trained on the crowbar. Don't shine it in my eyes or nothing."

Dookie nodded. "I won't."

Perry grabbed the sledgehammer, steadied his aim, and swung. The broad hammerhead struck the end of the crowbar with a loud metallic clang. Both tools shuddered. Leo flinched, but his hands remained steady, holding it in place. Perry swung again and again—a dozen times. He didn't think they were making any progress, but then Leo told him to stop.

"Look there," the boy said. "It's underneath the metal. Give it a few more whacks."

Licking his lips, Perry struck the crowbar a half dozen more times. Each blow rang out down the street, but if anyone heard the commotion, they didn't show up to investigate. When he was finished, he glanced toward his home, hoping to see the flashing red lights of a police car or other emergency vehicle. Instead, all he saw was darkness.

Leo stood, flexed his hands and fingers, and then pushed down on the crowbar. He grunted with exertion and the veins in his neck and forehead stood out, but the steel barricade didn't move.

"Here," Perry said, gently ushering him aside. "Let me give it a try."

He applied his weight to the crowbar. At first, it didn't budge, but then slowly, with a loud groan, the metal began to slide upward.

"That's it," Leo said. "Keep going, Mr. Watkins!"

Perry pressed harder, grunting with the effort. The barrier slid higher. Judging by the feel, he guessed that it was affixed to some type of hidden pulley system. He wondered who had manufactured it and why.

"Get underneath it," he gasped. "Heavy."

The boys darted forward and slid their fingers into the crack.

"Hold it there," Perry said. "Don't let it fall. If it starts to slip, jump clear. Don't need any of you getting your fingers chopped off."

When he was sure they had a firm grip on the door, Perry released the crowbar and moved to help them. The metal slid back down an inch, but the boys managed to hold it aloft. Perry grabbed the edge, wedging himself between Markus and Jamal. The surface was cold and rough.

"Okay," he said. "Count of three, let's lift it as high as we can. One . . . two . . . three!"

Moving as one, they strained and groaned, lifting the heavy slab of metal higher. They stood slowly. Perry's knees popped with the effort. The door squeaked as it rose over their heads. They gave it one last shove and heard something click into place. The steel barrier disappeared, held aloft by some hidden mechanism. The house stood open to them, a yawning, black mouth. Perry peered into the darkness and saw some kind of foyer.

"Okay." He sighed and wiped his forehead with the back of his hand. "Y'all ready?"

The boys nodded, but none of them spoke. They stared straight ahead, as if hypnotized.

Perry retrieved the handgun from Leo and gave him the crowbar. Markus hefted the sledgehammer. Chris, Jamal, and Dookie wielded the flashlights. Taking a deep breath, Perry stepped inside. He moved cautiously, licking his lips as he walked. His breaths were slow and deep, his pulse fast. The pistol trembled in his hand. The kids followed him one by one.

The dark foyer smelled of mildew and rot. A hallway and multiple closed doors led off from it into other parts of the house. The walls were covered with peeling yellow wallpaper and splotches of black mold. Rat holes riddled the baseboards. The floorboards were warped, and chunks of plaster dangled from the ceiling. Also hanging overhead was a string of construction lights, rigged together with an extension cord. They weren't on. Perry wondered idly if they were still functional.

The house was utterly silent. No voices. Nothing attracted by their noisy entrance. Not even the ever-present sound of rats or insects scurrying in the walls—something each of them would have expected. Even the distant sounds of traffic and other noises from up the block seemed nonexistent despite the open doorway out to the street, as if the house was muffling all outside sounds.

The soles of their feet stuck to the floor. When Dookie shined his light onto the floorboards, they saw why. They were standing in the middle of a large brown stain. It looked like somebody had dragged something across the floor. Perry knelt, trying to figure out what the stain was. He touched it with his index finger.

"Shit."

"It's shit?" Dookie asked, his voice tinged with disgust and disbelief. "Fuck. I'm standing in it!"

"No," Perry said. "It's not shit. It's blood. Still tacky, too. Fresh. Not quite dried yet."

"Motherfucker . . ." Jamal stepped out of the bloodstain and wiped his feet on the wall. His shoe sank into the plaster.

"Hello," Leo called. "Anybody here?"

His voice seemed oddly muffled, as if the walls were sucking it up.

"Hello," he tried again. "We're here to help you."

"Hey, white kids," Markus bellowed, grinning. "Where you at? Come on out!"

Chris elbowed him in the ribs. "What the fuck is wrong with you?"

"Nothing."

Still grinning, Markus approached one of the closed doors. The floorboards creaked as he crossed the foyer. He held the sledgehammer in one hand and opened the door with the other.

"Wait," Perry warned. But before he could move, the door swung open, creaking on rusty hinges.

Markus peered inside the room and shrugged. "Ain't nothing in there."

"Let me see." Perry moved past him, motioning at Dookie to follow him with the flashlight. They stepped inside the darkened room, and Dookie shined the flashlight into the corners, sweeping it around in a wide arc. The interior was desolate, just like the foyer. There was no furniture or appliances, just a few scraps of dirty cloth, crumpled pages from an old newspaper, and a crushed soda can. Otherwise, the room was barren. It smelled musty. Dust swirled in the flashlight beam. Perry wrinkled his nose.

"So what now?" Leo asked.

"We look around," Perry said. "Try to find them. Judging from that blood out there, at least one of them is hurt."

"We should split up," Jamal suggested. "That would make things a lot easier."

"Oh hell, no!" Chris shook his head. "Splitting up is

the stupidest thing we can do. I say we go back outside and call the po-po again. Tell them about the blood and shit."

"We're not splitting up," Perry agreed, stepping back into the foyer. "You go on back and call them again if you want. I'm gonna follow this blood trail. Hand me that flashlight, Dookie."

Dookie clutched the light protectively. "If it's all the same to you, Mr. Watkins, I'll hold on to it. I'll come with you, though."

"Okay. Good. Anybody else coming?"

Leo stepped forward, as did Jamal. Markus shrugged and then nodded. Jamal and Chris looked at each other.

"You go ahead if you want," Jamal told his friend. "I'm staying."

Chris's shoulders sagged. "Guess I'm staying, too. I ain't no punk."

They started down the hallway. Dookie was in the lead, with Perry just a few steps behind him. Markus and Chris followed them, while Jamal and Leo brought up the rear. Dookie kept his flashlight trained on the floor, and they followed the blood smear through numerous twists and turns. The house's layout made no sense. To Perry, it seemed like someone had added walls and rooms and passageways at random. Doors opened into walls. Hallways terminated in dead ends. The whole thing was bewildering and disconcerting. Occasionally they called out, hoping for an answer to guide them in the right direction, but the house remained silent.

All six of them jumped when they heard a thunderous crash behind them. The echoes vibrated through the walls. Plaster and dust rained down on them. Perry's finger jerked. If he'd had it on the trigger, the gun would have gone off. The crowbar slipped from Leo's hand and clattered on the floor. Chris dropped his flashlight and it rolled away from him, coming to rest in the rust-colored blood slick.

"What the hell was that?" Jamal shouted.

"I think it was that metal door," Perry said. "Come on. Let's get back to the front."

"But what about them kids?" Leo asked.

"Fuck them kids," Markus said. "This place is a motherfucking death trap."

For once, Perry agreed with the belligerent teen. He'd seen enough of the house's interior to know that it was even more dangerous than he'd suspected. It would be too easy for them to lose their way in here, too easy to be injured in an accident—or worse. He grabbed Dookie's arm and herded him past the others, then turned around and motioned at them to follow. Chris bent over and retrieved his flashlight, grimacing as he wiped the blood on his shirt. Leo picked up the crowbar.

"Come on," Perry urged. "Let's go."

Before they could move, however, they heard footsteps. It was impossible to tell what direction they were coming from. They seemed to issue from everywhere at once. The walls shook with each thudding step, and the makeshift lighting system overhead swung back and forth.

Perry grabbed Dookie's arm again and led him back the way they'd come. Leo and Chris followed him. Markus and Jamal hesitated. The footsteps grew louder.

"What are you doing?" Markus asked. "They're coming from that way!"

"No, they're not," Perry argued. "They're coming from down that hall."

"The hell they are."

"Listen." Perry scowled. "We don't have time for this. Now, let's go."

"I'm telling you," Markus insisted, "they're coming from that direction. Y'all heard that big crash. Whoever it was, they shut the fucking door on us. Come on, Chris."

Perry stepped toward them. "Goddamn it, you get back here. I'm responsible for you!"

"Yo," Dookie whispered, "do y'all smell that all of the sudden? It's like something died up in here."

"You ain't responsible for shit," Markus told Perry, turning away from the others and ignoring Dookie's comment.

Perry started to respond, but he paused. Dookie was right. There was an ammoniacal stench in the air—shit, sulfur, sweat, and worse. Then he noticed that the footsteps had stopped, replaced by the sound of harsh, heavy breathing.

Oblivious to the noise or the stench, Markus and Chris started down the hall. Chris glanced back over his shoulder once. His eyes were haunted and pleading. Then he wrinkled his nose. He turned around, and Perry saw a massive, looming shadow fall over them both. As Perry and the others watched, Chris raised his flashlight. Reflected in the beam was the biggest man Perry had ever seen—if indeed it *was* a man. He had to be over seven feet tall; his bald, misshapen head brushed against the ceiling as he stood there staring at them. His shoulders and chest were bigger than any professional wrestler Perry had ever watched on television—easily the width of several men. He was almost naked, except for some garbage bags tied together with silver duct tape. His pale skin, while covered with sores and growths, rippled with slabs of thick muscle. Most disturbing was the creature's genitals, which were obviously swollen and suppurated with some type of infection. Pus dripped from the tip of its penis like water from a leaky spigot.

He's so big, Perry thought. *How could someone so god-damned big just appear out of nowhere like that? I mean, sure, we heard his footsteps, but how did he just pop out of the darkness like this?*

Markus leaped back in alarm. Chris had time to stutter in surprise, and then the giant figure raised some sort of crude weapon—a boulder tied onto an iron pipe. The stone was crusted with blood. Without a word, the hulk swung the makeshift club up over his shoulders and down onto the top of Chris's head. The sound it made was like nothing Perry had ever heard. It sort of reminded him of when he was a kid. He and his friends had dropped a watermelon out the third-story window of an apartment building in North Philly. The sound the melon had made as it splattered across the sidewalk was similar to the sound Chris's head made as the club smashed through it—but this was wetter. The explosion coated Markus and the walls with blood and brain matter. Bits of Chris's skull flew across the corridor and were embedded into the wall. The mallet reached his neck and pounded what was left down into his chest. Amazingly, his body remained standing, clutching the flashlight in one jittering hand. The boy's sphincter and bladder both released, adding to the noxious stench in the passageway.

Perry cried out in horror. Jamal did the same, screaming his friend's name. Dookie trembled next to Perry, clinging to his arm and babbling nonsensical words. Incredibly, Leo charged forward, shrieking with rage, the crowbar held above his head like a spear. Perry's senses returned as he saw the boy charge forward. Shoving Dookie behind him, he brought the handgun up and tried to aim. Jamal's and Dookie's flashlights were shaking too badly to be of much use, and although Chris's standing corpse still held his, it was pointed at the floor. Perry did his best to draw a bead despite the bad lighting, but Leo got in his way.

"Leo," he hollered. "Get the hell out of there!"

If Leo heard him, he didn't react. Cursing, Perry took a few steps toward them, trying to get a clearer shot. As he did, Markus wiped the blood out of his eyes and stared upward, just as the looming monstrosity swung at him. Markus had enough reflexes to raise the sledge-hammer. The two weapons clashed against each other. The beast grunted in surprise or amusement—Perry couldn't tell which. Then it shoved Markus off his feet. The boy landed on his back with a jarring thud but managed to hold on to his hammer. The creature stepped over him and faced down Leo.

"Get the hell off him, motherfucker!"

Leo slashed at it with the crowbar. The tool glanced off the hulk's massive bicep, digging a shallow furrow in the flesh. If the thing felt pain, it gave no indication. It pivoted, swiping at Leo with the hammer, but he danced out of range, narrowly avoiding the bone-crushing strike.

"Goddamn it, Leo," Perry yelled. "Move aside!"

This time, he did as Perry asked, dropping flat to the floor. The thing in the hallway bellowed laughter and glared at Perry, Dookie, and Jamal, with round black eyes, as if it had just noticed their presence. Grinning, the creature stuck its tongue out at them. The organ looked like a pale, wriggling worm. Its smile grew wider, revealing broken, blackened teeth. Worse was the obscenely large penis dangling between its legs. As they watched, the swollen, infected organ began to dance and bob, spraying more pink and yellow pus. Perry was grateful for the dim lighting. He didn't think he could take seeing things any more clearly than he already was.

The stench wafting from between the man-thing's legs was nauseating.

The monstrosity laughed again, and Perry pulled the trigger. He hadn't planned on it, wasn't even aware that he'd done it until the gun leaped in his hands and the boom filled the room. The brass jacket flew out of the side of the gun and clattered onto the floor. The echo continued, deafening Perry to everything around him. The vibration ran up his forearms. Not waiting to see if he'd hit the giant, he squeezed the trigger again, this time making a conscious effort to aim for the bastard's chest. His opponent jerked and staggered, but then stood back up as if shrugging it off and raised its hammer high. Blood ran from a dime-sized hole in its chest.

"Jamal? Dookie? You still back there. If so, get those lights on it."

Perry couldn't hear whether they responded. His ears were still ringing from the gunshots. But a second later, two jittering flashlight beams crisscrossed the beast. It squinted at the light.

How the hell can it still be standing?

Perry's eyes grew wide as he saw Markus clambering to his feet behind it. The boy hefted the sledgehammer, eyeing his attacker coldly.

"Yo, turn your bad-cheese-smelling ass around, you skinhead motherfucker."

"Markus, no!" Perry lowered the gun in frustration as the ringing in his ears faded. "I can't shoot if you're behind it."

The giant spun around and swung its hammer again. Markus raised his to meet the attack. Once more, the two weapons smashed into each other with a loud crash. The head broke off Markus's hammer and crashed to the floor, narrowly missing his foot. Although Markus had deflected the killing blow, the force once again knocked him to the floor. His attacker's hammer glanced off the wall, shearing and gouging through plaster and studs. Markus dropped his weapon and scrambled backward across the floor. The giant raised a foot and stomped on his chest. Perry heard a sound like twigs snapping, and then realized it was Markus's ribs. Blood flew from the hapless boy's mouth. He made a choking, gagging sound. Perry tried once again to get a clear shot at the madman, but Leo darted between them and struck Markus's foe on the back of the head with the crowbar. Grunting, the hulk slapped him aside with one free hand. Although Perry could see the blood welling up on its bald scalp, the thing seemed unfazed by Leo's blow.

"The hell with this." Perry glanced back at Jamal and Dookie. "Get your asses out of here now! Go back the way we came. Get to the door and see if you can escape."

Without waiting to see if they'd listen to him, Perry turned around and ran down the hallway toward the battle. Leo was crawling to his feet and searching for his crowbar. He seemed dazed. Markus whimpered in terror and agony as the giant grabbed one of his arms and lifted him off the floor. It let go of the hammer, and the heavy weapon crashed to the floor, stirring up dust and sending vibrations through the boards. Then the bruiser grabbed Markus's other arm and began to pull them in different directions. Markus shrieked. Still pulling, the creature slammed him into the wall again and again. There was a horrible popping and tearing sound, and then Markus sagged in its grip as one of his arms ripped free. The giant flung him to the floor and then turned to face Perry and Leo. It grinned.

Without pausing to aim, Perry shot it in the face, sheering away part of its chin and cheek. Squealing, the attacker swiped at Perry with Markus's severed arm, splattering him with the teen's blood. Perry fired again. The bullet tore through the giant's shoulder. It paused, swaying back and forth on its tree-trunk legs. Then it surged toward them again. Perry realized that he could see its teeth and tongue through the bullet wound.

Why won't it fall? he thought. *Why the hell won't it die?*

He squeezed the trigger again. The gun jumped in his hand, and the shot went high, cleaving the monster's bald skull. Behind it, Perry heard Markus gasping for breath. He realized that the teen's struggles must be very loud indeed if he could hear them over the gunshots. Growling through its ruined mouth, the monstrosity charged, still wielding Markus's arm like a club.

Perry was suddenly aware of Leo standing beside him.

"Aim high," the boy shouted, and then dropped to his knees.

Before Perry could get off another shot, Leo jammed the crowbar forward, impaling their assailant directly in the middle of his grotesque, infected penis. A rush of foul air blasted from the creature's lungs. It cupped its ruined groin with both hands, dropping its grisly weapon. Blood and pus gushed from between its sausagelike fingers. Its round, black eyes rolled up into the back of its head, and then, uttering a small, quiet whine, it toppled over backward with the crowbar still jutting from between its legs.

"Get back," Perry told Leo.

Leo turned aside and threw up.

Perry leaned over the giant and emptied his weapon into its head. Again he was reminded of the exploding watermelons. This time, the image satisfied rather than horrified him. He kept squeezing the trigger, even after the pistol was empty. He couldn't seem to stop himself. From the neck up, the corpse was nothing more than pink and white chunks, but some small part of him still expected it to sit up or grasp at his ankles. His hands and wrists stung. His ears rang. The air was thick with gun smoke. Empty brass casings littered the floor, glinting in the flashlight beams.

"Damn . . ."

Perry wheeled around, and saw Dookie and Jamal still standing there, staring at the scene in shocked disbelief. Leo retched again, his vomit splattering across the floorboards, mixing with Chris and Markus's blood. Still trembling, Perry walked over to him and gently put his hand on Leo's shoulder. They stayed like that, not speaking, until Leo was finished.

"Damn," Dookie repeated, his voice barely a whisper.

"Check on Markus," Perry said, his voice hoarse with emotion. "See if he's still breathing."

Dookie made a choking noise. "Ain't no way—"

"Just do it! Please?"

Perry squeezed Leo's shoulder. The teen turned and looked up at him with tears in his eyes and puke on his lips and chin.

"You gonna be okay?"

"Yeah," Leo whispered. "I just . . . Markus was a dick, but he was my boy, too? You know what I'm saying?"

"I do."

"And Chris . . . damn, I've known Chris since we was in diapers. He can't be dead. He just can't."

Perry turned back to the bodies. Dookie was kneeling next to Markus, staring into his face. Markus stared back at him, unblinking, unmoving.

"Is he dead?" Perry asked.

Dookie nodded.

"What the hell was that thing?" Jamal sobbed. "I mean, what the fuck?"

Nobody answered him.

Perry helped Leo to his feet and then addressed them all.

"Somebody must have heard the gunshots. The cops may not have shown up before, but they'll have no choice now. I say we go back to the exit, find our way outside again, and wait for them to arrive."

"What about Markus and Chris?" Leo asked. "We just gonna let them lie here?"

"There's nothing we can do for them now. This is a crime scene. Best thing for all concerned is to just leave it alone until help arrives."

Jamal pointed at the mutant's corpse. "You're worried the po-po are gonna arrest you for capping him, aren't you?"

"No," Perry said. "I'm not. It was self-defense. Any fool can see that Chris and Markus were killed by that fucking freak. What I'm worried about is the rest of you. Now let's go."

He ushered them back down the hall. Leo stopped, turned and cast a longing, mournful glance back at his friends. Perry grabbed his arm and urged him to follow.

"Ain't nothing you can do for them now."

"It's my fault," Leo said. "I was the one who insisted we come in here. We should have never gotten involved. Should have minded our own damn business."

"It's not your fault," Perry said. "It's nobody's fault, except maybe that big naked fucker's. Things just happen sometimes. There's not always a reason or explanation, no matter how bad we want there to be. Now, come on."

Leo silently pulled the crowbar out of the giant's back. It came free with a wet squelch.

Perry led them back down the twisting hallway. They'd only gone a few dozen yards when they heard the patter of feet running toward them.

"Get behind me," Perry said, leaping in front of the teens. "Be ready to run."

A tall, misshapen form erupted from the shadows and charged down the passageway. Dookie raised his flashlight, shining it directly into the creature's face. The thing squealed but didn't slow. Perry stared at the lanky creature as it approached. It was some kind of horribly deformed human. One of its eyes was covered with thick, scabrous scar tissue. Its teeth were sharp and pointed. Its tongue had recently been severed. The raw, red stump flicking around inside its open mouth still leaked blood.

"Fuck me," Perry groaned.

He raised the handgun and pulled the trigger, remembering too late that he was out of bullets.

"Shit!"

Leo stepped in front of him and struck the mutant with the crowbar. Its nose and teeth crunched under the force of the blow. The thing tumbled to the floor, shrieking. Leo swung again. Then a third time. The monster flung its misshapen hands into the air in a feeble attempt to ward off the blows. The crowbar crashed down again and again.

"Die," Leo shouted. "Die, you motherfucker. Die, die, die, die . . ."

He chanted it over and over. Even after the thing's head had burst open. Even after the tip of the crowbar had punched a dozen holes in its body. Even after it lay still. Perry reached out and seized his wrist. Blood dripped from the weapon. Leo glanced at him, eyes blazing. Perry shook his head.

"It's dead now. You can stop."

"Can I?" Leo's voice was barely a whisper. "Can I really, Mr. Watkins? Because I gotta be honest with you. Right now, I don't think I'll ever be able to stop again."

CHAPTER NINETEEN

They didn't stop coming. Heather thought for sure that they'd give up, but even with the distance she'd put between them, the nightmares kept chasing after her. Their bizarre, unsettling cries echoed in the darkness.

She felt around the room, trying to remember where the exit had been. She wished now that she hadn't tossed her lantern at the horde. She was pretty sure the room was still unoccupied. She didn't hear any breathing, and there was no sour, telltale stench indicating one of the creatures was hiding there. But it wouldn't be empty for long. She tiptoed forward, trying to remain as quiet as possible, but the discarded papers and photographs rustled beneath her feet. She bumped into the table with her hip, wincing at both the pain and the sudden sound.

Biting her lip, Heather desperately considered her options. Where could she go from here? There were monsters in front of her and monsters behind her, and there seemed little chance that the police or anybody else were going to come down into the tunnels and rescue her or her friends. For a moment, she considered just hunkering down where she was. Just hiding in the darkness and waiting for the inevitable.

While she was thinking this, Heather spotted a light up ahead, coming from the tunnel that led into the larger cave complex and back up to the house. It grew bigger and brighter as she watched, enough that she could make out the room's interior again.

Oh good, she thought, *now I'll be able to see them clearly before they fucking eat me.*

The noises coming from the crevice grew louder. Heather quickly crossed the floor and peeked inside. The tide of in vitro deformities squawked when they saw her and began crawling faster. She ducked back into the room again. The light was closer and brighter still.

She was trapped.

Heather glanced around the room wildly, searching for anything useful. She knocked aside the remaining paperwork and overturned the table in a desperate race to find another weapon. There had to be something, even a fork to go with the butter knife she'd found earlier.

The first of the baby monstrosities tumbled into the room with a wet, squelching sound. Even in the semi-darkness, she could see the massive pupils in its watery eyes focusing on her immediately. It had no legs—just two short, stubby arms. Amazingly, the creature balanced on its hands and waddled toward her, mewling like a cat. Heather grabbed one of the old blankets and tossed it over the creature. Its cries increased as it fumbled around beneath the blanket. Heather drew back her bare foot and kicked it. The creature was soft and yielding beneath her toes. She raised her foot and brought her heel down. The baby screamed. She stomped it again and again, feeling tiny bones snap beneath her weight. It squealed and thrashed and then lay still.

In response to its cries, she heard footsteps coming from the direction of the light. The room grew brighter. More of the creature's brothers and sisters tottered out of the crevice. One by one, they poured into the small room. All of them were deformed. Most should never have lived, yet here they were. Some of the monstrosities were missing limbs. Others had bodies that were so twisted and ruined, she wasn't sure how they functioned. Their faces were the stuff of nightmares. Some were missing eyes or had too many. Others had gaping holes where their noses should have been and rotted cavities in place of mouths. Each of them was bathed in filth, crusted with vile sludge like pigs that had wallowed in mud and shit. Incredibly, many of them had mold and tiny, pale mushrooms growing in their body's crevices and crannies.

As if following some silent, communal command, the mutants fanned out, trying to surround her. Terrified and disgusted, Heather picked up the half-rotten table and flung it at them. The furniture exploded, slamming into a tightly clustered knot of the things and shattering, spraying both shards of wood and splatters of blood. The babies screamed. Down the tunnel, the light grew brighter still, and the footsteps increased their pace, running now.

"Goddamn it! You leave those young ones alone, bitch."

Heather recognized the voice immediately. It was the same one who had confronted her earlier, in the darkness. The one who had boasted of taking Brett's belt from Javier. As if to confirm her suspicions, she heard the belt crack as the light drew closer.

She had to move fast. If she delayed any longer, they'd trap her here, inside this grotto. Heather didn't want that to happen. If she had to die tonight, she didn't want it to be at the hands of these hideous, infantile freaks. Better to bash her own head against the cave walls until she lost consciousness. She needed to find a way out. For a second, she considered retracing her steps and going back up into the house, but she decided against it. The house was the hunting ground for these things—or more accurately, for the adults. Even if it was deserted now, there was no telling how many more traps lay in wait up there, and there was no guarantee that she'd be able to find an exit that wasn't blockaded. No, her best bet was finding another way out of the tunnels. There had to be other entrances and exits, because otherwise, the things would have starved a long time ago. They couldn't possibly live on just what prey came into the house.

"Hey, woman, do you hear me? Just give up now. I'll be quick. Bleed you before you even know what happened. You're only making it worse on yourself!"

The voice was closer. Clearer now. Less echo and distortion, but still as terrible as before.

Making it worse, Heather thought. *How could it get any worse? Her friends were probably all dead, and she was trapped beneath the streets of Philadelphia with a bunch of inbred mutant freaks.*

The infants recovered from her attack and began to regroup. Their frantic, mewling cries increased. The belt cracked again, echoing down the corridor. Heather darted forward and grabbed a splintered table leg, momentarily placing herself within striking distance. Several of the more daring creatures swiped and spat at her, hissing with rage. The smell wafting off them was enough to make her eyes sting and water.

She swung the table leg and sprang backward, halting their advance. The light grew even brighter—close enough now that she could make out the circular beam of a flashlight and the shadowy figure behind it.

There had to be a way out. That was what mattered. All the freaks and monsters and filth and death and stench in this place wouldn't matter if she made it to the other end and escaped. Heather kept telling herself that as she gagged at the stench in the air and eyed her attackers. The rejects and nightmares hopped, flopped, and sputtered as they tried to surround her again.

One of them—an emaciated thing with pasty skin between patches of filth and clay, bulging eyes and bared, oversized, yellowed teeth—charged at her, reaching with both skeletal hands. Screaming, Heather swung with her club. The table leg connected with moist skin, making a squelching sound that reminded Heather of a shoe sinking into mud. The thing grunted and then screamed, the long, bony fingers of its hands grasping at her ankle before Heather could pull back.

The cold, tiny fingers were unnaturally strong, and before she knew what was happening, the monster was upon her. Powerful hands gripped her leg and the dead white face of the thing lunged forward, the oversized teeth clamping down on her ankle and biting savagely, cutting through the denim of her jeans and into her skin. Teeth scraped over bone and peeled away flesh. Heather groaned as pain coursed up her leg. She swung the club, smashing it against the monster's back and shoulder. She half expected the rotten wood to fall apart in her hands, but instead, it held solid, thrumming with the force of her blows. Each strike delivered ugly purple and red welts on the creature's pasty white skin. It released her leg and hopped back, shrieking and batting at the air. Heather hissed in delight as it writhed in obvious pain. The rest of the swarm, which had been preparing to charge, now held back. Heather could see the caution and uncertainty in their eyes.

All of that vanished a second later as the figure with the flashlight entered the room.

"Oh my God . . ."

The figure smiled. "Like my suit, do you? Think it's pretty? Go on, take a good look. You're going to be my new Sunday dress."

The figure wore a dead woman's skin over its body. Crude, black stitches ran up the legs and abdomen, encircling the waist and neck. The flat breasts hung low. The skin was smooth and shiny, and pulled taut across the maniac's chest and arms. She could see his own muscles rippling and bulging beneath the second skin. Perhaps most shocking was the killer's groin. His penis jutted from the folds of the dead, tanned vagina, fully erect. She glanced back up at his face and saw him lick his lips as he appraised her.

"It's more than a suit," he whispered. "It's me. It's my skin. My second skin."

"Scug," Heather said, recalling his name from their earlier meeting.

"Yeah," the killer said. "That's my name. Don't wear it out."

He laughed, and Heather stepped sideways, favoring her injured leg. Immediately, the other mutants began to growl. She froze.

"You'll make a fine new addition to my wardrobe," Scug said. "But enough pussyfooting around. Might as well get to work, right? Let's get this over with. I've got lots to do tonight, and you and your friends have already got me off schedule."

His tone was matter-of-fact, his gravely voice almost bored. His eyes flicked to the table leg in her hand, and he laughed. Then, moving quickly, he lashed out at her with the belt. It cracked toward her. Heather felt the breeze from its passage as it narrowly missed her cheek. She managed to avoid the blow, darting to the side, but she stumbled and lost her footing. She fell to her knees, wincing in pain as the rough stone floor dug into her flesh. Scug lunged toward her, still cackling with laughter. Without thinking, Heather reached out with one hand, grabbed one of the smaller infants by the arm and stumbled to her feet. She swung the squalling baby, smacking Scug in the side of the head with the flailing infant. Both adult and baby tumbled to the floor. Scug stirred. The baby did not.

Heather ran for the exit. She gritted her teeth, ignoring the pain flaring in her ankle.

Behind her, Scug and the other mutants went berserk. They shrieked their anger, bellowing and lashing out wildly, slamming fists, flippers and stumps against the grotto's walls and staggering about in fury.

"You're gonna pay for that," Scug bellowed. "Oh, you are going to hurt for that!"

One of the creatures slithered in front of Heather, blocking her escape. It had crude, bony flippers instead of legs, and its arms seemed more like tentacles than anything useful. She wheeled around, searching for an opening. Howling with rage, Scug threw the flashlight at her. It smashed against the wall, plunging the room into darkness again. Heather was facing the crevice when the blackness returned. Swallowing hard, she ran straight ahead, plunging blindly, arms outstretched in front of her.

"You bitch," Scug yelled. "You scraggly little bitch! I'm gonna knife-fuck you. I'll pull out your intestines and stick my dick in them. I'll pop out your eyeballs and fuck the sockets."

Heather's bare foot came down hard on one of the babies. She slipped but maintained her balance. Something warm and wet squished between her toes. The infant wailed, thrashing beneath her foot. She stepped over it and limped on.

"Stop it," Scug shouted. "Leave them alone! I swear to Ob, when I get my fucking hands on you, I'm going to give you to Noigel and let him do what he does best."

Heather didn't know who Ob was, or what Noigel's specialty might be, and she didn't care. She didn't intend to stick around long enough to find out. Her fingers brushed against the wall. She groped around, found the crevice, and plunged into it. Behind her, the sounds of fury reached a deafening level. Heather scrabbled back up the slope, ignoring the sharp rocks beneath her hands and feet. She kept low, so that she wouldn't bump her head on the low ceiling. When her knee came down on a shard of broken glass from her lantern, she barely winced. Panic and adrenaline drove her onward.

She estimated that she'd reached the point where she'd first encountered the infant hordes before pausing to listen for pursuit. Sure enough, they were following. Scug was in the lead, judging by the sound. Heather scurried on, crawling through the darkness, not knowing what lay ahead, nor bothering to consider it.

The stench grew worse. Whatever it was that the baby freaks had been crawling around in, the source lay up ahead. Heather breathed through her mouth and refused to stop. Her entire body trembled, and now the pain started to creep in. She ignored it and gritted her teeth.

Her pursuers had grown quiet, but she could still hear them back there, relentless in their goal. They crawled and slithered without speaking. All she heard now were fingernails and claws on stone. She felt a breeze on her face, and when she patted the tunnel walls, she got the perception that it was widening again. Heather tried standing. While she couldn't straighten up to her full height, she managed to get into a sort of crouch. Her shoulders and back brushed against the ceiling. Ducking down a little bit more, she continued on until the passage broadened even more. Then she stood and stretched.

Heather paused. The stench grew more powerful. She could no longer hear the sounds of pursuit behind her, but Heather had no doubt that Scug and his minions were still there, creeping stealthily forward in the dark, intent on sneaking up and catching her unawares. Her only chance was to keep moving forward. Still, she hesitated, scared of what lay ahead. She was hoping for a way out, yes, but not one that led even deeper into the darkness. What if the blackness grew so dense and so complete that it snuffed her out? What if she simply ceased to exist?

I'm losing it. The darkness isn't a living thing. Keep moving, Heather. You owe it to Javier and the others. Go, damn it. Just go!

She shuffled forward, her body aching with every hesitant step. Her feet came down on something soft. Frowning, Heather knelt on the cavern floor and reached out experimentally. The material felt like a mix of newspaper strips, scraps of cloth, and fiberglass insulation. When Heather had been younger, she'd owned two hamsters named Tweedle-Dee and Totally-Dumb. The bedding in the bottom of their cage had consisted of newspaper scraps and pine shavings. This reminded her of that.

The stench was at its strongest here, but so was the breeze. Both washed over her, seeming to cling to her body. Heather coughed, unable to control the urge any longer. She froze, listening for any sign that she'd given her position away, but the tunnel remained silent behind her. Heather started to wonder if maybe she was wrong. Maybe Scug and the others had given up. Or maybe they were waiting. Maybe this was a dead end and they knew she'd have to come back.

She coughed again, gagging. It occurred to her that if she dropped lower, perhaps the nauseating odor wouldn't be as bad. After all, wasn't that what firemen said to do during a fire? If you dropped to the ground, the smoke couldn't reach you, because it climbed higher. Maybe the same thing would work in this situation. Anything was better than kneeling here and breathing it in. She could taste the reek in the back of her throat—oily and sour.

She hunkered down on her hands and knees and crawled forward. The material on the floor rustled beneath her, but Heather pressed onward, deciding that it was too late to change course. Her eyes still watered and stung, and her throat still felt coated, but the stench seemed more tolerable at ground level. Heather didn't know if it was her imagination or not. Then her hand came down on something hard and cylindrical. Cold metal. A flashlight!

Oh please let there be batteries in it. Oh please oh please oh please . . .

She debated whether to try it. If her pursuers were still there, the flashlight would undoubtedly lead them right to her. On the other hand, if they weren't, having some visibility would help her escape that much quicker.

If it even works. Don't know until I try it.

Holding her breath, Heather found the button on the side of the flashlight and pressed it. She almost passed out when the light came on. It was weak, but compared to the utter blackness she'd found herself in a moment before, the beam flooded the space with dazzling brilliance. Spots floated in front of Heather's eyes. She closed them for a moment and then opened them again, squinting and letting them adjust. When she could see again, she looked around.

She was in a large, round chamber, with tunnel openings on each end. The floor was indeed piled high with bedding—shredded newspapers and magazines, strips of old blankets, sheets and clothing, rolls of fiberglass insulation, and other soft material. Heather felt a bizarre surge of pride that she'd been able to identify the assortment just by touch. Scattered among the litter were old, broken toys—a dump truck missing a wheel, a doll with stuffing leaking from its seams, wooden blocks covered with mold.

With dawning horror, Heather realized that she was standing in some obscene nursery.

She climbed to her feet and hurried onward, stumbling for the exit. The smell was like a wall, but she no longer cared. She put her head down, breathed through her mouth, and forced herself to keep going.

She left the nursery and continued on. The passageway was short—more of an alcove than an actual tunnel. It opened into an even larger chamber. She stopped and shined the flashlight around. The landscape became clearer, but no less unsettling. There were heaps of refuse in front of her, islands of filth and ruined furniture, as well as broken, waterlogged lumber, rusted tin cans, glass bottles, scraps of cloth, and what looked like leather. None of it was new. Most of the debris was decrepit with age and rotten to the point of being almost unrecognizable. All of it stood in water deep enough to hide the floor below. Heather fanned her nose. The water was the worst—more sludge than liquid. She shined the flashlight across it and saw faint discolored rainbows of stagnated pollution and lumps of feces. Then she noticed something else.

Bones.

The water was full of human remains—all of them skeletal and picked clean, none of them complete. A shattered femur here. A broken rib cage there. A splintered half skull grinning at her from the muck.

Heather stifled a scream and trained the beam of light on the reeking mounds of garbage. To her surprise, the piles were honeycombed with holes—manufactured caves. They were igloolike structures made of refuse and filth, lined with old newspapers and scraps of other debris. Deep within those black hidey-holes, shapes began to stir, clearly disturbed by her sudden intrusion.

At one time in her life, Heather had planned on becoming a veterinarian. That dream had faded in quick succession when she decided to become a nurse, a hairdresser, and then a lawyer, before ultimately admitting that she had no clue what she wanted to be when she graduated—not that the admission had stopped her parents and the school guidance counselor. But during the brief time that she'd considered a career in veterinary services, Heather had watched every nature show she could find on television and absorbed every detail. There had been certain rules among the animals, and thinking of those rules while looking into the vile warren in front of her, she understood that the rules of nature had not merely been broken, but discarded completely.

Nature took care of certain things. In the wild, if a malformed cub was born to wolves or bears, it was most likely immediately put to death as a mercy, because life was not kind and certainly did not favor the weak. As the creatures emerged from their dens, Heather understood at last what she'd walked into. The things she had seen before, the ones that had killed her friends and chased them through the house and the caverns, and even the mutated infants from the previous tunnel—all of those had been healthy. Deformed, obviously, but healthy. The creatures that lived here in this festering pit were the things that nature would have killed in the wild. These were the children that could not fend for themselves, the rejects and the weaklings. The mutant mutants. But for whatever reason, they had not been killed.

Heather looked at the squalor around her, caught the scent of rotting filth and decay, glanced down at the bones, and felt a chill work through her whole body.

Not killed. They had been thrown away instead.

Discarded like trash, rather than living beings.

Left to their own devices. Maybe occasionally thrown some scraps of food—or maybe the skeletons just belonged to someone like herself, unlucky enough to escape the house and the caverns unscathed, but then stumble into this part.

The chamber before this one had been a nursery. This place was an orphanage—or a garbage dump. Or both.

Somewhere to her right, one of the castoffs mewled and dropped into the water with a loud splash. She missed its dive but spotted the ripples that radiated from the point of impact.

"You better stay the hell over there if you don't want to get the crap beat out of you."

Her shaky voice echoed around the chamber. The things living in the heaps and slithering through the sludge made reciprocal noises. She let her eyes roam around the pit, searching the garbage for anything useful, but saw nothing that she could use. There were ripples spreading out from several places in the water now, and tiny, shadowy forms moved beneath the surface. Her feet were at the very edge of the foul muck, and Heather stepped back, unsettled.

"I mean it," she shouted. "Keep the hell away from me!"

Again, her voice echoed, and again, the things responded

with more whines and chirps. Something rustled above her. Heather glanced upward, shining the light toward the ceiling. She couldn't see it. It was too high, and the flashlight didn't penetrate the shadows. The rustling sound was repeated. Dirt fell from above and drifted down, landing in Heather's eye and bouncing off her cheek. She flinched at the unexpected pain and closed her eye against the irritation. Her eye stung and watered, and she had to resist the urge to put down her flashlight and rub it.

A moment later a larger amount of dirt pattered across the top of her head. Blinking, Heather looked up—

—just as something dropped out of the shadows and landed on her upturned face.

It was about the size of a groundhog and had scaly skin and sharp teeth and claws, but beyond that she had no time to see it clearly before it was upon her. Tiny claws dug into her cheeks and neck, clinging tightly. Tiny, needlelike teeth chomped into her nose. The sudden weight and pain hit her hard and drove Heather to her knees. The flashlight slipped from her grip and rolled toward the murky waters. She grabbed the small creature and tried to pull it off, but its teeth and claws sank deeper. Blinded, Heather stumbled to her feet and beat at the clutching, smothering beast. Too late, she realized she was teetering at the edge of the water. One foot dangled in empty space, and then she fell.

The water was deeper than she'd suspected. She plunged beneath the surface. As the oily sludge covered her head, Heather's attacker dislodged itself from her face and swam away. She opened her eyes and saw only darkness. Then she remembered what that darkness consisted of—feces and sludge and other nastiness. She clenched her eyes shut again. The taste of raw sewage filled Heather's mouth and sinuses as she instinctively tried to inhale. Her lungs burned. Her pounding head felt like it would explode. In the blackness, jagged, unseen debris poked her skin and clothes.

Heather kicked for the surface, assuming that it couldn't be that far above her. Before she could reach it, though, another small hand pressed down on the back of her skull and shoved her farther into the depths. A desperate heat bloomed in Heather's chest as her oxygen faded and the urge to breathe moved toward desperate. She pushed with her hands, trying to dislodge the thing and failing. It moved above her and then lowered its face onto her scalp. She felt scaly skin and sharp teeth against her head. Heather opened her eyes. The creature tugged her hair and slipped its mouth lower, inching toward her neck, as if it was trying to decide where to kiss her. Heather flailed as she tried again to knock it free. This time she only partially succeeded. The body shifted, but it still clutched her hair.

Something else in the water scraped painfully across her rib cage and the side of her breast. Heather bucked again and twisted her arm behind her back, aiming to hit the thing with her elbow, but the angle was impossible. All she did was strain the muscles in her shoulder and back. But the effort must have frightened the creature, because it suddenly released her hair. She felt the black water surge as it moved. Then something bit into the meat of her other shoulder, drawing blood.

Heather opened her mouth to scream, losing what little air she had in her lungs in the process. More of the foul sludge poured into her throat as she tried to inhale. Violent shudders racked her body. Her head pounded and her ears rang as the vile waters filled her mouth. Heather fought more frantically, using the last of her strength. The teeth that had ripped into her shoulder came free as she turned and pushed and punched madly, desperate to live, regardless of the agony or damage her struggles caused.

The thing vanished, and Heather's head broke the surface. At first, she couldn't see anything. Gasping for breath, she wiped the sewage from her eyes and her vision returned. Her flashlight still lay at the water's edge. She kicked toward it. Nearby, a small figure glided through the water with decidedly sinuous grace.

"No . . ." Her voice was nothing more than a whisper.

Retching, she trailed her hands through the sludge, feeling it push between her fingers as she searched for something to defend herself with. This time, she got lucky. Her left hand caught a hard object, slicked with filth, but heavy. A feral grin split her face at that moment. The sound of her own laughter shocked her. She pulled the object out of the water, ignoring the reek of sewage that permeated the air and waited for her opponent. She glanced around, searching for it in the dim light.

The sound of water shifting was her only warning. Heather held tight to her weapon and slid her other hand along the uneven shaft, ignoring the odd slippery spots as she cocked the club back.

Three heartbeats, and the splashing sounds were closer.

Two, and she could feel the water surge around her as the abomination approached.

One, and she put her weight behind the swing, listened to the sound of whistling air and then the satisfying crack of her weapon against flesh and bone. The impact ran up her hands, and then her wrists and forearms before terminating in her shoulders. Her breasts swayed and heaved with the effort.

The mutant yelped in a high and jittery voice. She brought her club down again in a hard, violent arc. The impact numbed her hands and left her fingers throbbing in counterpoint. Sludge and sewage splashed her arms and face. Then something else sprayed, as well. Heather pulled back and felt the splatter of warm blood rise with her weapon, felt it christen her face in a baptism of blood and shit. She screamed her anger into the darkness, and listened to her voice echo as she shook with adrenaline and rage.

The next thing that attacked her swam in low and struck her hip. She bobbed beneath the surface for a moment before surging up again. Heather brought the club down in a hard thrust, striking a solid blow against the new opponent. Despite her attack, the thing wrapped a long, thin arm around her ass, and she felt spidery fingers clawing at her jeans underwater. Heather screamed again and prodded at the offending limb with her weapon until it withdrew. She swung again at where she thought the rest of the thing might be, but missed completely. The creature broke off the attack. Heather heard it swimming away.

Turning again, she focused on the shore as she coughed and forced herself to take deep breaths, eagerly taking in oxygen and expelling the vile taste of filth. Her lungs felt like they'd been splashed with acid, and her muscles felt like they had been replaced with live wires that shook and jittered but refused to work properly. Her face hovered barely an inch above the surface as she continued coughing and did her best to reach the edge. She grasped at the hard stone surface. For one panicked moment, she wasn't sure she'd have the strength to pull herself out of the pit, but then she heard more mewling cries and splashes. The noises were coming from all over the place, too many directions for her to even guess at their location. Spurred on by fear, she pushed herself up on her hands and pulled her lower half free of the muck. Then she collapsed, turned her head to the side, and vomited. Wet sludge dripped and ran from her body, pooling around her. The stench was incredible.

In the waters behind her, the sounds of activity increased again. Heather vomited again and then sat up, wiping her mouth and reaching for the flashlight. She shined it out over the pit and saw the waters churning. She grimaced in understanding. The mutant offspring were no longer interested in her. They were eating their brothers and sisters—the ones she had killed or injured. Heather smiled at the realization.

Good, she thought, *let them eat each other instead of me.*

She watched them feast and retched a few more times. Then, satisfied that she'd live for at least the time being, Heather turned to search for a way out.

She collided with Scug, who was standing silently behind her.

"Bitch," he spat, slapping her face with the back of his hand. "I should have known I'd find you down here with all the other trash."

Heather didn't utter a sound as she swung the flashlight around and smashed him in the side of the head. Grunting, Scug stumbled backward, swaying on his feet.

"No more, you fucker," she said, her voice low and predatory. "No more of this shit. It's my turn now. My turn!"

She struck him again, rocking his head back even harder. The air rushed from his lungs. Scug swayed more. For a second, she thought he might fall, but he maintained his balance. Heather darted in for a third blow, but Scug straightened up, rubbed the side of his head and stared at her, grinning. She faltered, halting in mid-swing.

"You think so?" he asked.

Heather felt her anger waver. Doubt crept back in. Her fear bloomed anew.

Scug's smile grew larger. "Do you *really* think so?"

"I m-mean it," she stammered. "Stay the fuck away from me, you sick freak."

"Come on, girlie. Give it your best shot."

Screaming, Heather charged. Rather than dodging or trying to block her attack, Scug met it head-on, stepping toward her. He caught her swing with one hand. His other arm grabbed her left breast and squeezed. Heather's enraged cry turned into a shriek of pain. Still twisting her breast, Scug wrenched her arm downward and twisted it at the same time. The flashlight slipped from Heather's grip and clattered onto the floor. The lens shattered, and the flashlight rolled away, plunging into the water.

Scug hissed. His foul breath was hot and humid on her face. His fingernails dug into her wrist and through her shirt into the meat of her breast as he squeezed harder, forcing her down to her knees until she was eye-level with the horrid penis sticking out of the leathery vagina he wore at his waist.

"You're not good enough for a new suit of clothes," he spat. "You're no good for anything. You're just another piece of garbage, washed down to us from above. You're trash."

"Please," Heather pleaded. "Please please please please . . ."

Scug laughed, his face hidden in shadow. "You gonna

beg now? You gonna offer to suck my dick or something if I promise not to kill you?"

Heather choked out a sob, unable to respond. Scug's penis twitched, coming to life.

"Is that what you're gonna do? You gonna beg for it?"

Behind her, Heather heard a great commotion in the water—splashing and a chorus of tiny, hungry voices. Her thoughts turned to Javier and the rest of her friends. She wondered where they were now, and if any of them were still alive.

"Well, guess what?" Scug let go of her breast and grabbed a fistful of her hair. He jerked it hard, and Heather screamed again. "I wouldn't let you put your mouth on me. What do you think of that? You're not good enough for it. Not good enough to eat. Not good enough to wear. Like I said, you're just another piece of garbage from up above. And down here, we throw our garbage away."

"No . . ."

"Yes. I bet your boyfriend tastes better, anyway. He's a fighter. I'll eat his heart first and gain his strength."

Laughing, he dragged her by her hair to the edge of the pit. Heather twisted and fought and clawed, but Scug refused to let go of her hair or her arm. Her feet kicked the ground, but to no avail. Scug grunted with effort and Heather felt herself falling. One moment, there was hard stone underneath her. The next, she splashed into the noxious pool again. She had the presence of mind to gasp a lungful of air before she sank beneath the surface, but that was all.

No, she thought. *I'm not dying this way. Not after all I've been through. Fuck that. No way.*

The waters fairly teemed with activity. Heather felt

them churning all around her as she kicked for the surface again. Her foot struck something hard that rolled and twisted under her heel. For a moment, she thought it might be her flashlight, but then she realized that it was too large for that.

Flashlights didn't have tails.

The tail was thick and long, and reminded her of a tentacle. It whipped up fast and slapped into her thigh with enough force to break her femur. The pain was worse than anything she had ever experienced in her life. Meat and bone were sheared away. The appendage tore through her arteries and nerves.

Heather sank fast and hard. She stared upward, hoping to see light, but all she saw was blackness. The shadows beneath the surface were too dense for her to be able to make out her attacker. All she could see clearly was a small shape with a large tail, rocketing toward her. More of the mutant babies swam behind it, all closing in on her position.

She instinctively threw up a hand to block the attack, and the tail sliced through her arm, severing it halfway between her elbow and wrist. Heather stared at the stump. Blood flowed slowly from the wound, clouding the water like ink. The tail came down again and shattered her sternum, chopping into her chest. One of her breasts floated, attached only by strands of gristle and flesh. Then it was torn free of her body by dozens of eager little hands.

Not going to die like this. I refuse, goddamn it! This isn't how I'm supposed to die. It's not fair. I've got stuff to do. This just doesn't make sense . . .

She looked to the surface again, hoping to see the light one last time, hoping to see Javier coming to save her. Hoping to see her parents. Her siblings. Her friends. God.

Instead she saw the tail lashing toward her face.

Then the darkness enveloped her, and Heather saw no more.

CHAPTER TWENTY

Javier closed his eyes. Not because he wanted to, but because the adrenaline surge that had fueled him ever since his escape from his captors had now left him, leaving him weak and shaking. Blood loss, shock, and fatigue had all finally caught up with him. He knew that if he was going to find the others and make it out of here alive, then he needed to rest, if only for a moment. His stomach growled. He was hungry. It seemed absurd after everything that had happened, but it was true.

A soft breeze blew across his face, coming from somewhere to his left. It reminded him for a moment of how he'd felt as a child when his mother's breath whispered over his skin as she sang him lullabies. He realized now just how precious those memories were, those odd little sensory recollections that made up the sum of his existence. They were what it meant to be alive. If he died tonight, those memories would cease to exist. Javier had no intention of allowing that to happen. He stayed where he was, crouched against a large boulder, not wanting to continue on just yet, not wanting to forget his mother because as long as he remembered her, he couldn't die.

He opened his eyes as another breeze dried the sweat on his forehead and cheeks. It had a different scent—not the stench of the mutants or the reek of sewage. This was something else. Something he couldn't identify. It was not unpleasant. He thought of some of his other favorite smells—gasoline and Heather's perfume and the pot-pourri his mother had all around the house and the char-broiled aroma that always seemed to drift out of Burger King restaurants. His stomach growled again. God, he was hungry.

So were his opponents. He needed to get moving again.

He wondered how they had managed to live for so long down here. What else did they eat? Rats? Bugs? Did they hold captives in pens like livestock? Or worse, force their prisoners to breed and then eat the offspring like some perverted form of lamb chops? Human veal? How did the creatures subsist? They couldn't have survived just on people who blundered into the trap above. Not everyone was foolish enough to run into a condemned house and offer up his friends as a fucking buffet.

That was Tyler's fault, he thought. And then, *No. No it wasn't. Not really. It was my fault. They're dead because of me. I led them in here. I couldn't protect them. I got them killed.*

How could he have been so careless? So callous?

Realizing what was happening, Javier pushed away the thoughts. He did not have time for self-loathing. The re-criminations and guilt could come later. If he was going to escape this place, he had to get his head back in the game. He needed to stay psyched. He checked himself over, making sure that the cuts on his wrists were still clotted and not bleeding. He was satisfied with what he saw. He still needed medical attention, but he wouldn't bleed out. His swollen lip had stopped bleeding, too. He'd live.

But for how long?

Javier rose carefully from his spot behind the boulder and moved slowly toward the soft breeze. The air was mostly still, and the breeze was easily lost if he moved too quickly. He assumed it might lead to a way out. He needed to know. If so, then he'd have two choices— escape and go for help, or plunge deeper into the cata- combs, find Heather, Kerri, and Brett, and then, with the girls and Brett in tow, hope to hell he could find the exit again and get them all to safety. But what if they were still all split up? Or what if one of them had been captured? That would make things even more difficult.

The unidentifiable smell grew stronger, as did the breeze. He felt around in the darkness and soon discov- ered a new passageway. It was carefully concealed, a sim- ple wooden door that slotted into runners. The handiwork was the same as in the house above. Further exploration with his fingertips told him that the door had been cov- ered with mud to help conceal it. The breeze was drift- ing out of a gap at the top.

What's behind door number one, he wondered. *Their war- ren? Pens for their prisoners? The subway, maybe, or some stairs to the surface?*

There was only one way to find out. Working as qui- etly as possible, Javier pushed. The door slid into its recess to the right. The faint breeze grew much stronger, nearly blasting out of the open space. The mysterious scent be- came more obvious. There was water nearby, and judging by the strength of the smell, a great deal of it. Not chlori- nated, processed water, but an earthy, more primordial aroma, the way a lake smelled when you got close to it. That was exactly what it reminded him of. Brett's father had once taken Javier, Brett, and Tyler on a weekend fish- ing trip to Raystown Lake. It had smelled just like this. He wondered what lay up ahead. Runoff from the Dela- ware, perhaps, or even from the sewers—trickling down into the caverns and condensing, forming an underground pond or lake. If so, what might be lurking around that watering hole? Still, he had to go somewhere. He couldn't just stand here in the dark and wait for Scug or one of the others to find him. There were the girls to think about.

And his own survival.

Javier stepped through the threshold and slid the door closed behind him. He shuffled along the corridor for a few minutes, the fingers of one hand trailing along the wall. He heard the sound of running water, faint but distinct. Then he paused, staring with his mouth agape. He squinted in disbelief. There was a light up ahead, weak and wavering, but there just the same. He approached it cautiously, and with each step, his surroundings became clearer.

Unlike the previous area, this section was obviously manmade. He was in a wide concrete access corridor that opened into an even larger sewer tunnel. He approached the opening and stared. A thin river of water ran along the curved bottom of the larger tunnel. He was surprised by the strength of the flow. It moved swiftly, surging out of sight into the shadows at the end of the tunnel, yet, despite its speed, the river flowed quietly, almost whispering. Javier licked his parched lips and considered drinking from it. He was so thirsty.

He knelt by the river and cupped the water in his hands, sniffing it experimentally. It looked okay. Then he saw the tiny, almost invisible tadpoles squirming in it. They reminded him of sperm. Thirsty as he was, Javier had no intention of consuming tadpoles. He had no idea what they were, but guessed that they were parasites of some kind. Last thing he needed was a family of them swimming around in his intestines. Choking in disgust, he emptied his hands and wiped them on his pants. His thirst was momentarily forgotten.

Javier turned his gaze upward, searching for the source of the light, and gasped again. There were several crude dwellings above the river, each built into the upper curve of the massive concrete tunnel, pushed out from the edges like giant wasp nests, suspended over the water and clustered together with little apparent care. They were fashioned from mud and wood and other debris. He stared at the structures with a mixed sense of dread and wonder. They didn't look like they could possibly be secure in their positions, and yet they were. Above the huts were seemingly endless strings of Christmas lights. Some of them blinked and twinkled. Others burned steadily, almost ominously. They ran through the walls of the hovels and were strung over various pipes and conduits. There were also several yellowed lights that had probably been placed by the sewer system's original builders, but only a few of them still functioned and the light they gave off was feeble at best.

Javier shook his head and stepped back a pace, crouching in the shadows. There might be a way out through the sewer tunnel, but could he risk being seen by whatever might be inside the huts suspended above him?

Do I really have a choice?

He glanced back up the tunnel to the point high above where the water washed down into the area from a hole in the wall. The pipes leading up to the hole were too steep for him to climb, and covered with slime and fungus. No way could he scale them. Even if he could manage to get to the top without slipping, the hole's opening was too small for him to fit through. Javier shuddered, imagining getting stuck in the fissure, waiting for Scug, Noigel, and the other cannibals to show up and gnaw on his legs. It was possible that Kerri or Heather could fit through the opening, but even then, there was the problem of actually reaching it without falling.

He turned in the other direction and watched the river disappear into the shadows. The tunnel was dark down there. He wondered if the creatures had removed the lights on purpose, or if they'd simply burned out over time. The water had to go somewhere, true enough, but there was no promise that it was an actual escape route. What if the river plunged farther into the bowels of the earth, or what if it deposited him right into the hands of more of these things, or into some kind of sewage tank?

"Damn it."

Javier eyed the nests. If they were occupied, their inhabitants must be sleeping or oblivious to his presence. He decided to search for the girls, bring them back to this location, and then try the river. It wasn't very deep and looked easy enough to navigate. If it led them somewhere they didn't want to go, they could always wade out.

Above him, something coughed. He ducked into the shadows and watched as a shape stepped from the opening of a suspended hovel. Javier caught a quick glimpse of filthy skin, and then the creature vanished back inside. He froze, his muscles tensed, wondering if the thing had seen him. If so, it gave no indication. There was no cry of alarm. No horde of mutants came charging forward.

Breathing a sigh of relief, Javier turned and started back into the depths of the maintenance corridor, heading back the way he had come. Something squeaked in the darkness. He jumped. A small, furry form scurried along in front of him. Relief washed over him. It was just a rat. Javier grinned. His stomach growled again.

"You better get out of here, dude. If they don't eat you, I just might."

As if in response, the rat paused, turned its head toward him, and stood up on its hind legs. It batted its forepaws at him, baring its teeth. The animal's eyes glittered in the darkness.

"Go on," Javier said. "Scat!"

He stomped his foot. Instead of running, the rat charged him. Before he could move, it had sunk its teeth into his shoe. Shouting, Javier kicked it into the air. It slammed into the wall, slid to the floor, and then sprang up and ran away. Javier stood there, panting. Too late, he realized that his cry was echoing down the tunnel.

Then the echoes were answered by other cries. Behind him, a chorus of howls and screeches erupted from the nests.

"Oh, shit!"

Javier moved faster, not running—he didn't want his footfalls to give his exact location away—but jogging back toward the door. He slid it open, hurried back into the cavern, and then shut the door behind him, muffling the onrushing creatures' frantic cries. The sounds still carried, though, echoing down the corridor behind the door. Javier plunged into the darkness, arms outstretched in front of him, wondering once more how the hell he was going to find the girls and Brett under such conditions. How large was the network of basements, caverns and tunnels? How deep into the earth did they go? How far did they travel? Was it possible that he could run far enough to wind up under his home back in East Petersburg without ever surfacing?

"Shit, shit, shit . . ."

Tight bands of fear cinched around his chest and for a brief moment, Javier thought he might be having a heart attack. He stopped, bent over, and took deep breaths until the feeling had passed. Then he straightened up again and quickly took stock of his environment. Even though it was dark, he knew which direction he'd come from and where he could go, at least to a limited extent. He knew there were probably more hidden passages out there. There could be any number of camouflaged entrances to other tunnels and other nightmares. Each step in a new direction increased his chances of stumbling across one and encountering whatever lurked inside. But if he was going to succeed in finding Heather, Kerri, and Brett, then he had to risk it. They weren't in any of the places he'd already checked.

And there were things in here with him. Maybe human, maybe not. He wasn't sure anymore. But they ate humans, whatever they were.

For a brief moment, he considered just forgetting about Heather and the others, and getting out while he still could. The thought shamed him.

He heard the door creak open from somewhere behind him, followed by the soft, whispered patter of feet as his pursuers poured into the cave. He wondered how many there were. It was impossible to tell by sound. None of them spoke. Their cries had ceased the moment they entered the darkness.

Holding his breath, Javier tiptoed forward. He thought about his mother. He thought about Heather. About Kerri. About Brett and Tyler and all their other friends. He thought of his teachers and the girl he'd kissed in summer camp when he was eleven and the guy he'd punched in the nose during fourth grade. He thought of everyone he'd ever known, everyone who had ever impacted his life for good or for bad. Everyone who mattered, convincing himself once again that as long as he remembered them, he wouldn't die, because then their memories would die with him. When that didn't work anymore, his thoughts returned to Heather. He focused on her. Summoned her in his mind, saw her face, her smile, the scattering of freckles across her nose, and felt his resolve return. He needed to find her, keep her safe. He used the goal to protect himself from the panic and fear that chewed on his mind and heart.

Javier took four more paces and then heard them coming, spreading out all around him. It sounded like there were a lot of them. He heard claws on stone, the rustle of hair, snorted grunts and whispered sighs. Something panted nearby, close enough that he could feel its breath on his back. He stopped in midstride and held completely still. He knew that if he remained standing there, his chances of being discovered were almost absolute. One of the things would bump into him in the dark or smell him. Hear his breathing. Sneaking forward wouldn't work, either. They'd hear his furtive footsteps, or he'd stumble on something in the darkness and they'd fall on him before he could recover.

Steeling himself, and hoping to momentarily startle and confuse his pursuers, Javier let loose with a bellow so loud that it hurt his vocal cords, and ran straight into the blackness as fast as he could. He pushed his fears aside, shoved away visions of crashing headlong into some unseen obstruction or tumbling into some hidden hole, and charged ahead. The darkness exploded all around him with cries and howls of furious alarm. Footsteps echoed around the cavern, sounding like thunder or gunshots. Javier hoped that in all the confusion, they'd be unable to tell his sounds from their own.

A shape leapt in front of him—a human-sized black spot against the darkness. It lunged for him, and Javier slammed his elbow into its throat as he ran by. The figure grunted and fell to the ground. Javier did not pause to see if it recovered. Instead, he ran even harder. He bit down on his swollen lip, bringing a fresh flare of pain. It spurred him on. Blood filled his mouth. His pulse raced. A stitch cut into his side, twisting and searing under his ribs. He tried to ignore the pain, and focused only on fleeing and breathing. The grunting and chattering increased, but sounded like it was behind him now. He summoned his strength and put on another burst of speed.

In that moment, Javier again considered backtracking—sneaking around behind them and heading back into the sewers. Then he could follow the river and hopefully find the exit. He was ashamed once more at the thought, aghast that even for a second, he'd consider leaving the others behind.

He heard something loping along beside him. Javier dodged to the right. He saw the shadowed outlines of a curved wall in front of him, but he didn't compensate fast enough. His left shoulder scraped painfully along the rough, pitted surface and he felt his shirt tear. His skin followed suit. Javier felt a hot flare of pain, and a moment later, a warm trickle ran down his arm. He shrugged it off and plunged back into the gloom. There was no way to know how deep the scrape was or how much damage he'd done to himself, but the pain made him forget all about his plight for a second. His pursuers cried out again to remind him.

Were they closer? He couldn't tell for sure. They sounded closer, but the darkness and the cavern's structure had bizarre effects on sound. Either way, this had to end soon. He couldn't keep going on the way he was. It was either fight, hide, or die, and Javier was no longer certain he could hide without the monsters spotting him.

That only left him two choices, and one of those choices was simply unacceptable.

Javier looked over his shoulder and saw the shadowy forms behind him. They were, indeed, much closer.

He spun around and charged straight at them.

"Come on, motherfuckers!"

He couldn't tell how many he faced. Some ran, perhaps startled by his sudden attack. Others held their ground, waiting for him to come to them. A third group ran to meet him head-on, and Javier laughed aloud as they crashed into each other. He punched and kicked, knowing full well that the slightest pause or error would lead to his death. Despite the knowledge, he felt a certain peace of mind from the simple desire to hurt as many of them as he could before he went down.

If he went down.

His left fist caught one of his enemies—a female—in the side of the neck. Her breasts swayed in the darkness, brushing against him. The woman coughed violently, clutching at the spot where he'd struck. Javier barely noticed. She was merely a blur to him, a target that, once struck, was no longer important. The rest of them closed in, grasping and pushing. He shoved them away, shifted his weight and jumped high, trusting that the maneuver would throw them off guard. It did. As the creatures scattered and cried out in alarm, Javier's heel struck bone and flesh. Something broke under his shoe. His grin grew wider. The target—male or female he could not tell—slammed into three of its fellow mutants. All four fell down, sprawling.

Javier's landing was not elegant, but he kept his feet and smashed his forearm into the face of the next in line, before reversing his hips and using his leverage to drive the opposite arm's elbow into the same target. The thing did not fall, but instead grabbed Javier's arm and bit down on the exposed flesh. Javier screamed and pulled hard, yanking his arm back and leaving a wedge of flesh in the creature's mouth. He punched again, catching the cannibal's nose, which snapped under the impact. Javier's stomach churned. The pain was making him nauseous.

His next swing missed as the shadow ducked below his fist, and then shoved forward. Male, and big, apparently, as he lifted Javier from the ground and rammed him into the cave wall. Javier's body was pinned. He gritted his teeth, hissing as his opponent raked its clawed fingers across his chest and ribs, scratching and slicing with the same savagery as a rabid cat. Javier drove his knee up hard into the thing's balls, and then kneed it again as it fell backward. Javier kicked the bruiser again as he hit the ground.

Suddenly, Javier realized that the others around him had fallen back, grunting and hooting as their larger companion rolled around on the ground. Javier's eyes narrowed. He glanced down at his opponent. He wasn't as big as Noigel, but his size was still ominous. As he watched, the creature staggered and then began to right itself.

Javier paused a moment, considering the situation. His enemy was bigger, older, and much stronger. He was also influential. There was no mistaking what was occurring here. The rest of the—what? tribe? pack? whatever— were stepping back and letting the big guy take care of business. They were deferring to their leader, or at least their champion. Javier wondered where this new arrival ranked in the pecking order. Obviously, Scug was a leader of sorts. Noigel seemed feared. Who was this one, and how would the others react if he was defeated?

In the darkness, a lantern flared. Javier squinted, shielding his eyes. His opponent chuckled. Javier dropped his hand and glared. He noticed now that his opponent was naked. The beast's looks were apish, his eyes sunken into a doughy, pockmarked face beneath a thick brow. His nose was barely discernible as anything more than nostrils, and his yellowed teeth were bared in an angry leer. Javier had bested him—hurt him—and he was very obviously pissed off about it. His intent was clear. He meant to kill.

Javier had different ideas.

He spat blood on the ground and let the big guy come to him, steeling himself, trying to prepare himself mentally. The mutant charged. Despite the gloom, Javier saw that his head was low and his arms were out at his sides. This thing wasn't used to prey that fought back. It had exposed itself, made itself vulnerable in an effort to look even larger than it already was.

Javier dropped back and darted to the side, letting his opponent have the space he'd occupied a moment before. Adrenaline surged through Javier's veins, boosting another wave of strength into him. The freak spun fast, roaring, and swung his arm in a wild arc. This time Javier did not dodge, but deflected the blow, slapping it aside and pushing the thing's hand away from his body. Exposed and overbalanced, the creature stared down at his hand as if it had deliberately betrayed him. Javier grabbed his attacker's wrist and pulled him further off balance. Then he drove his foot into the mutant's chest as hard as he could. He felt the ribs break under the blow and grunted his satisfaction. The brute let out a yelp and stumbled. Javier twisted his hand until the bruiser had two choices, follow the direction Javier forced on him or risk a broken wrist. The thing yelped and moved the way Javier wanted. Javier turned him around.

"Fuck you," he spat. "Think you're king of the fucking cave cannibals?"

Javier drove his knee into the man's kidney as soon as

his back was exposed. The thing's muscles were hard, and Javier felt the reverberation run through his heel. The fighter yelped and Javier struck again, taking no chances. This time, his opponent wailed and dropped to his knees. Using both his hands, Javier pulled the mutant's arm high over his head and twisted.

The brutal face went down, slamming into the rocks. Javier landed on his foe's back, knees first, driving them as deep as he could. The creature howled and thrashed. Javier had to struggle to maintain his grip on the muscled arm. He twisted again, stopping only when he'd separated the killer's shoulder from its socket—ending the fight. Moaning, the creature shuddered once and then lay still, unconscious.

Javier seized the thing's neck. The rest of the cannibals stepped back, hooting with cautious tones. While they watched, Javier twisted his enemy's head, snapping his neck. Then he let the corpse fall and stood up slowly. The warped faces around him stared first at the dead man and then at Javier.

"Who's next?" Javier's voice was a broken croak. "Who wants it?"

He could tell that they were momentarily stunned—surprised by the unforeseen turn of events, the hunted becoming the hunter.

"Come on," he taunted. "Who wants a piece of this?"

The pack shifted nervously. One of the creatures growled, low and menacing. Javier knew that their hesitation wouldn't last much longer. He could sense them working themselves back up into a frenzy. The air felt charged. Electric. He had to take advantage of their confusion while he still could. The lantern light seemed to flare brighter.

Javier backed away slowly. He'd gone four steps when

one of the females dropped down and grabbed the corpse. Her thick fingernails hooked into his skin and ripped long, bloody lines across his abdomen. Another of the creatures knelt and did the same, rooting between his legs. Javier kept moving, understanding what was occurring. It wasn't leadership or his display of strength that had saved him just now. It was simple economics. These things weren't as smart or developed as Scug, Noigel, and some of the others he'd encountered. They were more savage. Bestial. They hunted because they were hungry, and if Javier wasn't going to eat his kills, then they would.

He turned around and limped away as fast as he could. He didn't want to run. He was afraid that the sudden movement might attract their attention again, the way a running rabbit attracted a fox or a dog. He heard the sound of flesh tearing behind him, accompanied by eager grunts and smacking lips. Given the number of creatures and the ravenous way they attacked their meal, it probably wouldn't take them too long to finish. He needed to be long gone before the hunt began again.

Once he was safely out of range, Javier began to run again, retracing his steps and heading back toward the basement—intent on finding the girls and then following the river out of these catacombs once and for all. He was beginning to fear that if they didn't leave the warrens soon, he'd become just like these creatures.

Or possibly transform into something even worse.

CHAPTER TWENTY-ONE

"Give me that damned crowbar," Perry told Leo. "We need to get this door back up before more of them come."

"You think there's more of them in here?" Dookie asked, glancing around the foyer.

"Probably. Hold that flashlight still."

"I can't," Dookie said. "My hands won't stop shaking."

"We need to find the light switch," Jamal said. "Turn them back on so we can see and shit."

"No," Perry told him, taking the crowbar from Leo. "They turned the lights off for a reason. We flick them back on again, and they'll know where we are. What we need to do is focus on getting this goddamned door open again."

He tried wedging the crowbar under the edge of the metal slab, but it wouldn't fit.

"Damn it. I wish Markus's sledgehammer hadn't been broken in that fight. Too bad none of us could lift the freak's big-ass hammer, or we could just smash the door down with it. Leo, come over here and help me with this."

Perry heard snuffling behind him. He looked over his shoulder and noticed that Leo was staring at the floor. Tears ran down the teen's cheeks.

"Leo?"

The young man glanced up at him and wiped his nose with his hand. "Sorry. What's up?"

Perry's voice softened. "Give me a hand. I'm going to push on the door. You see if you can wedge the crowbar underneath it."

Nodding, Leo took the crowbar back from him. Perry stood up, glanced down the hallways to make sure they were still alone, and then pushed on the door. His sweaty palms slid against the cool metal surface. Spreading his feet apart, Perry pushed again, trying to simultaneously shove the door backward and lift it, even just a crack. He grunted and strained, but it refused to budge. Frustrated, Perry balled his fists and punched the door with both hands. The noise rang out, vibrating through the foyer. Perry grimaced as pain shot through his hands.

"Damn it!"

"Did you break them?" Dookie asked.

"No." He turned to the teens. "Okay, we need to look around. Remember when we came in and it slid shut behind us? We all heard that sound, right? There has to be some kind of switch or mechanism around here that controls it. All we have to do is find that."

"Before they find us," Jamal added.

Perry nodded. "Right. We're not gonna split up. That would be stupid. I don't want any of you going off by yourselves. I'm guessing it's nearby, either here in the foyer or the hallways. Dookie and Jamal, you guys search the foyer. Leo and I will search the hall. If you see or hear *anything*, call out. Got it?"

They nodded. Perry and Leo stepped into the corridor, searching both sides from floor to ceiling, while Dookie and Jamal combed the foyer. Perry's nose wrinkled as he inhaled dust. He eyed the dry, yellowed wallpaper curling back from the cracked plaster. Despite the persistent damp-ness in the air, this house was a firetrap waiting to happen. All it would take is one single match.

Maybe that would be for the best, he thought. *Rid the neighborhood of this thing once and for all. It's like a scab that never heals. Just sits here at the end of the block, all ugly and infected.*

"You see anything?"

"No," Leo whispered, his tone maudlin. "Just spider-webs, rat shit, and mold. It would help if I knew what we were looking for. Know what I'm saying?"

"I don't know what we're looking for. A switch of some kind. Could be hidden, or it could be something simple. There has to be some kind of trigger mechanism to raise and lower the trapdoor. We'll know it when we see it."

"Mr. Watkins?"

"Hmmm?"

"Those white kids are probably dead, aren't they?"

Perry paused before answering. "I don't know, Leo. It's certainly not looking good for them, though."

"We're gonna die in here, too, aren't we? Just like Markus and Chris."

"You just stop that kind of talk right now. I'm gonna get us out of here. Believe it."

"Yeah," Leo replied.

Perry heard the doubt and resignation in the teen's voice, and it broke his heart. His thoughts turned to Lawanda and the kids they'd never had.

And then a series of sharp, high-pitched screams echoed down the corridor.

"Shit . . ."

Leo turned ashen. "That's Jamal and Dookie!"

"Come on!"

Perry charged down the hall, his footsteps thundering. Leo ran along behind him. They barged into the foyer, but it was empty. Leo began opening doors, frantically looking in the vacant rooms.

"Dookie," Perry hollered. "Jamal! Where are you?"

More screams drifted down from upstairs.

"Oh Jesus . . . what the hell are they doing up there?"

He leaped up the stairs, taking them two at a time. Leo ran along right behind him. The stairs creaked and cracked beneath their feet and the worm-eaten banister trembled at their passage, but neither Perry nor Leo slowed. As they reached the second floor, they heard Dookie shriek again. Jamal was strangely silent. Another long hallway stretched out before them. Both sides were lined with doors—some open and others closed. The floor was covered with a frayed, mildew-stained, burgundy carpet. Dookie's flashlight beam winked at them from the end of the hall. They ran toward it and found him standing outside an open door. Dookie was pulling his own hair with one hand. His other hand waved the flashlight around in wide, excited arcs. His eyes bulged and his mouth was open in shock. He gasped for breath, preparing to scream again when Perry and Leo reached him. Perry grabbed his flailing arm and Dookie, shrieked, clubbing him repeatedly on the head and shoulders with the flashlight.

"Ow! Stop it. Dookie, it's us. It's Mr. Watkins and Leo! What's wrong? Where's Jamal?"

Dookie wrapped his arms around the older man and squeezed tight, burying his face in Perry's chest. When he tried to speak, all that came out was a muffled sob. He shuddered against Perry.

"Dookie," Perry tried again, "where's Jamal?"

Still not looking up, Dookie pointed through the open door with the flashlight. Perry and Leo glanced at each other. Then Leo peeked through the open door. He didn't speak. Didn't move. He suddenly seemed frozen in place.

Perry could tell by his stance that something was terribly wrong. Gently disentangling himself from Dookie, he crept up behind Leo and looked inside the room.

At first, Perry didn't understand what he was seeing. It came to him in bits and pieces. Jamal was levitating several feet off the floor with his back against the wall. There was a large sheet of plywood holding him in place. A length of thick rope had been attached to the plywood, suspending it from the ceiling. Perry followed the rope to the point where it disappeared into the darkness above. Then he glanced back down at Jamal. The teen hung there, pinned against the wall, silent and still. There was blood on the edges of the plywood. Blood on the wall behind Jamal. Blood pooling on the floor at his feet.

"Oh," Perry whispered. "Oh . . . Jesus."

He crept closer, and with slowly dawning horror, Perry realized what had happened. Someone had driven an assortment of kitchen knives, broken pipes, jagged shards of hard plastic, and rusty iron spikes into the plywood. Then they had winched it up in the ceiling. Somehow, Jamal had triggered the device when he entered the room. And, Perry assumed, since they'd heard both Jamal and Dookie screaming originally, the trap hadn't killed Jamal immediately.

"Those motherfuckers," he muttered. "Those sick motherfuckers."

Not holding much hope, he stumbled over to Jamal, reached up, and checked the unmoving teen's pulse. It was as still as the house.

"Is he?" Leo asked.

Perry nodded. "I'm afraid so."

"I tried to stop him," Dookie sobbed. "I told him to stay downstairs, but he figured there might be a light switch up here. Then he decided that maybe we could try one of the windows."

"They're bricked up," Perry choked. "Why would he—"

"But they're not, Mr. Watkins." Dookie pointed with the flashlight. "Look."

Perry swiveled his head, following the beam of light across the room. There were two windows in the wall. Both were barricaded with thick sheets of moldering plywood, but unlike the downstairs windows, they hadn't been bricked over. He glanced down at the floor. The half-rotten floorboards were covered with a thick layer of dust and dead insects. The only signs of disturbance were their own footprints and Jamal's blood, spreading out in a pool. Obviously, the room hadn't been entered in a long time. With the pervasive dampness in the air, it was possible that the plywood had weakened somewhat, and if so, whoever had boarded up the windows in the first place hadn't checked them lately.

Fingers crossed, Perry strode across the floor and tapped on the plywood sheet covering one window. It was solid. He checked the second window. The plywood covering this one was streaked with mildew and mold, and moist to the touch. Holding his breath, he shoved the sharp edge of the crowbar against it. The blade sank into the wood easily enough.

Perry started to cry. He turned to Leo and Dookie, tears of relief streaming down his dirty cheeks.

"It's rotten. Not all the way, but enough that I think I can get it off."

They stared at him blankly, as if not understanding what he was saying.

"We can get out," Perry whispered. "Through the window. Come here, boys. Quickly now."

Dookie's stunned expression crumbled, replaced by one of numb disbelief. Leo seemed unsure, as well. But they did as he asked and crossed toward him. They stood there, arms at their sides, looking at everything but Jamal.

Perry jammed the crowbar between the barrier and the wall, and wiggled it back and forth. A small chunk of wood broke off, splintering. He let it fall to the floor and pried off a bigger piece about the size of his fist. Grinning, he attacked it with abandon, no longer caring if he made any sound. They'd be free in minutes.

He'd cleared about half the plywood away, exposing a little less than half of the window before hitting solid wood. After that, his progress became harder. Because of how it had been constructed, Perry found it difficult to get any leverage. He began to grow winded.

"Damn it."

"What's wrong?" Leo asked. "Why'd you stop?"

"The rest of it is solid," Perry gasped. "I can't get it loose."

He wiped sweat from his brow and studied them both for a moment. Then he turned around and tried unlocking the window hasp. It was rusted into place and wouldn't move. Instead, Perry smashed the glass out of the portion of the window that they could see. Immediately, a cool breeze washed over them. To Perry, it was one of the most pleasurable sensations he'd ever experienced. He turned back around again. Leo and Dookie's expressions were terrified.

"Somebody's gonna hear that glass breaking," Leo scolded. "You'll lead them right to us."

"I know," Perry said. "That's why we've got to do this quickly. Dookie, you're the only one skinny enough to fit through that window. Go for help."

"You're fucking tripping, Mr. Watkins."

"Don't you get smart with me, boy."

"Who you calling boy?"

"We don't have time to argue, Dookie. Get out that fucking window and go for help. The police must have arrived by now."

"Don't be so sure," Leo said.

Perry sighed, exasperated. "If they haven't, then tell my wife what's happened. Tell her to call 911 again and stay on the line with them until somebody comes. She's got to make them send somebody. And then, while she's doing that, you start banging on doors and waking people up."

"And tell them what?"

"Tell them that we're fucking trapped in here with a bunch of psychos. Tell them to get their torches and pitchforks, just like in those old monster movies, and bash that fucking door in! Now get going, Dookie."

Still wide-eyed and stunned, the nervous teen peered out the window. Then, swallowing hard, he nodded.

"Okay. I'll do it."

"You're damn right you will," Perry grumbled. "Just hurry. And be careful. You won't do us much good if you break your neck on the way down."

"I'm on it, yo." Confidence crept back into Dookie's voice. "Don't worry about a thing."

Perry and Leo hoisted him up and helped him through the hole. They watched his head disappear, then his shoulders and chest, and then the rest of him, until finally, Dookie was outside on the arched roof. He turned around, pressed one hand to the remaining glass, and then crawled away. They watched him leave until the darkness ultimately swallowed him.

"Think he'll make it?" Leo whispered.

"He damn well better," Perry muttered. "Now let's get back downstairs and find someplace to hide, before any more of them show up."

They left the room and slowly made their way back down the hall to the top of the stairs, listening as they proceeded. There was no sign that Jamal's death or Dookie's escape had attracted any more attention. The house was utterly silent, as if holding its breath.

As they started down the stairs, Perry wondered what would happen when it exhaled. What would come crawling out of the woodwork looking for them?

CHAPTER TWENTY-TWO

There was nowhere left for her to go.

Kerri had searched, trying to find an exit from the endless, confusing network of tunnels, but with the darkness and the predators haunting her every step, finding one had been impossible. And so, in the long run, she chose to go for the only exit that she was sure existed. An unreasonable exit, but a way out all the same. She chose to return upstairs, to the house where everything had started, and hope that she could find a way past the barricaded entrance and the traps and the wooden walls that had appeared from nowhere. She had no idea what had happened to Heather and Javier, but she feared that they were dead. If they were alive, she reasoned, then she'd still hear them screaming.

Her legs shook with exhaustion. The scratches and cuts on her body ached. She felt feverish, and her mouth was parched. Miserable and numb, Kerri shuffled onward. Her heart seemed to echo in her chest as if she'd been hollowed out. And in a way, maybe she had been. She'd seen her boyfriend and her friends slaughtered tonight, and in return, she'd killed and survived. There was no way she'd ever be able to return to the life she'd had before the concert. That life was dead. That old

Kerri was dead, lying on the floor alongside Tyler and Steph with her brains bashed out.

She would survive, yes, but could she live with her survival? That was the question Kerri considered as she moved along cautiously, listening for sounds of pursuit or any possible hint that her friends were still alive. Instead, the caves were unsettlingly quiet.

Kerri emerged from a tunnel and after a moment, she recognized the landscape. She was back in the cavern that connected to the basement. She breathed a sigh of relief. It looked and sounded deserted. The rest of the killers must be searching for her deeper in the catacombs. All she had to do now was make it upstairs and then find a way outside. And if she couldn't do that—

—well, if she couldn't do that, she'd return to the room on the first floor where she and Javier had originally hidden. That was a safe place. The freaks hadn't found them there. She'd go back to that room, curl up in the darkness, and just go to sleep for a little while. When she woke up again, things would be better. She'd be able to think clearer.

Smiling at the prospect, Kerri began softly humming the beat of a song from the concert they'd seen earlier in the evening. She crossed the cavern, not bothering to be furtive or cautious. Nothing could touch her now. She had a hiding place in mind, and she'd be okay.

It wasn't until her humming turned into quiet giggles, that Kerri realized what she was doing. Stifling herself, she shook her head, trying to clear it. A new wave of terror washed over her. Was she crazy? Had she snapped? Or was this just some kind of delayed shock—a bizarre reaction to the pressure of the situation? Kerri became aware that she was trembling and that her arms were wrapped around her shoulders, squeezing tightly.

She'd twirled her hair with her fingers and then chewed on it, the way she'd done when she was a little girl. She forced herself to stop it and tried to shake the dread threatening to overwhelm her.

I'm losing it, she thought. *I'm really losing it. Got to get a grip on myself, or I might as well just give up now and lie down right here.*

She straightened up and started walking again. Her hand trailed over the wall, partly for guidance and partly for comfort. A prayer came to mind, and she opened her mouth to recite it. Then she crushed it instead, before it could form. If the Lord existed, then He had a lot to answer for, as far as Kerri was concerned. She would never forgive the people—things—who had killed her friends, and she would not allow herself to forgive God either. Just because He'd written the rules, that didn't mean He got to break them. Some sins were inexcusable. What He'd allowed to happen to them tonight was at the top of the list.

Kerri reached the cellar without incident, emerging into it from a large crack in the wall. Red clay squished between her fingers as she entered the dank room. She wiped her hands on her pants, glancing down as she did so. When she looked up again, there was a figure standing in front of her.

Kerri screamed, and the figure rushed toward her and clamped its hand over her mouth. Its palm was coated with dirt and dried blood, as was the rest of its body. It wore clothing, but the garments were almost invisible beneath the grime and gore. So were its facial features. She didn't recognize Javier until he spoke, and even then she wasn't sure.

"K-kerri?"

His voice was strained and hoarse. Kerri struggled

against him, and he pressed his hand tighter against her mouth.

"Sssshhhh. Kerri, don't! It's me. It's me, Kerri. Javier."

She stopped resisting and let her body go slack. Javier slowly removed his hand from her mouth, and Kerri stared at him, gasping. She took one faltering step backward.

"It's me," he whispered again, holding up his hands in reassurance. "Are you okay?"

"Oh my God . . . Javier?"

"Yeah, it's me. It's really me."

"Holy shit. I can't believe . . ."

She ran to him and wrapped her arms around him, ignoring the blood and filth. She squeezed him tightly, and Javier returned the gesture. Neither of them broke the embrace.

"Are you okay?" he asked again.

Kerri nodded against his chest. "Yeah. Cuts and scratches, mostly. I almost got . . ." She tried to say *raped*, but the word got stuck in her throat. "I'm okay. What about you? All that blood!"

"Most of it isn't mine."

"But your wrists. Jesus Christ, that looks really bad, Javier."

"They're fine. I'm fine. They've clotted now. Soon as we get out of here, I'll go to the hospital and get some disinfectant and a few stitches and be good to go."

Kerri's spirits soared, and her head cleared. "Did you find a way out?"

"Yeah. I was looking for you guys in areas that I hadn't been to yet, but then I got the idea to come back up here, thinking that maybe one of you had circled back around or hid her all along. But, yeah, I found a way out. There's a sewer tunnel. These things living down here hacked their way into it. It's got a little river running through it. We can follow the water, after we find Heather and Brett."

"Is it far?"

"Bit of a hike, but I remember the way. Have you seen the others?"

"Well . . . Brett's dead."

"Oh, shit. Are you sure?"

Kerri nodded, wiping her eyes. "Pretty sure. That thing, Noigel—the one who killed Steph and Tyler—had Brett when we all ran away. He smashed Brett against the wall right below the basement stairs. Brett stopped screaming after that."

"Goddamn it."

"Yeah. I should have . . . I should have helped him, but I couldn't."

"It's okay." Javier smoothed her hair. "What about Heather? She's got to be okay. Have you seen her?"

"No. Not since we all got split up."

"She's right here," said a voice in the darkness.

Startled, Kerri and Javier broke their embrace and glanced frantically into the gloom. The voice was distinct. Rough and gravely.

"Scug," Javier said. "You sick fuck."

Chuckling, Scug stepped out of the shadows, carrying Heather's decapitated head in one hand. Her glazed eyes stared sightlessly. Her mouth was open, as if begging for help. One of her cheeks had been torn so that it hung down in a flap of loose skin. Her cheeks were the color of bruised fruit. Strands of tissue dangled down from her mangled neck.

Javier closed his eyes and sighed. Kerri's hands went to her face. Her fingernails dug into her cheeks as she stared at her friend's head in horror.

"So you two recognize her then?" Scug asked. "Good.

That's real good. Had a hell of a time getting her head back from the rest of the garbage. They wanted her for themselves, you know? But that's how the trash are. Greedy little bastards. That's why we keep them down there. By the time I got to her, this was all that was left. Damn shame, really. I was going to use the rest of her, too. Ain't got any use for just her head, except to maybe put it on the end of my pecker and dance around a little. Maybe fuck the neck hole. What do you say there, lover boy? Want to give her one last go?"

"Fuck you." Javier's voice was thick with grief, barely a whisper.

Scug laughed. "Not so tough without your little belt, huh? You've caused us a lot of trouble tonight. Don't know how you got away. You were supposed to be skinned and gutted by now."

"Shit happens." Javier stepped between Kerri and Scug, putting Kerri behind him. "That's always sort of been my philosophy. You and your sick friends really put it to the fucking test tonight, though. Anyway, yeah, I escaped. Sorry to disappoint you. I killed your two nasty-ass girl-friends, though, before I got away. They died slow."

Scug shrugged. "Plenty more where they come from. I may even have a turn with the little miss standing there behind you."

"Not tonight, you won't. You'll have to go through me."

"I'm gonna go through you anyway, boy. Gonna slit your belly open and pull out your guts and show them to you. Then I'm gonna squeeze the shit out of them and smear it all over you before you die."

"Kerri." Javier kept his voice calm and level. "Run for the stairs. Don't stop."

"But you said the river—"

"You'll never find it yourself. Now get going. I've got him."

"Javier, you can't!"

"Do you see what he has in his hand?" Javier exploded. "Go, goddamn it!"

Kerri turned and ran. When she glanced back, Scug and Javier were still facing one another. She dashed on, and when she turned around again, both men had been lost in the darkness. She looked for the stairs and found them. Panicked, she didn't see Brett's corpse until she tripped over it. Kerri went sprawling across the stone floor, scraping the skin on her knees and elbows. Crying, she glanced over at what was left of her friend. His skull had been cracked in half and it looked like something big and round had drilled into what was left of his brains. Both of his eyeballs were missing, and the bloody sockets had been split and widened, as if whatever had been stuck in his brain had been inserted into them, as well.

Retching and sobbing, Kerri stumbled to her feet and fled for the stairs. When she opened her mouth to breathe, a scream slipped out. It echoed through the chamber long after she was gone.

"She won't get far," Scug said.

"We'll see about that. She might surprise you."

"Doubt it. Noigel's upstairs, dealing with some more guests. He likes the ladies, Noigel does. Of course, he likes the boys, too. Hell, he likes anything he can stick his pecker in, long as it's dead first."

"You're a twisted bag of shit, aren't you?" Javier shook his head in disgust.

"Here," Scug said. "Have a go."

He tossed Heather's head at Javier. He flinched as it slammed into his chest, recoiling in horror and disbelief.

The head thumped onto the floor and rolled away, leaving a wet stain. A part of him was disgusted, and he immediately felt ashamed for that reaction. How many times had they made love in his car or at her parents' house or at his house when his mother wasn't home? Or that one time backstage after the school play? She'd been so warm. Smelled so good. Felt so soft. Now the girl he loved had been reduced to this. Turning away from her, Javier glared at Scug. His hands curled into fists. His lips felt swollen and his ears and cheeks burned.

"Good," Scug teased. "That's good. Get all mad now. Think you can take me?"

"It's just you and me, you sick fuck. Your little mutants aren't here to help you."

Scug wagged his index finger in the air and then whistled. The darkness came alive with rustling shadows. One by one, more of the freaks stumbled, slithered, and loped into sight, slowly surrounding Javier. Some carried flashlights and lanterns. Several more had weapons—everything from crude stone clubs to expensive cutlery. They circled him, snarling like a pack of dogs.

Scug grinned. "What's that you were saying?"

"Pussy." Javier tried to sound unafraid. "You scared to fight your own battles?"

"If I was going to eat you by myself, then yeah, you'd be my kill. But I think the rest of my family would like a piece of you. And besides, I don't want to mess up my clothes."

Smiling, Scug ran his hands over the tanned human hide he was wearing, as if smoothing out the wrinkles.

Adopting a ready stance, Javier studied his opponents. These were not the same as the others he'd seen. He could tell that immediately. They were malformed, yes, but they seemed more symmetrical, more balanced.

More normal. One edged closer to him. It was sleek and muscular, with a broad jaw line and a wide mouth filled with teeth. The eyes were spaced too far apart and had no whites at all, but only the massive dark pupils.

"Sic him, boy," Scug said. "And some of the rest of you get upstairs and help Noigel. Tell him I want her skin, so he's not to fuck it up. It's been a long night, and I'm getting tired."

The thing with the dark eyes closed the gap. It did not growl as it came toward him. It roared, the sound of its voice blasting around the cellar as it charged. The rest of the creatures shouted in response.

Javier acted purely on instinct, and that simple reflex saved his life. He dropped back as the mutant attacked, and kicked the slavering thing in the stomach. It slammed into the wall and then shook off the blow, prepared to attack again. Before Javier could react, a second cannibal came for him. Sharp teeth ripped into his thigh, slicing through the heavy denim of his jeans and into the skin and muscle beneath with appalling ease. Javier jabbed his elbow down and struck the back of the monster's head. It was like striking stone. His elbow thrummed from the impact.

A third creature attacked, even as the second gnawed his leg like a dog with a rawhide bone. Javier threw up his arm to block it, but thick fingernails cut into his forearm. The strike happened so fast that for a moment he thought it had missed. Then the deep gashes started to bleed. The pain followed a second later—hot and nauseating.

Javier dislodged the thing gnawing on his leg, bringing more agony as he did so. He backed up to give himself room and immediately realized his mistake. In stepping away from his attackers, he'd moved closer to the rest of the things.

They seized him as one. Powerful teeth clamped down on Javier's shoulder. Claws lashed across his face, running lines of fire over his lips and nose, flaying his mouth open, cutting into his gums and fragmenting his teeth in one savage stroke. He managed to reach out with his fingers and return the favor, slashing across the deep set eyes of the beast. Javier bared his ruined teeth in a grimace as the fangs in his shoulder dug deeper, pressing together deep inside the meat of his arm and drawing a thick spray of blood. More teeth sank into his thigh, his waist, and his breast. Something cold and jagged and sharp pierced his buttocks. He tried to scream, but there was something wrong with his throat. Blood spilled into Javier's eyes, blinding him. He shook his head from side to side in an effort to see.

His vision cleared in time to see a creature with a wide, hinged mouth lunge forward. He'd never seen so many teeth in a mouth before—multiple rows, all jagged and sharp. The thing snapped its massive jaws shut around his face. Javier jittered and thrashed as the mutant broke bones and pulped his jaw and forehead, carving a massive trench down the front of his skull.

He had time to think one last thought before he died.
Wait for me, Heather. I'm coming. I'm—

CHAPTER TWENTY-THREE

Leo and Perry reached the foyer and huddled together in front of the metal door, waiting for Dookie to return with help or for more of the house's weird inhabitants to show up. Leo prayed for the former but was dreadfully certain it would be the latter. So when a door suddenly opened and a female figure stumbled out of the darkness, he leaped to his feet, ready to fight. Mr. Watkins sprang up beside him a second later, an unlit cigarette tumbling from his open mouth. Both men yelled in surprise and fright.

So did the girl.

They stared at each other. Leo frowned and blinked, trying to understand what he was seeing. She was dressed like one of the kids that had run away from him earlier in the evening, but she couldn't be one of them. The girls in that group had all been white. This girl was red. Scarlet. She was covered in blood from head to toe. It matted her hair and crusted on her cheeks and stained her clothes, and although he could see some superficial wounds on her arms and face, Leo was fairly certain that most of the blood wasn't hers. Leo shook his head slowly, and reached out a hand.

"Hey. Are you okay?"

The terrified girl jumped at the sound of his voice and

shrank away from them, cowering against the wall. She whimpered, but did not speak.

"It's okay," Leo murmured. "We ain't gonna hurt you. We're stuck in here, just like you are."

"Are you hurt?" Mr. Watkins asked her.

She stared at them, wide-eyed, but still refused to speak. Her chin trembled.

"Where are your friends?" Leo asked. "Them kids who ran in here with you? Are they okay? Do they need help?"

The girl flinched as if slapped. Then she opened her mouth and moaned. It was the most heartbreaking sound Leo had ever heard.

"Sssshhh," he whispered. "Don't do that, now. You'll lead them right to us. We need to be quiet and shit."

"Help is on the way," Mr. Watkins explained. "Somebody went for help. They should be here any minute."

As if in verification, they heard muffled voices from the other side of the door. It sounded like there was quite a large crowd outside. A moment later, Dookie yelled to them.

"Yo! Leo? Mr. Watkins? You alright?"

"Yeah," Leo called as loudly as he dared. "We're fine. Just get us the fuck out of here, dog. And hurry!"

"I got everybody out here. Angel and the crew and Mrs. Watkins and—"

"Dookie," Mr. Watkins yelled, "I don't care if you got all of Blackwater out there, along with a Navy SEAL team. Just get us the hell out of here. Now!"

"Get back from the door," Dookie shouted. "Angel's got a blowtorch!"

The men backed away. The girl hesitated, her eyes darting from them to the door and then back to them again. After a moment, she stepped toward them.

"That's it," Leo urged. "We ain't gonna hurt you. What happened earlier was just a misunderstanding. It's all gonna be okay now."

Through the steel barrier came the hissing and spitting sound of the cutting torch. Within minutes, the smell of scorched metal filled the air. Then they heard something else. Footsteps.

From inside the house.

A lot of them, judging by the sound.

"Oh, shit," Leo yelled. "Hurry up, y'all! We got company!"

"Quiet," Mr. Watkins said. "They'll hear you."

"They'll hear us anyway," Leo countered. "You telling me they ain't gonna hear the others outside or smell that blowtorch?"

"Coming in," Dookie called. "Just hang on!"

There was a great commotion as the men outside on the porch grunted and jostled and shouted orders to one another. Then, slowly, the metal door was hauled away, revealing dozens of faces peering in at them in shock and concern. Dookie stood at the front of the crowd, arms crossed over his chest defiantly.

"Told you I could do this shit," he said, grinning.

Leo and Mr. Watkins hurried forward. The bloody girl limped along between them. They hovered in the doorway, shrugging off the multitude of hands that reached for them.

"Damn," Leo said. "The whole neighborhood is here."

"Seems that way," Mr. Watkins agreed, grinning as he spotted his wife amidst the throng.

Dookie's eyes widened when he saw the bloodstained girl. "Are her friends still in there?"

"We don't know," Leo said. "She ain't talking. I think

she's in shock or something. Way she's acting though, I'm betting that they're all dead."

Behind them, the pounding footsteps thundered closer, seeming to come from all directions and behind every door. The walls and floorboards vibrated with the sound. Dust drifted down from overhead. The lights swayed.

Mr. Watkins snapped his fingers in front of the girl's eyes and got her attention. She stared at him blankly.

"Are the rest of your friends alive?"

She blinked at him. Mr. Watkins glanced at Leo, frowned, and then looked back at the girl.

"Listen to me, girl! Are any of your friends still in there?"

She shrugged almost imperceptibly and whimpered, low and mournful.

Mr. Watkins turned to Leo. "Take her outside and get her some help."

Leo flinched. "What are you gonna do?"

"I'm gonna do what somebody should have done years ago. I'm gonna finish this place once and for all."

"Are you crazy? They're coming."

"Do as I say, now, Leo. Get her to safety. It's time to start cleaning this neighborhood up."

The crowd parted, allowing Leo and the injured girl to get through. People gasped when they saw her condition. Most of the assembled throng followed along behind them, shouting questions. Perry shook hands with Angel, the chop shop owner.

"Thanks. Glad you brought that cutting torch along."

"Don't mention it. What the fuck is going on, Mr. Watkins?"

"Can I bum a smoke off you first?"

Sirens wailed in the distance. The mechanic fumbled

out a crumpled pack of cigarettes and handed one to Perry. He popped it into his mouth, unlit. The sirens drew closer. So did the commotion from inside the house. The hurried footsteps were accompanied by a chorus of howls and grunts now. Perry saw Dookie shudder at the sound.

"The police finally decided to show up?" Perry asked him.

The teen nodded nervously, his eyes flicking over Perry's shoulder. "Yeah, they said they were on the way. We'd best go, Mr. Watkins. Don't you think?"

Angel frowned at the increasingly louder noises coming from inside the house. "What the hell is that?"

"Call 911." Perry took the blowtorch from the chop shop owner's hands and stepped back into the house. "Tell them we're gonna need the fire department, too."

Perry adjusted the flame so that it was low, and lit his cigarette with it. He closed his eyes and inhaled.

"Ah, that's good."

"Are you fucking crazy?" Dookie shouted. "Get the fuck out of there, Mr. Watkins."

Perry ignored him. "Go do what I said. Call 911 now. Get some fire trucks down here."

Without another word, he turned the sputtering blue flame up high and touched it to the walls. As he'd suspected, they went up quickly, despite the pervasive dampness.

Perry tried not to think about the other missing kids. Judging from the girl's condition, they were probably dead. Most likely they'd been slaughtered the same way Markus, Chris, and Jamal had been.

"They've got to be dead," he whispered around the cigarette. "They've just got to be."

He repeated it to himself over and over again, trying

to assuage his conscience. This had to be done. How many years had this place been a blight on the neighborhood, spreading its poisonous roots through concrete and steel? How many people had gone missing in here over the years? It had to end. If the kids were alive—and he doubted very much that was the case—then they'd be the last victims the house ever claimed.

Perry bent over and applied the torch to the carpet and floor, feeling a serene sense of peace as the bloodstained floorboards blackened and smoked, then erupted into flame. Thick smoke curled toward him. The fire grew louder, drowning out the footsteps and growls. Perry caught a glimpse of something on the upstairs landing—a diminutive, naked figure, horribly deformed. Then the smoke obscured it. He stepped back and ran the blowtorch all around the front door's splintered frame. Then, finished, he handed the torch back to Angel and Dookie and hurried them down the porch.

"Thought I told you to go call the fire department. I guess it doesn't matter, though. Maybe we should just let it burn down into the ground first. Then we'll call."

Angel stared, dumfounded. Dookie shook his head and grinned.

"You are one badass motherfucker, Mr. Watkins."

"Thank you. And watch your mouth, son. No need to talk about my mother."

Only when they'd reached the street and he was holding Lawanda in his arms did Perry turn around. The open doorway was choked with thick, black and white smoke, and already the blaze was flickering higher, touching the roof overhanging the porch and climbing toward the second story. Within minutes, he expected the entire structure would be engulfed in flames.

He thought he saw several deformed shadows in the

doorway, dim against the swirling clouds of smoke, but when he looked again, they were gone.

Perry guided Lawanda and Dookie through the crowd, refusing to answer anyone's questions, including his wife's. When they reached Leo and the girl, the five of them looked back at the inferno.

"You set it on fire?" Leo asked. "Ain't the cops gonna know it was you, Mr. Watkins? All these people saw you do it."

"Maybe," Perry said, smiling sadly. "But I suspect they'll keep it to themselves. That's the way things are down here."

"True that," Dookie agreed. "And besides, ain't nobody here gonna be sad to see that place gone."

"If they ask," Perry said, "I'll just tell them that I don't know who started the fire. We'll blame it on one of the killers. After all, the place was old and rotten. A real firetrap."

"Yeah," Leo said. "That's true."

"You know what they say," Dookie chuckled. "Shit happens."

Then the girl standing next to Leo stiffened and began to scream.

She was still shrieking when the police and paramedics arrived.

Turn the page for an early look at
Brian Keene's next terrifying novel

DARKNESS ON THE EDGE OF TOWN

Coming from Leisure Books
February 2010

CHAPTER ONE

In the beginning . . .

That's how stories always start, right? I guess mine should, too.

In the beginning was the word. I know this because the Bible tells me so. The Bible tells me a lot of things. It says that Jesus loves me, that you shouldn't suffer a witch to live, and in the beginning was the word.

Words have power. So do names.

This is important stuff, so remember it. Names. Words. Witches. I'll come back to all of this later, if there's time. Who knows? It just might save your life. I wouldn't have believed that a month ago, but I do now. Things have changed.

My name is Robbie Higgins. There. Now you have power over me. It's Rob or Robbie to my friends. Robert to the cops or my teachers or anyone else who has ever hassled me.

Anyway, in the beginning was the word, and it existed alone in the darkness. The Bible tells us that, too—tells us about the darkness. And this wasn't just regular darkness, either. No, sir. This was the complete and total absence of light—a darkness so deep and dense that it would have made your eyes hurt. A heavy darkness. Thick. At least, that's how I imagine it was. I mean, I can look out my window for inspiration and see the darkness pretty fucking clearly. I can't see much of anything else, but I can see the darkness.

According to the Bible, here's how it all went down. You've got the word and the darkness and not much else. The two of them are just sort of hanging out together. The word and the darkness, chilling together in the void. And then the word says, "Let there be Light," and there was. And things continued just fine after that, for the most part.

Then, millennia later, some asshole comes along and fucks it all up. Someone else says another word, maybe a bad word or a different word, maybe, "Let there be Darkness again," and in doing so, effectively reverses the entire act of Creation—erasing the light. No, not just erasing it. Obliterating it. The light is fucking gone, man. Light doesn't exist anymore.

And who knows? Maybe we don't either.

Christy says that we're all dead. That's her theory, anyway. She says it explains everything—why the phones don't work, why there's no electricity, no contact with the outside world, no television or radio signals, why we can't see anything out there beyond the darkness, and most importantly, why nobody new has come into town since it all began and why none of the people who went out into the darkness have returned. Christy says that we're all dead and this is limbo. Purgatory. We can't move on to Heaven or Hell, because we're trapped here. Stranded. According to Christy, this is why ghosts always hang around the place where they died—because the darkness prevents them from leaving.

The problem is, Christy does a lot of drugs—or did, up until she ran out of them—so her conclusions are kind of suspect. Now, don't get me wrong. She wasn't into the hard stuff. She never did heroin or meth or anything like that. She just loved smoking weed and enjoyed the occasional line of coke or a tab of Ecstasy. So did I, truth be told. In any case, my point is this. Scientific method is not Christy's strong suit. But I love her anyway—and not just because she's got a great set of tits. Before the darkness, she made me smile every day. She made me happy. For guys like me, that's rarer than you might think.

Christy's wrong. We're not dead. I know this because dead people don't die. And every single person who has left town since the darkness descended, every single one of us who ventured out into that black space, has ended up dead. You can't die if you're already dead. So, that means they weren't dead and they weren't ghosts. They didn't die or become a ghost until *after* they left town.

Of course, Christy disagrees with me. She says I'm just speculating. Well, fuck that noise. I *know*, man.

I know.

Sure, I didn't see them die. Not personally. I mean, you can't see anything beyond the barrier. But I *heard* them. Heard them die. I heard their screams.

And the other sounds. The sounds the darkness makes.

Sometimes it whispers. If you stand too close to it, right there on the edge where the candlelight is swallowed by shadow, the darkness talks to you in a voice not its own—a voice you've probably heard before. A lover. A parent. A friend.

Ghosts.

But the darkness does a lot more than just talk. If chattering was all it did, we could just put cotton in our ears and be done with it.

The darkness bites. The darkness has teeth—sharp, obsidian fangs you can't see. But they're there just the same. The darkness has teeth and it's waiting to chew us up until there's nothing left. The darkness kills us if we venture out into it, and if it can do that, then we ain't fucking dead.

Therefore, the darkness is alive, and so are we.

We don't try to leave town anymore. Nobody does. But staying here has become a problem, too, because this town has gotten teeth of its own. The darkness is getting inside of us now, and the results aren't pretty.

We have a plan—me, Christy, and Russ. I'm a little apprehensive about it because the last time I came up with a plan a lot of people ended up dead as a result of it, and I became sort of a pariah afterward. That was early on in the siege. I've avoided trying to be a leader since then. But the three of us came up with this new idea today. It's not necessarily a good plan and it probably won't work, but our options are pretty fucking limited at this point. We came up with the plan after what happened with poor Dez. That was the last straw—the final indication that things will not be returning to normal. Game fucking over, man.

Anyway, we'll be leaving soon, but before we do, I figured maybe I should leave some kind of record. An accounting, just in case. So I'm writing it all down in this notebook, and I'll leave it here before we take off. I guess I should tell you about everything that led up to this. Tell the entire story from the beginning.

Names. Words. Witches.

Darkness.

In the beginning . . .

CHAPTER TWO

I'm not sure how long we've been here because I quit looking at calendars a long time ago, and my cell phone won't give me the date—or anything else. The battery is dead and I've got no way to charge it. Before the battery died, I'd occasionally flip the phone open and scroll through my contacts and try calling people, but it never worked. There was no recorded message telling me their numbers were out of service or one of those short beeps you get when the cell phone you're calling from is out of range of a tower. The phone didn't even ring. Each time I tried, it was like placing a phone call to the afterlife. All I heard was the sound of nothing.

Judging by the length of my beard and hair, I'm guessing we've been trapped here for about a month, give or take a few days. I'd never had a beard before. I hated the way it felt after a few weeks—itchy and tight, and all those little ingrown hair bumps that popped up beneath it, red and swollen and full of pus. But I'm too lazy to boil water, and shaving without hot water is a fucking pain in the ass. Plus, some dickhead looted all the shaving cream from both the grocery store and the convenience store. Then, not satisfied with that, they took the shaving cream from all of the abandoned houses. Who does that? Food, batteries, and water I can understand. Hell, we took stuff, too. But in our case, it was stuff that we needed. Who takes all of the fucking shaving cream? And so methodically, too. Taking the time to go house to house and abscond with it? I mean, that's just crazy.

But there are crazy people everywhere these days, and stealing shaving cream is the least of their bizarre behavior.

Anyway, I guess it doesn't really matter how long we've been here. All that matters is how this all began and what's happened since then.

What happened was this. Early one Wednesday morning in late September, me and Christy and everyone else in the bucolic little town of Walden, Virginia, woke up and found out that the rest of the world was gone.

Not destroyed, mind you, but gone.

Just . . . *gone*.

Walden was still there. That hadn't changed. Our homes and stores and schools, our pets and loved ones, our cherished keepsakes and personal belongings, our streets and sidewalks—all of those still existed. But the outside world, everything beyond the town limits, had been replaced by an unbroken wall of black. A curtain of darkness surrounded the town. It stretched east and west, from the sign on Route 711 that said YOU ARE NOW ENTERING WALDEN, POPULATION 11,873 to the rocky, tree-covered hills behind the senior high school, and north and south from the Texaco station on Maple Avenue to the vacant lot behind the half-empty strip mall on Tenth Street. Everything inside that radius still existed. Everything beyond those boundaries had been swallowed up by a heavy, impenetrable darkness. It was dark inside the town limits, too, but not as thick as on the exterior. Inside Walden, it just looked like night. Out on the edge of town, the blackness seemed deeper. Denser, like congealing grease or motor oil.

Some folks didn't even notice the darkness at first. They woke up to find that the power, gas, water, and other utilities were off. That was alarming, of course. But it wasn't until they stumbled outside to see if their neighbors were having the same problem that they discovered what was really happening—except that none of us were sure just what that was.

Personally, at first, I thought it was an eclipse, but Russ nixed that idea. He said that if it had been an eclipse, he'd have known about it, and I didn't doubt that. Russ lives in the one-bedroom apartment above Christy and me. He's an amateur astronomer and before the darkness came, he spent most nights up on the roof, staring at the stars through his telescope and bitching about all the streetlamps. He said they caused light pollution and made it hard for him to see anything clearly.

These days, he doesn't have to worry about light pollution anymore. The only problem is, there's nothing up in the sky for him to see. The stars are gone. He says it's like staring into a pool of tar.

House by house, apartment by apartment, Walden woke up to find out that sunrise had been canceled. Their reactions were interesting. A few people insisted that it wasn't a big deal. They were convinced the darkness was just some freak weather occurrence, some bizarre atmospheric phenomenon that would dissipate in a few hours. They climbed into their cars and trucks and SUVs, and started off on the day's commute. Other people caught one glimpse of the darkness, panicked, and decided to flee. They chalked it up to everything from a terrorist attack to the Second Coming of Jesus Christ himself, come back to judge us all. They loaded up their cars and trucks and sped away, convinced it was the end of the world.

Here's what I don't get about either of these groups. The first group, the ones who went to work like it was just any other day—what the fuck were they thinking? I mean, how much of a fucking drone do you have to be to just go about your regular, everyday business like that, ignoring the reality of what's happening around you? Were they that consumed with their mortgage payments and promotions that they willingly just blanked out everything else, hoping that once they arrived at work, the world would right itself again? And the second group, the people who were convinced it was Judgment Day and fled—where the hell were they going? If Jesus really had come back to judge us all, were they rushing off to meet him, or were they trying to hide? If it really was the end of the world, then what possible destination did they have in mind? What place wouldn't be impacted by the planet's destruction? Think about that for a moment because it's important. Where do you go to hide from the end of the world?

In both cases—those who took it in stride and those who freaked out—they drove out of town and into the darkness.

None of them were ever seen again.

That was how we first found out that the darkness had teeth.

Back again. I took a break from writing this and finished off the last of my whiskey. Basil Hayden's Kentucky bourbon. Christy got me a bottle of it for my birthday. Damn good stuff. Expensive as all hell but worth every penny. I drank the last because I figured if I was going to write all of this out, I should have a little bit of a buzz to get me through it. Grease the wheels, you know? Face my fears, because a lot of what I'm going to tell you is pretty fucking grim. And now my whiskey's gone.

Want to hear something funny? I'm reluctant to throw away the empty bottle. Booze is even scarcer than shaving cream these days. Walden was always a dry town, and the only place within the city limits that served liquor was the local Knights of Columbus hall—and you had to be a member to drink there. Not surprisingly, when the looting started, one of the first things to disappear was the booze. The Knights of Columbus got hit first, of course. Then people raided empty houses—and sometimes they broke into houses that weren't empty—and cleaned those out, too. These days, a bottle of Smirnoff or Jim Beam is better than cash. Hell, anything is better than cash. The only thing you can do with paper money is burn it to stay warm. Doing so is more psychological than anything else because the temperature in town never fluctuates. Sometimes it just feels good to be warm. So people burn their paper money. Liquor keeps you warm, too, and without all that annoying smoke or the risk of burning your house down while you sleep. Like I said, Jim Beam rules over the green. And coins? The only thing you can do with coins is put them in pipe bombs. They make excellent shrapnel.

But I don't want to throw the empty bottle away. I'd like to cap it and then, once in a while, I could unscrew the lid and smell the leftover vapors. Breathe what once had been. But I guess that, like everything else, would eventually vanish.

It's nighttime again. There's no way to tell what time of day it is, really, unless you own a battery-operated clock or a watch that still works. Daylight is a thing of the past. I'm going by my internal alarm clock, and that's telling me it's around ten o'clock at night.

I've always been a night owl. It's when I'm most awake. Alive. Part of that is because until recently I worked second shift at Giovanni's Pizza. The pizza parlor, a little redbrick building, used to sit just past the outskirts of town. Now it's part of the darkness. When I worked there, I came in at three in the afternoon and made deliveries until eleven most nights—later if there was something special like the Super Bowl or New Year's Eve. When my shift was finished, I was usually wide awake, jazzed up on Red Bull and coffee and Mountain Dew. So I'd stay awake until dawn, playing video games or talking to Christy if she was still awake. She usually tried to stay up until I got home, but it was tough on her. She worked part-time at the little New Age shop downtown, and her shifts were generally during the day. But we made it work.

I used to love the night. The darkness was like an old friend. I embraced it. Welcomed it. Nighttime was peaceful and serene and calming. It hummed with its own energy and possibilities.

I don't feel that way anymore, and now the darkness hums with something else.

Since back in the day when we were still cavemen, wandering around picking bugs out of one another's hair and trying not to get eaten by saber-toothed tigers, mankind has been afraid of the dark. I never understood why, until now.

I'm sitting here whistling a tune by Flogging Molly and wishing there was still electricity so I could listen to my iPod. I'd fucking kill to hear some music again— something other than Cranston down on the first floor strumming away on his warped, out-of-tune guitar, or the local juvenile delinquents rapping bad hip-hop to one another around the rusty burn barrel on the sidewalk. Yeah, I could go for some Flogging Molly right now. Or Tiger Army. Or The Dropkick Murphys. A little bit of that would chase the darkness away.

No. No, it wouldn't. Who the hell am I kidding? Music's no good. The darkness would just swallow that up, too.

Okay, I've stalled long enough and this whiskey buzz ain't gonna last forever. If I'm going to tell you about this shit, I suppose I should get down to business. Christy is sleeping in the next room, and Russ is upstairs packing for the trip. We try to avoid each other these days, so that none of us angers one another. We can't risk turning on each other, and the slightest perceived insult could easily lead to that. See, the darkness amps up our negative emotions. You might not understand that now, but you will.

There's not much time left. Soon as Christy wakes up, we're leaving.

Hopefully we can keep the outer darkness at bay just a little bit longer.

And keep the darkness inside of us at bay, as well.

CHAPTER THREE

You know those coming-of-age books and movies? The ones where a bunch of plucky kids have all kinds of adventures during the summer and it ends up being a major turning point in their lives? They defeat the monster, bully, bad guy, abusive parent, insert your own antagonist here, and afterward, they are changed forever as a result of that confrontation, and when they look back on it as adults, they realize how it shaped and molded them?

Yeah, you know what I'm talking about. I mean, who hasn't seen one of those movies or read one of those books? We all love that kind of story because we can all identify with it. We've all been kids and we've all faced our own monsters.

Here's the thing about those stories, though. Ninety-nine point nine nine nine percent of the time, they take place in a small town and in a simpler time—usually the fifties or the sixties. Back when things were supposedly gentler and more innocent. I mean, it's a real slice of Americana, isn't it? All you need to do is add some baseball and apple pie. Coming-of-age stories are supposed to represent America at its core—everything that is good and decent and moral about us as a nation.

But they're not really all that accurate anymore, are they? In those stories, everybody knows everyone else in town. People say hello when they pass one another in the street. The town has a real sense of history—the populace knows who founded it and when and why, and all of the things that have happened there since. Can you say the same thing about where you live?

Before all this, Walden wasn't like that. Yes, we were your stereotypical small town, but we were also a town of strangers. I can count on two hands the number of people I actually knew here. Christy and Russ. Cranston downstairs. My boss at the pizza place and the other delivery drivers. And Dez. But Dez doesn't count because everyone in Walden knew who he was. You couldn't miss him. He was the only homeless guy in town—by choice, really. Because of that, everyone knew Dez. He was the exception.

In Walden, you didn't stop and talk to people on the street about the events in your lives. Oh sure, maybe you nodded, acknowledging their presence. Maybe you even commented on the weather or asked for the time of day. But that was all. There was no five-and-dime store selling chocolate malts or comic books off a squeaky spinner rack. No kindly pharmacist dispensing medicine and grandfatherly advice in equal measure. No mom-and-pop stores of any kind, because those were a thing of the past. The only things that existed in Walden were the same cardboard-cut-out chain stores you found in every other American town—Wal-Mart, KMart, McDonald's, Best Buy, Burger King, Staples, Red Lobster, Bath and Body Works, Barnes and Noble, Bass Pro, Target, Subway, and a Starbucks on every corner. That might seem like a lot for a population of just over eleven thousand, but there were other small towns nearby and we'd become their hub. The only independently owned businesses in town, other than the new-age health food store and the comic book shop, were the Lutheran, Methodist, and Catholic churches—and they didn't see much traffic.

I bet it was the same everywhere in America. Those old coming-of-age stories are a lie.

Fire-hall bean suppers and pancake breakfasts weren't the hub of social activity and families didn't gather around the dinner table or the television because the kids were online and the parents were divorced or working two jobs. At traffic lights, drivers were unknown to the motorists in other cars. A yellow signal meant speed up, rather than slow down. Doctors didn't make house calls because the insurance companies wouldn't let them. The local waitresses didn't know their customers' names or ask them if they wanted "the usual." Kids didn't ride their bikes all over town or build forts in the woods because parents didn't let their kids do things like that anymore. In the twenty-first century, your next-door neighbor was somebody you didn't know, and they might have been a child molester or a serial killer, so you let your kids stray as far as the backyard, and even then, it was under your watchful eye.

Isn't it strange? Before the darkness, this was supposed to be the information age. People talked about the planet being a global fucking village. We lived in a world where you could hop online and play chess with some guy in Australia or have virtual sex with a woman you'd never met and never *would* meet because she lived in Scotland— and maybe, just maybe, she wasn't even a woman, but a dude pretending to be female. But despite breaking down all those social and global barriers, more than ever, we were a nation of strangers. Of secrets. We knew somebody online who we'd never met in person. Knew them by their screen name and their avatar and called them a friend, but we didn't know the people who lived next door. We hung out with people on message boards, rather than at the bar. We didn't drop off apple pies when our neighbors were sick or compare lawn mowing techniques over the white picket fence. We didn't know what our neighbors were up to behind closed doors or what they were really like in private.

Until the darkness came. Then everybody unmasked. Everybody showed their real faces, because it just didn't matter anymore. And in most cases, their real faces were ugly and monstrous. Not evil. Not really. Evil is too strong of a word. Evil is nothing more than an idea, a moniker we use to describe things that are otherwise indescribable. Anytime we can't explain a person's actions, we attribute them to evil. But all the shit that went down after the darkness came—calling it evil would have been too easy. It was brutal and savage, but it wasn't evil. It was just humans being. Like that? Pretty clever, if I do say so myself. Gallows fucking humor.

But it's true. All the rapes and murders and arson and everything else that's happened since the darkness arrived—it was all just humans being human. People reverting back to type. Turning primitive. Devolving back to how we behaved when we were still afraid of the dark. It didn't happen right away. At first, we were all too scared and we still had hope. But by the first long night, when that hope ran out and all we had left was fear, things went downhill quick.

I can't tell you what everyone else did because I don't know their stories. I can only tell you what happened to us. What we saw and heard and experienced ourselves.

In the beginning . . .

W. D. Gagliani

"GAGLIANI REDEFINES THE WEREWOLF MYTHOS FOR
A JADED TWENTY-FIRST CENTURY AUDIENCE."
—*SCI-FI HORIZONS*

Some people are afraid there's a wild animal
on the loose, savagely tearing its victims apart.
Others, like Nick Lupo, know better. Lupo knows
a werewolf attack when he sees one. He *should*,
since he's a werewolf himself, though he's been
able to control his urges and maintain his secret.
He's also a homicide cop, so it may be up to him
to hunt down one of his own kind. It looks like
there's a new werewolf in town, a rogue out only
for blood. But looks can be deceiving.

Wolf's Gambit

ISBN 13: 978-0-8439-6249-9

"If you've missed Laymon, you've missed a treat!"
—STEPHEN KING

RICHARD LAYMON

Something deadly has come to town—a slimy, slithering . . . *thing* like nothing anyone has seen before. With its dull eyes and its hideous mouth, it's always hunting for a new host to burrow into, and humans are the perfect prey. But the truly shocking part is not what it does to you when it invades your body— it's what it makes you do to others.

FLESH

"One of horror's rarest talents."
—*Publishers Weekly* (Starred Review)

ISBN 13: 978-0-8439-6139-3

☐ **YES!**

Sign me up for the Leisure Horror Book Club and send my FREE BOOKS! If I choose to stay in the club, I will pay only $8.50* each month, a savings of $7.48!

NAME: _____

ADDRESS: _____

TELEPHONE: _____

EMAIL: _____

☐ I want to pay by credit card.

☐ **VISA**   ☐ **MasterCard**   ☐ **DISCOVER**

ACCOUNT #: _____

EXPIRATION DATE: _____

SIGNATURE: _____

Mail this page along with $2.00 shipping and handling to:
Leisure Horror Book Club
PO Box 6640
Wayne, PA 19087
Or fax (must include credit card information) to:
610-995-9274
You can also sign up online at **www.dorchesterpub.com**.
*Plus $2.00 for shipping. Offer open to residents of the U.S. and Canada only.
Canadian residents please call 1-800-481-9191 for pricing information.
If under 18, a parent or guardian must sign. Terms, prices and conditions subject to change. Subscription subject to acceptance. Dorchester Publishing reserves the right to reject any order or cancel any subscription.